Nick's lips curved in a faint smile. "This isn't going to happen, darling."

She raised her eyebrows. "Meaning?"

"You and me…sleeping together."

A laugh slipped out of her mouth. Well, this was a first. She found Nick's lack of interest oddly refreshing.

And total bull.

"Oh, really?" She injected a teasing note into her voice. "So you're saying that you're not attracted to me?"

Nick let out a breath. "No, because I'd have to be a monk *not* to be attracted to you. What I'm saying is that I won't sleep with you."

"I see."

"It's nothing personal," he added, looking and sounding awkward. "I can't focus on anything other than fixing this mess. I'm also not the kind of man who does the casual fling thing, so…"

"I totally get where you're coming from." She pursed her lips. "There's just one problem."

"What's that?"

"I'm the kind of woman who wants what she can't have."

Dear Reader,

Well, this is it, the third installment of the Hunted miniseries. I'm sad to say goodbye to my sexy Special Ops soldiers, but I am happy to finally bring you Nick's story!

From his introduction in *Soldier Under Siege,* Nick captured my heart with his sweet and laid-back personality. But in *Special Forces Rendezvous,* we caught a glimpse of Nick's not-so-sweet side as he vowed to bring down the people hunting him.

The more I got to know Nick, the more I realized that this good guy was packing a bit of an edge beneath the surface. Foreign correspondent Rebecca Parker, the heroine of this final book, discovers the same thing. She thinks getting a scoop out of nice-guy Nick will be a piece of cake and that she can have him wrapped around her little finger in no time—but the gorgeous soldier proves to be more stubborn, and far more seductive, than she ever would have dreamed.

I hope you enjoy the conclusion to the Hunted trilogy. And make sure to check out the first two books if you haven't done so already—Tate and Sebastian's adventures await you!

Happy reading.

Elle

BK

ELLE KENNEDY

Special Ops Exclusive

HARLEQUIN® ROMANTIC SUSPENSE

Recycling programs
for this product may
not exist in your area.

ISBN-13: 978-0-373-27823-7

SPECIAL OPS EXCLUSIVE

HARLEQUIN®
™ www.Harlequin.com

Printed in U.S.A.

Books by Elle Kennedy

Harlequin Romantic Suspense

Missing Mother-To-Be #1680
★Millionaire's Last Stand #1686
★The Heartbreak Sheriff #1690
Colton's Deep Cover #1728
★★Soldier Under Siege #1741
★★Special Forces Rendezvous #1749
★★Special Ops Exclusive #1753

Silhouette Romantic Suspense

Silent Watch #1574
Her Private Avenger #1634

Harlequin Blaze

Body Check #458
Witness Seduction #637

★Small-Town Scandals
★★The Hunted

Other titles by this author available
in ebook format.

ELLE KENNEDY

A RITA® Award-nominated author, Elle Kennedy grew up in the suburbs of Toronto, Ontario, and holds a B.A. in English from York University. From an early age she knew she wanted to be a writer, and actively began pursuing that dream when she was a teenager. She loves strong heroines and sexy alpha heroes, and just enough heat and danger to keep things interesting.

Elle loves to hear from her readers. Visit her website, www.ellekennedy.com, for the latest news or to send her a note.

For Cyndi, Rochelle and Susan for rooming with me and still thinking I'm fun even when I'm on deadline!

Acknowledgment

Thank you to Rochelle French, Grace Callaway, Vanessa Kier, Karin Tabke, Joyce Lamb, Cyndi Faria, Susan Hatler, Kristin Miller and Sacramento Sheriff's Deputy Paul B., for your help with this one.

Chapter 1

Mala, Cortega

The crowd was growing disruptive. Angry shouts boomed in the afternoon air as hundreds of protesters raised their fists and chanted their outrage, standing united outside the parliament building. The mob's hostility was palpable, the first stirrings of violence coming as no surprise to Nick Prescott, who watched the scene without comment.

Standing under the pillared entrance of the coffee shop across the street, he examined the throng of people and swallowed a frustrated groan. Just his luck. After nearly two weeks of coming up empty, he finally got a real lead to investigate, only to find himself in the middle of a protest involving an election that didn't even concern him.

No way would his informant show up for their meeting today. Salazar was a member of the private guard that protected Cortega's president and government officials, and judging by the chaos in the streets, the countless news vans and story-hungry journalists, the man probably wouldn't be able to find time for a clandestine meeting.

Sure enough, Nick's cell phone buzzed less than ten minutes later, indicating a text message from Salazar.

With a muttered curse, he read the message, then dialed a number. When Captain Robert Tate picked up the phone, Nick got right to the point.

"Salazar bailed, but he said he'll try to meet with me tomorrow. Let's hope the protesters realize how futile this cause is and will have dispersed by then."

Not that he blamed the irate people. They'd gone to those polls in good faith, their votes bringing a new liberal party into power, and rather than be rewarded with a more democratic way of life, they were now being told the votes had been miscounted. Surprise! The *real* winner of the election was the oppressive regime they'd endured for the past five years! Anyone with half a brain could see through that line of bull, and Nick wholeheartedly supported the citizens' decision to make their unhappiness known.

He just wished their big stand hadn't fallen on the same day he'd hoped to get some answers.

After nearly a year of hiding out on foreign soil, Nick was pretty damn exhausted. He was tired of lying low, tired of discreetly digging around to figure out who wanted him dead instead of plowing full speed ahead and *demanding* answers, consequences be damned. But although he was no longer an active-duty soldier in the United States Armed Forces, he still followed the orders of his former commanding officer, who maintained that this entire mess needed to be handled delicately.

"So what's on your agenda, then?" Tate asked in that gruff voice of his.

"I'll hit the streets and see if I can track down the forger myself, but without a name it'll be tough. This city is crawling with shady characters, most of who dabble in fake IDs."

"Which is probably why Waverly made a pit stop there."

"Or this could all be an elaborate trap," Nick replied, a hint of aggravation in his voice. "Maybe Waverly never showed his face in Cortega at all. Maybe someone tricked us to think his credit card was used to charter that plane."

"To lure us out."

He gave a grim nod even though Tate couldn't see it. "To lure us out," he confirmed.

There was a beat. "You've been in Mala for two days. Did you get a sense that you were being followed? Have you heard about anyone asking questions about us?"

"No," he admitted. "And I've been keeping my eyes and ears open."

"So either your instincts have failed you, or the bastards who want us dead have no idea you're in Cortega."

Intuition was a soldier's greatest asset, and Nick held his in high esteem. Not only was his gut telling him he was in the clear, but he also hadn't seen or heard anything to indicate that his presence had been detected or expected. Which meant that Paul Waverly, the man they were hunting, had most likely been here.

And once he figured out what name Waverly was now going by, finding the little bastard would be much, much easier.

"All right, well, I'll keep looking," he told Tate. "Any news from Sebastian's friend at the Department of Defense?"

"None. Davidson has been trying to track Waverly down, but to no avail."

A wave of deafening cheers swept through the mob, drawing Nick's attention to the black wrought-iron fence separating the capitol from the street. Several protesters were attempting to scale the bars, egged on by the enraged crowd below them.

A second cacophony rocked the air—loud shouts and booing as law enforcement officers on the scene began setting up barricades in an attempt to steer the people out of the road to let the line of honking cars through. Several uniformed officers wielding batons swarmed the fence with sharp orders for the climbers to descend.

He suppressed a sigh and tried to focus on the deep voice grumbling in his ear.

"What the hell is going on there, Prescott?"

"The people are pissed," he replied flatly. "They got screwed over by their government again."

"Yeah, I feel their pain," Tate muttered.

Nick clenched his teeth. He wanted so badly to contradict the captain, but he couldn't, not when the evidence of his own government's betrayal kept piling up.

Once upon a time he'd believed in honor. He'd believed that the government didn't harm or oppress, but that it protected its citizens and kept the country safe from outside threats. Damn naive of him maybe, but he'd been raised to respect and find value in the system. Sure, there would always be a few bad apples, but that didn't mean the entire tree was poisoned. If his father had taught him one thing, it was that society couldn't function without the support of a strong government, and he'd always had faith that *his* government truly cared for each and every citizen.

Clearly that wasn't the case, seeing as how his entire unit had been sacrificed—all so a mysterious high-ranking official could conduct biological weapons testing on innocent people.

Nick had been horrified when that gruesome truth had come to light. He'd known something had been off about his unit's last mission, and those internal alarms had only grown louder and more urgent after his teammates started dropping like flies. Mugging, cancer, DUI—Nick hadn't bought the line of crap Commander Hahn had tried to sell him. All those men had been murdered, and once Nick had a close call of his own, he'd realized he couldn't afford to stay in D.C., not if he valued his own life.

Joining forces with Tate and Sebastian Stone, another member of their unit, had seemed like his best course of action. The three men had decided to band together to find out who wanted them dead, and after ten months of digging, they were finally getting somewhere.

And Nick, once an advocate for the importance and integrity of the government, had officially become disillusioned.

"Anyway," Tate was saying, "Davidson also assured Seb that the antidote to the Meridian virus is being developed by the CDC. If the virus somehow does get released again, they've got measures in place to get the treatment out as quickly and efficiently as possible."

Nick felt a spark of relief. Although he hadn't seen the effects of the disease firsthand, more than a thousand people had succumbed to the Meridian virus ten days ago after a terrorist group released it in a small town in New York. The terrorist cell had been neutralized, but not before Sebastian nearly lost the woman he loved to the virus. Fortunately, Julia had been administered the vaccine just in time, and the sassy doctor was now in Ecuador with the others, helping them figure out who'd authorized the creation of the virus in the first place.

Their best hope of learning the truth lay with Paul Waverly. After attempting to infect Sebastian with the virus, the DoD aide had fled Washington and hadn't been heard from since, but the man's ties to the Pentagon confirmed that someone in the current administration had given the order to kill Sebastian.

That same someone had also allowed a biological weapon to be engineered, tested on a remote South American island and placed in the hands of terrorists.

"Check in after you meet with Salazar, okay?"

Tate's command snapped Nick back to the present. "Sure thing," he answered.

After the two men hung up, Nick edged away from the concrete pillar. His temples were beginning to throb, and the noise levels weren't helping. Car honks, shrieks from the crowd, the earsplitting police whistles.

"I can't see a darn thing!"

Somehow, the melodic female voice penetrated the din and succeeded in snagging Nick's attention.

He shifted his gaze in time to see a pretty redhead stalk down the sidewalk. She wore blue jeans, a black T-shirt and white sneakers, and although she was petite as hell, she looked like a force to be reckoned with, carrying herself with confidence and single-minded purpose. A tall, muscular cameraman with a shaved head trailed after her, an amused look in his eyes.

"Stand on the van," he suggested.

From their accents, and the fact that they were both

speaking English, it was easy to deduce they were American. Nick searched the news vans in the distance, wondering which network these two worked for.

A few yards away, the reporter halted, spun around and propped her hands on her hips. "And I suppose I'll interview the protesters by shouting out questions while I'm standing on top of the gee-dee van?"

Gee-dee?

Nick furrowed his brows, trying to decipher that.

"Or," the cameraman countered, "maybe you don't do *any* interviews." When she balked, the man's expression grew serious. "I'm serious. I don't like the looks of these people, Becks. They're starting to get riled up."

No sooner had the words left his mouth than the sound of shattering glass filled the air and a fresh wave of cheers rolled through the mob.

Nick's heart dropped to the pit of his stomach when he glimpsed the source of the commotion. A dozen protesters had ambushed one of the cars attempting to drive through the clogged street. A man in ratty jeans and a sweat-stained tank top had driven a crowbar through the windshield and was now going to town on the hood. His cohorts were rocking the car and pounding their fists on the windows while the family inside the vehicle let out terrified screams.

This really *was* getting out of hand. Nick glanced at the police officers, who were trying to control the crowd, then at the armored van that had just arrived on the scene. Black-clad soldiers, the equivalent of an American SWAT team, poured out of the van, their shouts to cease and desist getting swallowed by the infuriated protesters.

"Crap," the cameraman blurted out. "The rubber bullets will be making an appearance soon. And those things *hurt,* damn it! Remember the riot in Johannesburg last year?"

The redheaded reporter laughed, and for some reason, that twinkle of sound made Nick's heart do a strange little flip.

"We made it out of there alive," she replied. "And we'll make it out of this alive, too."

And then, to Nick's surprise, the curvy little woman marched *toward* the commotion rather than away from it.

He tried to keep his gaze on her, but it was a difficult task, especially when she seemed determined to push her way into the swarm of screaming people. The crowd did not part for her like the Red Sea, it just swallowed her whole, and only that gorgeous red hair made it possible to see her. The afternoon sunlight caught in those long wavy tresses, making them shine like burnished copper. Because most of the protesters were of South American descent, boasting swarthy complexions and dark hair, the American reporter, with her bright hair and fair skin, stood out like white at a funeral.

Becks.

Something suddenly clicked, making Nick suck in a breath. Damn, that wasn't just *any* reporter. That was Rebecca Parker, the star foreign correspondent for ABN, the American Broadcast News network. Known for her gutsy coverage of the world's most dangerous conflicts, Parker was a news heroine, hailed as the next Christiane Amanpour, and one of the main reasons Americans tuned in to ABN.

Especially men aged twenty-one to forty-nine.

Hell, make that any male, any demographic. With those gorgeous good looks, sharp green eyes and a perpetual smirk that was half mocking, half sensual, Rebecca Parker was appealing as hell.

"Down on the ground!" boomed a member of the tactical team. The order was spoken in Spanish and had been directed at the vandals surrounding the damaged car, none of whom followed instructions.

Nick watched the rising tensions with uneasiness, feeling the threat of impending violence building in the air. As usual, his instincts didn't lead him astray. When chaos broke out, he was expecting it, and yet it still managed to catch him off guard.

The mob turned savage, attacking the vehicles on the road, attacking the police officers and SWAT members, attacking each other. Bottles and food items and garbage sailed through the air, glass smashing on the pavement, police whistles blaring as the officers tried to subdue the suddenly ferocious crowd. The protest had turned into a full-blown riot, and Nick quickly ducked away from the coffee shop as a dozen enraged people stormed the café and proceeded to throw bottles at the plate-glass window.

He could barely hear his own thoughts because the noise was so loud. The situation had grown critical in the blink of an eye, and Nick's pulse sped up as he suddenly remembered that Rebecca Parker was splat in the middle of all that anarchy.

Squaring his shoulders, he took a decisive step forward. Although he made no move to grab the 9 millimeter tucked under the waistband of his cargo pants and hidden by his T-shirt, he was acutely aware of the weapon. Any hint of trouble, and he'd shoot his way out of this damn riot if need be.

He swept his gaze over the sea of people, searching for that telltale flash of red. Where the hell was she?

And what kind of woman willingly placed her neck on the line? Didn't she have any concern for— *There*. Relief coursed through him as he spotted her.

She was thirty feet away, being jostled and manhandled by the people around her as they attempted to charge the fence in front of the parliament building. The woman was pushing her way through the crowd, trying to make it to safety. Her cameraman was nowhere in sight, much to Nick's dismay.

He quickly threw himself into the fray. Within seconds he was surrounded by hundreds of people. The scent of sweat and body odor and fury filled his nostrils, the heat of all those bodies making his T-shirt cling to his chest. He kept his gaze locked on the redheaded reporter, focusing on his target like a heat-seeking missile.

The uneasy flicker in Rebecca Parker's green eyes was evident, but it wasn't the flash of panic he expected to see. The woman was holding her own, throwing elbows like a street fighter. For a moment, he even questioned the decision to come to her rescue, because she seemed to be doing just fine on her own.

Or at least she was until a beer bottle flew through the air and collided with the side of her head.

Nick's gut went rigid as he watched her stumble. A second later, the redhead went down like a light and her body crumpled to the pavement.

In perfect position to be trampled by the mob.

Chapter 2

Rebecca felt like someone had pulled the carpet out from under her feet. One second she was totally vertical, the next she was flat on her back, pain shooting through the side of her head and black dots marring her vision. She sucked in a deep breath, blinking wildly, trying to get her bearings. The pain in her temple didn't abate, but her vision cleared to reveal just how precarious a situation she'd found herself in.

Angry faces and moving bodies whizzed above her. She braced both palms on the hot pavement and tried to stand up, only to fall backward when someone bumped into her. Someone else stepped on her foot, bringing a jolt of pain. Uh-oh. This was bad. Each time she succeeded in unsteadily climbing to her feet, she got knocked right back down, and now she was seeing stars again. Her eyes couldn't seem to focus and shapes were beginning to look blurry.

The fear finally hit her, clogging her throat and making her heart pound.

Agony burned up her arm as she got stomped on again.

God.

She was going to get crushed in a stampede.

With a burst of adrenaline, she made another attempt to hurl herself to her feet—and this time it worked. She was off the ground and hovering over the crowd—wait, hovering *over* it? Blinking a few times, Rebecca realized the reason she felt like she was floating was because she *was* floating. She was tucked tightly in a man's arms, a man who'd taken it upon himself to carry her away to safety, Kevin Costner–style.

"Who are you?" she murmured, but the inquiry got lost in the rioters' shouts and the rapid popping noises of rubber bullets being fired into the crowd.

Jesse. Where was Jesse? Her out-of-focus gaze roamed the area but she couldn't spot that bald head of his anywhere. She prayed he was okay, that he'd found his own savior to whisk him to safety.

She suddenly became aware of the most intoxicating scent, and she inhaled deeply, filling her lungs with that spicy aroma. It was *him,* she realized. God, he smelled good.

She glanced up to study the face of her rescuer, catching glimpses of a strong, clean-shaven jaw. Sensual lips. A straight nose. She wanted to see his eyes, but the angle was all wrong, so she focused on his incredible chest instead. Jeez, the guy must work out. His torso was hard as a rock, rippled with muscles that flexed at each purposeful step he took.

As much as she wanted to question this man, Rebecca decided to exercise some patience and wait until they cleared the mob. Shoot. She was going to receive a big fat *I told you so* when she reunited with her cameraman. He'd warned her not to venture too deep into the crowd, but at this point, she wasn't sure why he bothered with the warnings anymore. After five years of working together, Jesse ought to know that Rebecca did what she wanted, when she wanted.

She hadn't gotten to where she was by standing meekly on the sidelines; her reputation had been forged by her ability to throw herself in the middle of the action. She was only twenty-seven years old and she'd reported from countless war zones, covered everything from political scandals to genocide, and once she sank her teeth into a story, she refused to let go until she got to the heart of the matter.

She was Rebecca Parker, darn it. She didn't cower from danger or allow something like a measly riot to slow her down.

Says the woman who nearly got trampled to death.

Rebecca ignored the mocking internal voice and clung tighter to her rescuer's shoulders. Man, he had big shoulders. And he was *tall.* At least six-one, and she felt downright tiny in his arms.

Fine, so maybe she'd required a little assistance to get out of this latest jam, she amended, but for the most part, she usually managed to get in and out of tight spots with her own quick thinking and determination.

"You okay?"

The concerned male voice broke through her thoughts. She looked up at her rescuer, finally getting a good look at those elusive eyes.

Boy, were they worth the wait. At first glance they were brown—until you looked closer and realized they were the color of warm honey with flecks of amber around the pupils. And they were so magnetic that she felt hypnotized as she gazed into them.

"Ms. Parker?"

She blinked, forcing herself back to reality. "Oh. I'm fine," she answered. "A little bruised, but I'll live. And you can call me Rebecca. I think it's only fitting I be on a first-name basis with the man who saved my life."

His lips curved. "If you say so."

It didn't escape her that he hadn't introduced himself in return, but before she could press him for a name, foghorns started blasting and a male voice blared out of a megaphone. A member of the police force, urging the demonstrators to disperse or else extreme measures would be taken. The crowd only got noisier, booing and yelling in response.

Rebecca stifled a sigh. She'd borne witness to enough riots to know that these people weren't going anywhere. Now that the mob had gotten a taste of blood and violence, things would only escalate.

And she wouldn't be there to cover it.

"Crap," she muttered. "You have to put me down."

Her rescuer didn't miss a step. He kept bearing ahead at full speed.

"I'm serious." She wiggled in his arms, trying to get free, but his grip tightened, making her realize just how strong this man was.

Struggling didn't make a lick of difference. In the end, she gritted her teeth and clutched those broad shoulders. There wasn't a darn thing she could do until he put her down.

A few minutes later, when they were well away from the screaming protesters, her personal bodyguard finally set her on her feet. Before she could say a word, he captured her chin with one hand and angled her head while his other hand lightly touched her left temple.

Pain jolted through her.

"The wound stopped bleeding," her rescuer murmured in that deep, sexy voice of his. "But you've got a hell of a bump. How's your vision? Any nausea? Follow my finger."

As he moved his finger back and forth in front of her face, Rebecca's lips tightened. "I'm fine," she insisted.

"Follow my damn finger."

Ah, he was one of *those* men, huh? Mr. Alpha.

Deciding to humor him, she tracked the movement of his finger with her eyes. She knew she didn't have a concussion. She'd had several of those in the past, and although she'd taken a good knock to the side of the head, she was already feeling better, more oriented. Her surroundings were in perfect focus now, and aside from a slight throbbing in her temple, she felt alert.

Her savior must have reached the same conclusion, because he let those big hands drop from her face.

"You could've been killed," he said flatly. "That was damn reckless of you, strolling right into the middle of that mob."

A note of disapproval rang in his voice, making her roll her eyes. "Danger comes with the job," she said with a shrug. "Although if I'm being honest, I wasn't expecting this assignment to be so exciting. Election coverage tends to be boring."

There was a screech of tires as several police cars skidded to a stop ten feet away from them. Her rescuer planted a hand on her upper arm and led her farther away from the street, dragging her along the cobblestone sidewalk toward the end of the block. Only a handful of curious bystanders loitered here, peering at the violent spectacle down the road while a few uni-formed officers stood nearby, making sure the riot didn't spread outward.

Rebecca allowed him to drag her to the corner, then shrugged his hand off and spun around. She squinted, searched the handful of news vans in the distance, and hitched a happy breath when she spotted Jesse. Smart-ass was actually standing on top of the red-and-white ABN van, just like he'd encouraged her to do earlier.

Chuckling, she dug her cell phone from the back pocket of her jeans and pressed a button on speed dial.

"I have to let my colleague know I'm all right," she explained to her rescuer, who was watching her with those sharp amber eyes.

For a moment, she faltered, a sense of familiarity washing over her, but before she could examine that strange do-I-know-you-from-somewhere? feeling, Jes-se's voice came over the line.

"Becks! Where the *hell* are you?"

"I'm at the end of the block, just east of you. And don't worry, I'm fine. I made it out alive."

"Barely," she heard her rescuer say.

Ignoring the angry mumble, she raised her arm and waved a few times. "You see me?"

"I see you." Jesse sighed. "Don't move. Dave 'n' I will make our way over to you."

"No, stay there," she said, shoving a strand of hair out of her eyes. "Get some footage of the riot. I'll head back in a minute and do a live report."

"Are you frickin' *kidding*—"

"From the van," she quickly cut in. "Promise."

"Fine. Get back here, Becks. This crowd is nuts."

They hung up, and Rebecca glanced at the man

who'd saved her life. "So…" She tilted her head. "You still haven't told me your name."

"I'm Nick. Nick Prescott." He ran a hand through his hair, which was dark and thick, with a slight wave to it.

Again, that appealing scent floated in her direction. Subtle aftershave, soap, pure masculinity. She studied him, taking in the dark blue T-shirt that clung to every ridge and contour of his defined chest. The long legs encased in olive-green cargo pants. That classically handsome face.

It was odd—the man moved and behaved like a soldier, yet he gave off an aristocratic air. He came from wealth. She'd wager anything on it, even her most prized possession: the certificate listing her as a Pulitzer prize finalist, which was pinned to her bulletin board back home. Because she'd worked the White House beat when she'd first started out, she'd grown skilled at figuring out who was rich and who wasn't, sometimes from just one quick look.

And this man was definitely rich.

Nick.

The name suddenly registered in her head. Wait a minute…

"What?" he muttered, seemingly uncomfortable by her scrutiny.

"Nick Prescott," she echoed, fighting a rush of suspicion. "And what exactly do you do, Nick?"

He shrugged. "I'm a journalist, same as you."

Bullcrap.

She narrowed her eyes. "Print or television?"

"Print. Freelance." He answered smoothly, his previous discomfort having vanished. "Most of my pieces are featured in smaller publications. Nothing quite as impressive as your résumé."

He flashed her a boyish grin, but Rebecca saw right through it. Ha. Did he honestly think he could distract her by stroking her ego? She was a shark, for Pete's sake. And sharks never got distracted from their course, not after they'd caught a whiff of blood.

That feeling of familiarity grew stronger, teased her, nudged the back of her mind. Darn it. Where the heck did she *know* him from?

She swiftly scanned her mental databases, recalling the sources she'd relied on over the years, the conflicts she'd covered, the political figures she'd interviewed, the—

Back it up, Becks.

She frowned. Political figures. All right. Was this man a politician? A member of an influential family with fingers in the White House pie?

As far as she knew, there weren't any powerful Prescotts in D.C. She worked the name over in her head a few times. Nick Prescott. Prescott. Nick. Nick Pres— Recognition slammed into her like a tidal wave.

No, she wasn't familiar with a Nick Prescott.

She did, however, know of a Nick *Barrett*.

Holy crap!

Rebecca nearly gasped, but managed to curb the reaction at the last second. She couldn't let him know she'd figured it out. If he was using a fake name, then that meant he didn't want to alert anybody to his presence, and if he was going out of his way to hide his presence, then that meant…

Oh yeah, there was a story here, all right. No doubt about it.

And there was also no doubt in her mind that she

was, at this very moment, in the company of Nick Barrett.

The son of America's secretary of defense.

Chapter 3

Damn, this woman was appealing. Her mouth fascinated him entirely too much. Sexy and pouty and rosy-red, with a plump bottom lip that made Nick's own mouth tingle with the urge to kiss her. And his fingers itched to explore those delectable curves. Her jeans and T-shirt weren't skintight, but they hugged a set of round, high breasts and a pair of shapely legs that would probably feel incredible wrapped around his waist while he thrust into her and—

Whoa.

The wicked images had come out of left field, flooding his mind and making his mouth water. He'd been celibate for so long that the force of his lust didn't surprise him, but his lusty urges didn't normally catch him off guard like this. He quickly forced his libido in check, hoping Rebecca hadn't noticed that flare of heat in his eyes.

Her tiny smirk revealed that she'd noticed all right.

"So…Nick," she said, his name rolling off her tongue like a sensual melody. "How can I thank you for what you did back there?"

Half a dozen naughty responses came to mind, but he was nothing if not a gentleman. He all but tipped his imaginary hat and smiled graciously. "No thanks necessary. Saving you from that stampede was my pleasure."

Her lips twitched as if she were fighting a laugh. "Uh-huh. Well, even so, my daddy taught me that every debt must be repaid. So how about I buy you a drink tonight?"

When her voice took on a Southern drawl, a smile tugged at his lips. "Do I hear Georgia in your voice or is that just a damn good fake accent?"

"Atlanta born and raised," she confirmed.

"I didn't know that. I always assumed you were from D.C."

"The network forced voice lessons on me when I got hired. They wanted me to tone down the accent because it was too *low-brow*." A twinkle lit her green eyes. "And I can guarantee that there are many other interesting things you don't know about me."

He didn't doubt it one bit. This woman was intriguing as hell, and he was swiftly realizing she was much more than the fearless correspondent he'd seen on the TV screen countless times before. In person, it was hard to miss the laughter in her eyes, or the subtle sexuality radiating from her petite frame. And even though he hated stereotyping people, he was fairly confident that Rebecca Parker's flaming red hair was a surefire sign that the woman was stubborn as a mule.

"We'll get to know each other over drinks," she said

in a tone that brooked no argument. "I won't take no for an answer, so don't bother turning me down."

Yup, stubborn.

Nick couldn't help but chuckle. "Should I be insulted that you immediately assume I don't have other plans?"

She arched her brow. "Do you?"

He grinned. "No."

"You also aren't wearing a wedding ring," she pointed out, "which leads me to believe you're not married." She cocked her head. "Unless you're that breed of a-hole that hides the ring in his suitcase when he travels?"

"I assure you, I'm not that kind of a-hole."

Her answering laughter was a sweet song that made his pulse speed up. "You're a good boy, aren't you, Nick Prescott?" Now her expression went shrewd.

Heat rippled through him, pulsing in his blood and stirring his groin. If she could read his dirty mind at the moment, she might be inclined to alter that opinion, but he decided not to voice that thought out loud.

"Something wrong with good guys?" he said lightly.

Her eyes grew pensive. "I don't know. I've only ever gone out with bad boys." She shrugged. "But I guess I'll find out tonight. What hotel are you staying at?"

"The Liberty."

Those sexy lips quirked. "What do you know? That's where I'm staying, too. We'll meet downstairs at the bar, then. I'd ask you to dinner but I eat with my crew—it's sort of a tradition. How's nine o'clock for drinks?"

Nick knew he ought to say no. He was here to track down that snake Waverly, not to go out with a beautiful redhead he suspected might be nothing but trouble.

Yet as he met Rebecca Parker's expectant green eyes, he couldn't find the willpower to turn her down.

"Nine o'clock," he agreed.

Pleasure washed over her pretty face. "Good. I'll see you tonight." She took a step back, then met his eyes and grinned. "And thanks again for helping me out of that little jam back there."

She dashed off while he stared after her with a combination of disbelief and amusement.

Little jam? She'd nearly been trampled to death, for Chrissake. He didn't think he'd ever met a woman as blasé about danger as this one. That recklessness was definitely a turnoff—if he was planning on *marrying* the woman.

But if he planned on taking her to *bed*…well, then he could totally see the advantages of having a wildcat like Rebecca Parker between the sheets.

Nine o'clock didn't come soon enough. Nick had been holed up in his hotel room for the past two hours, watching the clock and mentally urging it to tick faster.

The rest of his afternoon and most of his evening had been a total wash. None of the forgers he'd questioned had recognized Paul Waverly's photo or admitted to procuring any documents for him, but Nick wasn't discouraged. The men he'd spoken to were small players in Cortega's shady underworld. There was really only one person Waverly would've gone to, a criminal kingpin known only as El Nuevo Diablo.

The New Devil.

The moniker made Nick roll his eyes. Damn melodramatic. According to the grapevine, though, El Nuevo Diablo was the man to talk to if you wanted to get something done. Enrique Salazar had been supposed to arrange the meeting between Nick and the crime boss, but the corrupt government guard had rescheduled their rendezvous for tomorrow, so Nick had no choice but to wait around for Salazar's phone call.

But at least he could amuse himself while he waited.

Anticipation gathered in his groin as he left the room and crossed the carpeted hallway toward the elevator. Fine, so he might be getting ahead of himself here. Chances were, his date with Rebecca Parker would begin and end with drinks and not a foray into the bedroom, but he sure as hell wasn't going to complain if they somehow wound up naked.

Which was shocking in and of itself, because he wasn't the kind of man to indulge in casual flings. The other guys in his former unit used to rag him mercilessly about his self-proclaimed gentleman status. Whenever they were stateside, Diaz and Berkowski would attempt to drag him out on the town in search of a hot piece of ass, but although Nick often tagged along, he usually went home alone.

He was twenty-eight-years old, but he'd never sown any wild oats. Never had the urge to either. Hell, if he found a woman who made him *half* as happy as his mother had made his father, then he'd consider himself the luckiest man on earth.

Tonight, though…he could totally be satisfied with a casual lay. It had been *that* long.

Swallowing a rush of frustration, he rode the elevator down to the lobby and headed for the hotel bar.

The Liberty was one of the nicer hotels in Cortega, boasting clean marble floors, expensive furnishings and extremely professional staff. Nick hadn't visited the bar yet, and when he strode in, he was surprised to discover how cozy it was. The large room offered plush sofas, big armchairs and low tables situated in a way that provided patrons with the illusion of privacy. Huge ceramic planters containing green leafy ferns added to that feeling of seclusion.

Nick spotted her immediately—it was hard to miss all that gorgeous red hair tumbling down her shoulders. She was sitting with her back turned to him, but her head shifted as he began walking in her direction.

Their eyes locked, and he went hard so swiftly that he was actually taken aback. He'd never been turned on from *eye contact* before and he might've laughed at his own pathetic eagerness if he weren't so entranced by the woman across the room.

She wore a dress, an emerald-green number that swirled around her bare knees as she stood up to greet him. The bodice wasn't low cut, revealing only a modest amount of cleavage, yet the sight hit him with a punch of lust.

Rebecca looked amused. "You okay there, Nick?"

His mouth had gone dry, so he was forced to gulp a few times before he could make his voice work. "I'm fine." He swept his gaze over her once more. "You look amazing."

Pleasure colored her cheeks. "Thank you. You clean up well yourself."

His gaze lowered to his khaki cargo pants and plain white T-shirt, the nicest items of clothing he'd packed in his go bag. "If you say so," he said wryly.

"Oh, I say so."

Their eyes met and held again. Awareness crackled in the air between them.

Nick cleared his throat. "Let's sit down."

They settled in the armchairs, which were positioned side by side but angled in a way that allowed them to sit face-to-face. When Rebecca demurely crossed her legs, the bottom of her dress rode up her thighs, drawing Nick's attention to her creamy white flesh. Her skin looked so soft he had to press his palms on his thighs to stop himself from putting his hands all over her.

Fortunately, a waiter approached the table before Nick committed a major faux pas on the first date he'd had in nearly a year.

Nick ordered whiskey, and he wasn't at all surprised when Rebecca ordered the same. The woman was bold and fiery—of course she'd order a drink that matched that personality of hers.

"No appletinis for you, huh?" he said with a wry smile.

"Do I look like a sorority girl to you?"

He laughed. "Not in the slightest."

"Good, because I'm not." A gleam of challenge crept into her eyes. "How did the rest of your day go, by the way? Did you stick around to report on the riot?"

"Nah, I came back to the hotel to write. But I caught the tail end of your segment on ABN. That was a great interview with the leader of the tactical team."

"Thanks." She twined a strand of hair around her fingers, tilting her head pensively. "What angle are you using for your piece? Big bad government or ungrateful out-of-line citizens?"

He lifted his brows. "Uh-uh, Parker, you know we're not supposed to show bias. Journalism 101."

She snorted. "That's bullcrap and you effing know it."

A laugh flew out of his mouth. "Okay, before we debate this, you've got to explain the weird nonexpletives. I don't think I've heard you utter a single curse word since we've met."

"That's because I don't curse." She gave a self-deprecating sigh. "I used to swear like a sailor, but I had to rid myself of the habit after I accidentally dropped an F-bomb on air. I almost got fired for it, and I knew I couldn't let it happen again, so I quickly learned to clean up my language. But I still swear creatively. Shoot, fudge, eff, crap, gee-dee—" When he looked at her questioningly, she lowered her voice to a whisper and clarified, "Goddamn. But don't tell anyone I just said that."

Nick laughed again. He couldn't remember the last time he'd been this entertained. Rebecca Parker was not at all what he'd expected her to be. On camera she came off as assertive and serious, though she did reveal a sassy, seductive side on occasion. Still, she was clearly sassier and more seductive than her audience knew, not to mention playful, funny, intelligent, outrageously sexy....

"Anyway, let's skip the bias debate," she said with a dismissive wave of her hand. "Because we both know every reporter's got one. Where are you from, Nick?"

To his relief, the waiter returned before he could answer. With a quick thanks, Nick slipped a twenty into the man's hand, all the while going over his cover story in his head. Tate's fiancée, Eva, had used her hacking skills to create an entire fake career for Nick Prescott the journalist, and his "work" was all over the internet. He'd read most of the articles on the plane ride here, but he sincerely hoped that Rebecca wouldn't ask any specific questions.

He had a sinking suspicion that she would. The woman was a lot sharper than he'd given her credit for.

"I'm from Vermont," he replied before taking a sip of his drink. The alcohol heated his gut and fueled his confidence. "But my family moved around a lot when

I was a kid. I was a military brat." He paused. "What about you?"

Rebecca brought her glass to her lips and downed half her whiskey, then proceeded to chat about herself for a few minutes. She told him a few stories about growing up in Atlanta, explained how she'd wanted to go into journalism ever since she was a little girl, and then she promptly steered the conversation back to him, much to his discomfort.

If it were any other woman, he would've felt better about his responses, confident that she was buying his bogus backstory, but this was *Rebecca Parker*. Each time he answered a question, those green eyes narrowed slightly, as if she were analyzing every single word that left his mouth.

"What about you?" he asked after he'd told her he'd studied journalism at Columbia. "Where did you go to school?"

"Northwestern." She lobbed another query his way. "How did you like living in New York?"

Nick stifled a groan. The back and forth went on in the same fashion for the next twenty minutes. It was like a game of ping-pong. Question, answer. Question, answer.

By the time they'd finished a second round of drinks, it became glaringly obvious that Rebecca had an agenda.

She's fishing.

Crap. She was absolutely, indisputably fishing.

Nick's shoulders stiffened, his guard shooting up as he studied Rebecca's knowing expression.

"Everything okay, Nick?" she drawled.

His hackles rose. The little minx knew he'd figured her out.

"Everything's great," he responded.

He polished off the rest of his drink, but didn't signal the waiter for another. Nope, because it had become imperative that he keep a clear head.

So much for getting laid tonight.

What started out as a promising evening had turned into an aggravating battle of wits. Did Rebecca know who he was? Was she somehow connected to the people who'd killed his unit, the people trying to kill *him?* Or did she think he was simply a rival journalist and was trying to unnerve him for some reason?

"Anyway, what were we talking about? Oh right, finding material to report on," she said casually. "You know where to find the best scoops? D.C. Seriously, all you've gotta do is walk down the street and you'll stumble across no less than ten scandals." She met his eyes. "Have you ever been to D.C.?"

"Of course. I wouldn't be a good freelancer if I didn't pay frequent visits to our nation's capital." He kept his voice light.

She cocked her head. "What do you think of our current administration? A little too military-focused, wouldn't you agree?"

He shrugged. "Defense is important."

"Of course it is. But should we really spend so much money on it?"

According to his father, hell to the yes. In fact, Nick's dad was partially responsible for the president's defense-focused platform.

But he kept that tidbit to himself.

"Where do *you* think the funds should go?" he countered, yet again pitching the proverbial ping-pong ball her way.

"Education, health care, social reform." Her tone was

absent, and frustration creased her forehead, as if she couldn't decide the best way to regain ground.

He suppressed a chuckle. "Everything okay, Rebecca?" he mimicked.

Annoyance ignited those big green eyes of hers, but it faded fast. As the corners of her mouth lifted in resignation, she leaned forward and set her glass on the table, then straightened her shoulders and met his gaze head-on.

"All right, let's cut the crap," she announced. "I know *exactly* who you are, so save your lies for a woman who's stupid enough to believe them. All I want to know is, why did you lie about your name and what on earth are you doing in South America?"

Chapter 4

For a moment, Nick considered playing dumb, but Rebecca must have read his mind, because she crossed her arms and scowled at him. "Don't you dare insult my intelligence by denying it." She smirked. "Mr. *Barrett*."

A sigh lodged in his throat. He'd known showing up to a place that was crawling with American journalists would be risky, but the alternative had meant letting Tate or Sebastian handle it, and Nick wouldn't have felt right about that. Tate and Seb had more to lose nowadays—women they loved, and in Tate's case, a three-year-old boy to protect.

Nick, on the other hand, was not as emotionally encumbered. No woman or children to mourn him if he died, just his father and older sister, Vivian.

Of course, his father was the reason he was currently facing off with this too-smart-for-her-own-good news correspondent. He'd been making an effort to stay out of sight and avoid the journalists covering the election. The only reason he'd made contact with Rebecca in the first place was because the foolish woman had decided to almost get herself killed.

But because he couldn't *un*rescue her, he had no choice but to deal with the consequences of his hero complex.

"No response?" Rebecca arched her brow.

Nick just shrugged. "What do you want me to say? You've got my number. Give yourself a gold star."

"So you're confirming that you *are* Nick Barrett?"

He appreciated that she lowered her voice when she posed the question. A glance around told him that nobody was particularly interested in him and Rebecca, but he kept his voice equally soft as he replied with, "I am. But I would be grateful if you didn't mention to anyone that I'm in town."

That sassy little smirk made another appearance. "Only if you promise me an exclusive."

He stifled a groan. "I'm not giving you an exclusive—because there's no story here."

"Yeah, then why are you in Cortega?" she challenged.

"It's personal."

"Why did you lie about your name?"

"I always use a fake name when I'm traveling."

"And do you always lie about your profession?" Defiance flickered in her eyes. "Is this about the election? Did your father send you here as a representative of sorts? Maybe to talk to President Garza or General Alves about…" She furrowed her brow. "About what? What could your presence possibly accomplish?"

"Exactly," Nick said triumphantly. "Nothing. My

presence is totally unrelated to this travesty of an election, okay?"

She went quiet. He could see that sharp brain of hers working, dissecting, dismissing. Her pretty face conveyed both curiosity and suspicion, the latter becoming more prominent the longer she remained silent.

"This has to be political," she announced.

"It's not."

Her chin lifted stubbornly. "I don't believe you."

A grin sprang to his lips but it didn't stay there long. He didn't like the predatory gleam that entered her expression. It told him that she wasn't going to let it go. She'd sunk her teeth into this "story" and Nick suspected that nothing short of death would persuade her to drop it.

Unfortunately, he couldn't exactly kill the woman. All he could do was placate her, try to steer her away from this potentially dangerous path.

"Look," he spoke in a quiet voice, "obviously you know who I am. But can you tell me what I've been doing the past nine years?"

Rebecca looked baffled. "Um…well…"

"Exactly," he said again. "I've been off the political radar. Why? Because I'm no politician, darling. Aside from a few obligatory appearances I make with my dad, I avoid that whole scene, and these last five years, I've been off the media grid completely."

"Why?"

"Because public appearances weren't conducive to the unit I served on."

"Army?" When he nodded, her eyes narrowed. "Special Forces?"

Although he hated confiding in a woman he'd just

met, he knew he had to offer a few more details if he wanted to convince Rebecca to back off.

"When I joined the army, my father and I decided it would be wise if I didn't use my real name. As much as I hate admitting it, the offspring of well-known public figures tend to have an easier ride, whether it's in the corporate world or in government or the military." Nick shrugged. "I wanted the other recruits to treat me like an equal, and I didn't want preferential treatment from my commanding officers. Not only that, but I'd always intended on becoming Special Ops, and that's hard to do when your last name is Barrett."

"I imagine a lot of our enemies would love it if they found out they'd captured the son of America's sec def."

"Yep. That's why I used my mother's maiden name—Prescott."

Now she looked fascinated. "And throughout your entire career, nobody knew the truth?"

"Some people did. My father, obviously, and a few high-ranking army officials, including my unit commander. But none of the men I served with knew."

"So, what, you're here on some supersecret army mission?" Rebecca's tone took on a skeptical note. "Are the rest of your men here?"

"No to both of those questions." Nick paused, knowing this was where he needed to tread carefully. "I can't give you any more details, and it's not because I'm trying to be difficult or coy or a jerk. This is a matter of life and death."

She grinned. "Sounds like my kind of story."

"There's no story," he said darkly. "I mean it, Rebecca. I need you to pretend you never saw me. You can't tell anyone that we met, okay?"

"Why? What's going on here, Nick?"

Frustration climbed up his throat. "I can't say any more than what I've already told you, but this is no joke. If you value your own life, you need to let this go."

Her lips tightened. "Are you threatening me?"

"The threat isn't coming from me, darling. But believe me when I say that if the people involved discover you've been in contact with me, your life *will* be in danger."

Alarm washed over her face. "What the heck have you gotten mixed up in?"

Without answering, he rose to his feet. "Good night, Rebecca."

She shot up like a light, her hand darting out to curl over his biceps.

"You can't just leave," she said in a hushed voice. "Let me help you. Whatever crazy situation you've found yourself in, I can help. I've got sources and—"

"You can help by forgetting you ever saw me." He gently removed her hand from his arm and took a step back. "I mean it, Rebecca. You *need* to let this go."

"But I—"

She was still protesting as he walked away.

Rebecca gaped at Nick's retreating back. She fought the urge to hurry after him, knowing that chasing the man wouldn't achieve a darn thing. He wasn't going to confide in her—he'd made that very clear.

If you value your own life, you need to let this go.

A tremor of fear ran through her, and yet it didn't come close to overpowering the excitement building in her gut. Her instincts were humming, her brain already working over the meager details Nick Barrett had fed into it.

He was mixed up in something big.

Life-and-death big.

And he was the son of the secretary of defense.

There was a story here. A huge, potentially Pulitzer-winning story.

You need to let this go.

Nick's voice continued to buzz in her head like a persistent fly, but Rebecca yet again ignored it. She wasn't the kind of woman who let golden opportunities pass her by. How could he possibly expect her to walk away from what could quite possibly be the scoop of a lifetime?

Grabbing her purse, she left the bar and rode the elevator up to her sixth-floor room. Jesse and Dave were sharing the suite next door, but she wasn't ready to fill them in yet. Instead, she strode into the living room of her suite and fished out her cell phone.

Harry Drexler picked up on the third ring, sounding harried as usual.

An award-winning editor and producer, Harry had been Rebecca's mentor ever since her freshman year of college when he'd been giving a guest lecture in one of her journalism seminars. She'd approached him afterward to gush about his speech and ask if he had any advice for an aspiring broadcast journalist, and they'd ended up having lunch the following week, a get-together that had become a ritual once Harry decided to take her under his wing.

Harry was the one who'd helped her land the highly sought-after internship at ABN, and no matter how impatient and prickly he could be, Rebecca adored her grumpy old mentor.

"What is it, Becks?" he barked in her ear.

"The story of the year." She paused. "Maybe."

"We don't put maybes on the air, sweetheart," Harry replied in a droll voice.

"Duh. That's why I'm calling you. I need you to look into something for me."

She sat down on the small couch, balanced the phone on her shoulder and reached for her laptop case.

"What is it?" Harry asked briskly.

"Find out why the secretary of defense's son is in Mala."

Harry went quiet, then let out an amazed curse. "Nick Barrett is in Mala? Are you sure about this?"

"Dead sure. I just had drinks with the man."

"You had drinks with the sec def's son."

"Yep."

"Why?" Harry's tone grew bewildered. "Why is Barrett in Cortega?"

She had to laugh. "That's what I need you to find out. Supposedly he's been serving in the army for the past nine years. Special Forces, under the name Nick Prescott, and I guess he was discharged? I don't know. Maybe your army contacts can shed some light on it."

"Are you thinking he's still active duty and carrying out a mission? That he's there for something unrelated to the election?"

"I have no idea what I'm thinking," she admitted. "Just get me some background info on the guy. There's something here, Harry. He was rattled, and he ordered me to pretend I never saw him. He said he was involved in something dangerous."

"Dangerous how?"

"I don't know." Frustration rose inside her. "I'm calling you with the bare bones here. This is nothing more than a hunch based on some cryptic comments from Barrett aka Prescott. Will you do some digging?"

"Of course. Let me run a quick surface search right now. I'll call you back."

After Harry hung up, Rebecca opened her laptop and typed in her password so she could do her own digging. A quick Google search brought up several news articles, all of which focused on Secretary Kirk Barrett, Nick's father. Most of the pieces offered only a brief mention of Barrett's children—Vivian, a married homemaker living in Arlington. And Nick, who served in the U.S. Armed Forces.

"So you weren't lying about that," she murmured to herself.

She keyed in a new search, hoping for Nick-centered results, but the man hadn't been kidding. He really *did* stay out of the limelight, save for a few public appearances at charity events. There were absolutely no details about the man's military career, but that made sense if he'd been using a different last name during his army stint.

Her image search was a tad more successful—but only because it allowed her to drool over the guy.

Whoa, baby.

Rebecca's tongue was practically hanging out as she stared at a picture of Nick and Kirk Barrett at a political fund-raiser in D.C.

Okay, the man filled out a tux like nobody's business. His body was so broad and muscular that her pulse sped up at the mere sight of it. And those eyes. Gosh, he had amazing eyes.

Realizing her mouth had gone dry, Rebecca gulped a few times and tried to drag her head out of the gutter. She needed to focus. Nick Barrett's sheer sexiness wasn't the headline here.

Well, it should be.

She ignored the naughty voice in her head and resumed her fact-finding mission, but the data she managed to acquire didn't help her solve the puzzle.

Nick Barrett was twenty-eight years old. He'd grown up in upstate New York, attended college at Princeton and was an active duty officer in the army. Rebecca didn't know how current that information was, because Nick had implied he no longer served in the military. So which was it? Current or former military?

The answer to that came when Harry phoned back less than twenty minutes later.

"You got something already?" she demanded in lieu of greeting.

"Yeah, a lot of red flags." His voice took on that suspicious note that told her he smelled a conspiracy.

Sure enough, Harry's next words were, "I smell a conspiracy."

She had to smile. "Hit me."

"I just spoke to an army buddy based on the East Coast. He did a search on Nick Prescott. Turns out Prescott *did* serve, but there's nothing in his file for the past five years, which is most likely confirmation that he did indeed go the Special Ops route."

"Okay, what else?"

"The file says he was honorably discharged a year ago, but I couldn't find any trace of him since then. Nick Prescott, that is."

"What about Nick Barrett?"

"That's the fishy part. According to my source at the Department of Defense, Nick Barrett was also discharged from the army last year, which makes sense if he really did use the name Prescott. But Barrett is allegedly playboying it up in the Caribbean since he left the army. Supposedly he's in St. Barts at the moment."

Rebecca frowned. "Is your source reliable?"

"He works under the deputy secretary, and he's basing this intel on a conversation he personally had with Secretary Barrett—*yesterday*."

"So yesterday, the sec def told someone that his son, Nick, was in St. Barts."

"Yessiree."

"But we know for a fact that Nick is not in St. Barts. He's here in Cortega." She chewed on the inside of her cheek, trying to make sense of it all. "Why is he here, Harry?"

"Looks like we need to dig deeper, sweetheart. I'll keep looking into it. In the meantime, try to get another meeting with Barrett."

"If he hasn't skipped town already," she muttered.

"Well, see what you can do. Oh, and word came from upstairs—the powers that be want more riot coverage. You in the middle of the action, if possible."

"Tonight?" she said in alarm.

"Tomorrow morning, but only if the crowd is still unruly."

Rebecca suppressed a sigh. Wonderful. Get Trampled in a Stampede, Part Two.

"Fine. Call me if you find out more about Barrett, okay?"

"Of course. Good night, Becks. Great reporting today."

She hung up the phone and stared at the picture of Nick on her computer screen. Lord, the man was *delicious*.

A part of her almost wished she'd saved the big I-know-who-you-are reveal until *after* she'd slept with the man.

A shiver rolled through her as she wondered what

he'd be like in bed. He looked and acted like such a gentleman, but she'd glimpsed the passion in his amber-colored eyes as they'd swept over her body. Would he be sweet and gentle beneath the sheets? Or did he leave his chivalry at the door when it came to sex?

Disappointment filled her belly as she realized she'd never get the chance to find out.

What's more important, Becks—sex or a Pulitzer?

Right. She definitely needed to focus on the latter. No matter how attractive Nick Barrett was, his delectable body wasn't the ultimate prize.

No, his secrets were what she was after.

The call came to one of his private cell phones. Not the one reserved for business or the one he used for personal calls. This phone was for *personal business.*

The kind of business that every last man in D.C.'s political arena dabbled in—and would deny to their last breath.

"What is it?" He kept his voice low and his gaze fixed on the closed office door.

Although he was burning the midnight oil, there was always an overeager aide or two beyond that door, just waiting to do some ass kissing.

"We might have found them."

He didn't need to ask *who?* The hunt for those bothersome soldiers had been the proverbial thorn in his side this past year.

"Which one slipped up?" he demanded.

"If the intel checks out? Barrett."

Frustration seized his insides. Damn it. Barrett was the *last* man he wanted to kill.

Hell, he had no desire to kill *anyone.*

"Where is he?"

"Cortega. He met with a journalist who's covering the election crisis down there. Rebecca Parker."

Christ. A reporter? And Parker, in particular? That woman was far too smart for her own good. And damn ambitious.

Why would Barrett be talking to her?

He shifted uneasily in his chair. Had the soldiers found something to connect him to the Meridian virus?

"Parker's producer has been making phone calls all night," the man on the other end of the line continued. "He raised several flags when he started asking questions about Barrett." A pause. "If Barrett is in Cortega, what would you like to do about it?"

He went silent, mulled it over, sighed in reluctance. "Send a team down there. Take care of the problem— but not until he gives up the location of the other two."

"Sir, with all due respect…"

He clucked in irritation. "Spit it out, Carraway."

"Our primary concern was that the soldiers would realize the deaths in Corazón were caused by a virus rather than the ULF rebels. At that point, the goal was to silence the unit before they questioned what happened in the village." Another pause. "But now the whole country knows that a virus was being tested in San Marquez."

Bitterness clamped around his throat. The whole country *did* know, a fact that continued to infuriate him. Project Aries had been shrouded in secrecy from the get-go. Nobody was ever supposed to know that an American-engineered biological weapon was being tested on foreign soil, and the truth would have stayed hidden if it weren't for that greedy scientist at the lab that created the Meridian virus.

That slimeball Stephen Langley had sold the virus to

a terrorist group, who in turn revealed to the world that the virus was U.S.-made and government-authorized. And now, thanks to Langley's betrayal, the DoD had formed a damn task force to determine who was responsible for Project Aries.

Not that he was worried about it leading back to him—he had several fail-safes in place.

Several scapegoats, too.

"Now that the truth is out, the soldiers aren't a threat," Carraway went on. "It's not like they can expose us."

"Not a threat?" He chuckled harshly. "Special Ops soldiers are a different breed. They're ruthless, smart, unforgiving. They won't stop until they find the person responsible for ordering the elimination of their unit."

"A unit that shouldn't have been sent to Corazón in the first place," was the embittered response. "A cleanup team was already on its way. The rebels would've been taken care of and the deaths of the villagers and the medical staff would've been blamed on Hector Cruz and his men. But no, thanks to a communication mix-up, a Special Forces team was sent to answer Dr. Harrison's SOS."

"There's nothing we can do about that now," he said with a heavy breath. "Mistakes were made. The unit was erroneously dispatched, and now we have three loose ends to take care of. So send a team to Cortega and deal with it."

"What about Parker?"

He thought it over, his stomach going rigid with anger. Damn it. Why had Barrett met with Parker?

And what the hell had he told the woman?

"Take care of her, too," he finally replied.

A long beat. "It will be difficult to separate her from

her crew, and any sort of interrogation would have to be handled delicately. She can't know why she's being questioned."

"Then don't question her. The woman is smart. She'll see through any phony interrogation attempts, and she'll keep investigating, especially if she's asked to stop."

"What are you saying, sir?"

"The protesters are still causing trouble in Mala, are they not?" he said slowly.

"As far as I know, yes."

"And Parker is right in the middle of the action." He released a weary sigh. "Take her out of the equation. Make it look like part of the riot. Her whole crew, if possible." He paused. "The producer, too."

"This is risky. Has the potential to blow up in our faces."

"We don't have any other choice."

"I suppose." Carraway sounded unconvinced.

He suddenly felt incredibly frazzled, like this entire situation was slipping out of his control. "Just get it done," he snapped. "Barrett, Parker, their associates... get rid of them all."

Chapter 5

Much to Nick's displeasure, Salazar texted the next morning to reschedule their meeting. Again. With the streets of Mala still in uproar, the presidential guard was committed to keeping the country's leader safe from the unruly people who refused to acknowledge Garza's power.

Cortega's military and law enforcement officers weren't equipped to deal with a riot of this magnitude. Barricades were being knocked down by the angry mob, all attempts by the tactical team to control the crowd had gone nowhere, and more and more people continued to arrive; some hailed from Cortega, others came from all over the world to show their support for the struggling citizens.

Nick had had enough of it all. He'd spent the morning in one of the city's most dangerous and derelict neighborhoods trying to track down El Nuevo Diablo. Nearly every man, woman and child living in those projects had refused to speak to him. Those who did demanded compensation for their time, but once he told them who he was looking for, they swiftly handed him back the cash and claimed ignorance. They were so terrified of El Nuevo Diablo that they wouldn't even accept a cash bribe that could've put food on their tables for months.

Now Nick was once again riding the elevator up to his hotel room. He had nothing to do but wait for Eva to get him the name of a con man who supposedly sold fake IDs down by the docks, but Nick doubted Paul Waverly would've used anyone less than the best. It was still worth looking into, though.

The elevator doors opened with a loud chime and Nick headed down the carpeted hallway toward his room. He was ten steps from the door when his instincts began to buzz and the little hairs at his nape stood on end.

Something was off.

Without slowing or altering his pace, he continued his approach, his gaze immediately noting the barely visible scratches around the keyhole on the doorknob. Someone had picked the lock.

Nick kept walking. Right past his room. All the way to the stairwell door at the end of the hall.

His hand slid beneath his long-sleeved shirt and down to the waistband of his cargo pants where he'd tucked his 9-millimeter SIG SAUER. He'd just gotten a grip on the weapon when a door flew open from behind.

He spared a hasty glance over his shoulder and saw a tall, muscular man filling the doorway of Nick's hotel room.

As their eyes locked, triumph lit the stranger's eyes

and his hand whipped up to reveal a .45 handgun with a suppressor affixed to its muzzle.

"We've got him!" the man shouted.

Son of a bitch.

Nick dived into the stairwell, adrenaline burning in his blood and fueling his actions. He raced down the stairs, his boots slapping the concrete floor with each hurried step. He'd just reached the third-floor landing when he heard the fifth-floor stairwell door burst open from above.

Footsteps thudded on the stairs, spurring him to move faster. His breathing didn't change. His heartbeat remained steady. One foot in front of the other.

There was no time to be afraid. No time to panic.

No time to dwell on the metallic *pop* that echoed in the stairwell as a bullet lodged into the wall above Nick's head.

He made it to the lobby, throwing the door open with such force that it slammed into the wall with a loud crash. Ignoring the startled looks of the clerks at the front desk, Nick tore out of the hotel. He didn't turn around. Didn't check to see if anyone was behind him.

"He's on the move!"

The male voice had come from the passenger side of the unmarked black van parked at the curb. A second later, a man in camo pants and a black tee flew out of the van and gave chase.

Damn it.

Nick ran faster, dodging people left and right. He made a conscious effort to keep his gun tucked beneath his shirt, but the man chasing him didn't deem it important to conceal his weapon. Several passersby gasped when they glimpsed the gun in the goon's hand. A woman screamed, and then several shrieks pierced the air as more people on the sidewalk became aware of the gun-wielding man running by.

Goddammit! Nick didn't dare turn around, but he knew his pursuer wasn't too far behind. Fortunately, the Liberty happened to be two blocks from the city's renowned antiques market—which was precisely why Nick had chosen that particular hotel. The market was an enormous maze of endless booths and tables and curtained kiosks, the perfect place to disappear.

Relief poured into him when the marketplace came into view. Less than a minute later, he was lost in a crowd of antiquers. A glance behind showed his frustrated pursuer elbowing his way through the throng of people.

Everything about the man said *mercenary*. The clothes, the shaved head, the military precision of his movements.

Nick reached a large area where hundreds of carpets hung from various clotheslines. He ducked behind a dusty Persian rug and began weaving his way through the canopy of carpet, which provided perfect cover.

He didn't turn around, didn't slow down, just moved through the market with quick methodical strides, not stopping until he was certain he'd lost his tail.

He ended up at a corner bar twenty blocks from the antiques market. His mercenary friend was nowhere to be seen, and the back of Nick's neck wasn't tingling anymore, a sure sign that he was no longer being hunted.

The bar was deserted save for the stocky bartender and a lone patron at the far end of the counter. Both men eyed Nick in suspicion as he approached the counter.

"What can I do for you?" the bartender asked in Spanish.

Nick responded in the same tongue. "A pint. What-ever you've got on tap."

As the burly, olive-skinned man moved away to pour the beer, Nick slid onto a tall stool, positioning himself so that he wasn't close to the front window but still had a line of sight to the door. The small television hang-ing over the bar was turned to a local news channel, the male reporter on the screen covering the downtown riot that was going strong. The looting had started in the wee hours of the morning, and there was now talk of Cortega seeking aid from the Brazilian army to con-trol the mobs.

"Crazy people," the bartender muttered, his disap-proving gaze fixed on the TV. He set a tall beer glass nearly overflowing with foam in front of Nick.

Nick paid for the beer and thanked the man, then fished out his cell phone and called Tate.

"They found me," he murmured, keeping his gaze trained on the door. He kept a close watch on the peo-ple beyond the plate-glass window, but the merc with the shaved head was nowhere in sight.

"Who?" Tate asked sharply.

"Mercs. They broke into my hotel room, then chased me for ten frickin' blocks."

"You sure they were soldiers for hire and not U.S. military?"

"They were too bold to be military. The one on the street was waving a gun around in front of pedestrians. He wasn't trying to be covert. If Uncle Sam had sent these guys, they would've used some stealth."

"Did you lose the tail?"

"Yeah. I'll head to another hotel, hole up there until Salazar gets in touch."

A familiar voice suddenly caught Nick's attention, drawing his gaze back to the television screen.

Rebecca Parker.

She was doing a live report from outside the parliament building, shouting over the roar of the crowd.

A spark of concern lit Nick's gut, but at least the woman had the sense to stick close to the news van this time. As she spoke, the camera panned to the furious mob, then focused on a car that was engulfed in flames thirty feet away. The sheen of sweat on Rebecca's forehead told him that she must be hot as hell standing near that conflagration, but she sounded cool as a cucumber as she addressed her viewers.

"As you can see, the violence has escalated overnight. Two members of the armed guard were nearly beaten to death by five youths who have since been taken into custody, and several vehicles have been set on fire in the past hour. We're seeing Molotov cocktails being thrown at the parliament building and—"

"—still looking into it, but Harrison was the only member of the team who spoke to Waverly."

Nick jerked his gaze away from the screen as he registered Tate's last remark. "Sorry, what was that?"

"I said that the scientists at the lab that created the virus, D&M Initiative, are being questioned, but they all maintain that they don't know who contracted them to work on Project Aries. Apparently Richard Harrison was the point man for the project—all he told his staff was that they were working on a top-secret government project."

"He didn't give them any names?"

"Nope, but his phone records indicate that he was in touch with Paul Waverly."

Wariness flooded Nick's chest. "Do we think someone in the Department of Defense authorized the virus project?"

"Maybe." Tate paused. "Secretary Barrett has always been gung ho about defense. I can easily see the man green-lighting a biological weapons project like this."

Nick bit back an indignant denial, but inside, he was seething. His father would *never* allow a deadly virus to be tested on innocent people. Kirk Barrett was the most honorable man Nick had ever known. A man who cared not only about the American people, but also about *all* people, a man who considered it his duty to help those who needed it, no matter what.

Not only that, but Nick's father possessed an iron-clad sense of right and wrong. It used to drive him nuts when he was growing up—every mistake he'd made required punishment, even if he'd learned his lesson from it. Kirk Barrett didn't tolerate wrongdoing, whether it was breaking curfew or forgetting to take the trash out or telling a little white lie.

Nick knew without a shred of doubt that his father was incapable of being involved in something as despicable as Project Aries, but he couldn't say anything to Tate. Not without confessing that he'd been lying about who he was in the five years they'd served together. Although his commander had known who Nick was, the other men in the unit had been kept in the dark, and he wasn't ready to confess to the deception. Not now, anyway.

"You've gotta light a fire under Salazar's ass, man," Tate went on. "The more time you spend waiting, the less chance we have of finding Waverly."

"Trust me, I know."

On the TV, Rebecca was urgently informing the audience that a Molotov cocktail had just been hurled at a member of the tactical squad.

"We've got a man on fire!" she said sharply. "Folks, these images are graphic. Please, if you've got young children, I urge you to move them away from the screen."

The camera shifted to provide a gruesome tableau of a uniformed man engulfed in flames as he rolled on the pavement. Two policemen were desperately attempting to stomp out the flames that were devouring the man, who was screaming in agony.

Nick blanched. Christ, this was *insanity*.

"Anyway," Tate was saying.

A deafening boom and a horrified scream blared out of the screen.

Two seconds later, glass shattered as the bartender dropped the empty beer pitcher he'd been drying with a dishrag.

"Oh, blessed mother," the man said in Spanish.

Nick sucked in a breath and watched the scene in horror. "Oh, Jesus." He shot to his feet, nearly dropping the phone. "Tate, I'll call you back."

Flames. Orange flames. Filling the screen.

Nick's heart hammered out a frenetic rhythm. The camera was no longer aimed on Rebecca. It had clattered to the ground, tilted at an awkward angle that made it hard to decipher what was happening.

A familiar female voice cried out in terror. "Jesse! *Jesse!*"

Rebecca.

With trembling palms, Nick glanced at the bartender and said, "Turn it up!"

The man did as he was ordered, and Rebecca's voice got louder. She was panicked. Freaking out. Nick couldn't see her, but he could hear her. He suspected everyone in the world was hanging on Rebecca Parker's every word.

"The van's been hit! It's on fire! Jesse's down! Oh God, *Jesse!*"

A blur of movement flashed past the lens, followed by a second explosion that yet again altered the camera angle.

Sneakers. Nick made out a pair of women's sneakers, a soot-covered hand whizzing past the camera.

"Jesse, open your eyes! Look at me!"

And then the screen went black.

"Go to a different channel," Nick snapped. "Now!"

Again, no hesitation on the bartender's part. The second news channel they tuned in to was already covering this latest catastrophe, and they caught the male anchor midsentence.

"—several incendiary devices thrown at the American Broadcast News van."

The anchor was sitting behind a news desk in the studio, and a picture of Rebecca appeared on the screen next to his head.

Nick's pulse sped up at the sight of her familiar green eyes and tousled red hair.

"We've just received confirmation that the driver was killed in the explosion. Parker's cameraman has been badly injured—we're getting reports that he's being rushed to the hospital with third-degree burns. There is no word on Parker yet. We simply do not know if she—" The man halted, touched his earpiece. "Wait, we've got an update. Rebecca Parker, award-winning correspondent for ABN, was not injured in the explosions. She just departed the scene in the ambulance with her cameraman, who has been identified as Jesse Williams."

Relief crashed over him like a tidal wave. Rebecca wasn't hurt. Thank God.

But her driver was dead. Her cameraman with third-degree burns.

Because a few protesters had thrown Molotov cocktails at the ABN crew.

Why?

Nick's gut went rigid as the question floated into his head. Why would the protesters try to harm the very people who were shedding light on their cause?

On the TV, the news anchor was attempting to make sense of it, as well. "Officials on the scene suspect that the explosive devices were intended for the tactical team that had just pulled up near the ABN van. The three Molotov cocktails, however, missed their mark."

Three Molotov cocktails?

And all three had failed to hit the intended target? Either those protesters had the crappiest aim on the planet, or…

Or the SWAT team *hadn't* been the intended target. *Rebecca.*

As the alarming thought sliced into his head, Nick glanced at the bartender and said, "Is there a back door I can leave out of?"

The man nodded, his shocked gaze still glued to the screen. He absently pointed to the corridor leading to the restrooms. "Emergency exit, back there."

With a nod of gratitude, Nick hurried to the corridor. He'd all but forgotten about the trigger-happy mercenaries who were currently pursuing him; all he could focus on was Rebecca. Her cry of horror. Her shaky pleas for her cameraman to open his eyes and look at her.

The hospital. He had to get to the hospital ASAP.

His inner alarms were ringing, his instincts screaming for him to get to Rebecca—and fast.

She was in danger. Whatever went down just now, it had been no accident. Someone had intentionally tried to blow up Rebecca and her crew. Nick knew it with a certainty that ran bone-deep.

And he got the feeling that it was all his fault.

Numb. Rebecca was utterly numb. She couldn't think, couldn't breathe, couldn't move. Each time she tried to snap herself out of it, the image of Jesse going up in flames assaulted her mind and nausea scampered up her throat. The odor of burned flesh still permeated her clothes, her hair, her nostrils. The look of terror and agony in Jesse's eyes was one she would never forget.

People were talking to her. Yelling at her. She could hear their voices, but they sounded so very far away, like they were coming from the other end of a long tunnel. It wasn't until she felt the sting of pain on her arm that she registered what was happening—the emergency room nurses were forcibly pulling her away from Jesse's gurney.

"You can't go in there with him, Ms. Parker," one of the nurses snapped. "Please, let us handle it."

She nodded weakly and stepped back, her gaze glued to Jesse's face.

Or what used to be his face.

Sickness churned in her belly and she swallowed hard, trying to keep the nausea at bay. She'd encountered some gory visuals in her career, but this…this…

Rebecca tore her eyes off her friend's charred, blackened flesh. Sorrow tightened her throat as the reality of the situation sank in.

Jesse wasn't going to make it.

Nobody could possibly survive the severity of these burns.

"Fourth-degree burns," she heard a male voice bark.

Shifting her head, she spotted a doctor in green scrubs rushing alongside the gurney, which was being rolled toward a pair of double doors bearing a restricted-access sign. The medical workers flocking Jesse disappeared through the swinging doors, but not before Rebecca heard the words *hypovolemic shock* being tossed out.

That didn't sound good.

God, none of this was good.

She still couldn't believe it. One second she'd been delivering a routine report into Jesse's camera, the next she was watching her cameraman engulfed by flames.

And then another explosion. The explosion that rocked the van.

Dave's screams of pain as he burned to death.

Rebecca gagged, choking on bile. She glimpsed a sign for the ladies' washroom at the end of the hall and dashed toward it, throwing herself into the first available stall and flying to her knees. She threw up, her eyes watering, her throat burning.

She didn't know how long she huddled over that toilet, but her insides felt raw and achy by the time she unsteadily rose to her feet. She left the stall and approached the sink where she rinsed out her mouth, then studied her ravaged appearance in the mirror.

Soot smudged her face, and she had a tiny nick on her left cheek from the pebble that had dug into her skin when she'd hit the pavement. Her white T-shirt was singed, streaked with black and gray—and red.... Blood. A quick investigation revealed that she had a minor scrape on her left hip.

Drawing in a shaky breath, she bent over the sink again and washed the ash off her face, but the smell of smoke continued to linger in the air.

That bone-numbing paralysis followed her out of the bathroom. She couldn't seem to focus on a single thought. She knew she needed to find a doctor and ask about Jesse. She needed to call the network. She needed to contact Harry.

But she was so unbelievably *numb*.

She stood in the fluorescent-lit corridor and sagged against the white wall, then slid into a sitting position and wrapped her arms around her knees. Five minutes or five hours—she could've been down there on the floor for either amount of time for how out of it she was.

"Ms. Parker?"

She lifted her head at the sound of the subdued male voice and found the doctor who'd been treating Jesse looming over her.

Rebecca took one look at his face and let out a soft moan. "Oh, God."

"I'm sorry," he said gently. "Mr. Williams's burns were simply too severe. We were dealing with burns on more than twenty-five percent of the total body surface area and I'm afraid that…"

She tuned him out.

Because really, what was the point in listening anymore?

Jesse was dead. Dave was dead.

When you spent ten months of the year on assignment, you didn't have much time for socializing, and these past five years, Jesse and Dave had been her only friends. The two men, both in their mid-forties, had taken Rebecca under their wing, treated her like the little sister they'd never had, shown her unfailing support and provided her with endless hours of laughter.

And now they were both gone.

"Ms. Parker?" the doctor prompted.

She absently met his gaze. "Sorry, what was that?"

"I was saying that the release of the body can be arranged with the coroner."

Tears stung her eyes. "Right. Okay."

With a sympathetic look, the doctor conveyed his apologies again, then walked away.

Wiping her eyes, Rebecca got to her feet, knowing she had to get it together. She would grieve later. Right now, she needed to be strong.

"Rebecca Parker?"

She turned around and saw two unfamiliar men in black suits approaching. The taller of the two flashed a gold badge, then offered a rueful smile. "Detective Raoul Flores," he introduced. "This is my partner, Dante Valleti. We're with the Mala P.D."

Valleti, a stocky man with a shaved head, shot her a grave look. "We're sorry to bother you in your time of grief, but we need to get a statement from you regarding the events that transpired."

She stifled a sigh. "Does it have to be now?"

"I'm afraid so," Flores said briskly. "It's imperative that we question you while the details are still fresh in your mind—"

Fresh in her mind? She almost burst into hysterical laughter. God! Like she would ever forget seeing Jesse devoured by flames.

"—if we want to find the culprits responsible for the bombing."

"Why don't we do this in the commissary rather than

the station?" Valleti suggested in a kind tone. "If you'd be more comfortable with that."

She finally nodded. "Fine. But let's make it fast. I have to contact Jesse's family and…" Her throat squeezed. "I…have things to take care of."

"We understand," Flores said, his dark eyes flickering with sympathy.

And annoyance. She definitely didn't miss the tiny spark of annoyance in the detective's eyes.

Rebecca's lips tightened as she followed the two men toward the elevator. The last thing she wanted to do was drink a cup of coffee and describe how she'd just watched her friends die before her eyes, and these policemen were insensitive jerks for making her do this. The only reason she'd agreed was because she wanted the people responsible to be punished for what they'd done to Jesse and Dave.

As the elevator doors opened, the trio stepped into the car. Valleti punched the button for the lobby, causing Rebecca to knit her eyebrows together in a frown. "The cafeteria is on the second floor," she told the detective.

He ignored her.

Suppressing an angry retort, she reached out and tried to press the right button, only to freeze when something hard suddenly jabbed her tailbone.

A gun.

"Detective" Raoul Flores had pulled a gun and was now pressing the muzzle into Rebecca's lower back.

As fear pummeled into her, Flores's low warning hung in the elevator car. "One more move and I put a bullet in your spine, sweetheart."

Chapter 6

Nick came to a screeching stop at the curb in front of the hospital entrance, ignoring the no-parking signs and the frowns from the scrubs-wearing, cigarette-holding hospital workers loitering at the nearby smoking area. He'd tuned into the radio on the drive over, and although there had been no further updates about Rebecca or her cameraman, that feeling of urgency refused to leave him.

Rebecca had nearly died—the morning after she'd met with him. It was too big a coincidence to ignore, and when you factored in the hit squad that had ambushed Nick at the hotel earlier, it didn't take a genius to figure out that his location had been compromised.

Shutting off the engine, he threw open the driver's door and jumped out of the tan-colored sedan, but he'd barely taken three steps when his gaze collided with a startling scene.

Rebecca had just walked through the automatic doors at the entrance. She was flanked by two men in dark suits—one of whom happened to be the mercenary that had popped out of Nick's hotel room less than an hour ago.

Rebecca's green eyes widened in recognition when she spotted Nick across the narrow roadway. "Nick!" she shouted, the fear and panic on her face unmistakable.

The mercenaries on either side of her immediately swiveled their heads in Nick's direction, and a second later, two guns were aimed at him.

Yet again, the sheer boldness of these bastards amazed him. They had no qualms about opening fire—in public—and Nick found himself diving behind the sedan for cover as the mercenaries started shooting.

Screams erupted from the smoking section near the curb. Nick ignored the din and drew his weapon. Sitting on the asphalt, he flattened his back against the passenger-side door, took a deep breath, then risked a glance at the shooters.

Metallic pings echoed in the air as a spray of bullets embedded into the side of the sedan. The men were using silencers. So was Nick, and his next shot came out as a sharp hiss. He hit one of the mercenaries square in the chest, and satisfaction ignited in his gut as he watched the man go down.

More horrified shouts cut the air. It was ten o'clock in the morning, too bright and sunny for a goddamn shoot-out outside a hospital. A swift peek around the front bumper revealed the remaining mercenary dragging Rebecca toward the police cruiser parked near the E.R. entrance. Nick didn't know how the mercs had managed to get their hands on a cop car, but these men sure as hell weren't police officers.

"Rebecca!" Nick yelled from his position behind the car. "Get down!"

Rather than obey, the stubborn woman did the exact opposite—she suddenly lunged at the man who was glued to her side, disarming him with a nifty little kick-boxing move that would've made Nick grin if he wasn't so frickin' furious.

Both Rebecca and the merc dived after the falling weapon, but the redhead reached it first. She pointed the gun at her almost-abductor and bounced to her feet, tossing Nick a frantic glance over her shoulder.

The questioning look in her eyes told him she was debating whether to shoot the mercenary, but Nick quickly vetoed that idea by shouting, "Get in the car! I'll cover you."

After a beat of hesitation, Rebecca spun on her heels and raced toward the sedan while Nick kept his gun trained on the mercenary. The stocky man was stagger-ing to his feet, his eyes alight with rage as he watched his prey escape.

Nick would've liked to put a bullet in the son of a bitch's head, but the wail of sirens and the shocked faces of the crowd beginning to form stopped him from being stupid. This was a disaster. One merc dead, the other now fleeing the scene, his heavy footsteps thud-ding on the pavement.

Rebecca slid into the passenger seat and slammed the door, prompting Nick to move. Keeping his head down, he dashed to the driver's side and jumped into the car. Seconds later, he'd started the engine and was hightailing it out of there.

No media. He clung to the thought as he sped away

in a squeal of tires. There had been no cameras or re-
porters outside the hospital, so at least he didn't have
to worry about his pretty mug appearing on any television screens. But those people on the curb had seen
his face—what if one of them had recognized him as
Nick Barrett?

His gaze moved to the silent, ashen-faced redhead
beside him. No, Rebecca was the more recognizable
of the two of them. If anyone had been recognized, it
was her.

"Are you okay?" he asked tersely, keeping his eyes
on the road ahead.

She didn't answer.

From the corner of his eye, Nick saw that her hands
were still wrapped around the mercenary's .45 HK.
Steady hands. Jeez, the woman had nerves of steel.
She wasn't trembling, her breathing was steady, her
eyes alert.

Only that white-as-snow complexion revealed her
fear.

"Rebecca." He sharpened his tone. "Are you all
right?"

She blinked. Shook her head a couple of times. Then
she turned to meet his concerned gaze. "What the heck
is going on?" she blurted out. "Who were those men?
What did they want from me?"

"They were mercenaries. A private hit squad."

Her face went another shade paler. "Hit squad? They
were sent here to kill me?"

"Most likely."

Those green eyes blazed at his nonchalant response.
"Why? Why would they want to kill me?"

"Because you talked to me," he said simply.

Her breath hitched.

Nick drove through an intersection and executed a hard left, speeding through the narrow streets of Mala.

"I told you this would happen," he went on, his tone harsher than he intended. "You spoke to someone about me, didn't you?"

"Yes." There was no guilt in her voice, no remorse on her face, but she looked shaken as hell.

"Who?"

"My producer, Harry Drexler." She let out a wobbly breath. "I asked him to dig around, find out why the sec def's son would be in Cortega."

Nick cursed under his breath. "He probably triggered a hundred alarms when he started asking questions."

Not to mention broadcasted Nick's location to the people who were hunting him.

Wonderful. Now it was even more imperative that he meet with Salazar and get the hell out of Cortega.

"I'm sorry," Rebecca said quietly. "You told me to forget I ever saw you, and I didn't listen, but you've got to understand, this is my job—"

"This is your *life,*" he cut in. "I told you that getting involved in this would put you in danger, but you just couldn't let it go, could you?"

"Involved in *what?*" she said angrily. "Maybe if you'd offered a few more details last night, I would have been able to drop it the way you asked—no, the way you *demanded.* But what the heck did you expect would happen when you dangled that gee-dee carrot under my nose? I'm a journalist! I don't stop asking questions, I don't stop digging, not until I have the whole story, and I refuse to apologize for being dedicated to my job!"

He sped through another intersection before turning to glare at her. "How clearer could I have been? I told you your life would be at risk if you told anyone about me."

"My life is always at risk," she retorted, her jaw tighter than a drum. "It was at risk when I got shot at by those rebels in Johannesburg. It was at risk when I covered the civil war in Congo and when I visited a warlord's prison in Nigeria and when—"

"I get the point."

"Do you? Because I don't think you understand what I *do* for a living." Her tone grew surly. "I don't walk away from a story. Period."

"Well, how's that working out for you right now?" he said sarcastically.

Rebecca fell silent, but he could feel the anger vibrating from that petite body of hers. Angry. She was frickin' *angry* at him. After he'd just saved her life.

She saved herself, buddy boy.

Fine, so she'd displayed some impressive skills when she'd kicked that gun out of her captor's hands, but if Nick hadn't taken down the merc's colleague, Rebecca wouldn't have had the opportunity to act. The woman ought to be showing him some gratitude instead of stewing there as if he'd wronged her.

Nick turned into the parking lot of a small plaza and drove to the alley in the back where he parked next to a black SUV.

"What are we doing?" Rebecca asked warily.

"Ditching the car."

"You're just going to abandon your car in this alley?" She sounded bewildered.

"This isn't my car."

"Then whose is it? Did you steal it?"

"Do you always ask so many questions?" he said irritably.

"I'm a *journalist*. Why do you keep forgetting that?"

Nick reached for the door handle. "Get out of the car, Rebecca."

They hopped out, and he quickly ushered her to the SUV and opened the passenger door for her. A suspicious cloud floated across her face. "Did you steal this one, too?"

He sighed. "No, this one is mine. I stashed it here before I went to the hospital. Now get in before I push you in."

To his dismay, amusement danced in her green eyes. "You're so bossy. I kinda like it. Sometimes."

He decided not to touch that remark. In fact, he was having a difficult time making sense of *anything* this woman said and did. Rebecca Parker was fearless. Terrifyingly fearless. She should've been far more shaken up over everything that had happened, yet she seemed unfazed by it all.

Or so he thought; it wasn't until they were in the SUV and on the move again that Rebecca's composed front finally began showing signs of cracking.

"I need to know what's going on." Her voice wavered. "Jesse…my cameraman…he's *dead*."

The chord of sorrow in her voice made his chest ache. "Ah, Rebecca, I'm sorry."

"Fourth-degree burns." Now she sounded angry again. "He's dead, Nick. Jesse's dead and Dave is dead, and *I* almost died, and I don't think it was part of the riot. I don't think it was an accident."

"Neither do I."

His hands slid over the steering wheel as he pulled onto the on-ramp of Mala's sole freeway. The road was littered with potholes, the pavement uneven, but it sure beat the narrow maze of streets that made up the city's core.

"Where are we going?" Rebecca asked as the SUV picked up speed.

"North. I've got a place where we can lie low until we figure out our next move. It's about an hour's drive."

"An hour, huh?"

He felt her sharp gaze burning a hole into the side of his face. Stifling a tired sigh, he gave her a sidelong gaze and said, "What?"

"Are you kidding me?" She shook her head in disbelief. "We've got an hour's drive ahead of us. So start talking, Nick! Tell me what the fu—*fudge* is going on, darn it!"

Rebecca couldn't remember the last time she'd felt this frustrated. It didn't help that the man beside her was more tight-lipped than a mob boss. Would it kill Nick to offer some insight on this messed-up situation? Two men had nearly abducted her in broad daylight. With the intent of *killing* her, if they truly were members of a hit squad like Nick claimed.

Leftover adrenaline traveled in her veins, making her feel light-headed. She suddenly became aware that she was still holding that hit man's gun, and she quickly opened the glove compartment and shoved the weapon inside.

Next to her, Nick still hadn't uttered a word.

"Start. Talking," she ordered through gritted teeth.

He let out a heavy breath. "It's a long story."

"And gee, we have an *hour* for you to tell it. So, for the love of God, tell me what's going on. Why do people want to kill you?"

Nick went quiet for a beat. "What do you know about the Meridian virus?"

The question succeeded in startling her. "Wait, this is about the Meridian virus?" When he nodded, she furrowed her brow in confusion. "Okay. Well, I know a lot about it. A terrorist group—some splinter faction of the ULF—released it in the water supply of Dixie, New York, two weeks ago, killing a thousand people. The group threatened to release the virus in a major city if America didn't remove its influence from San Marquez."

"Right," Nick said with a nod. "What else?"

Because she'd reported on the virus crisis directly outside the small town of Dixie, Rebecca had no shortage of details. "The ULF cell claimed that the virus was engineered in the United States, and that our government authorized the testing of it in San Marquez. They said we killed hundreds of their villagers."

"We did."

Nick's matter-of-fact response sent her eyebrows soaring. "Are you serious?" she demanded.

He turned his head to meet her surprised gaze, nodded, then focused on the stretch of highway up ahead. "The first test site was Corazón. It's a remote village in the western region of San Marquez. My unit and I were sent there to extract an American doctor who was supposedly being held hostage by the ULF rebels, but when we got there, the doctor was already dead. So were all the villagers."

"They were killed by the virus?"

"Yes, but we didn't know it at the time. My unit showed up to find Hector Cruz and his fellow rebels burning all the bodies."

Rebecca blanched. Before she could stop it, the

image of Jesse on fire flashed into her head, and her mind cruelly conjured up the acrid stench of smoke and flesh. It was so real she could swear she was smelling it in the SUV, and she had to take a deep calming breath before she fell apart again.

"What happened afterward?" she asked, trying to focus on Nick's story.

"Cruz got away, and we were recalled back to the States for debriefing. We were all operating under the assumption that Cruz and his men had killed the Corazón villagers." Nick's profile hardened. "But then my teammates starting dying. One accidental death after the other. It became obvious that someone was trying to eliminate us, but we didn't know why. When there were only three of us left, we decided to skip town and hide out until we could figure out why we were being hunted."

She wrinkled her brow. "And you tied it to the Meridian virus?"

He nodded again. "The Corazón villagers died from the virus. We think someone in the government wanted to shut us up, get us out of the way in case we gave too much thought to what we saw in that village."

"Who's we?"

"Me. My unit's captain, Tate. And Sebastian, another soldier. We've been moving around this past year, trying to make sense of it all. A couple of months ago, the virus was released in a new test site, another San Marquez village called Valero, and soon after that, one of the scientists responsible for creating the virus sold a vial of it to the ULF cell. Sebastian was actually part of the assault team that raided the terrorists' hideaway." Nick chuckled, but he didn't sound the slightest bit amused.

"Someone in the Department of Defense decided to thank Seb by infecting him with the virus."

Her eyes widened. "Your teammate died from the virus?"

"No, he's still alive." Nick's jaw tensed. "Sebastian's girlfriend accidentally ingested the water instead, but luckily she was administered the antidote in time. But the attempt on Seb's life told us that whoever authorized the creation of the virus still wants us dead."

"But why? The virus is common knowledge now," she pointed out.

"Yeah, but the identity of the person who green-lighted the project? That's still up for grabs, and that bastard knows my men and I won't rest until we track him down."

The lethal tone of his voice sent a shiver up Rebecca's spine. She studied his rigid profile, intrigued by the contrast between his handsome good looks and volatile expression. This man was a warrior. It was easy to forget that when you looked into those warm eyes, when you admired those classically chiseled features.

That cold shiver dissolved into a rush of warmth the longer she scrutinized Nick Barrett. His white T-shirt outlined every delicious ridge of his tight six-pack, and her fingers itched to stroke that hard, broad chest. To run through his messy brown hair, which looked so soft to the touch. She couldn't believe she was capable of getting aroused at a time like this, but apparently she was. So painfully aroused that her thighs clenched together involuntarily.

Nick seemed oblivious to her current state of agitation. "So that's it," he finished. "Someone in the government, most likely a big player in the White House, wants me dead."

She bit her lip. "And when I called Harry, I pretty much advertised your location to…let's just call him Mr. X."

Nick sounded annoyed again. "I told you to drop it."

"Well, I didn't, and now I'm a target," she said matter-of-factly. "So let's move past it and come up with a plan."

Shaking his head, he let out an amazed laugh. "Nothing fazes you, does it, Rebecca?"

"Not usually."

She swallowed hard as Jesse's agonizing screams rang inside her head. She swiftly banished the memories, forcing herself to focus. Grief would come later. Right now, her priority was staying alive.

A thought suddenly occurred to her. "You still haven't told me why you're in Cortega," she accused.

"Remember how I mentioned someone in the DoD tried to kill Sebastian? It was an aide named Paul Waverly, and he fled D.C. right after the attempt on Sebastian's life. We tracked him to Cortega," Nick explained. "Apparently he paid a visit to a man who rules the criminal underworld here, El—"

"Nuevo Diablo," she finished. "Yeah, I've heard of him. Mr. New Devil reportedly runs guns and drugs, dabbles in prostitution and deals with fake IDs. Is that what Waverly was doing? Getting papers?"

"I think so. But I can't be sure until I meet with Mr. New Devil for confirmation, and I haven't been able to arrange a meeting yet. My source has been distracted with the riot."

Rebecca pursed her lips. "All right. So we sit tight until your source is ready to meet us, then—"

"There is no us," Nick interrupted. "You're not a part of this."

Her jaw fell open. "Excuse me?"

"You heard me. You're not getting involved," he said in a tone that invited no argument. "I can handle this on my own."

"Oh, yeah? And pray tell, what am I supposed to do while you 'handle' this all by your lonesome?"

"I'll stash you somewhere safe and—"

"Stash me somewhere safe?" Disbelief hung from each word, and her pulse sped up in anger. "Are you effing *kidding* me?"

"Two men dragged you out of the hospital at gunpoint," he snapped. "Your cameraman and driver just burned to death!"

She flinched at the reminder.

"You're in danger, Rebecca. Whoever is after me probably thinks that I confided in you about this whole mess. You're a threat to him now."

"We don't even know who Mr. X is," she protested.

"But Mr. X doesn't know that. For all *he* knows, my men and I are fully aware of his true identity, and I came to Cortega to tell my story to world-renowned correspondent Rebecca Parker."

Nick flicked the turn signal and changed lanes, quickly speeding past a slow-moving truck that was chugging clouds of exhaust into the morning air.

Morning. Jeez, how was it only morning? Rebecca felt like collapsing and she'd only been up for four hours. God, so much had happened in those four hours—she'd lost two of her closest friends, she'd nearly been kidnapped and killed by a pair of mercenaries, and now she was fleeing the city with a gorgeous soldier who seemed intent on relegating her to the sidelines.

Well, too bad for him, because Rebecca had never spent a single second on the sidelines her entire life.

From this point on, she and Nick were in this together.

Whether he liked it or not.

Chapter 7

Rebecca Parker was the most aggravating female Nick had ever encountered. The woman had deemed it necessary to argue about every single sentence that came out of his mouth, and it was beginning to drive him crazy.

"We're here," he said curtly.

He came to a stop in front of the rambling old farmhouse that Rebecca had been eyeing with disdain ever since they'd turned onto the overgrown driveway half a mile back.

"This is your safe house? It doesn't look very safe." She paused. "Is this where I'm supposed to be *stashed?*"

Nick briefly closed his eyes and counted to three. *You cannot murder this woman,* he told himself.

He shut off the engine and yanked the keys out of the ignition. "It's safe enough," he said, then reached for the door handle.

Rebecca stuck close to his side as they approached the paint-chipped front door of the single-story farmhouse. The house had seen better days—its thatched roof looked ready to collapse, all the windows were boarded up, and the surrounding lawn was overrun with yellowing grass and tall weeds.

"Who owns this place?" Rebecca asked curiously.

"As of five days ago, I do. We bought the property online the day before I came to Mala. We've learned to take precautions over the past year. Now we always make sure to arrange for a safe house before we venture out into the world."

He reached into his pocket for the key he'd picked up from the Realtor's office the morning he'd arrived in Cortega.

"You really *bought* this farm?" Rebecca sounded amazed. "On the off chance that you might need a safe house?"

"Trust me, it didn't cost much," he said wryly.

As if to punctuate that, the front door creaked like a haunted house prop and released a cloud of dust when Nick pushed it open.

They walked in to find the house's interior as desolate and run-down as the exterior. The main room offered a wooden couch with ratty plaid cushions, a dining area with a broken table and appliances that were covered in a thick layer of dust. The entire place smelled like mildew, urine and sour milk.

Rebecca made a gagging noise as she breathed in the not-so-appetizing scent. "Okay, first thing on our to-do list? Open the gee-dee windows."

Nick didn't want to smile, but her backdoor expletives never failed to bring a grin to his lips. "Don't worry, we won't be here long," he assured her, but he did stalk across the room to crank open the kitchen window.

A warm breeze wafted into the room, making dust motes dance in the air. Nick dropped his go bag on the uneven wood floor and pulled his cell phone from his pocket. As he keyed in a quick text, he felt Rebecca's gaze on him.

"Who are you texting?" she demanded.

"Enrique Salazar. Telling him I need to meet him ASAP. I can't afford any more delays."

Rebecca offered a sweet smile. "You mean, *we* can't afford any more delays."

A frustrated groan lodged in his chest. Christ, this woman was tenacious. She refused to accept reality—he was *not* involving her in this quest for Waverly. In fact, the second he could make it happen, he was sending her to their base camp in Ecuador where Tate and the others could keep an eye on her. He'd already broached the idea in the car, but she'd shot it down so fast and so firmly that he hadn't mentioned it again.

Still, he had no intention of teaming up with this pigheaded redhead. For some inexplicable reason, he'd felt protective of Rebecca since the moment he'd seen her get swallowed up by that mob. He wasn't willing to put her neck on the line, especially because this entire mess had nothing to do with her.

He reiterated that now with a scowl. "This isn't your fight, and no disrespect, but if you tag along you'll only get in my way. I work better alone."

That stubborn chin of hers jutted out and he resisted the urge to march over and plant a kiss on her rosy-red lips. Even with her T-shirt streaked with soot and blood and her red hair a tangled mess, the woman was a damn knockout. His body reacted to the mere sight of her, prompting him to break the gaze and focus on the text he was in the process of composing.

After pressing Send, he held out the phone to Rebecca. "Call your producer," he told her. "Tell him to get out of town."

Anxiety filled her expression. "You really think Harry is in danger?"

Nick nodded gravely.

Her worry intensified, burning in her bright green eyes. With a shaky exhale, she accepted the cell phone, then hesitated. "What if Mr. X tapped your phone or something?"

"Don't worry, it's secure. Untraceable."

Rebecca dialed a number and brought the phone to her ear.

And then she waited. And waited.

The longer her call went unanswered, the uneasier Nick got.

"His cell went to voice mail."

Her tone was flat, her fingers shaky as she quickly punched in another number. She waited again, those pretty features straining with concern.

"Office line is going to voice mail, too." Her straight white teeth worried her bottom lip. "Harry's at his desk at 5:00 a.m., seven days a week. He should be at the studio. Why isn't he at the studio, Nick?"

He met her eyes. "You know why, darling."

"Bullcrap!" Her voice cracked. "He's probably at home. Let me call his house."

She called her producer's house.

No answer.

Her breathing grew shallow.

When she dialed another number, Nick swallowed a sigh and said, "Who are you calling now?"

"ABN's main switchboard," she said tightly.

He noticed that her fingers were trembling wildly as she gripped the phone. "Marlene," she said a few seconds later, "it's Rebecca Parker. I'm trying to get in touch with Harry, but he's not answering his phone. Do you know where he is?"

There was a long pause, and when Rebecca gasped in horror, Nick's heart dropped to the pit of his stomach like a sinking rock.

"When did this happen?" she whispered.

She looked so pale and stricken that Nick couldn't help but move closer. He rested his hand on her arm in a protective gesture, and when she leaned into him, he couldn't resist wrapping one arm around her shoulders.

He heard a tinny female voice emerging from the speaker, but he couldn't make out the words. Whatever was being said, it was bad. Very, very bad.

"I'm fine," Rebecca murmured into the phone. "Yes...I know...Jesse..." Her voice wavered. "I don't know yet. When is the memorial service?"

Nick gently steadied her when a shudder rolled through her body.

"I don't know...I'll be back in D.C. soon...Can you tell Stan and Bernie that I'm all right and that I'm taking some time to process everything?...Thanks, Marlene." Rebecca hung up without another word.

As another shudder racked her petite body, she shoved the phone into Nick's hand and for the first time since he'd met her, she looked truly affected by the tragic events of the past couple of days.

"Heart attack. Harry had a heart attack late last night." She spoke through ragged breaths. "His cleaning lady found him this morning."

"I'm sorry—"

"Harry was healthy as a horse! His heart was strong," she insisted. "He didn't die of a heart attack! He couldn't have."

"Rebecca—"

"He couldn't have," she repeated.

Tears brimmed in those big green eyes and she started shaking so hard that Nick knew it would be cruel not to offer comfort. So he yanked her into his arms and held her tight, stroking her tangled hair as she pressed her face against his chest and cried her heart out.

"It's okay, darling. It'll be okay."

His murmured words didn't seem to help, so he held her even tighter and offered every ounce of strength he possessed. The scent of smoke and death drifted up from her hair, bringing a deep ache to his chest. This woman had watched two of her friends get blown up this morning, and now another person she'd been close to had died.

"He was such a good man." Her agonized whisper heated the air, and then she was tilting her head to look up at him, her cheeks stained with tears. "This is my fault, Nick."

"It's not your fault." He cupped her chin and fixed her with a stern look. "You didn't cause this. If anyone's to blame, it's me. I shouldn't have gone for drinks with you. I shouldn't have put you in the position to snoop around."

Misery hung from her tone. "*I* asked Harry to look into it."

Nick swept his thumbs over her cheeks to wipe away the moisture sparkling there. Lord, even with her red-rimmed eyes and splotchy cheeks, Rebecca Parker was absolutely stunning.

"Mr. X did this, didn't he?"

The sharp bite that entered her tone, mingled with a note of rage, startled him. He wasn't sure he liked the glint of resolve that lit up her green eyes. Or the way her delicate hands curled into fists as she stepped out of his embrace.

"Whoever killed the other men in your unit is responsible for this," she said angrily. "He killed my crew, and now he sent someone to kill Harry."

"I told you—"

"Don't you dare say I told you so," she burst out. "I get it, all right? I shouldn't have gotten involved. But there's nothing I can do to change that. I can't rewrite the past. All I can do is deal with the present. And presently?" Fortitude blazed in her eyes. "We've got a corrupt DoD aide to track down."

As if on cue, Nick's phone buzzed. Satisfaction and relief rippled through him as he read Salazar's message.

"It's done," he told Rebecca. "Salazar arranged the meeting."

"With El Nuevo Diablo? When?"

"Tonight. Salazar will be there, too."

She responded with a dubious look. "How is it exactly that a member of the presidential guard is buddy-buddy with Mala's number-one criminal?"

"Do you really need me to explain the nature of corruption to you?"

When she rolled her eyes, she looked like her old self again.

The change of demeanor floored him, as did the determination lining her expression. This woman was no shrinking violet. She was tough as nails, and for a moment he was reminded of Eva and Julia, Tate and Sebastian's respective women. Those two possessed awe-inspiring strength that continued to take Nick's breath away, and now here he was, standing in front of another gutsy woman who seemed impervious to the danger around her.

"You know I'm coming with you to that meeting, right?"

Her no-nonsense tone brought a sigh to his lips. "No, you're not." He held up his hand before she could object. "And not just because it's too dangerous. Do you honestly think Salazar will be eager to talk to me if I show up with a journalist? He's a crooked government guard. You're a hard-hitting, very recognizable reporter. There's no way he'll risk his position by talking to you. So I don't care if I have to tie you up to that pipe over there—you're not going with me."

"Tie me up?" She smirked. "Let's save the kinky stuff for the bedroom, *darling.* And why don't you just relax? I see your point, and I concede to it."

He blinked in surprise. "Seriously?"

"I didn't get to where I am today by being a moron, Nick. You're right. Salazar will be less likely to talk if I'm there. We need to tread carefully here."

Again with the *we,* but Nick decided not to argue. Might as well pick his battles. Maybe if he humored Rebecca about their "partnership" for a bit, she'd be more agreeable later when he informed her she was heading to the Ecuador safe house.

Agreeable?

He nearly snorted as the thought entered his head. Yeah, he doubted that was a word that could ever be used to describe Rebecca Parker.

Salazar had arranged to meet at a bar situated halfway between Mala and the small village near the farmhouse. Nick had appreciated that Salazar had chosen a location outside the capital city, but now, as he arrived at the run-down rural cantina, he wondered if he ought to have insisted on meeting somewhere more…public.

Set away from the road, the bar was a one-story wooden structure with no discernible signs labeling it as a commercial venue. Moonlight reflected off a sloped tin roof, and although the place had no windows, the glow of lights spilled out from the front doors. Salazar said that Nick would know he was in the right place by the pack of dogs out front, and sure enough, nearly a dozen canines were lying on the reddish-brown dirt beyond the bar's entrance.

Nick parked the SUV next to a beat-up pickup truck that had seen better days. The dirt lot contained only a handful of vehicles, all in the same sorry state as the pickup.

As he hopped out of the car, several of the dogs lifted their heads and eyed him with mistrust. He eyed them right back, noting their scrawny bodies, visible rib cages and matted fur. Crap. Hopefully he wouldn't need to get a rabies shot today.

Luckily, not a single dog changed positions at Nick's approach. The canines just lounged there on the dirt, their eyes glowing in the darkness.

He headed for the entrance—a pair of waist-high swinging doors, Wild West–style—wishing he was carrying more than his SIG. He supposed he could've grabbed a few more choice weapons from the duffel in the trunk, but he hadn't wanted to scare Salazar away by showing up armed to the teeth.

There were a dozen men in the bar when Nick walked inside. A few single patrons sitting at the splintered, beer-stained counter, a small group playing dominoes at a corner table and another playing cards near the back. Every pair of eyes narrowed at Nick's entrance.

Ignoring the suspicious looks, he went over to the counter and met the bartender's cloudy gaze head-on. "I'm looking for Jose," he said in Spanish.

Almost instantly, the bartender's demeanor changed. Those dark eyes widened slightly, flickered with unmistakable fear, and his tall, lanky frame shifted uneasily.

Without a word, the man hooked a finger at the corridor across the room.

"Back there?" Nick prompted.

He received a quick nod in return.

Nodding back, he headed for the hallway, feeling every patron's cagey gaze glued to his back. He would've liked to say these men were being paranoid, but he got the feeling that the characters who frequented this cantina weren't exactly upstanding citizens. They probably treated every stranger who walked in here with extreme caution.

There were four doors in the hall—two were open, revealing a bathroom that stank to high heaven and a room full of metal cabinets. The third was marked *Storage*. Nick paused in front of the fourth and rapped his knuckles on the closed door.

A moment later, it swung open and he found himself looking into the dark brown eyes of Enrique Salazar.

"Prescott?" the man said sharply.

Nick nodded. He didn't need to ask if *he* had the right man—he recognized Salazar from the photos Eva had managed to compile. And just like the first time he'd seen Salazar's picture, he was surprised by how handsome the man was. Rugged features, tall, muscular body clad in jeans and a black leather jacket, a head of wavy black hair; the man seemed better suited for a career in Hollywood than the presidential secret service.

Salazar gestured for him to enter, and Nick stepped into a musty-smelling room that offered a green felt poker table surrounded by half a dozen chairs. Before he could take another step, Salazar began patting him down.

Nick's jaw tensed when the man confiscated his SIG, but Salazar simply shrugged and said, "Just a precaution, Mr. Prescott. You'll get it back when we conclude our business." He spoke in perfect, unaccented English.

"Fair enough."

"Let's sit."

They sat down on opposite ends of the table. Salazar leaned back in his chair and crossed his arms over his lean chest.

Nick was having a tough time battling his bewilderment. The man in front of him conveyed a calculated intelligence and understated charm that Nick had not expected. And he seemed incredibly...unruffled. Like he had no care in the world, which was seriously ironic considering he was betraying his president and government by dealing with El Nuevo Diablo, a wanted man in Cortega.

"So who's Jose?" Nick finally asked, referring to the name he'd been ordered to use with the bartender.

Salazar waved a careless hand. "Just a silly code. A man in my position doesn't want to advertise his presence—or his identity." He lifted a brow. "Do you have the money?"

"You mean you didn't feel that fat envelope of cash in my pocket when you were patting me down?"

He was rewarded with a genuinely warm laugh. "I

thought you were—what's the American phrase?—
happy to see me?"

Nick couldn't help but laugh, too. Reaching into the
pocket of his brown bomber jacket, he extracted the envelope and slid it across the green felt tabletop.

Without a word, Salazar picked up the envelope and
thumbed through its contents.

"It's all there," Nick assured him.

The other man kept counting.

Nick stifled a sigh. "Twenty grand, which is above
and beyond what I ought to be paying you to set up a
simple introduction."

A minute later, Salazar tucked the envelope into the
inner pocket of his leather jacket.

"Well?" Nick prompted.

"Well what?"

Impatience traveled through him, trailed by a rush
of annoyance. He was beginning to wonder if Enrique
Salazar was toying with him, purposely stalling just
for the hell of it.

"Where can I find El Nuevo Diablo?" he demanded.

Amusement filled Salazar's dark eyes, another hearty
laugh leaving his mouth. "You're looking at him."

Chapter 8

Despite an initial bout of shock, it didn't take long for Nick to realize that Salazar's confession was not shocking at all when you really thought about it. Members of the presidential guard carried a lot of clout in Mala—they had even more authority than the police. Salazar would have a mile-long list of connections, not to mention security clearance, and insider information about the president's movements and political agendas.

Nick released a rueful breath. "Why am I not surprised to hear that?"

The black-haired man chuckled. "There is something very devilish about me, no?"

Jeez. How was this man so damn charismatic? Every person Nick had spoken to in regard to El Nuevo Diablo had cowered at the mere mention of the infamous criminal. Drugs, guns, women—the man was involved in more than one shady enterprise. If you crossed him, you paid the price. If you did business with him, you were locked in for life.

And yet here he was, Mr. New Devil, sitting across the table with that dimpled smile and palpable magnetism.

"So you're not a middleman at all," Nick remarked.

"Clearly not." Salazar's lips twitched. "Now, tell me what you want with Mr. Waverly."

Nick's head jerked up. "So he *did* come to see you."

"Of course. There is no one else in Cortega worth seeing."

"Did you acquire documents for him?" A note of urgency echoed in Nick's voice. "Can you tell me what name he's traveling under? Or where he went from here?"

Salazar held up his hand to silence him. "First, let me tell you about the way I operate, Mr. Prescott. You probably already have an idea, considering you interrogated half the city about me these last few days."

He didn't bother asking how Salazar knew he'd been asking around. The man undoubtedly possessed more connections than the president he was sworn to protect.

"The people I do business with, they keep their mouths shut," Salazar began, his tone downright pleasant. "In return, I keep mine shut. Secrecy is the name of the game, as well as a sign of respect. Private transactions stay private—my clients trust me to deliver on that promise, and in return, I trust them to do the same."

"And if they don't?" Nick couldn't help but ask.

"They suffer the consequences." Salazar shrugged. "Not many men attempt to double-cross me these days, Mr. Prescott."

"No, I don't imagine they do." He slanted his head. "Is this your way of telling me that you won't sell out

Waverly? He's protected under your, uh, *confidentiality* agreement?"

"Not quite."

Salazar shoved a hand in his pocket and extracted two items. A Polaroid picture and a folded-up piece of white paper. He set them facedown on the table, but did not invite Nick to take a peek.

"I photograph every individual I do business with," Salazar told him.

"Another precaution, I presume?" Nick said drily.

"Of course. It allows me to keep my customers in line, should they think about selling me out or revealing my identity somewhere down the line. Oh, they all protest at first—'You can't take my picture!'—but I usually succeed in making them see reason. Now, as I said before, I don't typically betray my clients' identities. It's bad for business, and I am, first and foremost, a businessman."

Nick tried not to roll his eyes. "Of course."

"But the man you're looking for? Mr. Waverly?" Scorn flickered in Salazar's dark eyes. "I don't feel the need to extend the same courtesy to him that I do to other clients."

"He tried to double-cross you," Nick guessed.

"He tried to *negotiate*."

Salazar sounded so disgusted you'd think Waverly had done much worse than haggle for a better price. But apparently haggling was a big no-no in the eyes of El Nuevo Diablo.

"My fees are set in stone," the man harrumphed. "But that little prick thought he could mess with me. Rude, entitled bastard. I was happy to be rid of him."

"You arranged his new papers, then."

"I did." Salazar slid the Polaroid across the table. "This is the man you're seeking, is it not?"

Nick flipped over the photo and found himself looking at the pale face of Paul Waverly, former aide working out of the Pentagon, and the man who'd handed Sebastian a water bottle infected with the Meridian virus. Waverly's appearance had a very ghoulish vibe to it—with his light blond hair and vampire-white skin, he looked washed-out and sickly. But Sebastian had warned Nick not to be fooled by the man's outward fragility. Supposedly Waverly was built like a football quarterback—tall, muscular and strong.

"This is him," he said brusquely.

"My forger always makes sure to send me a photocopy of any documents he procures for me." Salazar gestured to the folded paper. "That's the passport he did for Waverly."

Nick unfolded the sheet and studied the photocopy, which showed the front page of Waverly's new travel document. It was a bogus British passport under the name William Neville, and impeccably done judging by the watermark and security features that showed up on the copy.

"Can I keep these?" Nick asked.

"The copy, yes. The photograph, no." Salazar swiftly reached for the Polaroid and pocketed it.

"Thanks," Nick told the unlikely criminal across the table. "You've been more than helpful."

Salazar flashed a rogue grin. "Who says I'm done?"

Nick lifted a brow.

"I assume your next move will be tracking down our friend William Neville?" When Nick nodded, Salazar's grin widened. "Lucky for you, the little prick required more than documents from me. I was also gracious enough to arrange for his charter out of Mala."

He sucked in a breath. "You know where he went from here?"

"Indeed." The man cocked his head. "Out of curiosity, what do you plan on doing to Mr. Waverly when you find him?"

Nick's jaw hardened. "Whatever it takes to make him talk."

Approval glittered in those dark eyes. "Interesting. You are often underestimated, aren't you, Mr. Prescott?"

Surprise jolted through him. "Pardon me?"

"You appear civilized on the outside, but there is a savage beneath that quiet, polished exterior. You are a man who will go to great lengths to right a wrong."

Now he felt uneasy. "How about you quit psychoanalyzing me and tell me where Waverly went?"

Salazar chuckled. "Ah, you're uncomfortable being scrutinized. Most Americans are. I won't press the matter, then." He paused, although Nick suspected it was done solely for effect. "Pista Olvidada. It's a coastal town in Costa Rica."

Because Nick's father had insisted his children be fluent in several languages, Nick relied on his knowledge of Spanish for the translation of the town's name. "Forgotten land," he murmured.

"Quite poetic, isn't it?" Salazar said with another grin. "But Waverly has not been forgotten, has he, Mr. Prescott?"

"No, he hasn't." Nick tucked the photocopy into his pocket and scraped back his chair, then extended a hand at Salazar. "Thanks again."

The other man rose as well, but he didn't shake Nick's hand. Not yet, anyway. First, he crossed the room and picked up the nylon backpack on the dirty linoleum, then unzipped the bag and pulled out a Polaroid camera.

Apprehension climbed up Nick's throat as he eyed the camera. "You weren't kidding about the photos, huh?"

"It must be done, my friend." Salazar gave a little shrug. "But know that the photographs are kept in my safe, and will never see the light of day."

"Not unless I try to stiff you, right?" Nick said drily. "In which case, you'll be flashing my pic around just like you did Waverly's."

Salazar's eyes twinkled. "Just be happy you didn't try to negotiate, and smile for the camera, my friend."

Rebecca spent the evening lying on the ratty couch and trying to get some sleep, but to no avail. Alone and in the silence of the isolated farmhouse, it was difficult not to fall victim to grief.

Jesse. Dave. Harry.

They were all dead because of her. And yet the messed-up thing about it? She knew that if any one of them could see her right now, they'd slap her upside the head for letting the guilt consume her. All three men had been dedicated to the quest for truth, Harry especially. And this particular truth—that someone in the government had allowed a biological weapon to be tested on innocent people? Her colleagues and mentor would have gladly laid down their lives if it meant exposing such a deplorable plot.

Her thoughts turned to Nick, who was so determined to keep her out of this investigation. He'd been gone for two hours, and she knew that when he returned, he would yet again put his foot down and declare that he didn't need her help.

She rose from the couch and paced the dusty floor, sighing as she glanced around the barely habitable room. This farmhouse had stood empty for years and the interior showed it, as did the lack of indoor plumbing and electricity. Nick had carted two huge jugs of water from the SUV, along with some Meals-Ready-to-Eat, which Rebecca had reluctantly scarfed down out of sheer hunger. She longed for a change of clothes, but she was stuck wearing her dirty T-shirt and faded jeans, which she now noticed boasted a jagged hole in the knee. When had that even happened?

Maybe when you were wrestling a gun out of a hit man's hands...

The reminder made her jaw clench. God, how could Nick possibly expect her to back off now? Someone had tried to kill her during that riot, and then attempted to abduct her from the hospital. The hospital where one of her closest friends had died from severe burns.

And now Harry was gone, too.

Her throat clogged as she pictured Harry's craggy features and snow-white hair. She'd loved that man like a father. And thanks to one foolish phone call on her part, he was dead.

The sound of a car engine interrupted her moment of self-reproach. She dashed to the window, but it was difficult to see through the thick layer of dirt coating the glass. And it was pitch-black outside, so all she could make out was the silver glint of the SUV's rims and then a blur of movement as Nick got out of the vehicle.

When he strode into the house a minute later, Rebecca swarmed him like paparazzi surrounding a celebrity. "Well?" she demanded.

His lips twitched in humor. "Hello to you, too, darling."

Despite herself, her heart skipped a beat as the husky nickname left his mouth. Normally she hated lovey-dovey terms of endearment—she'd always found them so very demeaning—but coming from Nick, the word didn't sound condescending. There was something sweet about the way he said it.

Snap out of it, Becks.

Yeah, she really needed to quit getting distracted by this man.

"What happened with Salazar?" she asked him.

Nick shrugged out of his bomber jacket and tossed it on the arm of the couch. A cloud of dust billowed in the air as the garment landed on the frayed upholstery.

"I got Waverly's location," he answered. "The bastard's hiding out in a small beach town in Costa Rica."

She wrinkled her forehead. "How does Salazar know where Waverly is? I thought he was supposed to hook you up with Mr. New Devil."

Nick's amber-colored eyes grew somber. "Is this off the record?"

"I'm insulted that you'd even ask me that," she huffed.

"Is it off the record, Rebecca?"

"Yes!"

"Salazar *is* El Nuevo Diablo."

Shock spiraled through her. "Are you serious?"

Nick nodded, then brushed past her and headed for the kitchen. At the counter, he untwisted the cap off one of the water jugs, lifted the heavy container and took a long swig.

"El Nuevo Diablo is a member of the presidential guard," she mused. "Now, that's an interesting development."

"I thought so, too."

"Okay, so Salazar is the one who arranged Waverly's new ID. And he's certain Waverly went to Costa Rica?"

"He chartered the guy's plane himself."

Rebecca nodded briskly. "Fine. Then we go to Costa Rica. I assume you've got contacts with a private air-field?"

A low laugh exited his mouth. Setting down the jug, he stalked back to her, stopping when they were nose to nose. Well, kind of. At over six feet, Nick towered over her five-foot-one frame, so it was more like they were nose to collarbone.

That was precisely why she habitually avoided dating tall men—they always made her feel utterly dwarf-ish—but Nick's size was a bit of a turn-on. She could easily imagine herself being sheltered in those strong arms, or clinging to his broad shoulders as he carried her to bed....

Snap. Out. Of. It.

Jeez, what was *wrong* with her? Why couldn't she quit fantasizing about this man and focus on the peril-ous situation they'd found themselves in?

"You're not coming with me," Nick said in a reso-lute tone. "I don't know how many different ways I can say it to make you understand that it's not happening."

She bristled. "If you don't take me with you, then I'll go without you. I'll track Waverly down myself."

Frustration burned in his eyes. "The only place you're going is Ecuador. My men and I have a base camp there, and you can stay with them until we deter-mine that it's safe for you to go back to D.C."

"No."

"Rebecca—"

"No," she repeated. She was so annoyed she had to fight the urge to kick him. "I get that you're trying to protect me, but I don't need your protection, Nick. What I *need* is to find the person who killed my colleagues. And no matter what you think, I can be an asset to you. I have sources in dozens of countries—" her tone turned smug "—including Costa Rica. And don't forget about D.C. I know every last player in that city, *darling.*"

"Are you always so difficult?"

"I'm not trying to be difficult. All I'm saying is, I'm already involved, okay? I was involved the moment we went out for drinks at the Liberty, and I refuse to be hidden away in Ecuador. Whether you like it or not, this is my fight, too, now."

She could see his resolve crumbling as a resigned look settled over his face. "I don't like this. You're too recognizable."

An incredulous laugh popped out. "And you're not? You're Secretary Barrett's son, for Pete's sake."

He sighed. "Touché."

"Look, you can keep putting up a fight, or you can just make it easy for yourself and accept that we're in this together from this point on."

There was no mistaking the reluctance creasing his handsome features, but after several seconds of silence, he finally capitulated. "Fine," he muttered. "You can come with me—"

She beamed at him. "Thank you. I knew you'd see it my—"

"—on two conditions," he finished.

Wary, she waited for him to go on.

"First condition, you follow my orders. If I say jump, you jump. If I ask you to stay behind the way I did tonight, accept that it's for a good reason and don't fight me every step of the way."

Although she hated answering to anyone, she shot

him a grudging look and said, "I will follow your or-ders." She paused. "Within reason."

"There you go, being difficult again."

She grinned. "Hey, I'm just sayin'. You can't expect me to follow you blindly. If I disagree with an order, we're darn well going to talk it out."

"You're a big fan of talking, huh?" He looked torn between laughing and strangling her.

"Yep. Now, what's the second condition?"

"Anything we might discover, every lead we stum-ble on, every gory detail—it's all off the record." His expression turned steely. "When this is over, we'll sit down and discuss the best way to get the story out. Before that, you don't write anything down, you don't put it on camera, you don't consult with your network. Deal?"

She had to admit that sounded fair. It wasn't like he was suggesting she sweep everything under the rug and pretend there *wasn't* a story, just that she ought to wait before making anything public.

Which kind of irked, because what did he take her for, an amateur? She would never go ahead with a story until every last *t* and *i* was crossed and dotted.

Nevertheless, she stuck out her hand so they could shake on it. "Deal," she agreed.

The second their palms touched, a jolt of electricity coursed from his hand to hers.

Actual sparks heated her skin, and he must have felt them, too, because he abruptly withdrew his hand and muttered, "Huh."

Rebecca gave him a knowing look, enjoying the tiny glimmer of heat that lit his eyes. "So when do we leave?" she asked brightly.

* * *

She wasn't expecting them to get a flight out of Mala so ridiculously fast, and yet three hours after Nick returned from his meeting with Salazar, the two of them were climbing into the back of a twin-engine Cessna in the most derelict hangar Rebecca had ever seen.

The scent of jet fuel, exhaust and rubber permeated the small cabin, and the blue vinyl seat she lowered herself onto was torn in several places. Their pilot, a stone-faced man with a head of long, oily black hair, didn't say a single word as he went through his preflight check.

Rebecca scooted closer to Nick and brought her lips right up to his ear. "How do you know this guy again?" she whispered. "Are you sure he won't murder us before we even get off the ground?"

Nick responded with a soft chuckle. "Relax, Red. Manuel is the most harmless man on the planet. He used to be a priest."

She raised her eyebrows. "Did you just call me *Red?*"

"Yeah." To her amusement, he actually flushed. "You didn't seem too thrilled with *darling.*"

"Says who?"

"Says the way you called me that earlier, all mocking like and whatnot." He offered an adorable shrug, then buckled his seat belt. "So Red, it is."

"I don't mind darling."

The admission slipped out before she could stop it. Shockingly, she felt herself blushing, too. Oh, for God's sake, what was she, a preteen with a first crush? She really needed to get a handle on her strange reaction to this man.

"Good to know," he murmured, and then their eyes locked, and Rebecca's heart did an excited little flip that made her want to make fun of herself.

"So...our pilot was a priest?" she said, quickly steering the conversation back to safe territory. "What happened? Did he lose his faith?"

"Something like that," Nick answered. "But there's no need to worry—he's a good pilot, and trustworthy. We've used him a couple of times over this past year."

At that moment, their priest-turned-pilot slid into the cockpit and started flicking knobs and buttons. The dashboard came alive with a multitude of lights, and then Manuel glanced over his shoulder and addressed Nick.

"Forecast calls for heavy cloud coverage," he said in Spanish. "Might be some turbulence, so it could get bumpy."

Rebecca's stomach churned at the thought. "Gosh, I hate turbulence."

"You speak Spanish?" Nick said wryly.

"Yep. And French. Russian. Hebrew. Passable Italian and Farsi. Not-so-passable Chinese."

Nick let out a soft whistle. "We've got ourselves a real linguist here."

"I travel a lot. I've picked up a few languages over the years."

A metallic whine reverberated in the cabin, followed by the roar of the propellers coming alive, and a moment later, the little plane chugged forward. They taxied out of the hangar and into the pitch-black night, taking flight less than two minutes later.

As the Cessna rose higher and higher into the dark sky, Rebecca glanced at the back of Manuel's head, then shot Nick a sidelong look. "How exactly did you convince our pilot to leave his bed at one in the morning and fly us to Costa Rica?"

"Money. Lots of money."

"Pays to be rich, huh?" she said glibly. "I bet you single-handedly bankrolled everything this past year."

"Yep."

"And your soldier buddies never asked where the money came from? You said they don't know about your family, so how did you explain all the cash?"

"I didn't, not really, anyway. I told them my family has some money, and they were satisfied with that. They didn't ask any other questions, which isn't much of a surprise, actually. We're private men, all three of us. We don't do too much talking about the past." He sighed. "Eva and Julia have been bugging me about it lately, though."

Rebecca narrowed her eyes. "Eva and Julia?" she echoed, and damned if she didn't experience a little pang of displeasure.

Who the heck were Eva and Julia?

Had Nick somehow managed to date not one, but *two* women during his year of hiding?

She didn't know whether to be impressed or ticked off at that.

"Eva is Tate's fiancée, and Julia is Sebastian's girl-friend."

The green-eyed monster swiftly retreated to the dungeon of jealousy in Rebecca's belly. Jeez. Why had she reacted so viscerally to the idea of Nick having some kind of harem?

Because you want him for yourself.

Yep, she did. She totally did. Then again, how could she not? The man was drop-dead gorgeous and his body was utterly droolworthy. Lord, she wanted nothing more than to run her fingers over every hard ridge of muscle and sinew. To nuzzle the crook of that strong neck and breathe in the woodsy, masculine scent of him.

To feel those sensual lips pressed against her own, his tongue sliding into her mouth while his hands tangled in her hair.

The naughty images sent a shiver dancing through her.

"You cold?"

In the blink of an eye, Nick removed his bomber jacket and was draping it over her torso like a blanket.

Rebecca stared at him in wonder. "You really are the consummate gentleman, aren't you, Nick?"

"So I've been told."

"Your girlfriend back home must miss you a ton."

He burst out laughing. "Is that your incredibly *un*-subtle way of asking me if I'm single?"

"Mmm-hmm."

He laughed again, a deep, sexy sound that had her shivering again beneath the warmth of his coat. "Well, I am," he said. "Single, that is."

Rebecca shot him a pointed look, then waited.

Nick furrowed his eyebrows. "What is it?"

"Aren't you going to ask me if *I'm* single?"

"Of course you're single."

The speed and conviction of his response made her frown. "What's that supposed to mean?"

"It means you're ambitious. I bet your career has come first your entire life, and relationships have always been somewhere on the back burner." When she didn't answer, he cocked his head in challenge. "Am I wrong?"

"No, you're not wrong," she admitted. "My career is important to me. I was never that little girl who fantasized about meeting her Prince Charming and then baking cookies all day long while he brought home the bacon. I was daydreaming about Pulitzers and fame and shedding light on the injustices of the world." She paused. "Not necessarily in that order, of course."

He chuckled. "And you achieved two out of the three, with the Pulitzer sure to follow. I imagine your parents are very proud of you."

"They are. My mom still doesn't quite understand the career thing, though. She's the ultimate Southern belle, spoiled rotten but with the biggest heart on the planet."

"And your dad?"

"More progressive than Mom. He's a criminal lawyer in Atlanta, and he desperately wanted me to go to law school and join his firm so we could practice together." She grinned. "I've assured him that he can represent me should I ever get in trouble—you know, if I wind up in jail for protecting a source or something."

"You mean that hasn't happened to you yet?" Nick teased. "Shocking. You seem like a total troublemaker."

"Maybe to some extent," she said impishly. "So, what about you? Why did you join the army?"

"I wanted to serve and protect my country." He wrinkled his forehead when he noticed her expression. "Why do you look so surprised?"

"Because your father is Kirk Barrett. *Barrett.* As in, big oil."

"Yeah, so?"

"And your mother was a Prescott. As in, the hotel empire Prescotts."

"Yeah, so?" he repeated.

"So you're loaded," she said in exasperation. "You could be spending your life drinking piña coladas on some yacht, traveling the world and suntanning and doing nothing but counting your big stack of cash. But instead, you chose to serve in the military. Special Forces, to boot, where the risk of dying is, like, astronomical."

"I wasn't raised to sit idle," he replied with a shrug. "Even if I chose not to go into the army, I wouldn't have been lounging on a yacht. My father instilled a solid work ethic in me and Viv."

"Viv...right, your sister, Vivian." Rebecca scanned her brain, but she couldn't summon too many details about Nick's older sister. "What does she do for a living again?"

"She used to be a teacher, but now she's a stay-at-home mom. Her husband, Jeff, designs airplanes." A sad look crossed Nick's eyes. "I haven't seen my nieces and nephew in a year. They're probably unrecognizable by now. Kids grow up so damn fast, you know?"

She impulsively reached out and touched his hand. "It must be hard for you, being away from your family."

"It is."

He spoke absently, and she noticed his gaze was focused on their joined hands.

Her own gaze followed suit, and unable to stop herself, Rebecca stroked his rough-skinned knuckles. Lord, he had such big hands, such long, graceful fingers. Strange to think that he'd chosen to hold a weapon in those hands rather than some monogrammed pen he could sign multimillion-dollar contracts with.

When she'd worked the White House beat, she hadn't given much thought to the Barrett family, but she'd always assumed that Nick Barrett would be a spoiled, superficial pretty boy who coasted through life on his father's wealth and accomplishments.

But there was nothing superficial about this man. He was so very...*real.* Strong. Genuine.

Gentlemanly.

There it was again, the G-word. But she couldn't help ascribing it to this man. Nick Barrett really was a bona fide gentleman.

Truth was, she hadn't been in the company of many gentlemen. Half the men in Washington were snakes, including the ones who worked at ABN. And for some foolish reason, she'd always been drawn to the bad boys, the men every woman wanted to tame, the ones who ended up being total jerks.

Chivalry wasn't sexy—or at least she hadn't thought so until now.

Nick slowly moved her hand away and placed it back in her lap. The cabin went silent save for the mechanical whir of the plane's engine and the soft hiss of the wind beyond the windows.

Their eyes locked again, and then Nick's lips curved in a faint smile. "This isn't going to happen, darling."

She raised her eyebrows. "Meaning?"

"You and me." As his gaze darted to the pilot five feet from them, he lowered his voice and clarified. "Sleeping together."

A laugh slipped out of her mouth. Well, this was a first. She couldn't remember the last time a man had gone out of his way to tell her he *wouldn't* take her to bed. Usually, men were hitting on her left and right, eager to say they'd slept with ABN's Rebecca Parker.

She found Nick's lack of interest oddly refreshing.

And total bull.

"Oh, really?" She injected a teasing note into her voice. "So you're saying that you're not attracted to me?"

Nick let out a breath. "No, because I'd have to be a monk *not* to be attracted to you. What I'm saying is, I won't sleep with you."

"I see."

"It's nothing personal," he added, looking and sounding awkward. "Like I said, the attraction is there, and I think sex with you would be off the charts, but I'm in the middle of a crazy situation right now and I can't focus on anything other than fixing this mess. I'm also not the kind of man who does the whole casual-fling thing, so…" He trailed off, as if that said it all.

"I totally get where you're coming from." She pursed her lips. "There's just one problem."

"Yeah, and what's that?"

"I'm the kind of woman who wants what she can't have." She heaved out a mock sigh. "It's my biggest flaw."

"Why does that not surprise me?" His smile was brief, quickly replaced by a suspicious look. "Where exactly are you going with this, Rebecca?"

She shrugged. "I don't really know. I'm just opting for full disclosure here. There *is* a chance I might seduce you."

His husky laughter brought another shiver to her body. "Fair enough. I'll just have to resist, then."

"That easy, huh?"

A smug note entered his tone. "That easy."

"If you say so, *darling*."

With a little grin, she snuggled under his coat and turned her head, resting her cheek on the cool upholstery of her seat. "I'm going to sleep for a bit. I'm exhausted."

"Good plan. I should probably catch some shut-eye myself."

"Wake me when we land?" she asked.

"Will do."

"Oh, and Nick?"

"Yeah?"

"I'll begin formulating my seduction plan tomorrow."

"I look forward to resisting it," he said solemnly.

Laughing softly, she closed her eyes and went to sleep.

Chapter 9

"We still haven't found them."

An aberrant vise of helplessness squeezed his throat as he paced the expensive carpet in his office. This was *not* the news he'd wanted to hear first thing in the morning.

"Where the hell are they?" he demanded. "And how have you not tracked them down yet? She's one of the most recognizable women in the world, for Chrissake."

"And he's one of the most skilled soldiers in the world," came the annoyed response. "Neither of them has surfaced in Mala since the shoot-out at the hospital."

He clenched his teeth, not in the mood for the reminder. Fortunately, the media hadn't uncovered the truth behind the shooting, so Rebecca Parker's involvement in the death of the mercenary was not common knowledge. And thanks to Parker's call to her network and her assurance that she was taking some time off to grieve, the ABN executives hadn't reported their star correspondent missing.

Yet.

"She told the receptionist she's coming back to D.C. soon." He stopped pacing and approached the desk. "I want people at her apartment, the network, her favorite haunts. If Parker steps foot in this city, I want to know about it."

"Of course."

"And what's the latest on Waverly?"

Carraway sounded aggravated. "No sign of him either, but I've got men looking into it."

He briefly closed his eyes. Bad enough that he had three supersoldiers breathing down his neck. He also had a missing government aide to deal with.

Paul Waverly should have never been allowed to leave the Pentagon after giving Sebastian Stone that tainted water; the man was supposed to be neutralized, damn it. But now Waverly had taken off, too, fleeing in a panic because he was smart enough to know that he would need to be eliminated for his part in this cover-up.

"Just find him," he grumbled into the receiver. "Call me later with an update."

He hung up and sat down at the desk. Took a deep, calming breath. All right. Time to push the headaches out of his mind and concentrate on doing the job people depended on him to do.

Leaning forward, he pressed the intercom button that connected to his secretary. "Bernice," he barked, "what's the first item on the agenda for today?"

They landed in Costa Rica just after 7:00 a.m. Despite the five hours of sleep, Nick didn't feel at all rested or refreshed. Rebecca, on the other hand, looked as chipper as a cartoon character. Bouncing off the plane, tipping her head to gaze up at the bright blue sky, shaking hands with Manuel as she thanked him with a broad smile.

He wondered if she'd still be in good spirits if she'd been forced to experience the same X-rated dreams that had taunted his subconscious all night.

Rebecca, naked, moaning and writhing beneath him. Christ.

His mind had managed to produce such vivid images that Nick felt like he'd actually been naked with the sassy redhead.

Banishing his wicked thoughts, he slung his duffel over his shoulder, shoved his aviator sunglasses on the bridge of his nose and rested a hand on Rebecca's upper arm to lead her into the hangar. The cavernous space smelled like oil, fuel and oranges, and it was devoid of life as they strode inside.

First things first—find a mode of transportation. This was the closest airfield to Pista Olvidada, but the town was still a good two-hour drive, and they didn't have a car.

Spotting two men in gray jumpsuits near a metal rack littered with toolboxes, Nick offered a casual wave and called out, *"¡Hola!"*

Both men lifted their hands in brisk waves.

Next to him, Rebecca's hand tightened over the strap of her canvas purse. "Do we have to show them our passports or something?" she murmured.

Nick laughed under his breath. "Does this look like a real airport? We won't be encountering any customs officials here, Red."

"Ah. Right."

They reached the two men, one of whom introduced himself as Javier, the owner of this less-than-legal airstrip. Javier was a stocky man with a thick black mustache and pockmarked olive skin, but even though he looked slightly menacing, he was surprisingly pleasant.

"What brings you to our little town?" He moved away from the mechanic he'd been consulting with and gestured for Nick and Rebecca to follow him.

As the three of them headed for the open doors where sunlight streamed into the hangar, Nick addressed the man's inquiry. "We're backpacking through Central and South America and decided to make a pit stop here to track down an old friend."

"I see." Javier's dark eyes seemed to be smirking at them. "And do you always travel by such…backdoor methods? Because not many tourists wind up in my airport, my friends."

Nick just shrugged. "We like to live on the edge."

Beside him, Rebecca huffed out an exaggerated breath. "Don't listen to him, Javier. My boyfriend is just trying to protect me."

The owner of the airfield lifted one bushy eyebrow. "How so?"

"I'm on a no-fly list," she said glumly. "There was an…incident…a few years back. Let's just say I lost my temper and now I'm paying the price for it. No commercial flights for me."

Now the man let out a genuine laugh. "This doesn't surprise me."

She narrowed her eyes. "No?"

Still laughing, Javier reached out and tugged on the end of Rebecca's long ponytail. "The red hair," he clarified. "Women with red hair are known to have ferocious tempers."

"Tell me about it," Nick said with a sigh.

They stepped out into the morning sunshine and Nick breathed in the scent of rain, earth and flora. The air was unbearably humid, which was what you got when visiting Costa Rica during the wet season.

He shrugged out of the jacket Rebecca had returned to him before they'd landed and tucked it under his arm, then glanced at Javier. "Our friend was in these parts about a week ago, but we have no way of contacting him."

"No cell phone," Rebecca said, shaking her head in amazement. "Who doesn't have a cell phone these days?"

"He called us collect from some little town. Pista Olvido? Olvida—"

"Olvidada," Javier filled in.

"Yeah, that was it. So he called and told us to come see him if we ended up here, but we have no idea where he's staying or if he's even still there."

"But he was here at your airport," Rebecca piped up. "He's the one who hooked us up with our pilot, Manuel."

Javier stroked his mustache with one meaty hand. "And he was here last week, you say?"

Nick nodded. "He's from London, but he's been living in the States so long that his accent might not be as pronounced anymore. His name is William Neville."

The flicker of recognition in Javier's eyes told Nick that Neville aka Waverly had indeed made an appearance at this airfield. "Yes, I remember him. Blond hair, blue eyes—"

"Vampire-white skin," Rebecca chimed in, grinning. "Yeah, that's Willie."

Although he had to hide it, Nick was ridiculously impressed with Rebecca's playacting. The woman was quick on her feet, handling Javier like a pro, and every word that left her mouth sounded like the honest-to-God truth; Nick himself would've believed her if he didn't know better.

"Well, I don't know where your friend is staying or whether he's still in town, but as of seven days ago, he *was* in Pista Olvidada," Javier confirmed.

Nick masked his eagerness. "Are you certain?"

"Quite certain. I drove him there myself." A frown puckered Javier's mouth. "He wasn't the friendliest of men. Slightly rude, if I'm being honest."

Rebecca sighed again. "Willie tends to get cranky after a flight. And he's a Brit—we all know those Brits are notoriously snooty. Don't take it personally."

Javier laughed again. "You're right about that. Damn Brits."

"So you drove him to Pista Olvidada," Nick prompted. "Did he say if he planned on sticking around?"

"He didn't say much, but he hasn't been back, so if he left town, he didn't do it by plane. Unless he flew commercial or drove to another private airport—the nearest one is about ten hours south of here."

Nice. So chances were, Waverly was still in Costa Rica, Nick thought with satisfaction.

He looked around, noting the three vehicles parked nearby on the dirt. "Is there anywhere to rent a car around here? Or is Pista Olvidada within walking distance?"

"Oh, no, my friend, it is a very long walk. Two hours by car, much longer by foot."

Nick and Rebecca exchanged a look, as if they weren't happy to hear this.

"Lucky for you, I also offer car rentals," Javier said

with a big, crooked-toothed smile. He hooked his thumb at an older-model Jeep. "Two hundred bucks a day."

Wow, that was steep, but Nick supposed a man had to make a living in this no-horse town any way he could. Besides, he couldn't imagine that they'd be in the country more than twenty-four hours.

Nick reached into his back pocket and pulled out a roll of bills. He peeled off two hundred-dollar bills and handed them to Javier. "Let's say one day for now. If it's more, I'll pay you when we bring the car back."

Javier accepted the bills and nodded in agreement.

"And if you could also arrange for a charter out when we return?" Rebecca asked sweetly. "We probably won't be visiting with Willie for too long, and we're eager to head south. Venezuela is next on our itinerary."

"I will see what I can do," Javier said as he handed Nick a set of car keys. "The tank is full. And it comes back full, yes?"

"Of course," Nick assured him.

The two men shook hands, and then Javier took Rebecca's hand and planted a wet kiss on her knuckles. To her credit, she didn't balk or convey any sign of disgust.

"I will see you soon, then," Javier told them before stalking back into the hangar.

They watched him go, then turned to each other with matching grins.

"He is astonishingly awesome considering he owns an illegal airport and probably smuggles drugs through here," Rebecca said wryly.

Nick suddenly thought of the charismatic Enrique Salazar and had to laugh. Seemed like none of the nefarious characters he was meeting these days were living up to their reputations.

He took a step toward the Jeep. "Come on, let's go. The sooner we get there, the sooner we find Waverly."

She nodded enthusiastically. "The game's afoot, then!"

He choked down his amusement. "Whatever you say, Watson."

"Watson?" Her trademark smirk returned. "Uh-uh, Nicky, I'm Sherlock. *You're* the sidekick."

"Whatever helps you sleep better at night, darling."

Nick was hyperaware of Rebecca during the ride to the coast. Excruciatingly aware, in fact. Erection-of-the-century aware.

It didn't help that the woman kept lifting her ponytail up, revealing the tantalizing arch of her graceful neck and the little red tendrils at her nape. Her skin glistened with a sheen of sweat, thanks to the humidity thickening the air and the sun beating down on their heads. The breeze that rushed through the open top of the Jeep did nothing to ease the fire in his groin.

Why did Rebecca Parker have to be so damn sexy?

And so damn intelligent?

He wasn't sure what he found sexier—those stunning looks of hers, or her astute, passionate rhetoric. He'd always had a thing for smart women, and Rebecca's endless well of knowledge and insight was a major turn-on.

"So yeah, they *steal* the eggs!" she was saying, sounding livid.

Nick snapped out of his thoughts and tried to remember what they were discussing now. Sea turtles. Right.

"And then these a-holes sell the eggs, thus contributing to the extinction of the species."

She angrily shook her head, and her wide-brimmed straw hat nearly flew off. Earlier, they'd stopped at the bustling outdoor marketplace they'd spotted along the way and picked up some supplies. Courtesy of his stack of cash, Nick was able to buy Rebecca a few changes of clothes and better shoes, and they'd also stocked up on water and fresh fruit.

Now they were about twenty minutes from Pista Olvidada, and Nick couldn't say he hadn't enjoyed the ride. Unceasing erection aside, he enjoyed Rebecca's company, even if she did tend to go on long diatribes about the injustices of the world.

"And then, to make matters worse, we've got all these resorts being erected—"

His groin clenched. Did she have to use the word *erected?*

"—effectively usurping the nesting grounds these turtles have been using for centuries. You know what, Nick? I hate people. I really do. People suck."

A laugh rumbled out. "Aw, come on, not all people are egg-stealing, resort-building villains."

"True," she relented. "There are some great folks working at the preservation society. I volunteered with them last year—we spent hours digging up sea turtle eggs and moving them to protected areas, that way those nasty thieves can't get their hands on the eggs."

The revelation impressed the hell out of him. He was quickly learning that Rebecca was more than a pretty face you saw on television. She didn't just report on stories—she interacted with them, lived them, breathed them. Which brought both a spark of admiration and a tug of dread, the latter because it was becoming less and less likely that she would meekly agree to go to Ecuador if he pushed the issue.

Up ahead, the road sloped upward, hugging a jagged cliff that overlooked the ocean hundreds of feet below. To their left was the jungle, emanating the familiar scent of earthy vegetation, wildflowers and acrid rot. Nick breathed it in, reminded of some of his earlier ops under Tate's command.

The road narrowed and curved, then dipped down after five or so miles.

"It's so beautiful," Rebecca remarked, her gaze focused on the sparkling turquoise ocean. "I'd love to live somewhere like this one day."

"And be away from the hustle and bustle of the city? I can't see you giving that up."

"No?"

He shot her a sidelong look. "Nah, I think you'd miss the excitement."

Her green eyes twinkled playfully. "I don't need to be in a heavily populated area for that. I can find excitement anywhere."

Something hot and sultry sizzled between them, and it had nothing to do with the stifling temperature.

Nick broke eye contact and swallowed a groan. His lower body was on fire. He was stiffer than a two-by-four, his blood humming with arousal. Fortunately, Rebecca wasn't looking at his crotch, otherwise he knew she'd flash that mischievous smile and tease him mercilessly.

New aromas permeated the air as they drove into the beach town of Pista Olvidada. Sweet flowers, dark spices, pungent coffee, and underlying it all was the salty scent rolling off the ocean. The town offered one main strip with a handful of shops, restaurants and bars. In the distance was a picturesque marina, and a long dock where vessels ranging from beat-up speedboats to gleaming white sailboats were moored.

Nick parked in a spot on the street and they hopped

out of the Jeep. "So how are we doing this?" Rebecca asked. "Same deal? We're looking for our friend Willie?"

"It worked with Javier. Might as well keep up the charade."

"So I'm your girlfriend again."

"Yep."

"Okay, then."

Before he could object, she rounded the vehicle and took his hand. When she interlaced their fingers, the warmth of her palm seeped into his already-feverish flesh.

"Couples hold hands," she informed him.

Her tone was light, but those green eyes were dancing again. Looked like her seduction plan had officially been launched.

Nick decided to play along. Truthfully, holding Rebecca's hand felt...nice. He couldn't remember the last time he'd held hands with a woman.

They fell into step with each other and crossed the street, heading for a corner bar that featured a green sign cleverly labeling it as "The Bar." Several patrons were seated on the outdoor patio, and the light breeze blew cigarette smoke in Nick and Rebecca's direction. Every person on the patio narrowed their eyes suspiciously when they glimpsed the approaching couple.

"The locals might not be too welcoming," Rebecca murmured.

"Nah," he murmured back. "They'll warm up once you unleash that sassy redhead charm."

Sure enough, his prediction proved correct. Within two minutes of meeting Rebecca, every man, woman and child they spoke to fell in love with the redhead. Unfortunately, nobody admitted to knowing, seeing or having any information whatsoever about one William Neville.

For the next hour, they struck out time and time again. After visiting every establishment on the strip, they drove to the marina where they finally hit pay dirt at a fish and chips restaurant right on the water.

The fishing boat captain they encountered turned out to be a Chatty Cathy, and more than familiar with Nick and Rebecca's prey.

"Neville! Yes, yes," the captain said with an enthusiastic nod. "He bought Rudy's place by the dump. I gave him a lift out there to check out the property."

Nick's chest tightened with excitement. "He's still in town, then?"

"Well, sure. Haven't seen him around the strip, but I saw him on the water early this morning. Fishing near the cove."

"He has a boat?" Rebecca asked in a careful tone.

The gray-haired captain gave a hearty laugh. "If you can call that flimsy dinghy a boat, then yes, he has a boat. The dinghy came with the house. So did the car. When old Rudy dropped dead, his kid sold everything in one bundle."

Nick chuckled. "Who exactly was this Rudy?"

"An American. He visited our town about thirty years ago and never left. Cranky son of a bitch, a real cheap bastard, too, but he had a knack for finding the fish. Whenever I had a bad catch, I'd take old Rudy out on the water the next day and that bastard would sniff out the fish like a bloodhound. It'd more than make up for the loss of the previous day." The captain sighed regretfully. "I'll miss that son of a bitch."

They ended up chatting with the colorful captain for several more minutes, but not about Waverly; they'd already gotten the intel they'd come here for, including directions to Rudy's beach house. But the captain seemed to appreciate the company, and Nick felt slightly bad when he finally had to cut the man off and announce it was time for them to go.

Rebecca's green eyes were filled with excitement as they left the waterfront restaurant and walked down the wooden pier toward the marina's entrance.

"So what now?" she asked. "Are we heading to old Rudy's place or should we wait until nighttime? You soldiers prefer the cover of darkness, right? Like, being one with the shadows and whatnot?"

"First I want to case the place." He shot her a stern look before she could open her mouth. "Just me. Alone."

"Aw, you're mean. I happen to be a *great* caser."

He rolled his eyes. "Yeah, I'm sure. But you're still not coming with me. You'll only slow me down."

"Have I slowed you down so far?" she challenged.

"No," he had to concede, "but this is different. It's recon. I prefer to do recon alone."

When they reached the Jeep, Rebecca paused by the passenger door and tightly crossed her arms over her chest. The pose pushed her breasts together and created a whole lot of cleavage in her tight white tank top. Nick's mouth went dry at the sight, and he had to force himself not to ogle the tantalizing swell of creamy white skin.

"And what am I supposed to do in the meantime?" she demanded. "Knit a sweater?"

He opened the door and slid into the driver's seat. "Take a nap. Read a book. I'm sure you can find ways to entertain yourself."

"I'm not tired, I don't have a book, and in case you haven't noticed, we didn't pass a single motel driving through town, so where exactly am I supposed to lie low and entertain myself?"

She raised a good point. And although he'd teased her about it, she was also right about that cover-of-darkness issue. He would much rather check out Waverly's place at night when he could blend into the shadows and move around unseen. Doing recon in broad daylight defeated the purpose of...well, recon.

But what other choice did he have? It was only ten o'clock in the morning. The sun wouldn't set until at least seven, maybe later. So unless they wanted to spend the next nine or so hours twiddling their thumbs, it looked like a daytime mission was in the cards.

Nick started the engine, then waited for Rebecca to get in and buckle up. "You'll have to stay in the car, then," he told her.

That elicited an unhappy frown, but she didn't protest. "Fine."

He gawked at her.

"What?" she muttered.

"Did you really just agree to my request without putting up an argument?" He pulled out of the marina lot and headed in the direction the captain had told them.

"Request? You don't request, Nick. You command."

He sighed. "Not usually. With you, the commands just come out."

"Oh, really? So you don't typically order women around?" She sounded extremely intrigued.

"Nope. I'm a gentleman, remember? Very polite and respectful."

"Are you saying I bring out the rude, disrespectful a-hole in you?"

"I guess so." Laughing, he stepped on the gas and

picked up speed as they drove away from the heart of town.

Waverly's hideout was only a ten-minute drive according to the fishing captain, and it required following a long, dusty road lined with towering trees and dense foliage on both sides. Five minutes in, the odor of garbage thickened the air and made them both wrinkle their noses.

"And there's the dump," Rebecca said, her gaze fixing on the wooden sign indicating the turnoff for the town's garbage dump. "Why would anyone willingly live near a dump?"

"Clearly old Rudy was a risk taker."

She laughed. "Clearly. Hey, did you also find it weird that the captain seemed to know a scary amount about Rudy?"

"Not really. I mean, Rudy was a genuine fish whisperer—of course he was popular around these parts."

Another melodic laugh left her mouth and tickled his ears. "I guess you're right. I kind of wish I got to meet him. It sounds like he was an interesting chara— Hey, you missed the turnoff," she suddenly said. "The captain said to turn at the red fence."

Now Nick was the one laughing. "We're not going to pull up right into his driveway, Red. We may as well wave around a big sign that says We're Coming for You." He snorted. "Ha, I knew you'd be terrible at recon."

She stuck out her tongue at him.

"Wow, real mature of you, Rebecca."

This time she gave him the finger.

"Even more mature," he said mockingly, but his lips were twitching with amusement.

Jeez. He was having way too much fun with this woman. He definitely needed to stop that.

He kept driving for another fifty yards or so, slowing down when he neared a section of road where the vegetation was thicker. "Hold on to the dash," he told her. "Might get bumpy."

She barely had time to respond when he'd veered off the road and drove directly into the thick canopy of trees. The Jeep bounced as it traveled over the tangle of vines and rotting undergrowth that made up the jungle floor, and the sun disappeared from view, hidden by the trees. Everything was green and lush in the rainy season, and the air smelled like fragrant wildflowers and damp earth.

Palm fronds scraped the sides of the Jeep as the vehicle skidded to a stop in a small clearing. The trees provided shade, but no protection in terms of bugs. The moment Nick killed the engine, mosquitoes swarmed the vehicle, whizzing past his ears with a high-pitched whine.

As Rebecca began swatting at the persistent insects and cursing in her noncursing way, Nick hopped out and grabbed his go bag from the back of the Jeep. He rummaged through it, found a can of heavy-duty bug repellent, along with a mosquito net that he tossed to Rebecca. Then he began to arm himself, sliding a pistol into his waistband, a knife sheath on his hip, a second pistol in his right boot and another deadly KA-BAR in his left one.

When he finished, he stalked to the passenger-side door and held out a 9-millimeter Beretta. "You know how to use this, right?"

She nodded. "I go to the target range every couple of months, and I have a permit to carry."

"Good. Safety's on, keep it that way. Move into the

driver's seat and don't get out of the car, no matter what. If I'm not back in an hour—"

Her eyes widened. "Why wouldn't you come back—"

"—I want you to get the hell out of here. Make your way to the airfield and call Tate. He'll arrange for a plane to take you to Ecuador. Understood?"

After a moment, she nodded again.

"With that said, I'll be back shortly," he assured her.

"You better be," she grumbled. "I can't do this alone, Nick. You're the Watson to my Sherlock, remember?"

He laughed again and resisted the urge to do something stupid, like lean in and kiss her goodbye. The mere thought of feeling Rebecca's pouty lips pressed against his own sent a bolt of lust straight to his groin, and he took a step back before he gave in to the overpowering urge.

"Remember, stay put," he said in a strict tone.

"Yes, sir."

He left her in the Jeep and disappeared into the trees, swiftly making his way through the heavy brush. His boots didn't make a sound as they stepped over the overgrown jungle floor; years of training and experience had honed his ability to move like a ghost.

The half-mile trek to Waverly's property didn't take long, and soon the house became visible through the trees. Nick found himself staring at a small shack constructed from an unusual combination of brick and wood, with a brown clay-tiled roof and a front courtyard overrun with dirt and sand. He couldn't see the ocean, but he could smell it, salt and seaweed and fresh air.

Flattening himself against a gnarled tree trunk, he drew his gun and examined the house. Through the blossoming foliage he made out a rust-covered sedan.

Someone was home, then, unless Waverly was out on that dinghy the captain had mentioned.

Nick crept closer, assessing, pinpointing entry points. Front door. One window.

Satisfied, he made his way to the back of the house, traveling silently through the brush. His grip on the 9 millimeter was solid; the weapon had become an extension of his hand over the years.

A rickety wooden deck graced the rear of the shack, ringed by a slatted railing with several broken posts. Nick's gaze zeroed in on the beer bottle sitting on the rail. Condensation dripped down the side of the bottle, hinting that it had been recently opened.

Footsteps.

His spine stiffened when he heard the footsteps. He edged backward, camouflaged by the trees, but he still had a clear line of sight to the man who'd just stepped onto the deck.

Paul Waverly.

Jackpot.

The tall, blond man wore khaki shorts and a white polo T-shirt, and the Costa Rican sunshine had brought some color to his normally pale face, which meant that he no longer resembled someone who'd spent his entire life locked up in an attic.

He had something in his hand. A cell phone. He was typing furiously on the keypad and he didn't look happy. Not by a long shot.

Nick shifted his gaze and noted the large window behind the blond man, then the screen door with its mesh torn to hell. When he concluded his appraisal, he made his way through the trees again, this time emerging at the side of the house.

Now he could see the ocean. About a hundred yards

away, and getting there required a trek down a rocky slope that opened onto black sand rather than white, a product of the volcanic rock much of the landscape had been carved out of. He glimpsed a small wooden dock at the water's edge where an old white motorboat was tied up.

Satisfied, he returned to the back of the house, but Waverly was no longer on the deck. A flash of movement in the window confirmed that the man had gone inside.

Nick stared at the screen door, thoughtful. There was really no reason why he couldn't make a move right now. The house was isolated, no neighbors for miles. And yes, it was daylight, but Waverly was indoors. Unless the DoD aide had ten bodyguards with assault rifles in there—which Nick highly doubted—gaining the upper hand on the man would be a piece of cake.

He checked the tactical watch on his wrist. Only fifteen minutes had passed since he'd left Rebecca. It shouldn't take long to handle Waverly. And if the man refused to talk, he could always tie him up and go back to the Jeep to grab Rebecca before his hour was up.

Decision made, Nick palmed his weapon and stepped out of the brush.

Chapter 10

Rebecca's arms were getting a real workout swatting at the relentless mosquitoes that were determined to possess her blood. Fortunately, the netting kept the annoying insects out of her face, and the bug repellent she'd sprayed all over herself seemed to be working. The bugs swarmed, but so far none had been brave enough to take a bite.

Nick had been gone for nearly thirty minutes. She kept checking the time on the screen of the secure cell phone he'd given her. The numbers for his friends were already programmed in, but she didn't plan on making any calls. No way was she abandoning Nick here. If he wasn't back in an hour, she had every intention of tracking him down and saving his butt.

She kept a comfortable grip on the Beretta in her hand, grateful for all those shooting lessons her father had forced on her when she was growing up. Theo

Parker, God bless his soul, had desperately wanted a son, a boy he could take hunting and fishing, a male he could groom to take over the law firm one day.

Instead, he'd gotten a daughter, and yet to his wife's dismay, it was the kind of daughter neither of them had expected. Rebecca was the furthest thing from a sweet Georgian peach. From a young age, she'd been fearless, feisty, daring. An absolute terror, in fact. She'd driven her parents crazy by running around with the boys and causing heaps of trouble around the neighborhood.

Bzzzzzzz.

Another mosquito flew by her ear. Ugh. She whole-heartedly believed that mosquitoes were the most useless insects on the planet. Who cared if they helped the food chain go round—the creatures that fed on mosquitoes could easily find something else to eat, in her humble opinion.

Bzzzzzzz.

She slapped away the next intruder. "For the love of—"

A gunshot sliced through the air.

Rebecca froze. As her pulse sped up, she peered in the direction Nick had gone in, but her sexy soldier didn't come bursting out of the trees.

That had been a gunshot, though.

Right?

Panic soared inside her, along with a rush of fear that seized her chest and made it difficult to breathe. She sucked a deep gust of oxygen into her lungs, forcing herself to relax. To think.

Okay, so she'd heard a shot. That didn't mean Nick was in trouble. Maybe he—

Maybe he what? an incredulous voice demanded. *He*

was only supposed to case the house! There's no reason for anyone to be shooting anything!

Her heart started beating even faster, pounding a frantic rhythm in her chest. Taking another deep breath, she jumped out of the Jeep, tore off the mosquito net and adjusted her grip on the Beretta. She aimed at the trees, but there was no movement, no sign that she was sharing this jungle with anything other than the pesky mosquitoes and the mysterious creatures that scuttled across the tangled undergrowth on the ground.

She took a step forward, then halted as Nick's order echoed in her head.

Don't get out of the car, no matter what.

Her teeth sank into her bottom lip. She stood there, torn. Did hearing a gunshot count as *no matter what*?

Probably, but darn it, she couldn't just do *nothing*. What if Nick was in trouble?

A quick peek wouldn't hurt, right? She'd check out the house, just to make sure that he was all right, and if everything looked kosher, she'd simply sneak back to the Jeep and Nick would never be the wiser.

With a decisive nod, she started to walk, making her way toward Waverly's property. She cringed each time a twig snapped beneath the hiking boots Nick had bought her. It was difficult to move quietly when the jungle floor was covered with vines and branches and dried leaves, all of which made so much noise it was like she was walking to the tune of her own personal sound track.

Several minutes later, she caught a glimpse of the house's clay roof, a flash of reddish-brown amid the greenery. She approached with caution, then ducked behind a tree and carefully peeked out. Her gaze swept over the back of the dilapidated shack, the open screen door, the curtainless window. No movement in front of the window or the door. Not a single sound wafted out of the house.

No sign of Nick.

She wasn't sure if that was a good thing or a bad thing. If he was still casing the place, then he'd probably be hidden away somewhere, so of course there'd be no sign of him.

But then what had that gunshot been about? Was Waverly doing target practice around the side of the house or something?

She bit her lip again, unsure of her next move. Did she keep looking for Nick, or did she head back to the car?

She was debating what to do when a second gunshot cracked in the air.

Nick.

As a rush of adrenaline sizzled in her bloodstream, Rebecca sprinted out of the trees and raced toward the back door without a single concern for her safety. She practically dived through the broken screen door, stumbling into a narrow corridor, then blinking wildly as she tried to orient herself.

God, where was Nick?

Had he been shot?

Panic, terror and worry jammed in her throat, but she managed to keep moving. When muffled thuds and male grunts greeted her ears, relief crashed into her with the force of an 18-wheeler. There was more than one person in this house. That meant Nick was still alive. She followed the sounds of a scuffle to the other side of the house and quickly emerged into a small living room.

Rebecca's heartbeat accelerated as she absorbed the

scene in front of her. Nick was on the floor, wrestling with a bulky blond man she knew had to be Paul Waverly. Angry curses and ragged breathing filled the air, then a loud snap as a fist connected with a jaw.

Heart pounding, Rebecca raised her gun and took aim, but she didn't dare fire a shot, not when there was the risk of hitting Nick.

Whether or not to pull the trigger became a moot point, because Nick gained control of the situation in the blink of an eye, flipping Waverly onto his back and straddling the man with a growl.

"Don't move," he snapped.

"Screw you!" Waverly spat out.

Nick jammed the muzzle of his gun into Waverly's throat. As the man made a loud gagging noise, Nick's shoulders suddenly stiffened and his gaze sharply moved to the doorway.

He swore loudly. "I told you to stay put!"

Rebecca offered a feeble shrug. "I heard a shot and…" She trailed off, knowing he wasn't in the mood to hear her excuses.

But she refused to apologize for disregarding his orders. What if he hadn't managed to subdue Waverly just now? What if he'd truly needed her help?

On the floor, Nick let out another curse. His brown eyes glared daggers at her before taking on a resigned light. "Well, fine. As long as you're here, see if you can find something to tie this son of a bitch up with."

Ten minutes later, Paul Waverly was secured snugly to a chair that Nick liberated from the man's dinette set. Using the roll of duct tape Rebecca had found in the kitchen, Nick had restrained Waverly's hands, feet and torso. The entire time, he'd been infuriatingly conscious of Rebecca's presence, but he'd forced himself to bite back his anger.

The woman seemed incapable of following orders, and at the moment, her presence bothered him on a whole other level. Who knew what he'd have to do to get Waverly to talk, and he didn't feel comfortable resorting to forceful methods of persuasion in front of Rebecca. Call him old-fashioned, but he'd been raised with the belief that women needed to be protected and kept out of harm's way.

Allowing Rebecca to witness a potential torture session didn't really adhere to either of those rules.

However, when he turned to ask her to leave the room, the stubborn woman just crossed her arms and said, "Don't even think about it. I'm not going anywhere."

The man in the chair suddenly sucked in a breath as his gaze shifted to the doorway where Rebecca stood. Waverly had been staring at her for the past ten minutes, and recognition had finally dawned on his face.

"Are you…you're Rebecca Parker!" he sputtered, his ice-blue eyes widening. "What the hell are you doing here?"

"Shut up," Nick snapped. "I'm the one asking the questions here."

"Screw you!"

Nick glared at the man who'd nearly blown his head off. He was pissed off beyond belief, but at the same time, he grudgingly had to give Waverly kudos for catching him off guard.

Standing on the back deck, the DoD aide hadn't revealed any indication that he'd realized he was being watched, and yet the second Nick attempted a stealth entrance, Waverly had popped out of a doorway with a gun in hand. Only the aide's piss-poor aim had saved Nick from a bullet to the head. As the bullet lodged into the wall five inches from his left ear, he'd quickly disarmed Waverly, but the other man had managed to make a run for the front door, unfazed by the warning shot Nick had fired at his feet. Despite Waverly's football-player build, Nick had finally brought the man down, and now he loomed over his captive, though he could have done without Rebecca lurking in the doorway like that.

"Who are you?" Waverly demanded with a scowl.

Nick's jaw tightened. "Take a wild guess."

The man's cheeks turned red. "If I knew that, I wouldn't have asked! They sent you to kill me, didn't they?"

He arched a brow. "Who's they?"

"You know damn well who I'm talking about." Waverly's gaze drifted to Rebecca and his resolve seemed to falter. "But why is *she* here? You can't kill me in front of a journalist."

"Nobody is killing anybody." Nick paused. "At least not yet. First, you're going to tell me everything I need to know. Then I'll decide if I'm going to let you live."

"Who *are* you?" A miserable note entered Waverly's voice.

"I'm a colleague of Sebastian Stone."

Waverly went even paler, a feat Nick would have deemed impossible.

"Stone," the man mumbled.

"Yes, Sebastian Stone. You know, the guy you tried to infect with a deadly virus?" Nick said sarcastically.

There was a long silence, and then Waverly's breath hitched and understanding dawned in his eyes. "You're one of them. One of the three soldiers who skipped town."

"Give the man a cigar." Nick moved toward the flower-patterned sofa and leaned against the arm, absently resting his gun on his thigh. "It bodes well that you know who I am. So now tell me, who authorized the killing of my unit?"

Waverly didn't answer.

"Come on, Paul. Or William. Or whatever you want to call yourself these days. Let's not play games. Who wants me and my men dead?"

More stony silence.

"Who decided it was a good idea to engineer the Meridian virus and test it in San Marquez?"

"I'm not saying a goddamn word," Waverly mumbled. "Go ahead and kill me. Either way, I'm dead."

"Yeah, how do you figure that?"

"If I talk, they'll know, and then they'll hunt me down and kill me—but it won't be fast. They'll drag it out, make me suffer...." The man's Adam's apple bobbed as he gulped. "So go ahead. Do it. Pull the trigger. At least with you, it'll be fast."

"Says who?" Nick asked softly.

In the doorway, Rebecca gasped.

Ignoring that squeaky sound of distress, Nick dragged the barrel of his gun over his thigh and fixed his gaze on the man bound to the chair.

"You underestimate me, Paul. See, I'm not the same man I was a year ago. I was chased out of town when a gunman decided to break into my apartment under the pretense of a home robbery, and I've been running ever since. Being on the run takes a toll on a man."

Nick slowly rose from his perch and approached the

chair. "Make no mistake, I will do whatever it takes to get answers from you."

"Bull! You're a soldier! A man of honor," Waverly said feebly. "You wouldn't resort to torture."

"You sound confident of that."

"I—I am," Waverly stammered. His blue eyes darted in Rebecca's direction. "You won't torture me with her watching. You wouldn't."

"You're right about that," Nick agreed. With a pleasant smile, he glanced over at Rebecca. "Darling, would you please give us a moment alone? Go take a walk on the beach or something."

She looked stricken, but to her credit, she didn't object or recoil in horror. "I can stay if you want," she said, her voice barely above a whisper.

"Nah, Red, trust me, you don't want to be around for what happens next." Nick's smile turned feral.

When Rebecca took a step away, Waverly made a panicked sound and shouted, "Wait!"

She froze.

Nick hid a grin.

"Tell her to stay," Waverly pleaded, his desperate eyes focusing on Nick. "I'll tell you whatever you want. Just ask Ms. Parker to stay."

Huh. Although Nick would never admit it to Rebecca, it looked like her presence did bring some advantages to the table. Waverly probably believed he could stay alive in exchange for giving Rebecca an exclusive or something.

"Hear that, Red? The man likes having you around," Nick told her.

A weak smile lifted her mouth. "I guess so."

She crossed the room and joined Nick near the couch.

He could sense she was ill at ease, but her expression was shuttered, her shoulders set in a rigid line.

They both turned to Waverly, whose face didn't look quite so ashen anymore. "What do you want to know?" the man asked in a defeated tone.

"I already told you what I want," Nick replied coldly. "I want a name."

Indecision flashed in those ice-blue eyes.

"Give me a name, Paul. Tell me who ordered the deaths of my teammates. Tell me who had that virus engineered. Tell me who—"

"Secretary Barrett!" Waverly burst out. "There! Are you happy now? The name you want is Kirk Barrett. The secretary of defense."

Chapter 11

An icy rush of dread skittered up Nick's spine. He stared into Waverly's blue eyes, unable to comprehend what the son of a bitch had just told him.

"No," he finally said, "I don't believe you."

"It's the truth," Waverly insisted. "Secretary Barrett was behind everything! I swear on my mother's life!"

He was lying. He had to be.

Nick refused to believe that his father had anything to do with this. Christ. But what if it was true? His palms went damp at the thought, his SIG nearly slipping from his grasp.

"Tell me everything," he ordered. "From the beginning."

Waverly visibly swallowed. "Project Aries was set up about two years ago. I was running double duty at the time, acting as the aide for Brent Davidson and Fred McAvoy, the—"

"The deputy secretary," Rebecca supplied with a frown.

"McAvoy's involved in this, too?" Nick barked.

"He's the one who approached me," Waverly replied. "McAvoy said that he and the sec def were growing concerned with President Howard's lenient attitude toward terrorism, that Howard wasn't taking enough precautions to protect our country from another attack. McAvoy confided in me that certain measures were being taken to prevent another terrorist attack on American soil, and that the department was dedicated to ensuring we had all the necessary weapons to fight the war on terrorism."

"Biological weapons, you mean," Rebecca said.

Waverly nodded. "He didn't give me many details about the project, but he put me in charge of communicating with Richard Harrison, the scientist at D&M Initiative. The lab was contracted to experiment with different biological agents and develop a weapon that was fast-acting and easy to release into a general population."

Nick scowled. "The Meridian virus."

Another fervent nod. "Harrison worked on it for more than a year, and when it came time to test it, Barrett and McAvoy knew the field testing couldn't be done on U.S. soil—"

Each time his father's name left the aide's lips, Nick flinched like he'd been shot by a rifle. He tried valiantly to hide the reaction, but from the sympathetic look Rebecca gave him, he knew she'd noticed.

"—so they struck a deal with the San Marquez government," Waverly finished. "Our troops would contain the ULF situation and help the country prosper, and they would sacrifice a few rural villages for the sake of national security. Your unit was sent to that village by accident—Harrison managed to get a call out before the rebels got a hold of him, and there was a communication mix-up in the military channels. You weren't ever supposed to be there."

"But we were, and we needed to be shut up, right?" Each word dripped with bitterness.

Waverly let out a weary breath. "The secretary believed it was necessary."

Bull! Nick wanted to snap, but he clenched his teeth to control the outburst. His father would never order the murder of his own son, for Chrissake. Kirk Barrett loved his kids. He was fiercely protective of them and always had been. Nick would believe in unicorns and leprechauns before he believed that his father had ordered someone to kill him.

"And when Sebastian was at the Pentagon, you were instructed to give him the tainted water bottle?" he said instead.

"Yes." Remorse flickered in the man's eyes. "I didn't want to. Hell, when they gave me the vial containing the Meridian virus, I agonized over it. I'm not a murderer, you have to believe that, but national security was at stake! They said that Stone and the rest of you were after revenge, that you planned on exposing the DoD's part in the virus crisis, and we couldn't let that happen. It would have been a scandal the administration could have never recovered from."

"God forbid you cause a scandal," Rebecca said, sarcasm oozing from her voice.

Nick shook his head in disgust. "Just so we're clear, you're saying that Secretary Barrett personally delivered a sample of the virus into your hands and told you to infect Sergeant Stone."

Waverly faltered. "Well, no, McAvoy was the one who gave me the vial, but he was acting under Barrett's orders. He said so himself."

Suspicion flooded Nick's gut, kicking his instincts into gear and causing a few puzzle pieces to slide into place.

"So you dealt only with McAvoy these past two years?" he said thoughtfully.

"Yes, but that's because Barrett couldn't officially give the orders. His connection to the project needed to remain a secret. McAvoy ordered me never to speak to the secretary directly."

How convenient. Some of the load bearing down on Nick's shoulders eased, making it easier to breathe. This entire situation sounded fishy as hell. The deputy secretary calling the shots, giving Waverly the virus, ordering him not to speak to Nick's father... Was Fred McAvoy the mastermind behind Project Aries, then?

Nick didn't know McAvoy too well, but he remembered his father praising the man's dedication to his country. Just like Nick's dad, McAvoy also placed great importance on defense, so it wasn't a stretch to think he'd created a biological weapon as a means to protect their nation.

"So that's it, the whole story." Waverly looked exhausted, and his head lolled to the side, as if his neck could no longer support the weight of it.

Nick glanced at Rebecca, who was watching him with wary green eyes. "What now?" she asked him. "What do we do with him?"

He thought it over for a second. "Call the DoD, I guess. Tell them we found their missing aide."

"No!" Waverly blurted out. "If they know where I am, I'm dead!"

"If they wanted you dead, they wouldn't have whisked you out of town," Nick said coldly.

"Nobody whisked me anywhere, you morons! There was a thug with a gun waiting for me in my apartment after I left the Pentagon that day." Waverly sounded utterly betrayed. "I was a loose end. Once Barrett told me to take care of Stone, I was no longer the lackey who simply made a few phone calls to Dr. Harrison—I was a murderer, and that bastard couldn't be connected to me anymore."

During his Special Forces stint, Nick had interrogated more than a few bad guys, and he'd developed a knack for knowing when he was being lied to. And the bitch of it was, Waverly genuinely believed every word he was saying. In Paul Waverly's mind, Kirk Barrett *was* behind everything.

But was that because McAvoy had orchestrated it to appear that way?

Or was it because Nick's father truly was the guilty party?

His heart squeezed painfully. No. There was no way his dad had allowed a virus to be tested on innocent people. No way his dad had tried to have him killed.

Now it was just a matter of proving it.

"Give me a sec," he told Rebecca before reaching into his pocket for his phone.

He stepped into the hallway and dialed Tate's number. When the captain picked up, Nick didn't waste any time in bringing him up to speed.

"I've got Waverly tied to a chair in the other room."

Tate's gruff laughter filled his ear. "Nice job, Nicky."

"I finished interrogating him, and now we need to figure out what to do with him. He swears he's being hunted for his role in the cover-up and he's terrified of getting offed by these people." Nick let out a frustrated breath. "Maybe we can try to arrange protective custody for him? I'm sure he'll cut a deal and testify if asked. This guy will do whatever it takes to stay alive."

"Did he give up a name?"

"Yes." Nick hesitated. "Secretary Barrett."

Tate's sharp breath echoed over the line. "Doesn't surprise me. Barrett is borderline obsessive when it comes to defense, and he's—"

"My father."

Silence.

"What?" Tate finally spoke, that one syllable laced with both shock and bewilderment.

"Kirk Barrett is my father, Tate."

There was another pause.

Followed by a muttered curse, a sigh and then, "Start talking, Nicky."

Rebecca approached the screen door and gazed out at Nick, who was on the deck brooding by the railing. Same way he'd been brooding for the past three hours. He hadn't said much since Waverly had dropped the Secretary Barrett bomb, and she knew the notion that his father might be the bad guy was tearing Nick apart.

"What's up?"

His gruff voice startled her. He was still standing there with his back turned, yet he'd detected her presence before she could even announce herself.

She stepped onto the deck and joined him. "Any word from Davidson?"

"Not since he called with an ETA for those federal agents he's sending."

Apprehension rippled through her at the reminder. She and Nick couldn't leave the beach house until the agents came to collect Waverly, and she continued to feel uneasy about that course of action. Nick had assured her that Brent Davidson, their contact at the DoD, could be trusted, but she didn't share his conviction. Davidson worked under McAvoy and Nick's father— how could they be sure he wasn't up to his elbows in this biological weapons scandal?

"Is our hostage still griping and complaining?" Nick asked her.

"Yep. Now he's demanding we feed him. I came out here to see what you wanted for lunch."

"You cook?"

"If making sandwiches counts as cooking, then yes."

He didn't even crack a smile, which told her he was even more upset than he was letting on.

Sighing, she placed her hand over his, which he'd rested palm-down on the splintered wooden railing. "You're going to drive yourself crazy if you keep agonizing over this. Reserve judgment until we speak to your dad, okay?" She tilted her head. "That *is* the plan, right? Head to D.C. to talk to him?"

Nick nodded, then spoke in a preoccupied tone. "I haven't seen my father in more than a year. I don't even know what he's been told about me."

Rebecca opened her mouth to respond, then slammed it shut.

Her sudden about-face did not go unnoticed. "What is it?" Nick demanded. "What do you know?"

She swallowed. "It doesn't matter. It's just…it doesn't matter."

"Tell me what you know, Rebecca." There was steel in his voice.

"Um. Well. Remember how I asked Harry to look into your background? Well, he spoke to one of his military contacts and the guy got a look at your file. It said you were honorably discharged last year."

A deep line appeared in his forehead. "I see."

"And another source said you've supposedly been sailing around the Caribbean ever since."

Nick let out a harsh laugh. "So that's the official story, huh?"

"Yeah."

"My dad would never believe that." His breath hitched. "He must know something is wrong, then. He's probably been trying to track me—"

Rebecca hated to interrupt, but she had no choice. "Your father was the one who told Harry's source the Caribbean story."

Nick's jaw tensed. "What?"

"Harry's source works at the Pentagon. He asked your father about you, and that was the answer he received."

As Nick fell silent, Rebecca's heart ached for him again. She knew exactly what he was thinking. Secretary Barrett was going out of his way to pretend he knew where his son was and that nothing was amiss. Why the lies?

"Maybe he really thinks you're traveling," she suggested in a feeble tone. "Maybe that's what he was told."

"My father knows I would never stay out of touch for an entire year. He *has* to suspect something is up." Nick paused. "Maybe he's playing along with the story they fed him about me, but secretly he *has* been searching for me."

Rebecca stifled a sigh, but she didn't contradict him. He needed this. Needed to believe that his father was the good guy, that Barrett was innocent. But Rebecca had been embroiled in politics for long enough to know that nobody in Washington was ever truly innocent.

"I guess we'll find out when we talk to him," she said softly. "And speaking of which, how are we going to manage that? People want us dead." *Possibly your father,* she didn't add. "We can't just waltz back to D.C. without anybody knowing we're there. Did you tell Davidson about our plans?"

"Yes, but Davidson can be trusted. He won't reveal to anyone that you and I are coming to D.C."

"Davidson answers to McAvoy and your fa—" she stopped guiltily, making a quick amendment "—he works for the Department of Defense. There's the risk that he's in cahoots with Mr. X. And even if he isn't, how is he going to keep our presence under wraps?"

"Davidson is part of the task force that's been set up to investigate the Meridian virus. Every government agency and employee is under the microscope right now," Nick told her. "Finding Mr. X has become a matter of national security, and Davidson is taking his role in the inquiry very seriously. He wants the person responsible caught as much as we do, which means he won't jeopardize our investigation by announcing to anyone that we're in town."

Rebecca remained unconvinced. "I'd still feel better if we continued investigating on our own. I don't want to rely on your buddy Davidson or these agents who are supposed to show up. I think we should make our way to D.C. without federal assistance."

He seemed to mull it over.

"Please, Nick. I'd feel a lot better if we did this alone."

"Me, too. Which is why we're not catching a ride

back with Davidson's men. Manuel will take us as far as Miami and we'll make our way to D.C from there."

She bristled. "You couldn't have just told me that off the bat? Why did you let me *beg* for it?"

The corners of his mouth lifted in the first smile she'd glimpsed all day. "Sometimes I like hearing you argue. It's fun."

She couldn't help a laugh, but the humor faded when she noticed that the cloud of sorrow had floated back into his honey-brown eyes.

"Nick, we'll find the truth," she said gently. "And if your father is involved—"

"He's not."

"If he is, then we'll deal with it."

She brought her hand to his face and stroked his cheek. It had been intended as a gesture of comfort, but almost immediately, the crackle of attraction heated the air and a wave of desire swelled in her belly.

With the gentlest of caresses, she ran her fingers over the razor-sharp stubble dotting his jaw, then swept her thumb over his bottom lip, which was surprisingly soft and incredibly sensual.

When she met his eyes, the hunger she saw in them made her heart beat faster.

He wasn't pulling away, wasn't moving her hand, and his acceptance of her touch spurred her next move. She stepped closer, stood on her tiptoes and pressed her lips to his in the softest, sweetest of kisses.

Again, it was intended as an offering of comfort, a token of her friendship, but she hadn't anticipated *Nick's* next move.

With a husky growl, he yanked her close and kissed the living daylights out of her.

Rebecca gasped against his mouth. Her legs buckled

as pleasure crashed into her, but Nick swiftly steadied her by clasping her waist and pulling her even closer. Her body melted into his, her breasts plastered against his rock-hard chest.

His tongue was greedy, demanding, licking its way into her mouth and robbing her of breath. Lord, the man could kiss.

He slanted his head to deepen the contact and when their tongues touched, he made a husky sound of approval deep in his throat and his fingers slid down to cup her bottom. He squeezed, devouring her mouth with his tongue as he ground his pelvis into the cradle of her thighs.

Moaning, Rebecca clung to his broad shoulders, her fingernails clutching the sleeves of his T-shirt. This wasn't how she'd imagined it to be. Nick was so reserved, so polite that she'd assumed she'd be the one in control if they ever surrendered to the attraction that had been brewing between them since they'd met.

But the control was all his. She was helpless, giddy, consumed with arousal that burned between her legs and coursed through her body.

When Nick finally tore his mouth away, she actually whimpered in disappointment.

They were both breathing hard, and she could see his pulse throbbing in the hollow of his throat.

Rebecca swallowed, still stunned by the dominating nature of that mind-blowing kiss. "That wasn't a seduction attempt," she said in a wobbly voice. "I was only trying to offer some comfort."

"I know," he said thickly.

Her heart refused to stop pounding. "I…"

I want to do that again.

But she couldn't voice the thought. The passion in

Nick's gorgeous eyes was beginning to dim, the glaze of lust reverting to that flicker of sadness.

"Rebecca," he started, and she knew he was about to apologize for the kiss.

To tell her it couldn't happen again.

Refusing to give him the chance, she pasted on a smile and said, "Come on, let's go feed our hostage."

The federal agents Brent Davidson had sent arrived mid-afternoon and promptly took Paul Waverly off Rebecca's and Nick's hands. She appreciated that neither agent attempted to strong-arm them into coming back to the States aboard the DoD jet. The two men didn't comment on her presence either, although one of them did confess to being a fan of hers.

By the time she and Nick returned to Javier's airfield in their rented Jeep, it was nearly four o'clock. Fortunately, Manuel and the Cessna were already waiting in the hangar and they managed to get in the air shortly after.

Nick was quiet on the journey home, leaving Rebecca to her own devices during the two-hour flight to Miami. The memory of this morning's kiss continued to echo in her mind like a seductive melody, and each time she glanced over at Nick's stoic profile, she had to resist the urge to jump into his lap and kiss him again.

She didn't quite understand why her hormones went on overload in Nick Barrett's presence. The man was hardly her type with his whole gentleman vibe and his determination to keep her away from the action. She'd dated men like Nick in Atlanta, the traditional types, the ones who believed women belonged barefoot and pregnant in the kitchen. Granted, Nick didn't seem like a chauvinist, but she knew he didn't particularly approve of the way she placed herself in danger's path.

But her job was dangerous at times. There was nothing she could do about that, short of quitting, and she had no intention of giving up her career.

And boy, wasn't she on a ridiculously premature train of thought?

Give up her career? She and Nick weren't even dating, for Pete's sake. They'd kissed. Once. And there probably wouldn't be a follow-up if Nick had anything to say about it. So really, there was no reason for her to be thinking about all the ways she and Nick Barrett were incompatible.

It was just past six when they landed in Miami, and it took another hour for Nick to secure a ride for them with the pilot of a cargo plane they encountered at yet another private airfield. As Nick handed over a stack of cash, Rebecca had to wonder just how much money the poor guy had spent this past year. All the charters, the weapons, the safe houses—it must have cost him a fortune.

On the other hand, when you came from Barrett oil and Prescott hotels, the word *fortune* probably held a slightly different meaning.

"Home, sweet home," Nick mumbled when their journey finally came to an end.

Rebecca peered out the window of the small plane and gazed at the twinkling city lights down below. The sun had set a couple of hours ago, but she could still make out the Washington Monument and the silvery glow of the Capitol as the plane began its descent.

She had a love-hate relationship with D.C. On one hand, the city was rife with scandal, which was every journalist's dream, but on the other hand, it was so hard not to become disillusioned in the face of all that corruption. Rebecca had lost her wide-eyed optimism years ago, and sometimes she missed that gung ho girl who'd believed that the truth always prevailed.

"Let me take your bag," Nick said ten minutes later, after the plane had come to a stop on the runway.

Rebecca passed him the large tote bag she'd picked up at the marketplace in Costa Rica, shouldered her green canvas purse, then accepted his hand as he helped her out of the plane. A perfect gentleman, as always.

To her surprise, a taxi was waiting for them directly on the tarmac. "When did you arrange for a cab?" she asked.

"When you were lecturing Javier about sea turtles." A ghost of a smile crossed his mouth.

Because smiles from Nick had been rare today, she welcomed the sight.

"Keep your head down as much as you can," he added. "I don't want the cabbie recognizing you."

"Same goes for you," she said wryly.

With Nick carrying their bags, they headed for the waiting cab and greeted their driver. Rebecca made a conscious effort to avert her eyes, casting her gaze downward and pretending to be fascinated with her dust-streaked hiking boots.

"Mr. and Mrs. Jones?" the Asian man inquired.

Nick nodded. "That's us."

As they slid into the backseat, Rebecca couldn't fight the yawn that overtook her. It felt like they'd been on the move from the moment she'd met Nick in Cortega three days ago. She longed for about twelve hours of uninterrupted sleep.

And a shower. God, she wanted a shower. She felt

grimy and gross, and her ponytail was greasy and kept sticking to her neck.

"You tired?" Nick said softly.

"Exhausted."

He patted his shoulder. "You can lean on me if you want."

Her heart skipped a beat. She couldn't remember the last time she'd snuggled up next to a warm male body. A couple of years at least. Right. She'd been seeing Jonas back then, the last bad boy she'd had the misfortune of dating. She hadn't gotten serious with anyone since then, although she had indulged in a weeklong affair last year with a lobbyist who turned out to be a complete jerk.

She really seemed to gravitate toward the jerks, didn't she?

Except this time.

No, this time she'd found herself drawn to a man who was so far from a jerk, so ridiculously nice, that he was probably too good to be true.

Resting her head on Nick's strong shoulder, she closed her eyes and tried not to overanalyze her feelings for this man.

She napped during the entire cab ride, and although she couldn't be sure, she could have sworn she felt Nick's lips brush the top of her head in a soft kiss before she dozed off.

When the car lurched to a stop about twenty minutes later, she jerked awake. Blinking rapidly, she turned to the window and saw that they'd arrived at a modest hotel not too far from Capitol Hill.

Nick quickly paid the cabbie and ushered Rebecca into the front lobby without giving her time to officially wake up. But she understood his haste. The two of them couldn't risk being seen in public; they were too recognizable, and the last thing they wanted to do was alert Mr. X and his thugs that they were stateside.

When they approached the front desk, she discovered that Nick had already booked their room over the phone—also when she'd been talking sea turtles with Javier—so it took no time at all to check in and collect their room key card.

Room. Singular. As in *one*.

She knew that Nick had purposely booked it that way to maintain the pretense that they were "Mr. and Mrs. Jones," but the delicious possibilities did not escape her as they rode the elevator to the second floor.

One room. One bed. Her and Nick.

All thoughts of seduction had been shoved to the back burner earlier, thanks to Waverly's accusations about Nick's father. But after that explosive kiss…well, she might have to forge ahead with that seduction plan. And conveniently, she had one hotel room at her disposal.

But first things first, they needed to find a way to reach Nick's father without tipping off Mr. X.

Unless Nick's father is *Mr. X….*

She banished the pessimistic notion, wishing for Nick's sake that Waverly was dead wrong about Barrett's role in the virus conspiracy.

"So how are we going to do this?" she asked as Nick dropped his duffel on the soft white carpet of their room. "Can we get a message to your dad somehow? Maybe through someone with access to the Pentagon?"

Nick flopped down on the edge of the king-size bed and pulled out his cell phone. "Or…I can just call him."

Rebecca glared at him. "You can't! What if his phone is bugged?"

"Trust me, it won't be."

Much to her horror, he was already dialing a number. Crap. Didn't he realize that in Washington, *everyone's* gee-dee phone was tapped?

"How do you know it's safe?" she demanded.

"Because this isn't a number anyone else knows about." He rolled his eyes. "My dad is the secretary of defense, darling. He lives and breathes covert."

As she watched, Nick pressed a sequence of numbers into the keypad.

And then he hung up.

"That's it?" she said in confusion.

"That's it," he confirmed.

"So now what?"

"Now we wait."

Rebecca shot him an exasperated look. "For how long?"

"Depends on what he's doing, but it shouldn't be long. It's ten-thirty at night, so he's either in his office or heading home. I doubt we caught him in the middle of a meeting, not unless the president requested a hush-hush powwow at the White House tonight."

"Hey, as long as we're waiting, do you think I should contact the network again? I haven't been in touch since I called about Harry."

Harry's name got stuck in her throat, causing her heart to clench. She'd tried so hard not to think about him these past couple of days. Harry, Jesse, Dave... But the grief made a swift appearance now, and it took all her willpower to choke it down and raise that shield around her heart again.

"You can't call anyone," Nick answered in a stern voice. "Anyone connected to you will *definitely* have had their phones tapped."

She sighed. "I wish I had a computer, at least then I could do some research. Or heck, even a pen and paper would be nice. I wouldn't mind jotting down some of my thoughts about all this."

When his gaze sharpened, she held up her hands in mock surrender. "Off the record," she assured him. "I'm not planning on publishing or airing anything until this is over. I made you a promise, remember?"

"I remember, but it's good to hear that you do, too." He relaxed, then stiffened right back up when the phone in his hand buzzed.

Rebecca watched his expression transform from calm to nervous as he studied the display.

"It's him," Nick said gruffly.

The phone kept buzzing.

She eyed him expectantly. "Well, pick it up already."

After a beat, he pressed a button and lifted the phone to his ear.

"Dad?"

The emotion thickening his voice brought a soft smile to Rebecca's lips. God, she was a total sucker for men who were close with their parents. She loved her own folks to death, and she'd never understood people who didn't appreciate the importance of family.

But Nick sounded so choked up that she felt like she was intruding on a private moment, so she ended up inching toward the bathroom doorway, needing to give him some privacy.

"I'm taking a shower," she whispered.

He nodded. Didn't even glance her way as he spoke into the phone again.

"Yeah, it's me," he said roughly. "I...hell, it's been a long time, huh?"

That was the last thing Rebecca heard before she

stepped into the bathroom. Her eyes were surprisingly damp, and she found herself praying that Kirk Barrett was the man his son believed him to be. Nick was such a good man, an honorable man. The last thing he deserved was to be saddled with a father who'd tried to have him killed.

She hurriedly stripped out of her dirty, sweaty clothes and nearly dived into the glass shower stall. The moment the hot water rushed out of the faucet and coursed down her naked body, she purred in pleasure and tipped her head into the spray.

She proceeded to spend the next thirty minutes scrubbing herself raw with the sweet-smelling hotel soap, washing her hair and shaving her legs and armpits with the complimentary razor she found on the ledge affixed to the tiled wall. By the time she stepped out of the shower, she felt like a new woman.

Grabbing a fluffy white towel from the rack on the wall, she dried off, then wrapped the terry cloth around her body and tucked the top in. She'd forgotten to bring a change of clothes into the washroom, which meant she had no choice but to walk out in the towel.

When she reentered the room, Nick was no longer on the phone, but sitting on the bed, lost in thought.

"Hey," she said quietly.

His head lifted in an abrupt motion, as if he truly hadn't realized she was standing there. His lack of vigilance said a lot about his state of mind.

"Hey," he murmured.

"So what happened? What did he say?"

"A lot."

The two-syllable response brought a rush of aggravation. "Um, care to elaborate?"

Nick let out a heavy breath. "He says he's been trying to locate me ever since I went off the grid, and that he didn't believe for a second I would be discharged and take off without a word. He suspected there was a conspiracy in play, but he had no idea what it could possibly be related to, at least not until news of the Meridian virus was made public."

"So he didn't know about the virus," she said.

"Dad insists he didn't. He thought my disappearance was related to an op, that I might have been a POW somewhere and the military was trying to cover it up." Nick hesitated for a second. "We're meeting in an hour. He has some business to wrap up, and then he's leaving the Pentagon and coming to meet me."

Rebecca's voice went dry. "And let me guess, you want me to stay put."

"No." He cleared his throat. "I want you to come with me."

Chapter 12

Nick didn't blame Rebecca for looking so surprised. Since the day they'd met, he'd been demanding she stay behind, lie low, stay put—pretty much anything that involved keeping her out of the line of fire. And now here he was, actively seeking out her company for a potentially dangerous situation.

"You actually want me to come?"

Nick nodded.

Her green eyes flickered warily, as if she thought he might shout "Gotcha!" at any moment. "Um. Why?"

Helplessness squeezed his chest so hard his lungs hurt. "Remember that discussion we had in Mala about bias?"

"Yes…"

"Well, I am totally, categorically biased right now." He stared at her in dismay. "This is my *father*. I believe with all my heart that he's innocent, but…am I fooling myself here? Do I just want him to be innocent so damn bad that I'm unable to objectively examine the evidence?"

Sympathy softened her gaze. She moved closer, and he suddenly became aware that she wore nothing but a towel. Despite the misery tightening his throat, his traitorous body actually had the gall to respond to Rebecca's scantily clad appearance. His groin stirred, thickened, throbbed. Pulse sped up. Mouth went dry.

"Then I'll be the objective one," Rebecca said in an earnest tone. "I have a talent for reading people and I can usually tell if someone is lying to me."

"That's why I want you to come along."

She looked pleased, but then something shifted in her eyes and her chin lifted in perplexing determination.

"What is it?" he asked, unable to keep the suspicion from his tone.

"When do we have to meet him?"

"Midnight."

She glanced at the alarm clock on the nightstand. Nick followed her gaze and saw the red numerals change from 11:32 to 11:33.

"How long will it take to get there?"

"Five or ten minutes. Why?"

"So we have some time, then."

His eyes narrowed. "To do what, darling?"

"To help you forget."

There was nothing ambiguous about her quiet, candid words. He knew exactly what she was suggesting, what she was offering. Heat stirred in his lower body, spreading through him until he was painfully hard again, but the indecision that hit him was as powerful as the lust.

He didn't do casual flings. He preferred there to be *some* emotion involved in his sexual encounters.

There is, a little voice pointed out. *You feel something for her.*

Nick tried to silence the voice, but it was too late. The thought had already cemented itself in his mind, and he couldn't deny the truth. He *did* care about Rebecca. He cared a lot. Maybe even too much.

"No more thinking."

Her stern voice penetrated his thoughts and snapped him back to the present. To the gorgeous redhead standing in front of him. In a towel. Just a little white towel...

Rebecca took a step closer. "I'm serious. I can see your brain conjuring up all the reasons why we shouldn't do this. Well, let me make it easy for you, okay?"

His mouth turned to sawdust when she reached for the knot holding her towel up.

"We're doing this," she went on.

She undid the knot.

"So deal with it, Nick."

The towel dropped.

An instant wave of red-hot lust slammed into him and set his body on fire. His gaze roamed every inch of her naked body, from her perky breasts and cherry-red nipples, to the sweet curve of her hip, to the shapely legs that looked so smooth to the touch. Her lily-white skin was still pink from the shower, and it turned even pinker as his gaze trailed over all of that tantalizing flesh.

When he focused on the strip of red curls between her legs, Rebecca's green eyes danced with humor. "Natural redhead," she quipped.

He choked out a laugh. "I never had a doubt. You've got that redhead stubbornness, remember?"

Despite the alarms going off in his head, he found

himself reaching out and touching her bare hip. Just the mere graze of his fingertips over her hip bone.

She shivered.

He quickly withdrew his hand. "This is a bad idea."

"No, it's not."

"We...can't."

"Oh, for the love of God, Nick. Stop being so difficult and let me help you forget for a little while."

With that, she climbed onto his lap, wrapped her arms around his neck and kissed him senseless.

As her tongue filled his mouth and her fingers dug into the nape of his neck, Nick surrendered.

He kissed her back. Long, deep, desperate. The next few minutes were a blur. All he could see was Rebecca, all he could feel and smell and taste was Rebecca. They fell back on the mattress, her curvy naked body still plastered to his fully clothed one, and all the pent-up desire he'd felt for this woman came spilling out like water from a broken dam. Their kisses grew hotter, more intense, until they were both gasping for air, and suddenly Rebecca was clawing at the hem of his shirt in an attempt to pull it up.

With a husky groan, he helped her out, ripping the shirt off in one smooth motion, then tackling his zipper and shoving his cargo pants and boxers down his legs. When they were skin to skin, they let out simultaneous moans, their hands taking on lives of their own.

Nick explored every sweet curve, every feminine secret. While his pulse drummed in his ears, he squeezed her breasts, kissed them, laved them with his tongue, toyed with her nipples. He loved the way she moaned in response to his sensual ministrations. The way she pushed her breasts into his palms and begged for more.

When he slid one hand between her legs and discovered the liquid honey pooled in her core, he nearly lost it.

He needed this woman more than he needed his next breath, and it took every agonizing iota of willpower to leave her so he could rummage in his bag for a condom. He returned to the bed in a nanosecond, sheathed himself, then covered her body with his.

No more foreplay. No lead-up. But Rebecca didn't seem to mind. She welcomed him into her wet heat and he groaned at the feel of her inner muscles clutching him like a glove.

"Oh, God. *Nick.*"

Her breathy words and the glaze of pleasure swimming in her eyes sent him soaring to a new level of *turned-on.* He withdrew slowly only to plunge back in fast, then met her eyes and murmured, "You're incredible."

She responded with a soft whimper and hooked her legs around his ass to deepen the contact.

The pleasure was unbearable. Unstoppable. He'd never been a selfish lover, but damn if he could stop this all-consuming train of lust. He needed it too badly. Wanted her too much.

His hips pistoned into her tight heat, his mouth fastening over hers. He kissed her until they were both breathless again. Despite that overwhelming need for release, he managed to hold off, to coax her closer to the edge by reaching down to rub her sensitive nub.

Only when Rebecca came apart beneath him did he let go. Closed his eyes, let the ecstasy consume him, let his mind go blissfully empty. When the waves of release finally ebbed, he collapsed on top of her. Drained. Sated.

Man, he'd needed that.

It took a few minutes to catch his breath, and then he rolled onto his side and drew Rebecca to him. Her hair tickled his left pec, her body warm and boneless as she snuggled close, but it wasn't until she let out a little sigh of pure contentedness that the guilt made an appearance.

Jeez. He'd taken her hard and rough like a goddamn caveman. Hadn't even taken the time to make her hot, to get her ready.

As he opened his mouth, armed with an apology, Rebecca suddenly grumbled in frustration.

"You think way too much, Nick." Sighing again, she disentangled herself from his embrace and sat up. "Don't you dare apologize to me. I wanted this. I *instigated* this."

It didn't surprise him that she'd read his thoughts and known exactly what he'd been about to say. "Right," he said. "I forgot about your little seduction plot."

She smiled ruefully. "This wasn't part of the seduction. I…I was trying to help. You looked so sad and broken and…" She shrugged. "I wanted to make you feel good, even if it was just a temporary fix."

Temporary. The word lingered in his mind, resonating with truth, reminding him of the reality of their circumstances. Whatever happened between him and Rebecca, it *would* be temporary. Eventually they'd have to say goodbye, and there was no way around that.

"But trust me, when I decide to full-on seduce you—" she stalked naked toward the tote bag she'd left on the carpet, tossing him a glance over her shoulder "—it'll involve a lot more than a quickie before we have to meet your dad."

Another rush of guilt rose inside him, but Rebecca yet again chided him before he could speak.

"No apologies," she repeated. "I *wanted* a quickie. So, please, let's just get dressed and get this meeting over with."

He couldn't figure out if this careless, no-biggie attitude of hers was a front, but there was no time to question her. She was right. At the moment, he needed to focus on this impending reunion with his dad.

The rest they could figure out later.

Secretary of Defense Kirk Barrett had already arrived when Nick and Rebecca emerged from the heavily wooded ravine bordering the park where they'd arranged to meet. Nick had spent the past fifteen minutes scouting the area to make sure a team of mercenaries or snipers wasn't watching the park, and he had just concluded that the coast was clear.

That he even had to take such precautions when meeting his own *father* brought a pang of sadness to his chest. He hated considering that his dad might have an ulterior motive or that he may have planned an ambush, but Nick hadn't stayed alive this long by being stupid. No matter how much he loved his father, he had to at least acknowledge the possibility that the man he'd always idolized could be involved in this conspiracy.

But that didn't mean he didn't feel a rush of relief when his recon turned up nothing out of the ordinary. As promised, Kirk Barrett had come alone.

"You ready?" Rebecca whispered as they stepped out of the woods where he'd forced her to wait until he determined it was safe to come out.

"Not really," he mumbled.

The residential park contained a small playground and a circular concrete fountain with several wrought-iron benches situated around it. He and Rebecca walked through the shadows toward one of the benches where a lone figure sat in wait.

Nick's heart soared, then got stuck in his throat like a piece of gum. A year. It had been a year since he'd seen his dad. Damn, he'd missed the old man.

At their approach, Kirk Barrett rose from the bench. Visible relief flooded those familiar brown eyes, and Nick was shocked to hear a choked sob slip out of his father's mouth.

"Nicky."

The next thing he knew, he was enveloped in his father's arms. He couldn't remember the last time his father had hugged him—the secretary rarely showed his affection in the form of physical contact. But here he was, hugging Nick so tight that his lungs started to burn from the lack of oxygen.

When they finally broke apart, Barrett urgently searched Nick's face. "Are you all right, son?"

Nick nodded, feeling a little choked up himself. "I'm good. Thanks for coming, Dad."

"Where the hell else would I be?" the secretary grumbled. "And where the hell have you been, Nicky? What the fu—" He stopped mid-expletive as he seemed to remember he was in the company of a woman. He glanced at Rebecca apologetically. "Pardon my language. I'm slightly rattled, in case you couldn't tell."

Rebecca smiled politely. "It's all right." She extended a hand. "Rebecca Parker."

"Yes, I recognize you." He took her hand. "Kirk Barrett."

"I recognize you, too, sir."

As they shook hands, Nick tried to gauge Rebecca's reaction to his dad. Her green eyes revealed nothing but cordial interest and slight caution, making it difficult to figure out where her head was at.

His dad, on the other hand, was easy to read. Concern was splashed all over the older man's face, those familiar handsome features that were so much like Nick's. Kirk Barrett was in his early fifties, but he looked a decade younger; people often mistook him and Nick for brothers rather than father and son.

The secretary gestured for them to sit, his brown eyes never leaving his son's face. "I thought you might be dead," he said frankly. His voice hardened. "Why the *hell* haven't you contacted me this past year?"

Nick let out a breath. "I couldn't risk it. I didn't know how high the conspiracy went, and I didn't want to endanger you in any way. I was trying to protect you."

"Endanger me? I'm your father, Nicholas! *I'm* the one who's supposed to protect *you*." Barrett held up his hand to silence Nick's objection. "You should have contacted me. End of story."

Nick couldn't help but smile. He really had missed his dad's deep, commanding voice and no-nonsense manner.

"But it's in the past and we don't concern ourselves with the past," Barrett said brusquely. "So, now tell me everything. Every last detail."

"That could take a while," Nick said with a sigh.

In the end, it took nearly thirty minutes to recap the events of the past year. Nick told his father about the mission in Corazón, Hector Cruz's confession that Dr. Harrison had killed the villagers, Sebastian's encounter with the virus in D.C., the break-in at the hotel in Mala. Through it all, the secretary of defense said nothing. Didn't blink, didn't move, just listened silently while wearing that shrewd expression Nick had grown up with.

When Nick mentioned the attack on Rebecca and her crew, his father finally reacted, sympathy filling his eyes. "I saw it on television. Those were some horrific images."

"Yes, they were," Rebecca said sadly.

"I'm glad to see you're all right. Everyone in the country was out of their minds with worry when that screen went black." The secretary turned back to his son. "So I assume you and Ms. Parker tracked down our missing aide?"

Nick nodded.

"And?"

He shifted in reluctance, dreading this part of the conversation.

"Talk to me, son," his dad ordered.

Letting out a breath, Nick told his father everything Paul Waverly had said in that beach house.

When he finished, a chasm of silence stretched between them.

The wounded look on his father's face caused guilt to tug at his insides, but Nick refused to apologize for voicing Waverly's allegations. This needed to be addressed. He needed to know the truth, damn it.

"Well?" he said when his father still hadn't answered.

The secretary arched one dark brow. "Are you asking me if I ordered a hit squad to kill you, Nicholas?"

He nodded.

"And if I allowed a deadly biological agent to be engineered in a U.S. lab and then tested on human guinea pigs?"

Another nod.

"And if I ordered Mr. Waverly to poison Sergeant Stone? And sanctioned an assassination attempt on three members of the ABN news team?"

Nick swallowed the lump in his throat. "Did you?" he asked hoarsely.

"No."

One syllable. One tired voice, one sad expression.

It was all Nick needed to hear. How could he have ever doubted it? Of course his father wasn't behind this.

On Nick's other side, Rebecca didn't seem as convinced by the secretary's quiet denial. She leaned in so both men could see her and fixed Barrett with a cool look. "Then who did, Mr. Secretary?"

With a gentle smile, he met her narrowed eyes and said, "I think we all know who's responsible for this."

Rebecca paused for a beat. "Fred McAvoy."

"Seems like the likeliest culprit." Disappointment and anger hung from Barrett's every word. "McAvoy gave Waverly the vial containing the virus. And because my deputy didn't have access to the vials confiscated in the raid—they were shipped directly to the CDC— then that means he procured his sample elsewhere."

"Directly from the D&M lab," Nick guessed.

"McAvoy was not acting on my orders. I need you to believe that, son."

"I believe you."

Barrett turned to Rebecca. "But I sense that you're the one I must convince, isn't that right, my dear?"

Her tiny shrug confirmed that he'd hit the nail on the head.

"So, Ms. Parker, what will it take to make you a believer?"

She met his gaze head-on, and Nick couldn't help but

be impressed. Not many people had the nerve to stare his father down like that.

Or to ask the question that smoothly left Rebecca's mouth.

"Would you kill to protect your country?"

The secretary rubbed his clean-shaven jaw. "If you mean would I kill someone who is a threat to the country, a member of a terrorist cell, a double agent, a threat to national security? Then yes, I would—at least if the justice system failed to competently handle the issue first, as it unfortunately often does." He held her inquisitive gaze. "But an innocent? An entire village filled with innocent people who did absolutely nothing to wrong this nation? Never."

The conviction echoing in Barrett's words was unmistakable, and Nick could swear he saw a gleam of approval flicker in Rebecca's expression.

"And never my son," the secretary continued in an impassioned voice. "Before my Jeannie died, I promised her that our kids would always be taken care of, always be loved and protected. Nicholas and Vivian are the most important people in my life."

"I believe you," Rebecca said softly.

Nick experienced a burst of relief. This was the reason he'd asked her to tag along. He'd needed that validation. *Her* validation.

And it startled him just how much he'd come to value Rebecca's opinion and advice this past week.

"So what now?" she asked, looking from one man to the other. "How do we expose McAvoy?"

"I'll deal with McAvoy," the men said unison.

Laughing, they exchanged a look, and then the secretary's features hardened. "You're officially out of this fight, son. Let me handle it from this point on."

Nick just laughed again. "Dad, I love you, but we both know that ain't gonna happen. I'll be the one talking to your deputy, same way I dealt with your fugitive aide."

His father's jaw went stiffer than stone. "I can get the truth out of Fred."

"So can I. And my way will be a lot quicker."

Nick didn't even bother sugarcoating it; his dad had been Special Forces himself, once upon a time. He knew the score. The methods a soldier sometimes had to utilize.

"Is McAvoy married? Kids?" Nick asked before his father had another chance to argue.

"He's single. He lives alone in Fairfax County," Barrett said grudgingly. "But he's out of town at the moment handling a delicate matter in Beijing. He'll be back in two days."

"Text me his address to this number." Nick recited the number for his secure cell so his father could key it into *his* secure cell.

The fact that both of them had untraceable phones for the sole purpose of covert communication made him want to laugh, but he fought the urge because, really, there was nothing funny about any of this.

"Don't do anything foolish, Nicky," his father warned. "And I want you to check in with me every few hours. You're not disappearing on me again."

"Don't worry, once I get the truth out of McAvoy, we'll handle the fallout through official channels. But I don't want you to act until we have confirmation that McAvoy was involved. If you make a move before that, or give any indication that you suspect something, you'll risk tipping McAvoy off, and then he might skip town just like Waverly did. Promise me you'll sit on this until I have more for us to go on."

Although the secretary didn't look thrilled about it, he gave a quick nod. "Fine. We'll do this your way, son." That authoritative gleam in his dark eyes made a swift reappearance. "For now."

Chapter 13

"Well?" Nick drove away from the side street where they'd left the rental SUV that had been arranged for them by the hotel concierge.

In the passenger seat, Rebecca released a little sigh. "I didn't lie back there. I believe your dad, Nick. Nothing about him triggered my B.S. meter."

She didn't miss the relief in his eyes, or the way his broad shoulders relaxed. "So it wasn't just me."

"No. I think he's telling the truth."

"Me, too."

"So what now?"

The question was becoming her new catchphrase, and she found it odd how readily she allowed Nick to call all the shots. Yes, she'd promised him that she would follow orders, but she normally wasn't so obedient—God knew her parents could vouch for that.

"Now we stay out of sight for a couple of days until

McAvoy returns from Beijing, and then I pay him a visit."

She rolled her eyes. "Back to *I,* huh? Now that you've conquered your bias, we're back to keeping me hidden away."

"I'm just trying to keep you safe. What's so wrong about that?"

"It's not wrong. Just…old-fashioned. It's the twenty-first century, Nick. Women aren't fragile, helpless creatures that require a man to protect them. We've *never* been that way, no matter what all those big manly men wanted to believe." She shook her head in aggravation. "Women are perfectly capable of taking on dangerous tasks, just like men. We can serve in the military, work in law enforcement, politics—"

"Are you really lecturing me on women's lib?" Nick sounded vaguely amused.

"Just seems like you forget about it sometimes," she answered with a shrug.

He changed lanes, making his way through the deserted streets of D.C. in the direction of their hotel.

"Darling, I have no doubt about a woman's ability to take on the same roles as a man. Trust me, I've met some pretty badass women, even got my ass kicked by one during basic training."

She grinned. "I would've loved to see that." Her grin faded as a thought occurred to her, and suddenly she felt wounded. "So wait, are you saying it's just me? You think *I'm* weak?"

"What? No, not at all. You're probably the strongest woman I've ever met." When he gave her a sideways look, the confusion in his brown eyes was evident. "Honestly? I don't know why I'm so overprotective of you."

Because you like me.

She quickly swallowed the words before they could pop out of her mouth. For some reason, Nick didn't seem at all comfortable with his attraction to her. Which brought a prickle of offense, because, really, what was so bad about liking her? She was smart and funny and pretty and successful—any man would be *lucky* to have her.

So what was Nick's problem? Was it just her job he didn't approve of? Or maybe he didn't like being attracted to a woman who wasn't his usual type?

Then again, he hadn't seemed to mind it a couple of hours ago when he'd been rocking her world....

The memory of their explosive joining sent a bolt of arousal straight to her core. God, the sex had been... thrilling. Amazing. Unexpected. Nick had been rougher than she'd thought he'd be. More intense. More passionate.

She'd loved every second of it.

"Penny for your thoughts?"

Warmth spread through her as his voice broke into her thoughts. Penny for your thoughts? Gosh, who said things like that? Why did Nick Barrett have to be so effing cute?

"Sorry," she said, "I spaced out there for a bit. Anyway, I know you feel protective of me, but I still think I should come along when you see McAvoy."

Nick turned left onto their hotel's street, then glanced over in reluctance. "I don't think it's a good idea."

"I think it's a *great* idea. My being there worked to our advantage with Waverly, remember? We could do that whole leave-the-room ploy again where you pretend you're going to torture him but can't do it in front of me."

"Pretend?"

At first she thought he was teasing her, but when she looked into his eyes and saw the feral gleam there, she realized he was dead serious.

"You actually would have tortured Waverly?" she blurted out.

"Yes."

Yes. That was it. He didn't say another word, and Rebecca sat there in silence for a moment, trying to make sense of this man. There were so many facets to him. One minute he was sweet and chivalrous. The next, he was devouring her body like a starved man. And then in the blink of an eye, he was a deadly warrior capable of torturing another human being.

She gulped, pushing away her confusion and focusing on the matter at hand. "Well, I still think I can be an asset. McAvoy might be more willing to talk if—"

It came to her attention that Nick was no longer listening to her. His shoulders had gone rigid, his handsome profile revealing the tense line of his jaw.

"What is it?" she demanded. "Is everything all ri— Hey, you just passed the hotel. What's going on?"

Nick turned with a grim look and said, "We've got company."

Rebecca battled a spark of fear. "Are you sure?" she demanded, twisting around in her seat to peer out the back window.

She didn't see anything out of the ordinary, but Nick's body language said otherwise.

He nodded stiffly. "Positive. The black van parked on the street was the same make and model as the one that was outside the Liberty in Mala. The driver was the merc with the shaved head, and the dude reading a newspaper in that bus shelter across the street was also a mercenary."

"How did they find us?"

"I don't know. Maybe the hotel clerk recognized one of us. You, most likely. She could've notified the press that you were staying there. Or maybe Mr. X paid off every hotel worker in the city to inform him if a couple matching our description checked in."

She shot him a dubious look. "That seems like a very expensive plan."

"Hey, I'm just throwing out suggestions here."

Rebecca felt terrible asking her next question, but she couldn't stop it from slipping out. "Did you tell your dad where we were staying?"

"No," Nick said curtly, "I didn't."

His foot slammed harder on the gas pedal and the SUV picked up speed, zooming away from the Capitol. Rebecca stopped talking and let Nick concentrate on driving, but her brain was still trying to make sense of this latest development.

She supposed the woman at the front desk could have recognized her and phoned one of the papers with a tip that Rebecca Parker had checked into a hotel with a strange man. Everyone in D.C. was looking to make a few extra bucks, and when a scandal landed in their laps, they weren't going to ignore it.

The alternative was far worse—Secretary Barrett had alerted the hit squad to the fact that his son was back in town.

But darn it, Rebecca had truly believed in Barrett's innocence. There had been nothing insincere about that man.

He's a politician, Becks. Politicians are good actors.

True, but Secretary Barrett wasn't a typical politician. He had been a soldier first and foremost. And he was a father. A good one, if the love shining in his eyes when he'd looked at his son was anything to go by.

When Nick slowed the SUV twenty minutes later, Rebecca lifted her head to examine their surroundings. They were on the outskirts of the city, pulling into the paved lot of an L-shaped motel with a flickering blue neon sign. Capitol Hills Motel. Not exactly an apt name, seeing as how they were nowhere near the Capitol and the landscape was flatter than a pancake.

"Stay in the car," Nick told her as he parked in front of the motel office.

He hopped out of the SUV and disappeared through the office door. Wooden blinds shielded the door and front window from view, so Rebecca couldn't see inside. She was on edge the entire time, unable to relax until Nick strode back to the car five minutes later.

"Did the clerk get a good look at you?" she asked.

"He didn't even get *a* look at me, let alone a good one. The kid's eyes were glued to the TV over my head. We should be fine."

Nick drove across the courtyard and parked in front of the room at the very end of the row.

"Stay here until I check it out," he ordered, and then he was out of the SUV and approaching the chipped red door of room 14.

Through the windshield, Rebecca watched as he withdrew his pistol and kept it flat against his thigh. A flash of silver winked in the darkness. The room key, which Nick stuck into the keyhole.

He crept into the dark motel room, and less than two minutes later, he reappeared in the doorway and gave her a nod of approval.

Nodding back, Rebecca unbuckled her seat belt and

slid out of the car, then waited for Nick to grab their bags from the backseat.

She'd teased him about it earlier, insisting it was pointless to constantly lug that duffel around instead of just leaving it in the hotel room, but now that the hotel had been compromised, she was eating her words.

They entered the motel room a minute later and Nick flicked a switch, shedding light on their shabby surroundings. The room contained a pair of twin beds, a frayed brown carpet, ugly flowered bedspreads and a minifridge that hummed like the engine of a jet plane.

"Cozy," she said lightly.

Nick didn't answer. He locked the door, flicked the chain, then approached the bed and dropped the duffel bag on the bedspread.

"What are we going to do now?" she asked when he didn't say a word.

He unzipped the bag. "Send a message."

Alarm skittered up her spine. "What does *that* mean?"

"It means these mercenaries are just gonna keep coming. See, Mr. X underestimates me. He thinks he can send some goon squad, they'll take us out like that—" he snapped his fingers "—and all will be swept under the rug. Well, it's time to prove his assumption wrong."

Rebecca didn't like the reckless glint in his eyes. "I'm not going to approve of this, am I?"

"Probably not." He promptly began removing a startling amount of weapons from the duffel bag.

They'd both donned all black for their meeting with the secretary, but Rebecca thought Nick pulled off the deadly look a lot better than she did. And he looked even deadlier now that he'd put on that shoulder holster and was strapping on so many weapons she didn't know whether to be terrified or turned-on. She was kinda digging the badass warrior thing he had going on, but at the same time, her heart was beating like crazy at the thought of Nick getting hurt.

She watched as he knelt down to slide a lethal-looking blade into his scuffed black boot. "Are you seriously going after these mercenaries all by yourself?" she said in disbelief.

"Yep."

"Fine, then I'm going with you."

"No."

"Nick, I'm serious. You can't take on a team of mercenaries by yourself!"

"Yes, I can," he said simply.

Okay, the confidence was definitely a turn-on. And it succeeded in chipping away at some of her terror. Looking at him now, dressed in black and covered with weapons, she had no doubt that this man really *could* take on a mercenary squad and come out triumphant.

Without another word, Nick stalked to the door, then halted as if remembering he wasn't alone.

"Lock the door behind me," he said softly. "And don't even think about leaving this room, not even to grab something from the vending machine. If you're hungry, choke down an MRE."

Rebecca sighed. "Is there any way I can talk you out of this?"

"Nope." His voice came out gruff. "And, Red, if something goes wrong…if for some reason I don't come back tonight, I want you to call Tate. Same drill as before, all right? Go to Ecuador."

Surprise filtered through her. "You don't want me to go to your dad?"

He shook his head. "We stick to the plan. Tate and Sebastian will make sure you're safe, and they'll handle the McAvoy thread, okay?"

"Okay."

Before he could reach for the doorknob, she dashed toward him and intercepted his hand. "Wait," she burst out.

"What is it?"

She threw her arms around him and hugged him.

After a beat, his arm came around her waist to hold her close.

"Be safe," she whispered, resting her cheek on his broad chest.

His warm hand stroked the small of her back. "I will."

"Promise?"

"I promise," he said huskily.

To her surprise—and pleasure—he dipped his head and dropped a quick kiss on her lips.

And then he was gone.

Nick was in warrior mode as he moved through the shadows. Unseen. Unheard. A predator closing in on its prey. It was three o'clock in the morning and the city was asleep. Not a single light was on in the residential street running parallel to the road where the hotel stood, making it easy for him to go unnoticed.

He crept along the narrow walkway between the two low-rise buildings across the street from the hotel. His initial sweep of the area had pinpointed the location of only one sniper, situated on the roof of one of these ivy-covered buildings. Ascending the fire escape took no effort at all, and then he was hauling himself over the concrete edge of the roof and landing silently on his feet.

On the other side of the roof, the black-clad mercenary lay on his belly like a snake, one eye focused on
the scope of what looked like an M40 sniper rifle. Standard issue rifle in the Marine Corps, which hinted that
the merc was former military.

Nick crept toward his prey, who was oblivious to the
fact that he was no longer alone on the roof. It was only
when Nick was a foot away that the sniper sensed his
presence and abruptly twisted around. His eyes widened
in surprise, his hand reached for the pistol strapped to
his belt, but not fast enough.

Nick got his hands around the man's throat and
snapped his neck with an efficient crack.

One down.

No remorse. The sniper had been ordered to put a
bullet in Nick's brain. In Rebecca's. He couldn't risk
knocking him unconscious and having the man wake
up before Nick could finish sending his message.

His heartbeat remained steady as he lowered the dead
sniper to the pebble-strewn rooftop. He arranged the
limp body to make it appear that the man was still peering into that scope, just in case one of his merc buddies happened to glance up with a pair of field glasses.
Then he descended the fire escape and locked in on
his next target.

Make that two targets. Both stationed behind the
hotel, one hunkered down behind a row of Dumpsters,
the other positioned on higher ground, trying to cam-
ouflage himself in the trees.

Nick maneuvered through the shadows and made his
way to the farther target first.

"Son of a—"

That was all the dark-skinned soldier for hire managed to get out before Nick got him in a chest lock and

dragged him backward into the brush. The man was struggling too much for Nick to get a solid grip on his neck, so he swiftly drew his knife from his hip and shoved the blade into the soldier's chest, slicing up toward the sternum to penetrate the heart.

Two down.

Lowering the body to the dirt, Nick dislodged his knife, wiped the bloodstained blade on his pant leg and headed for the Dumpsters.

Three minutes later, it was three down.

Jeez, these men were making it too damn easy for him. None of them had even seen him coming, which said a lot about their piss-poor instincts.

As he stashed the third body behind the enormous garbage bins, a crackling noise filled the air.

Crap. The merc's radio.

"Charlie, you copy?"

More static.

Stifling a sigh, Nick reached into the dead man's pocket and pulled out the small, compact radio. After a beat, he pressed the talk button, covering the speaker with his hand to produce a muffled response.

"Copy," he said briskly. "No sign of them."

He held his breath as he awaited a reply.

Another hiss of static, then "Copy that."

Relaxing, Nick shut off the radio and tossed it on the ground. That check-in ought to buy him some time, but not much. When "Charlie" didn't answer the next call—not to mention the other two radio-silent mercs— their buddies would undoubtedly come to investigate.

Nick followed the brick wall at the side of the hotel where steam rolled out of the vents that ran along the bottom of the building. He heard the murmur of voices beyond the service doors and quickened his pace. This next part was going to be tough. The van was parked only forty yards from the bus shelter where that soldier was not so covertly monitoring the hotel's entrance. If the men in the van made any noise, or managed to get a shot off, the bus shelter merc would be all over him.

This had to be fast. Like ripping off a bandage.

Drawing in a steady breath, Nick sheathed his knife, withdrew his SIG and sprang into action.

He rushed the back of the van and threw open the doors, eliciting shocked curses from the three heavily armed men sitting there. Before they could raise their weapons, he pulled the trigger. Once, twice, thrice. Three *pops* from his silenced SIG. Three kills.

There was no time to waste and no way to approach the brightly lit bus stop unseen, which meant it was time for a full-frontal attack.

Taking another breath, Nick bounded from the cover of the van and came out running.

The mercenary at the bus shelter instantly spotted him. Dropping his newspaper, the man flew to his feet and drew a black Glock from beneath his blue windbreaker. He proceeded to fire at Nick, who ducked and zigzagged as he sprinted forward, making it difficult for the soldier to connect with his target.

Nick was five feet from the bus stop when heat streaked through his left shoulder. Ignoring the sting of pain, he charged the mercenary before the man could take aim again and knocked the Glock out of his meaty hand.

In a heartbeat, Nick had the barrel of his gun pressed against the man's temple. "Don't frickin' move," he hissed.

The other man froze.

Nick knew he didn't have a lot of time. Despite the

late hour, the bus shelter was lit up like Fort Knox, and there was a chance that a bus would pull up any second.

Keeping one arm locked around the merc's chest, Nick jammed the muzzle of his SIG deeper into his captive's temple and said, "Let's not waste time. I assume there are a few more of you up in my hotel room, right? Luckily for them, I'm not in the mood to kill anyone else tonight."

With an angry curse, the soldier attempted to bring the heel of his boot into Nick's groin, but Nick simply shifted and tightened his hold.

"But you need to know that if I wanted to, I could kill every last one of you bastards," he went on. "And that's the message I want you to take back to your boss."

The other man released another dark expletive, but he had stopped struggling. "Go ahead and kill me. Carraway will only send another team."

Carraway. Nick filed the name away for future contemplation, then let out a chuckle.

"Good. I look forward to it," he said pleasantly. "I'll enjoy eliminating them, too, just like I eliminated ninety percent of your buddies tonight. And if your boss decides to send another hit squad after that, I'll take them out, too. And then the next hit squad, and the next one, and—well, you get the point. See, I'm getting damn tired of these games. Enough with this cowardly crap. Tell him if he wants me, he can come after me himself."

With the lightest of touches, Nick swiftly moved his other hand to the man's beefy neck and sought out the correct pressure point.

Then he chuckled again. "So when you wake up, please make sure your boss gets the message, okay, pal?"

"Screw y—"

He applied pressure on that delicate spot and the soldier went limp in his arms. Lights out.

Nick hastily lowered the man's heavy body onto the metal bench, then holstered his gun.

As he walked away from the bus stop, he kept his gait casual, relaxed, just a man out for a late-night stroll.

Your move, Mr. X.

Chapter 14

Rebecca launched herself at Nick the second he strode into the motel room. Their chests collided with a loud thump, and her panicked brain registered the sound of husky laughter and crinkling plastic.

Nick had barely been gone two hours, but she felt like she'd been waiting for an eternity.

She pulled back and searched his face, which revealed nothing. "What happened? Are you all right? Did you take care of the mercenaries? Was it—"

"How about one question at a time?" he cut in with a grin.

"Sorry. I was just worried."

"No need for that, Red. I'm perfectly fine."

"And the mercenaries?"

"Taken care of," was all he said.

"I see," she said warily.

"Oh, don't give me that look. I told you exactly what I planned on doing, Rebecca. It was necessary."

She released a sigh. "I know. Kill or be killed, right?"

Nick blinked in surprise. "And you're okay with that?"

"I have to be." Her jaw tightened. "Those men killed Jesse and Dave, and one of them probably slipped Harry some kind of drug that stopped his heart." She frowned. "I should really get my hands on Harry's tox screens. Shoot. I bet the hospital didn't even run any if Mr. X had anything to say about it."

Nick shrugged his holster off, then held out a brown paper bag she hadn't noticed him holding until now.

"What's that?" she asked suspiciously. "One of the soldier's heads?"

He burst out laughing. "This isn't the medieval times, darling. Jeez. I stopped at an all-hours deli and grabbed us some sandwiches. I know how much you hate those MREs, and I was worried that if I didn't put something tasty in your belly, you'd starve."

Warmth trickled through her. He'd actually stopped to buy her food? At four-thirty in the morning? God, this man was too thoughtful for words.

As if on cue, her stomach grumbled, officially betraying the fact that she had indeed forgone that MRE.

Rolling his eyes, Nick reached into the bag and said, "Ham, turkey or tuna?"

"Turkey," she said, holding out her hand.

He slapped a foil-wrapped sandwich in her palm.

Rebecca sank on the edge of the second twin bed and hurriedly unwrapped the food, then brought the sandwich to her mouth and took a big bite. The flavors instantly suffused her taste buds—lettuce, tomato, honey mustard, mayo. She chewed fast and swallowed faster, enjoying the first yummy meal she'd eaten in days.

On the other bed, Nick tackled his own sandwich. He finished it in no more than five or six bites, making Rebecca grin even as she chewed on a mouthful of turkey.

Nick stood up and grabbed two bottles of water, chugged one and handed her the other. She accepted it gratefully and took a long sip.

"I'm going to take a quick shower," he told her.

"Go for it."

He bent down and grabbed a fresh shirt, boxers and a pair of pants from his duffel bag, and he'd nearly made it to the bathroom door when Rebecca noticed the white first aid kit he'd tried tucking inside the pile of clothes.

"Stop right there, Nicholas!"

He glanced over, his lips twitching. "Did you really just call me that?"

Scowling, she hopped off the bed and marched up to him. "Did you really think you could hide the fact that you're *injured?*"

"I'm not injured," he protested.

"Yeah, right." Her gaze swept over him, up and down and side to side. She gasped when she noticed the wet spot on his shirt right over his left shoulder and the flash of red skin where the material had been torn away.

"Oh, for Pete's sake! Take off your shirt."

He looked extremely reluctant, but he must have seen the flames of anger in her eyes because he peeled off his long-sleeved black shirt without a word.

Rebecca paled when she saw the nasty red burn mark on his shoulder.

"Just a graze," he said gruffly. "It's no biggie."

She grumbled under her breath. "Why do men always have to act all macho?" She pointed to the bed. "Sit. Let me clean this up."

"Let me take that shower first."

"No. Because once you're in the bathroom, you'll lock the door and try to patch yourself up alone."

His tiny shrug told her she'd hit the mark.

"Fine, you want a shower so badly? I'll sit there until you're done."

"Are you serious?"

"Yep."

She grabbed hold of his uninjured arm and ushered him into the washroom. His tall, muscular body dominated the small space, and when she looked at their reflections in the mirror, she almost laughed at the difference in their sizes.

"Well?" She flopped down on the closed toilet seat and pointed to the shower stall. "Get in."

Heat flared in his brown eyes. "And what, you're going to sit there and watch?"

She lifted a defiant brow. "Sure am. Got a problem with that?"

"Nope."

He unzipped his pants and let them drop to the tiled floor.

His boxer briefs were next, and Rebecca sucked in a breath when his erection sprang up and bobbed against his navel.

He was incredible. So hard, so male, so virile.

He spun around to turn on the water, providing her with the most mouthwatering view of his spectacular ass. She went on sensory overload, unable to focus on any one detail for too long. Golden skin, roped muscles, heavy chest, muscular legs.

Nick Barrett was the sexiest man on the planet.

Rebecca was suddenly hungry again. God, she wanted him. Wanted to feel his hot mouth on hers. His rough hands on her breasts. His male hardness filling her.

"What are you waiting for?" Nick said mockingly, tossing her a knowing look over his shoulder.

He stepped into the shower stall, but didn't close the pink plastic curtain. Instead, he just stood there, his eyes locked with hers as water streamed down his naked body and clung to the defined ridges of his chest.

Rebecca knew she was supposed to be doing something important. What was it again? Um…letting him take a quick rinse so she could bandage up his shoulder. Right. That was it.

So why was she unbuttoning her jeans?

While her gaze stayed glued to Nick's naked, soaking-wet body, her hands continued to do their own thing. Taking her jeans off. Pulling her shirt over her head. Unsnapping her bra. Wiggling out of her panties.

Throughout her striptease, Nick watched in silence, the fire in his eyes burning hotter and hotter as each piece of clothing exposed a new body part.

"Get in here," he growled.

He didn't have to ask her twice. Rebecca slid into the stall and into his arms, tipping her head to welcome his blistering kiss. Their tongues tangled, breaths mingled with the steam that was beginning to fill the stall.

As the hot water rushed over their heads, their bodies became slick, plastering to each other as Nick brought her flush up against him and cupped her bottom. The position caused his erection to slide over her mound, bringing a moan to her lips.

Everything about this man drove her wild with desire. The bad boys she'd dated in the past didn't even compare to Nick Barrett—she'd thought those lovers were passionate, but she'd been wrong.

This was passion. Nick's heavy-lidded eyes. His features, taut with arousal. His deft fingers and talented tongue teasing her lips and breasts.

"Oh, that's good," she whimpered when he rolled her nipples between his thumbs and forefingers, getting them stiff, making them tingle.

Rebecca's head lolled to the side, the pleasure so intense she could barely stay upright. Her breasts had always been particularly sensitive, and it thrilled her that Nick enjoyed focusing so much of his attention on them.

"You like that, huh?" he rasped, his warm breath heating her lips as he bent down to kiss her again.

He squeezed her breasts, sweeping his thumbs over those puckered buds until she was moaning in impatience.

"What is it? What do you need, darling?" he said roughly.

"Your mouth," she squeezed out.

He gave her what she wanted without delay, dipping his head and capturing one nipple between his lips.

A jolt of hot pleasure seized her core.

Nick licked the distended nipple, then suckled gently. His tongue teased and explored, summoning moan after moan from her deep in her throat.

It wasn't long before she was shifting in agitation, desperate for more. She reached between their bodies and encircled his shaft, giving it a long, languid pump.

Nick's groan vibrated against her breasts. "Oh, that's good, darling. Tease me a little."

As she stroked him lazily, he brought one hand to the juncture of her thighs and did some teasing of his own. Rebecca's entire body hummed with pleasure as he stroked her hypersensitive folds, teasing that swollen bud. When he slid one long finger inside her, she gasped with delight and rocked into his hand, all the while quickening the tempo with which she stroked him.

"I need to be in you," he muttered, backing her into the wall.

She wrapped her arms around his neck and her legs around his waist, opening herself up to him, waiting for him to plunge inside. But he didn't. Instead, he made a frustrated sound and met her eyes. "No condom."

"I'm clean and on the pill." She blushed. Sometimes sex was so darn awkward, yet she still had to ask, "Have you been tested?"

"I'm clean, too. Do you… Are you sure I should…"

His awkwardness was adorable, and for some weird reason, it succeeded in turning her on again. He was such a good guy. So very thoughtful all the time. Which made the times when he lost control so much more satisfying.

Like now, as he drove into her and filled her to the hilt, his hips moving fast and furious. A thrill shot through her, followed by a rush of excitement as he pounded into her in a relentless rhythm that made her breathing go shallow.

She watched Nick's face through the haze of steam, loving the way his amber-colored eyes slitted with passion, the way the tendons in his neck strained, the way he muttered her name under his breath.

His mouth found hers again, his tongue sliding in with one greedy thrust and stealing the breath from her lungs. She clung to his strong shoulders, dug her heels into his firm buttocks and closed her eyes as a rush of pleasure consumed her body and sent her mind soaring. She felt Nick tense, heard him groan and knew he'd reached that same explosive pinnacle.

With a groan, he slipped out, then eased aside so she could duck under the spray, which had gone luke-warm. They quickly washed up before the water turned freezing, and then Nick shut off the water and pulled back the curtain.

Rebecca stepped out of the shower first, turning to shoot him a sheepish look. "FYI, when I followed you in here, that wasn't a seduction attempt either. I really wanted to take care of that wound."

"*Sure.* You keep saying that, but I don't think I believe you anymore." He slanted his head thoughtfully. "I think you're in seduction mode 24/7, Red."

"Well, it would be a lot easier to snap out of it if you weren't so darn tempting," she grumbled.

"You want to talk tempting?" He gestured to her naked body. "Because I'm pretty sure you're the most tempting woman on the planet."

She offered an impish smile. "I'm sorry?"

Nick offered a grave look in return. "Never apologize for your hotness. Ever."

Rebecca laughed, then grabbed two towels from the rack and handed Nick one. They dried off in silence, and the air in the bathroom went from comfortable to uneasy, echoing with questions that neither of them voiced.

What are we doing here? she wanted to ask. *Where will it lead?*

Nick had insisted he didn't do casual, and yet he'd stopped putting up resistance a long time ago. He'd pretty much commanded her to get into the shower with him just now, which told her he wasn't trying to keep her at arm's length anymore.

But where was his head at? She wished he would be

more forthcoming about the way he felt, about what he wanted from this, but it was clear that Nick Barrett, as sweet and gentlemanly as he was, did *not* like discussing his feelings.

On the other hand, maybe that was a good thing. Because she had the sinking suspicion that if she asked him about the future, she wouldn't like what he had to say.

So rather than force a serious discussion—at five in the morning to boot—she stood on her tiptoes and brushed her lips over his in a casual little kiss. "Come on, Watson. Let's bandage up this 'graze' of yours and get some much-needed sleep."

"We've got a problem. A very big problem."

What else was new?

With a sigh, he rose from his desk chair and walked over to the redbrick fireplace across the room. It was six in the morning, but he hadn't been in bed. After another night of elusive sleep, he'd finally given up and gone into his study with a tumbler of whiskey and a pack of cigarettes that his wife, God bless her soul, would have been horrified to see. She'd forced him to quit years ago, insisting she wanted him to live a long, healthy life.

How ironic that he, the one who'd been smoking for twenty years, was still alive while the love of his life was buried under six feet of dirt in a New York cemetery.

And now he had to listen to Carraway inform him of yet another problem. Another mess he'd no doubt be forced to clean up.

"What is it?" He could barely muster up interest; it

was too early in the morning to dwell on how out of control this situation had gotten.

"Six of my men are dead. Barrett took them out."

Shock slackened his jaw. "Are you sure it was him?"

"Positive, sir. He passed along a message to one of the soldiers he left alive. He wanted us to know that he'll kill any hit squad we dispatch to take him out." Carraway paused. "And he had a specific message for *you*."

"What is it?" he said warily.

Carraway sounded awkward. "For you to stop being a coward. If you want him, stop sending soldiers and come after him yourself."

His lips curled in a sneer. Coward? Who did that young punk think he was, accusing him of cowardice?

Would a coward have put his neck on the line for the sake of his country?

No, he didn't think so.

"So what's the order, sir? Do you want me to assemble another team?"

He mulled it over. "You might as well. Maybe the next crew will have better luck."

"Or maybe they'll die at Barrett's hands, too," was the bitter reply.

"Find better men."

"This crew was my best."

"This crew was garbage," he snapped. "Otherwise they'd have taken care of our little problem. So hire some soldiers who are more skilled, and get the job done."

He hung up without a word, angrily slamming the phone on the fireplace mantel. It required several deep breaths to ease the volatile emotions swirling in his gut.

Setting down his tumbler, he headed for the desk and peered at his calendar. Thursday's entry caught his eye, inspiring a nod of satisfaction. Good. McAvoy would be back from Beijing. His gaze shifted to the following day where the words *Veterans Gala* were penciled in.

Christ, the last thing he was in the mood for was a highly publicized event.

He shoved the annoying reminder aside and glanced at McAvoy's name again.

It might be time. As unhappy as the idea made him, he knew they'd officially reached a critical point here.

It was time to start distancing himself from this Meridian virus fiasco. Time to transfer the burden of blame onto someone else's shoulders.

Time to save himself.

Nick woke up to the feel of a warm, wet mouth encircling his shaft.

As wicked reality settled in, he nearly jerked three feet in the air, eliciting a soft laugh from the woman who'd decided to bestow him with a wake-up call never to be forgotten.

"What are you doing?" he croaked, even as his hips lifted and his arousal sought out that incredible mouth again.

"Seducing you." Her soft laughter tickled his engorged head. "Officially."

Then she took him deep in her mouth and sucked.

A wild groan burst out of his chest. She was trying to kill him.

Well, then you'll die happy. Now, shut up and enjoy this.

He decided to listen to that impatient voice. Closing his eyes, he thrust his hands in Rebecca's hair, loving the way those silky red strands slipped through his fingers.

Her enthusiasm was a major turn-on. She took the time to discover what he liked, though in all honesty, he couldn't imagine her doing anything he *didn't* like.

With featherlight licks, she dragged her tongue along the length of him and teased his tip, making him groan again. Then she brought her hand into play, wrapping it around his base and stroking firmly. She created a steady tempo with her hand and mouth, driving him to a level of arousal that had him clawing at the sheets.

When his body started tingling, an indication that he was perilously close to losing control, he shoved a hand in her hair again and stilled her eager movements.

Rebecca lifted her head and gave him a questioning look. "What's wrong?"

"Nothing's wrong. But it's my turn."

"What are you—"

He flipped her over before she could finish, bringing a startled squeak to her lips. He swallowed that adorable sound with his kiss, then pulled back and met her pleasure-hazy eyes.

"Mind if I do a little seducing of my own?" he murmured.

"Not at all," she said breathlessly.

"Good, because I've been dying to have my way with you since the moment we met."

And he proceeded to do just that. He kissed every inch of her hot, silky flesh. Nuzzled her neck, sucked on her ear. Her soft whimpers and husky moans told him exactly what she liked and he paid attention to the signs her body gave him—the way her nipples went impossibly harder when he flicked them sharply with his tongue. The shiver that rolled through her when he kissed that sensitive spot right above her hip bone.

The way she shuddered when his fingers grazed her warm mound.

He inched his way south, and when his mouth found her core, she cried out in delight.

As a spark of male satisfaction lit his gut, he focused on pleasing her. He licked her, slowly, lovingly, enjoying the way she sighed, the way she murmured his name. Her hips began to move and he followed her rhythm, bringing her closer and closer to the edge, refusing to stop until she toppled right over it.

"Nick." She said his name on a groan and clawed at his shoulders, urging. "I need more. I need you."

She didn't have to ask him twice. He swiftly covered her petite body, no longer fearful that he was crushing her. Whenever he tried to give her room to breathe, to raise himself over her on his forearms, she always pulled him down so that her breasts were crushed against his chest and held him in place. Truth was, he absolutely loved the way her body constantly strained to get closer to his.

And he loved the feeling of sheer completion that overtook him when he pushed into her welcoming heat. As usual, the need to take her hard and fast was ever present, but he forced himself to slow the pace and make it last.

"Oh, that's nice," Rebecca whispered as he began to move in slow, deep strokes.

"Very nice," he said hoarsely.

The mattress squeaked as they moved together, neither one of them racing to reach that finish line. Nick cradled Rebecca's head with his hands and kissed her deeply, his tongue matching the movements of his cock.

When release finally seized his body, it wasn't so much an explosion as little sparks of heat that danced through his nerve endings and shivered along every inch of his flesh. He knew Rebecca was feeling that same rush of bliss because her eyes had glazed over and she was rocking her hips with abandon.

Eventually they both went still, and a comfortable silence fell over the room. Nick rolled onto his back and twisted his head to look at her while a feeling of pure and utter content washed over him.

"Wanna go back to sleep?" he suggested.

"Kinda." She laughed. "Is that too decadent of us?"

"Well, McAvoy isn't back until tomorrow. What else are we going to do until then?"

She wiggled her eyebrows in an overly lewd way that made him smile. "How about more of what we did just now?"

"Well, duh, Rebecca. Of course we'll be doing that."

"A lot?"

"A lot," he confirmed. "In fact, we should definitely go to sleep. That way I can be the one giving *you* the wake-up surprise this time."

"Deal." She abruptly slid off the bed. "Gotta pee. BRB."

A laugh tickled his throat. Lord, he liked this woman. She was so full of life, so fun and sassy and entertaining—yet at the same time, focused and intelligent. It was an odd combination, but he liked it.

What he *wasn't* crazy about was the way his heart skipped a beat when Rebecca stepped out of the bathroom, or how his pulse sped up when she hopped back into bed and cuddled against him like it was something they'd been doing for years. Cuddling, having sex, laughing together.

Not that there was anything wrong with any of those things. He liked doing them with her, but...

But what? the voice in his head mocked.

After a moment, he gave up on trying to finish the rest of that thought. It was too early in the morning to be thinking about stuff like this.

Which was why he promptly rolled over again, spooned behind Rebecca and went back to sleep.

Nick wasn't kidding—three hours later, Rebecca was coaxed out of slumber by the feel of his tongue between her legs, which led to another round of incredible sex that left them both breathless. Afterward, they devoured the two remaining sandwiches that Nick had stashed in the fridge the night before, then returned to bed.

"I can't remember the last time I was this lazy," she confessed as she idly dragged a finger over Nick's bare chest.

"Me neither," he said in a contented voice. "I think I like it."

"I don't know. It feels wrong. I feel like we should be investigating, following up on a lead, looking for a clue. You know what I mean?"

"Yeah. But our only lead is still out of town. McAvoy's the one who dealt with Waverly, and chances are, he's Mr. X."

"And if he is?" she asked carefully. "You're not going to go all Rambo again and kill him, are you?"

Nick's pecs vibrated with his laughter, tickling her ear. "Relax, I'm not pulling a Rambo again. I promised my dad we'd handle the fallout properly, remember? McAvoy will be going to jail, not the grave."

"Good, because it would be better for my career if he was alive," she teased. "That way I can score an exclusive with the good old dep sec def."

She could swear Nick's abdomen tensed, but when

204 *Special Ops Exclusive*

she ran her fingers over his tight six-pack, his muscles were relaxed.

"I don't know how you have the stomach to interview people like that," he admitted. "I remember that segment you ran last year about America's child predators. I wanted to throw up listening to some of those sick bastards."

"Me, too," she said frankly. "Believe me, being in all those prison visitation rooms and hearing those men try to excuse their crimes was pure torture. Jesse almost had to pull me off one of them. I was two seconds from strangling the life out of him after he made an appalling comment about redheaded girls."

Now Nick *definitely* stiffened. "I probably would have killed the son of a bitch." He paused, hesitated. "Yet you still put yourself through that. Why?"

"People needed to be aware that predators like that existed. Sometimes when I run with a story, it's to shed light on an injustice, or to inspire others to act, or change, or contribute." She shrugged. "Other times, I just want to warn citizens that there are some messed-up people in this world. Those prisoners probably thought they were getting to defend their actions, but that's not why I put them on the air. I wanted to warn parents that predators are everywhere—in the playground, in schools, in grocery stores. And I wanted those parents to take better precautions when it came to their kids."

Nick dragged his hand over her bare back in a fleeting caress. "Do you want kids of your own?" he asked, curious.

"Definitely." She propped herself up on her elbow. "A boy and a girl."

He grinned. "Have it all planned out, huh?"

"Yep. I love kids." She grinned back. "I think I'd be a really fun mom."

"Will you quit your job once you have kids?"

She wrinkled her brow. "Of course not."

"So you plan on taking off and leaving your children at home with your husband or a nanny when you're on assignment?"

She couldn't help but laugh. "Taking off? It's not like I'm gone for years at a time. Other parents travel a lot more for their jobs. I'm gone for only a few days usually. Sometimes a few months, but only if I'm covering a war zone or something huge. I plan on being there for my children, don't you worry."

When he grew silent, she studied his troubled expression and smiled again. "By the way, I think you'd be a good father."

That grave look in his eyes faded. "A good one. Not a fun one?" he teased.

"No, you'll be fun, too, when you're not in father-hen mode."

Not that she was complaining about that particular quality of his. She was actually beginning to enjoy the way he fussed over her and how attuned he was to her needs. Bringing her sandwiches because he knew she hated those prepackaged meals. Surprising her with a pen and notebook he'd swiped from the deli—he'd stolen them right off the counter just so she'd be able to jot down her thoughts. Nick Barrett, committing theft to make her happy.

She'd never been with anyone like him, and she had to admit, she was finding her time with Nick a lot more rewarding than all her past relationships combined.

"What was your father like when you were growing

up?" she asked, suddenly curious to learn more about the man in her bed. "Was he fun?"

"Not really. He was strict. Very big on rules, and right and wrong, and taking responsibility for your actions. It's a military thing—he came from a long line of army generals. The drill-sergeant attitude is in his DNA."

"And your mom?"

"She followed my dad's lead when it came to discipline," Nick replied, absently running his fingers through her hair.

"Did she work?"

"Nah, she stayed home and took care of me and Viv. She was really into the domestic stuff—cooking and gardening and doing these dorky crafts. She'd always sucker me into helping her, too. My friends would be out riding their bikes and I'd be helping my mom paint a bird feeder, or making a collage out of found items in the woods behind our house."

Rebecca snickered. "I think you loved every second of it."

After a beat, he sighed. "You're right. I did. My mom was just so easy to be around, whereas my dad was so stern and composed, you know? She was like a ray of sunshine that lit up our house."

Hearing the pain in his voice, Rebecca stroked his chest in a soothing motion. "When did she die?"

"When I was fifteen, and my sister was seventeen. My dad never really got over it. He hasn't dated another woman in the thirteen years since Mom died. Whenever Viv and I bug him about it, he says he's not ready. Sometimes I wonder if he ever will be."

"He must have really loved her."

"He did. They had the kind of marriage you see in those cheesy family sitcoms. So in love, decades later."

And that was what Nick wanted—Rebecca suddenly knew it without a shred of doubt. Nick aspired for what his parents had shared. That everlasting love, the sunny housewife who spent time at home with her kids while her husband brought home the bacon.

Her heart sank to the pit of her stomach as she realized something else. She could never be the docile housewife that Nick wanted. She craved excitement, adventure, new experiences. Her genetic makeup didn't allow her to sit idle. She didn't want to experience the world looking out the window of her kitchen while she slid a fresh tray of cookies into the oven—she'd *never* wanted that.

But Nick did.

Question was, what did that mean for them?

Or better yet, what did she *want* it to mean? Did *she* want a future with this man?

Yes.

The answer breached her consciousness so swiftly she didn't know why she'd bothered asking herself the question.

She *totally* wanted to be with Nick Barrett. She was more than ready to say goodbye to the bad boys of the past and focus on the good guy in her future.

Now she simply had to convince him they could have one.

Chapter 15

Thursday didn't come soon enough for Nick. He definitely wasn't complaining about the explosive sex he and Rebecca were having at regular intervals, because that wasn't the problem. At all.

No, the problem was that he was starting to enjoy her company *way* too much.

He liked lying in bed with her. He liked listening to her childhood stories and work anecdotes and passionate tirades. He even liked the way she teased him mercilessly whenever he did something "overly" chivalrous. Although in his defense, how on earth was leaving the toilet seat down considered *overly chivalrous?* He'd shared a bathroom with his sister growing up—he was perfectly aware of what happened if you left that seat up.

What he also knew was that no matter how much he liked Rebecca, she couldn't be a part of his future. He didn't want to be in a relationship where he'd be worrying about the woman he loved 90 percent of the time. Each time she went off to cover a dangerous assignment, he'd be freaking out and climbing the walls with panic.

And yeah, he saw the hypocrisy in that, considering his military career had placed him in many dangerous positions over the years, but that didn't mean he wanted the woman in his life doing the same.

Besides, his career was over now. Once he put this mess behind him, he'd probably look for a civilian job. Maybe he could find a place at the DoD with his dad where he'd work his ass off to make sure nothing like this ever happened again.

If he got seriously involved with Rebecca, he'd go gray within the year. The woman was stubborn, reckless, bold. She gave no thought to her well-being, only the adventure, the next big scoop. When he'd yelled for her to get down outside the hospital in Mala, she'd done the opposite and gone for that mercenary's gun instead. When he'd ordered her to stay put in Costa Rica, she'd showed up in the doorway of Waverly's beach house.

How could he be with someone who would undoubtedly argue with him every step of the way? Challenge every decision or suggestion he made?

"Penny for your thoughts?"

Nick turned away from the window and found Rebecca smirking at him. She'd taken to mimicking his "good guy lingo" as she liked to call it, and he had to admit, hearing the outdated phrase leave her mouth made him realize how nerdy it was.

"I'm just watching the sunset—" he started.

"Aw, you big romantic, you."

"—because I can't wait for it to get dark so we can get out of here," he finished.

"Oh, like you haven't enjoyed every second we've spent in this room."

Said the beautiful, naked woman stretched out on the bed. Despite himself, Nick's body reacted to the tantalizing sight, and he couldn't have mustered up a denial even if he'd tried.

"Of course I have," he conceded, "but I'm also anxious to get this confrontation with McAvoy over with."

"Did your father message you again?"

"Not since he let us know that McAvoy landed three hours ago."

"He was supposed to meet McAvoy at the Pentagon, right?" Rebecca paused. "I hope he didn't give anything away. We can't tip McAvoy off yet."

"Trust me, my dad knows how to play the game. He lives and breathes secrets and lies."

"This is D.C. Who doesn't?" Her tone was dry.

She stretched her arms over her head, drawing his gaze to her bare breasts. His mouth immediately watered, his tongue tingling with the urge to taste those rosy nipples.

As she noticed where his gaze had landed, Rebecca's lips curved in a smile. "Hmm, I think I'd better get dressed before you ravish me again."

"Good idea," he agreed, because yep, he was in real danger of doing some ravishing.

After Rebecca disappeared into the bathroom, Nick donned a navy blue button-down over his black tee, then tucked his SIG into the waistband of his jeans. He didn't like the fact that Rebecca was coming along, but sometime in between all the sex they'd been having, she'd actually come up with a plan that Nick had grudgingly seen the merit of.

Her approach was far more diplomatic than the

course of action he'd planned on taking, but he still would've preferred to handle this alone.

Rebecca emerged from the bathroom a few minutes later wearing jeans, a blue T-shirt, an open plaid shirt and her brown hiking boots. Her red hair was loose and cascading down her shoulders, and she looked so damn pretty that his heart squeezed.

"What is it?" she said warily.

"Nothing." His voice came out so hoarse he had to clear his throat before speaking again. "Ready to expose some corruption, Sherlock?"

Her features relaxed, a broad smile stretching across her sexy mouth. "Heck yeah. Let's do this thing."

It didn't take long to reach Deputy Secretary Fred McAvoy's house. A quick trip on the freeway, a drive across the bridge into Virginia, and then they were on a residential street in Fairfax County staring at the gated entrance of McAvoy's Tudor-style home.

Rebecca eyed the wrought-iron barrier. "Should we buzz the intercom?"

"Nah," was all Nick said.

As she battled her confusion, he stopped at the curb a few yards from the gate and parked on the street. Shutting off the engine, he unbuckled his seat belt and said, "Give me a minute."

Now she was even more confused, especially when he twisted around and grabbed a small leather case from the duffel in the backseat.

Before she could ask what the little kit contained, Nick was out of the SUV and striding toward the house. Because the gate was set away from the street, she couldn't see what Nick was doing once he disappeared behind one of the concrete posts on either side of the gate.

But he stayed true to his word, returning to the SUV a minute later and gesturing for her to get out.

Rebecca's palms were unusually damp as she followed Nick. She couldn't believe he'd agreed to her plan; she'd been expecting to fight him tooth and nail about coming along, and she wondered if his willingness to let her risk her life was a sign that he was warming up to the idea of having her in *his* life.

Being with Nick in the motel these past couple of days had provided her with some real insight into his head—and heart. She was pretty sure she knew what he was looking for in a partner, but she hoped he would be open-minded enough to accept that sometimes what you were looking for was not what you *needed.*

Take her, for example: She'd always figured she'd end up with a daredevil like herself, but now, she would give anything to have such a sweet, honorable man like Nick in her life.

Focus, Becks.

She shoved all those pesky relationship thoughts from her mind and discovered that McAvoy's gate was now wide open. A glance at the electronic keypad affixed to the concrete wall showed that the cover had been removed to expose a tangle of wires.

"You hot-wired the gate?" she whispered in amusement.

"Yep."

They walked right through it, heading up the long driveway leading to McAvoy's two-story house. Flower beds lined the paved drive, and the late-night summer breeze rustled the stems of colorful flowers and the leaves of the lush green plants filling the beds. McAvoy had a good landscaper, that was for sure.

Rebecca inhaled the sweet scent in the air, taking a second to admire the array of red, yellow and white roses planted beneath the spacious porch. The second they approached the porch steps, a light flickered on.

"Motion sensor," Nick said with a nod.

She noticed he had one hand positioned slightly behind his hip, ready to draw his weapon in a heartbeat.

Before they could knock or ring the doorbell, the heavy oak door flew open, which told her that their approach must have triggered an alarm inside the house.

An angry-looking man in gray wool trousers and a black V-neck sweater appeared in the doorway. "How the *hell* did you get past the gate—" His jaw fell open as he recognized Rebecca. "Parker? What the hell?"

"Good to see you again, Deputy McAvoy," she said coolly. "It's been, what, two years since we met at that fund-raiser?"

Fred McAvoy had a pair of blue eyes that were a tad too close together and a long, thin nose that lent him a perpetually birdlike air. He also wasn't a very tall man, only four or five inches taller than Rebecca, who considered herself tiny.

"What the hell are you doing here at this hour?" McAvoy demanded. His suspicious gaze shifted to Nick, who hadn't uttered a word. "Who's this? And why are the two of you—" The man halted, eyes narrowed, and then his face lost all its color. "Barrett."

Nick's voice was deceptively cordial. "Yes, we've met, too, Fred. On at least a couple of occasions. Should I be insulted that you didn't recognize your own boss's son?"

"My boss is the president of the United States," Mc-

Avoy answered curtly. "And I don't give a damn whose son you are. It's ten o'clock at night—you don't show up unannounced at this hour."

"Yeah, we're sorry to barge in on you like this," Rebecca said, her tone conveying just how *not* sorry she was, "but we really wanted to give you a chance to respond before I took this story to the network."

McAvoy faltered. "What are you talking about? What story?"

"Well, the copy hasn't been written yet, but..." She shrugged. "I suppose I could give you a rough idea of what I plan on saying. It'll go something like this— *Some breaking news this morning, folks. Deputy Secretary Fred McAvoy has been implicated in the manufacturing, testing and release of the Meridian virus, which, as you all know, claimed more than a thousand lives in the small town of Dixie only a short time ago.*"

The remaining color drained from McAvoy's face, leaving him paler than snow.

"It has been confirmed," Rebecca went on cheerfully, *"that McAvoy was the mastermind behind the—"*

"I'm not the mastermind behind anything!" McAvoy burst out.

He was practically shouting, and he quickly lowered his voice and glanced in the direction of the gate just in case an evening jogger happened to be passing by.

"You have no proof of anything, Parker. The department will sue you for libel if you air any of your preposterous allegations."

"These aren't allegations. They're facts."

Nick spoke up. "Paul Waverly is in federal custody, Fred, and he's more than willing to testify against you. He's stated on the record that you gave him a sample of the virus to eliminate Sergeant Sebastian Stone."

McAvoy's outraged mask slipped, revealing a flash of uncertainty. "Paul Waverly left town."

That earned him a little smirk from Nick. "Yeah, and I found him. So now why don't you invite us inside, Fred, so we can have some privacy."

The other man's lips tightened with indignation. "Privacy for what?"

"For you to tell your side of the story to Ms. Parker." Nick shrugged. "No matter what she says on the air tomorrow, you're still going to jail, Fred. My father knows what you've done—"

The deputy's breath hitched in evident fear.

"—and he's not going to cover it up to save your ass. So if you want to explain why you did what you did, this may be your only chance before you're thrown into federal lockdown."

It was obvious McAvoy didn't want to let them in.

It was also obvious he knew he was beaten.

With a ragged breath, he opened the door wider and allowed them to step into the spacious front foyer.

"I need a drink," he mumbled.

McAvoy took off walking without checking to see if they were following. Rebecca exchanged a look with Nick, and then the two of them trailed after the deputy secretary, whose shoulders had sagged in defeat.

They entered a cozy den with wood-paneled walls, leather couches and a wet bar, which McAvoy made a beeline for. He didn't offer them a drink. Just poured himself a big glass of whiskey and sank onto the sofa as if his legs could no longer support him.

Rebecca sat down on the couch across from him while Nick stood behind her, watching the other man's every move.

"I'm not going to make a run for it," McAvoy said

in a bitter voice. "You think I want to get shot down by the SWAT team that's probably out on the street, waiting for your word to storm the house?"

Neither of them corrected him. Might as well let him think there was a team of government agents waiting to arrest him, Rebecca thought.

"I'm surprised Kirk allowed you to talk to me first," the deputy said gloomily before raising his glass to his lips and taking a swig. "He's usually more by the book."

Rebecca answered for Nick. "I can be very persuasive, and Secretary Barrett owed me one for helping him track down his son." She leaned forward and rested her hands on her knees. "Let's not waste any time, Fred. Tell me what compelled you to believe that testing that virus on innocent people was a good idea."

He blanched. "That wasn't my call. I didn't make any decisions regarding the testing of the biological agent. I only followed the orders given to me, made a few arrangements and pulled the right strings."

She raised a brow. "Orders, huh? And who gave you these orders?"

McAvoy just shrugged and took another sip.

"Come on, Fred," she cajoled, "don't get all tight-lipped now. You know you have a better chance of saving your own butt if you give up the person responsible for Project Aries. Who gave the order to engineer the virus?"

Slowly, McAvoy set his glass down on the handsome pine coffee table. "Who the hell do you think? It was Ferguson."

Rebecca tried to mask her shock. "You mean...the vice president?"

"Who the hell else would I mean?" he said irritably.

"Was he acting on President Howard's behalf?" She held her breath, slightly afraid of the answer to that.

"No. Howard has no idea what the veep has been up to." A fresh dose of bitterness splashed on the deputy's face.

Nick finally joined the discussion, his voice laced with incredulity. "You're saying that Vice President Troy Ferguson went behind the president's back and sanctioned the development of a biological weapon?"

"That's exactly what I'm saying."

Rebecca was still having a tough time controlling her shock, which was now joined by a pang of doubt. "Ferguson was all about social reform during both campaigns. He and Howard were in agreement that we needed to cut back on defense spending."

"That's what he wanted Howard to think," McAvoy said darkly. "Ferguson wanted his name on that ticket, and he lied through his teeth to get it there. His father was a navy admiral, for Chrissake. Of course he's pro-defense."

She had to admit McAvoy raised a good point. She remembered thinking the same thing during that first election—why would the son of a decorated admiral be so gung ho about cutting military spending?

"The veep loathes our commander in chief," McAvoy said with a sigh. "He thinks Howard's attitude is too tolerant, that he should be making decisions with a more high-handed approach. After the terrorist attack on that hospital in California a couple of years ago, Ferguson had enough. He's a big believer that ten years from now, wars will be fought solely with biological weapons, so he decided to create the deadliest one of all."

"And he cut a deal with the San Marquez government to test it in their country," Rebecca said in disgust.

"Sometimes extreme measures are necessary." McAvoy sounded defensive. "Those villagers died so millions of future Americans could live."

"Whatever helps you sleep at night," Nick muttered.

"I *don't* sleep at night," McAvoy shot back. "Why? Because any second, a plane could crash into my house, or a nuke could be dropped on my city—the war on terrorism continues to rage, and nobody's doing a damn thing to stop it. Innocent people are dying for whatever crazy cause these fanatics subscribe to, and nobody is doing—"

Rebecca cut him off in disbelief. "You're doing the same thing yourself, Deputy! Killing innocent people for your cause—in this case, the cause is national defense. Those villagers in San Marquez did nothing to harm us. You and Ferguson *murdered* them, just like you murdered the men in Nick's unit. And those men, by the way? They were Americans, the very people you're claiming to protect."

"Sometimes sacrifices have to be made," McAvoy said feebly.

The disgust rose in her throat once more, and she resisted the urge to clock him right in the face. Taking a breath, she glanced over at Nick, who seemed equally annoyed with McAvoy's reasoning.

"So now what?" McAvoy demanded, his wary gaze moving from her to Nick. "Can I at least phone my lawyer before I'm arrested?"

"Sorry, Fred, but we can't let you anywhere near a phone," Nick said.

He rounded the couch and approached the other man, whose blue eyes filled with panic. "What the hell are you talking about? What are you doing?"

"You must be jet-lagged," Nick interrupted pleasantly. "It's time to take a little nap."

Rebecca's eyes widened as Nick executed a lightning-fast karate chop to the back of McAvoy's head. A moment later, the deputy sagged backward. Unconscious.

"What the heck did you do that for?" she exclaimed.

Nick shrugged. "We can't leave him here and risk him calling Ferguson. And we can't have him arrested yet or Ferguson might be tipped off."

"So what do we do with him, then?"

Nick bent down and heaved the other man over his shoulder in a fireman's carry. "We take him with us."

Chapter 16

When four short knocks sounded on the motel room door an hour later, Nick hastily walked over to let his father in.

"Were you followed?" was the first question out of his mouth.

The secretary's answering laugh resonated with genuine mirth. "Son, what do you take me for, an amateur? I was avoiding tails before you were even born."

Nick rolled his eyes. "Right. I keep forgetting what an old fogy you are."

"Not old. Distinguished." Barrett's shrewd eyes examined the room. "Where is he?"

Without a word, Nick marched over to the narrow closet and turned the doorknob.

The door opened to reveal an unconscious McAvoy with a gag stuffed in his mouth, and his hands and feet bound.

Secretary Barrett released an unhappy breath. "I'm damn disappointed in you."

It took a second for Nick to realize his father wasn't talking to *him;* Kirk's brown eyes had been focused on his colleague when he'd voiced that bitter remark.

"How long has he been out?"

"About an hour," Nick replied as he shut the closet door. "He should be coming to soon."

Rebecca rose from the edge of the twin bed she'd been sitting on. "He gave us a name," she told Barrett. "The person responsible for authorizing Project Aries."

"I'm afraid to ask."

Nick shot his father a grim look. "Vice President Ferguson."

The secretary looked startled. "Troy? That's ridiculous. Fred must have been lying. I'll get the truth out of him when he wakes up."

"I think he *was* telling the truth," Nick disagreed.

"No. It's simply preposterous. Troy has never offered any support for the defense platform. Trust me, I've had to fight him tooth and nail on every decision these past six years. Remember the rebuttal he gave on the issue during the reelection debate?"

"Apparently he's a secret defense nut," Rebecca explained. "Which kind of makes sense, seeing how crazy Howard is about social reform. The president might have chosen a different running mate if Ferguson had revealed his fervent support on the matter of national defense. If I was Ferguson and I had my eye on that VP office, I'd second every last idea and endorse every last plan the president proposed."

"Yes, that's a good point, but..." The secretary appeared stricken. "But allowing a virus to be tested on innocent people? I can't imagine Troy initiating that."

With a sigh, Nick's father glanced at the closet door. "Then again, I never would have imagined Fred would be embroiled in something like it either, and yet here he is."

"So how do we want to handle this?" Nick asked.

"Clearly Ferguson's role in this needs to be exposed," Rebecca said firmly.

Barrett's gaze sharpened. "You can't be planning on putting this on the air without talking to Ferguson first."

"Of course not. But with all due respect, Mr. Secretary, if the VP is guilty, I won't be persuaded to cover it up."

His expression grew strained. "We're getting ahead of ourselves. First we need to determine if there's anything *to* cover up."

Nick's jaw hardened in fortitude. "I'll talk to Ferguson."

"No," his father said briskly. "This time it's my turn."

"Dad—"

"Don't challenge me on this, son. Everything needs to be handled delicately from this point on. I can't just accuse my vice president of engineering a virus that killed a thousand Americans after it wound up in the hands of terrorists. Troy deserves the chance to defend himself, to tell his side of the story before we jump to conclusions or make any allegations."

"You really want to be the one to confront him?" Nick asked his father, who nodded in response. "Then you're not doing it alone. I'm coming with you."

"I'll agree to that only if you agree to follow my lead."

"Fine. And it has to be somewhere public," Nick added in a stern voice he'd learned from his father. "If he's guilty, he might panic and try to take you out right then and there. I don't want you becoming another casualty in this mess, Dad."

"How do you plan on getting Ferguson to meet in public?" Rebecca asked. "The man is surrounded by Secret Service agents 24/7 and whenever he leaves his residence, a thorough security plan is enforced. He can't just meet you in a park or go for a stroll on the street."

"The Veterans Gala," the secretary said suddenly.

Nick wrinkled his forehead. "Come again?"

"Oh, right," Rebecca spoke up, sounding excited. "I RSVP'd for that months ago."

"There's a dinner and gala at the White House tomorrow evening to honor our Vietnam vets," the Secretary informed his son. "President Howard won't be in attendance, not unless his itinerary has changed, but Ferguson is supposed to attend. As am I."

Nick thought it over for a moment. "It'll be at the White House, so the VP won't risk making a scene. Which makes me feel a helluva lot more comfortable about exposing myself like that." He paused, then nodded. "I like it. We'll attend the event together and find a way to speak to Ferguson in private."

"What about Fred? He was scheduled to attend, as well."

"Tell everyone he's sick. And in the meantime, we'll leave him here in the motel with Rebecca."

"Excuse me?"

Rebecca's voice was laced with shock, and when he met her green eyes, he saw the anger glittering in them. Knowing he was about to get another argument, he stifled a sigh and said, "Dad and I can handle it. I need you here to keep an eye on McAvoy."

"I'll arrange for one of my guards to keep watch," the secretary offered. "In fact, I think I'll do that regardless. Connor can be trusted, and I don't like the idea of you two staying here without protection."

"Hear that?" Rebecca said with a bite to her tone. "*Connor* will watch McAvoy."

The sigh slipped out. "There's no reason for you to tag along, Red."

"You mean other than the fact that I was invited and already RSVP'd?" Sarcasm dripped from each word.

"Then call and cancel. We don't know what might be waiting for us there. What if there's another hit squad lurking around, waiting for another shot at us?"

She opened her mouth to argue, but Nick cut her off again. "I'm serious, Rebecca. You're staying here. I can't split my focus, okay? If you come, I'll be too busy worrying about your safety." At her dark scowl, he softened his tone. "You promised to follow orders, remember?"

Her mouth set in a tight line. "Fine. I'll stay behind, then."

As relief fluttered through him, he shifted his attention back to his father. "You should probably go now. People might start wondering about your late-night excursions."

Barrett nodded. "I'll send that guard to keep watch on McAvoy. I'd recommend renting out the room next door and—"

"Already done," Nick said with a crooked grin. "What do you take me for, an amateur?"

His dad's eyes twinkled with humor. "Walk me out, son. And good night, Ms. Parker," he told Rebecca.

"Night," she murmured, her green eyes conveying a whole lot of displeasure.

Nick followed his father outside to where a Lincoln Town Car with heavily tinted windows was parked.

"She's a feisty one, isn't she?" the secretary remarked with a soft chuckle.

"Yep. Not to mention headstrong, argumentative, infuriating…"

Barrett clicked a remote to unlock the car. "So," he said casually, "is it serious?"

Nick shifted in discomfort. "Nah, not really."

"You sure about that, son?"

His dad's piercing look was too shrewd, too knowing, and Nick found himself averting his eyes. "You know how it is in extreme situations, the whole adrenaline rush, the sense of urgency. Sometimes people get caught up in all those intense emotions." He shrugged awkwardly and repeated himself. "You know how it is."

"Actually, I don't. Your mother and I were quite boring."

Nick smiled. "The good kind of boring, though. You two were so in sync."

"We were. She was a good woman, your mother."

A lump rose in the back of his throat and he struggled to swallow it down. "I still miss her. Do you?"

"Every damn day." The secretary reached for the door handle, then halted. "Son…Ms. Parker seems like a good woman, too, you know."

Nick gulped again. "She is," he agreed. "But…" He gave a helpless shrug. "She's just not the *right* woman."

He could have sworn he glimpsed a flash of disappointment in his father's eyes, but then the older man offered a shrug of his own and opened the car door. "If you say so, Nicky. If you say so."

* * *

Rebecca went to bed early that night, miraculously finding the strength to resist Nick's advances even as her body begged her to indulge. But she couldn't. She was too upset. Too hurt. And even though she was a woman who usually met challenges and confrontations head-on, she couldn't bring herself to talk to Nick about what she'd heard him say.

She's just not the right *woman.*

He probably hadn't realized she'd been standing near the window. Or remembered that they'd left that window slightly open to air out the odor of mildew in the motel room.

God, when she'd heard him say that, it had been like a knife to the heart. The deep ache in her chest had ensured a night of tossing and turning, and that agonizing throb had been there when she'd opened her eyes this morning.

Nick seemed oblivious to her turbulent mood, or maybe he was just too distracted to notice. He'd been ducking next door a lot this morning to question McAvoy and get as many details as he could about Ferguson and any other potential players in this mess, and each time she watched his back disappear through the door, she imagined that it was for the last time.

Because soon it would be.

Because he didn't want to be with her.

He thought she was headstrong and argumentative and—what was the last one? Oh right, infuriating.

Sometimes people get caught up in all those intense emotions.

Those words had stung, too, and still did as they floated back into her head. Was that what he thought this was about? She was so jacked up on adrenaline and danger that she'd jumped into his bed without thinking it through?

Rebecca was so troubled she didn't realize Nick had returned to the room until his arms wrapped around her from behind.

She jerked in surprise. "Hey. I didn't hear you come in."

"You okay?" He planted a soft kiss on her shoulder, which was bare thanks to her spaghetti-strap tank top.

His lips were warm, firm, and that teeny little kiss sent a shiver of pleasure through her.

"I'm fine," she said absently.

Nick's breath tickled her ear. "No, you're not. You're still pissed off at me."

When she turned to look at him, the guilty cloud in his eyes was hard to miss. "I'm not pissed off. I'm just...tired, I guess."

"Tired of what?"

"Trying to convince you that I can take care of myself."

"I know you can. And maybe it makes me an alpha Neanderthal, but it's in my nature to want to take care of people. I..." Something oddly vulnerable flashed on his face. "I can't stand the thought of something happening to you."

Despite herself, her heart soared. He cared about her. Darn it, she *knew* he cared.

So why was he so against a future with her?

It can't work, Becks. Deal with it.

That painfully blunt voice sent another shooting pain to her heart. But it was true—it couldn't work.

Nick's protectiveness was cute, and sure, maybe it made her melt just a little, but she would never be that sweet, docile housewife who'd sit around waiting for

her husband to come home from work. That wasn't a
role she could ever play, a role that would ever suit her.
Nick's vaguely disapproving response to her admission that she wouldn't quit her job after she had kids
spoke volumes about the kind of partner he wanted,
and no matter how much she wanted to be with him,
she couldn't give him what he wanted.

Story of her life, huh? Her parents had tried to pi-
geonhole her, mold her into what they wanted her to
be, but Rebecca had always been that square peg that
didn't fit into the round hole. Even if she'd tried, she
wouldn't have been able to change her personality to
please her parents.

And she couldn't do it now to please Nick.

She had to end it.

She *needed* to end it.

But as she stood there in front of him, while he
stroked her cheeks with his rough-skinned fingertips,
she couldn't bring herself to say the words.

One more time. She wanted him just one last time.
Was that too selfish of her?

Heck, if it was, she didn't care.

Blinking to control the tears stinging her eyelids, she
slid her fingers into his dark hair and pulled his head
down for a kiss.

Nick could taste the desperation on Rebecca's tongue.
Something had upset her, he knew that, but she didn't
seem interested in talking anymore. Her mouth was eagerly devouring his, and he didn't have the strength to
break that passionate connection.

As he kissed her back, his hands explored those
delectable curves he was becoming addicted to. He
skimmed his fingers up her bare arms, then let them

travel down her body—over the sides of her breasts, the curve of her hips, the perfect roundness of her buttocks.

"I want you," Rebecca murmured.

She led him toward the bed even as she continued to kiss him with an urgency that sent his pulse careening.

They stumbled onto the mattress, with Rebecca straddling his body and bending over to kiss him again. Her long hair fell like a curtain around their heads, tickling his neck and getting stuck between their mouths. With a frustrated moan, Rebecca pushed her hair aside and moved her mouth to his neck.

When she sucked on his flesh, Nick groaned and thrust upward to rub his throbbing erection into her core.

She straightened up, her breathing heavy, her cheeks flushed with desire. As their gazes locked, she slowly peeled off her tank top, then unsnapped her bra so that her breasts came free. Her nipples were already hard, two tight buds of arousal pleading for his attention.

As his pulse thudded in his chest, Nick reached up to play with those mouthwatering breasts, knowing how sensitive she was there, how much she loved it. Sure enough, she moaned and pressed those firm mounds deeper into his palms, and he gave them a squeeze that made her squeak with pleasure.

"C'mere," he rasped.

He leaned forward on his elbows so he could capture one nipple with his mouth. The moment his lips closed over that rigid bud, she made a sexy little purring sound that sent a bolt of excitement straight to his groin. He kissed and tasted and nipped and teased, his stubble leaving red splotches on her perfect skin and bringing a rush of male satisfaction he probably should have been more ashamed of. He knew he shouldn't be getting so turned on seeing his mark on her skin, and yet he was harder than he had ever been.

Rebecca reached for his shirt and shoved it off him, and once his bare chest was exposed, she kissed him right between the pecs. The sweet brush of her lips sent a shiver rolling through him. That shiver became a full-body shudder when she moved her mouth to one flat nipple and her tongue darted out for a taste.

"Do you like that?" she asked in a breathy voice.

"Darling, I like everything you do to me."

"Good."

Nick went mindless with need under her sweet exploration. Every kiss, every teasing flick of her tongue evoked a new rush of heat and a new jolt of impatience. Anticipation built deep inside him as that sexy mouth started to move lower and lower.

"Off," she ordered when she reached the barrier of his pants.

Nick didn't need to be asked twice. He unbuttoned, unzipped and undressed like the good soldier he was.

Rebecca laughed at his eagerness, then wiggled out of her own pants and underwear and tossed them on the other bed.

As usual, the sight of her naked body got him so hot he could barely breathe. He drew her back into his arms, so she was draped over his chest, and proceeded to explore her curvy body. She explored right back, running her hands over his face, his chest, his abs. Christ, her touch drove him wild. Actually, everything about her produced that result.

Apparently he had the same effect on her, because when he slipped one hand between her legs, he found her drenched with desire.

Nick choked out a groan. "How are you always so ready for me?"

She wrapped her hand around his rock-hard shaft and said, "I can ask you the same question."

Then she brought him to her entrance and seated herself fully.

Nick shuddered with pleasure. Crap. He was so close to exploding and Rebecca hadn't even started to move yet.

Breathing through his nose, he willed away the oncoming climax and dug his fingers into her waist.

"Take us over the edge," he murmured. "Do it, darling."

Something tender and vulnerable passed over her face.

And then she nodded and began to move.

Nick watched her face the entire time. Her heavy-lidded eyes, flushed cheeks, parted lips. Tiny sounds of pleasure left her mouth as she rode him, slow, sweet, gentle. When her movements grew erratic, her body squirming in agitation, Nick knew she was close. He promptly moved his hand to the place where they were joined and began to stroke her, and soon she was crying out and sagging forward, trembling wildly as she toppled right over the edge.

His own release swept him away to a plane of body-numbing bliss, tightening his muscles and fogging his brain. When he finally crashed down to earth, he felt something wet on his shoulder. Alarmed, he tipped Rebecca's head back and saw the tears sparkling in her eyes.

"Did I hurt you?" he burst out.

"No. No, of course not."

She broke the intimate connection by sliding off his

lap, then reached for the box of tissues on the nightstand and hurriedly started cleaning up.

Nick studied her with growing apprehension. "Why are you crying, then?"

She didn't say a word.

"Talk to me, Rebecca. Are you okay?"

"Not really," she said in a small voice.

He was off the bed in a nanosecond, cupping her cheeks and wiping her tears with his thumbs.

"What can I do? Tell me what's going on, damn it."

Rebecca let out an audibly unsteady breath. "It's over, Nick. I'm done."

Chapter 17

Stunned, Nick stared into her green eyes, but he didn't see any hint that she was joking around. No, she looked more serious than a full-on stroke.

"Rebecca." He went to touch her cheek again, and discovered that his hand was shaking.

Rather than respond, she ducked out of his touch and went to search for her discarded clothes. When she started getting dressed in a hurry, he found himself doing the same. Somehow it felt wrong to have a serious conversation buck-naked.

He wanted to approach her, to take her into his arms, but she seemed to be intentionally keeping her distance. She walked over to the window and peered out, but he knew she wasn't looking at anything in particular.

"Rebecca," he said again, "what do you mean it's over?"

She turned to him with a sad look. "I mean it's over. You and me. This thing between us."

Nick was too afraid to try to interpret the burst of panic and fear that skated up his spine.

"Why?" he demanded, his tone harsher than he wanted it to be.

"Because I don't want to fall in love with you."

Her soft confession hung in the air for a moment.

He swallowed. "I see."

"Do you? Because I don't think you do." A chord of desperation rang in her voice. "I love being with you, Nick, and the more time I spend with you, the closer I come to falling. So we have to stop it, now, before I get even more attached to you. Because we both know there's no future for us."

His throat got real tight all of a sudden. "What makes you say that?"

"You," she said simply. "You have a vision of what your future should be like, and I don't belong in it. I won't quit my job, and I won't be a housewife, and I won't stop reporting on potentially risky events. Not just won't, but *can't*. It's my life, my livelihood, and not only am I great at it, but I love it."

"I know," he said hoarsely, because damn it, he couldn't deny that.

Rebecca Parker was talented as hell, and not only that, but she truly *cared* about the stories she reported on. She wasn't one of those jaded correspondents who'd given up on the concept of truth and justice. She belonged on that television screen, informing people about the corruption and greed and horrors of this world.

"I'm not the right woman for you."

His chest went rigid as she repeated the same words

he'd told his father last night. When he met her eyes, the weariness in them said it all.

"You heard me and my dad talking last night," he said flatly.

She nodded.

"Christ." He raked both hands through his hair in a gesture of frustration. "I wish you hadn't heard that, but...I don't know what to tell you. I love being with you, too, but you're right. I *do* have this mental image of my future. I want what my parents had, damn it."

She sighed. "I know."

"That's all I've ever wanted," he said roughly. "The other guys at school, they'd be looking for that next lay, and I'd be the guy looking for *the one*. Call me a wuss, but I want that perfect life my folks had."

Her answering smile was gentle. "There's no such thing as perfect, Nick."

"Perfect is what you make it," he countered.

"And you and me...we're not that vision of perfection, huh?"

The pain in her voice tore at his insides. He wanted nothing more than to assure her that they could make it work, but each time he pictured a future with her, he saw Rebecca taking off to parts unknown and possibly getting killed by, say, a frickin' Molotov cocktail being hurled at her head.

He swiftly banished the gruesome image. "I'd end up trying to change you," he confessed. "And I don't want to be the man who puts out that spark in your eyes, darling. I can't be that man."

Now it was anger coloring her tone. "Wow. My personality is so undesirable to you that you'd actively try to *change* it?"

"That's not what I meant," he said in frustration. "It's

more about your job than anything. I wouldn't want you to take on dangerous assignments. I'd be a mess whenever you left town, consumed with fear and worry, and I never want to place you in the position where you had to choose between me and your career."

"What about me?" she challenged. "What if you choose to return to active duty? I'd be in the same boat worrying about *you*."

"I'm done being a soldier," he said quietly. "When this is all over, I want a civilian job. Probably here in D.C., so I can be close to my dad and sister."

Rebecca fell silent for a moment. "There's really no point in talking about this anymore. We both know it won't work."

His throat burned, but he couldn't figure out why this hurt so bad. He'd known from the start that this affair wouldn't amount to anything long-lasting.

So why did he feel like the damn world was ending?

"I…" Nick stopped, not sure what he wanted to say. Not sure if there was anything left to say. "I guess you're right. There's nothing left to talk about."

Rebecca's expression grew veiled. "You should call your father and make sure he's made all the arrangements for tonight."

"Yeah, I should."

Their gazes locked.

Another silence descended.

As his gut clenched in sorrow, Nick broke eye contact and reached for his phone.

The secretary's limo picked Nick up at eight-thirty that evening. Because his dad was traveling with several DoD agents who made up his security detail, Nick didn't want them knowing about McAvoy and Rebecca, so he'd arranged for the pickup seven blocks from the motel.

The dinner portion of the veterans' event would be wrapping up around now, and because his father's presence hadn't been required, the two men had agreed it would be better to show up just as the gala was getting under way. They planned on catching Ferguson right before he delivered his speech to the veterans.

When Nick slid into the backseat of the limo, his father immediately leaned forward and handed him a garment bag. "I grabbed the tux you left in the guest room closet," Kirk Barrett said.

"Man, I can't remember the last time I wore this."

With a rueful grin, Nick unzipped the bag and stared at the tailored tuxedo jacket, black trousers and crisp white dress shirt it contained. He was suddenly grateful that he'd decided to shave the scruff he'd been sporting since Mala. Rebecca had persuaded him to do it, pointing out that he was attending the gala as good-guy Nick Barrett and not the badass Nick Prescott she'd been traveling with all week.

Don't think about her.

Crap. He'd promised himself he wouldn't let thoughts of Rebecca distract him tonight. Although he knew ending it had been for the best, the troubling emotions swirling in his gut made it impossible to feel good about the decision.

But he couldn't dwell on that now, which meant forcibly shoving Rebecca from his mind.

His father, however, hadn't gotten the memo. "So is our sassy Ms. Parker still unhappy about being left behind?"

"A little, but she'll get over it." Nick avoided his father's eyes before the older man could do that mind-reading trick he excelled at.

He shucked his camo pants and stuck his legs into the tuxedo trousers, yanking them to his hips and zipping up. As he put on the shirt and started buttoning it, he felt his dad's shrewd gaze boring into him.

"What?" he said defensively.

The secretary's eyes flickered with what resembled disappointment. "What are you doing, Nicky?"

"What are you talking about?"

"With Rebecca Parker."

"Nothing." He hesitated, fought another burst of pain. "In fact, we ended the affair earlier this afternoon."

Kirk looked surprised. "Why on earth would you do that?"

"I already told you why last night."

Feeling more than a little uncomfortable—he and his father didn't normally discuss Nick's love life—Nick reached for the small box inside the garment bag and flipped it open. The velvet bed contained a pair of monogrammed cuff links his dad must have grabbed from their home safe.

"We're not right for each other," Nick added when his father didn't say a word.

More silence.

Sighing, he snapped on the cuff links and fixed his sleeves, then shrugged into his tuxedo jacket. His fingers were unusually ungainly as he tackled his bow tie. He was acutely aware that his father was still watching him, and that silent stare-down left him feeling frazzled.

"Oh, spit it out, Dad. What's on your mind?"

"I think you're a fool."

The frank words made him raise his eyebrows. "Wow, don't hold back any punches."

"You asked what was on my mind—well, that was it." The secretary shook his head. "For the love of God, son, that woman is so right for you I want to grab you by the shoulders and give you a firm shake for being so damn blind."

A tornado of shock spiraled through him. "What?"

"You heard me. She's the one. And you're letting her go? I know it's been a year since we've seen each other, but when did you become such a dumb-ass, Nicholas?"

Nick was having an impossible time making sense of this conversation. "She's not the one," he sputtered. "She can't be. All she ever does is challenge me and argue and drive me absolutely nuts with her complete disregard for her own safety. Half the time I want to strangle her for being so damn stubborn, and the other half, I want to throw her over my shoulder and carry her to bed—"

He quit talking when he realized his father was laughing at him. Loudly. And for a very long time.

"Care to fill me in on the joke?" Nick said with an edge to his voice.

"You don't see how lucky you are, do you, son?" Kirk continued to chuckle. "What you're describing? It's *passion.* Lord, what I would have given to have had just a fraction of that in my own marriage."

Nick sucked in a stunned breath. "What?"

"Don't get me wrong. I loved your mother. I loved her with every fiber of my being, but let's not kid each other here—Jeannie was a yes-woman. She agreed with every word that came out of my mouth, approved of every decision I made, took every suggestion I gave her." A flicker of shame crept into Kirk's eyes. "Honestly? Sometimes I'd make the most outrageous demand in hopes that your mom would argue with me about it—and more than half the time, she wouldn't! She'd go along with whatever stupid thing that came out of my mouth, because that was the kind of woman she was."

Nick shook his head a few times to clear out the cobwebs of shock. He'd never heard his father say a negative word about his mom, so this was a startling first.

"Are you saying you weren't happy with her?" he heard himself ask.

"Of course not. All I'm saying is, our marriage was not as perfect as it seemed. And your mom, as much as I loved her, wasn't perfect either. She was too damn passive. Usually I loved it, you know, because I tend to be dominating—"

Nick snickered. "No kidding."

"But like I said, sometimes I wished she stood up to me more. Challenged me, excited me." The secretary shrugged. "You lucked out, son. I know you don't see it that way, but honestly, marriage can be boring. You *want* that passion, Nicky. I see the way you look at Rebecca, and I see the way she looks at you, so trust me when I say that letting her go will be the biggest mistake you could ever make."

The Veterans Gala was being held in the White House's East Ballroom, a stunning room with magnificent crystal chandeliers, a sleek terrazzo floor and gold-colored silk draperies gracing the walls. There was a mixed crowd in attendance—decorated soldiers, their wives and girlfriends, White House staff, politicians and movers and shakers. The guests chatted and mingled, sipped on champagne and munched on appetizers and stole glances across the room to where Troy

Ferguson was holding court with two senators, an army general and a supreme court judge.

Nick stuck close to his father's side, wishing the secretary hadn't initiated that disturbing heart-to-heart right before they were due to confront the vice president of the United States. Nick's head was all over the place now, and he had to make a serious effort to concentrate on the task at hand.

He accepted a champagne flute from a passing server and studied Ferguson, whose trim body and youthful features never failed to surprise him. Only the threads of silver in Ferguson's thick dark hair hinted that the man was older than he looked. He'd served in the military, too, a decorated soldier in his own right, and several of the uniform-clad veterans were ushered by White House staff to chat with the VP.

"He seems to be in good spirits," Nick murmured.

"Indeed," his father murmured back.

The two of them started to walk, but they hadn't made it two steps when they were intercepted by a congressman who wanted to talk to the secretary of defense. When they finally managed to pry themselves away, they ended up being intercepted again, this time by a female senator whose eyes widened at the sight of Nick.

"And is this your son?" she asked. "Where have you been hiding him, Kirk?"

"I just got in from a yearlong sailing trip last night," Nick lied.

"Yes, I can tell you must have been out on the boat. You look very tanned."

He did? Uh, okay, if she said so.

"And what are your plans now?" she asked in a conversational tone.

"Not sure yet," he said, keeping his response vague.

His father touched his arm. "Nicholas, there's someone else I'd like you to meet. Excuse us, Susan."

They moved away from the curious woman, only to be stopped by someone else. Needless to say, it took twenty minutes for them to make their way across the ballroom.

At their approach, Vice President Ferguson sharply turned his head. He looked startled to see them, and his dark gray eyes lingered on Nick for so long that his shoulders tensed.

Was Ferguson surprised to see him here because he was the one trying to kill him and he'd been hoping Nick would already be dead? Or was the VP just genuinely surprised that the secretary had arrived with his traveling nomad of a son?

"Kirk," Ferguson said warmly as he shook the secretary's hand.

Two stone-faced agents stood a few feet away, keeping a vigilant eye on the ballroom and everyone in it. In fact, the whole room was swarming with agents, all boasting that same alert posture and hawklike gaze.

"Mr. Vice President, you remember my son, Nicholas," Secretary Barrett said, gesturing to Nick.

"Of course. Pleasure to see you again, son."

Nick reached out to shake the vice president's hand.

Hmm. Firm shake, steady hand, dry palm. If Ferguson was nervous, he wasn't showing any outward signs of it.

"I thought your father had mentioned you were out of the country," the VP said with mild interest.

Yeah, because that was the lie you fed him.

Nick restrained the biting response, quickly reminding himself that Ferguson might not be guilty.

And yet something about the man was triggering his internal alarms. Ferguson was too poised, his expression too contemplative as he gazed at Nick.

"I was. I only got in last night," Nick explained.

"I see. And did you enjoy your travels?"

Nick thought about this past year—the safe houses, the frustration, the rage...

He met Ferguson's silver-gray eyes. "More or less."

Next to him, his father took a small step forward and lowered his voice to a grave pitch. "Mr. Vice President, we were hoping to get a moment alone with you."

The other man made a clucking noise with his tongue. "I'm afraid that might be difficult. I'm due to give a speech in less than an hour, and there are several people I have yet to speak to."

"It won't take long," the secretary insisted.

Ferguson's eyes narrowed with suspicion. "What's this about, Kirk?"

"It's a matter that would be best discussed in private, sir. My son has come to me with some very troubling news."

Nick didn't miss the spark of alarm that lit the VP's eyes. Question was, was it genuine or false?

And if that was real alarm, what was Ferguson worried about? National security...or that he might be exposed?

"I wouldn't ask this if it wasn't of the utmost importance," Nick's father said in a coaxing tone.

Finally, the vice president nodded. "Yes, of course. I suppose I can spare a few minutes."

He glanced at his Secret Service agents, gave a curt nod, and a moment later, their little group was heading for the door.

Two agents took the lead, stepping out of the ballroom first. The three men trailed after them while three more agents took up the rear. The entourage walked the quiet halls until they reached the office the VP used when he was at the White House; his day-to-day office space was located on the Naval Observatory grounds, which Nick remembered getting a tour of when his father first became the secretary of defense.

The Secret Service agents entered the office to make sure it was secure before allowing the vice president to enter.

"You and your men can wait in the hall, Alfred," Ferguson barked at the lead agent.

The tall, silent man nodded and left the room, closing the door behind him.

Ferguson didn't make a move for the desk or the couch. He stood in the center of the room instead, fixing both Barretts with an impatient look.

"Well? What is it?"

"I'm afraid something very troubling, and slightly unbelievable, has come to my attention," Secretary Barrett began. "Regarding the Meridian virus."

Ferguson didn't even blink. "I'm going to need you to be a little more specific, Kirk."

"How's this for specific? Deputy Secretary McAvoy has admitted to being involved with the development of the virus—and he names you as the individual in charge of the project."

Nick watched the vice president's expression for any change, any indication of guilt, but the man had a phenomenal poker face. Nick couldn't tell if Ferguson was surprised or angry or who knew what, at least until that carefully composed mask broke away and unexpected resignation filled those gray eyes.

With a heavy breath, Ferguson rounded the commanding mahogany desk and sank into the plush chair. He clasped his hands on the desktop and said, "I was afraid something like this might happen."

Chapter 18

When the cell phone on the bed started to buzz, Rebecca lunged for it with the speed of a professional athlete. She'd been alone in the motel room for the past hour, impatiently waiting for word from Nick, and now it had finally come.

"What happened?" she demanded rather than saying hello. "Did he confess?"

"Not quite."

The sound of Nick's deep voice caused her heart to splinter in yet another place, but Rebecca forced away the pain and focused on the aggravation she detected in his tone.

"What does that mean?"

"It means that the vice president is denying all involvement."

"Shocking." She didn't bother controlling her sarcasm. "Where are you now?"

"The West Wing. I'm out in the hall. My dad's still talking to Ferguson, but the VP isn't changing his story."

"Which is?"

"That Fred McAvoy is the brainchild of this entire operation. Ferguson claims that the deputy secretary approached him about two years ago with the idea of engineering a biological agent that would be easier to handle in terms of contagion, and easier to release into a large population. Apparently McAvoy insisted that his contacts at D&M were confident that a successful waterborne virus could be engineered—typically, weaponized bioagents tend to be airborne, but McAvoy wanted to try something new."

She raised her eyebrows, even though nobody could see her. "This sounds sketchy."

"Tell me about it. Anyway, Ferguson says that he unequivocally vetoed the idea on the spot and told McAvoy in no uncertain terms to drop it. Ostensibly, McAvoy went ahead with the project without authority."

Rebecca pursed her lips, a rush of irritation rising inside her. "And of course we can't challenge that story, because there's no proof of the VP's involvement aside from McAvoy's word."

"Yep."

"What do *you* think? Is Ferguson guilty?"

"Yes," Nick said without delay.

"You sound sure of that."

"I am." She could hear the frustration in his voice. "I can't put my finger on it, but something about him rubs me the wrong way. It isn't anything specific. His body language and facial expressions and even his words— they all seem sincere. But my instincts are humming, Red. Humming big-time."

Red. Her heart throbbed painfully at his easy use of that nickname. Lord, at least he hadn't called her *darling*—she was liable to burst into tears if he did that.

And wasn't that just pathetic? She was Rebecca Parker, for Pete's sake. She'd never cried over a man in her entire life.

"I'll go talk to McAvoy," she said. "Maybe he can be persuaded to give us some more details about Ferguson if he knows that the VP is letting him take the fall for this."

"Keep me posted. Dad and I are still here for the time being."

They hung up, and Rebecca left the room and knocked on the neighboring door.

A lock clicked, and then Barrett's bodyguard, a beefy man in his late thirties, appeared in the doorway.

"I need to talk to McAvoy," she told him, entering the room without waiting for an invitation.

McAvoy was on the bed, and he glared daggers at Rebecca when she walked in. He was no longer bound and gagged, but one hand was handcuffed to the wooden headboard of the bed.

"You can't keep me here like a prisoner!" he spat out. "This is a violation of my rights!"

Rebecca glanced over at Connor. "Do you mind giving us a few minutes alone?"

The bodyguard nodded. "I'll be right outside the door."

Once he was gone, she turned back to McAvoy and shrugged. "Fred, if I were you at the moment, I'd stop worrying about my rights and start thinking about saving my butt."

Those sunken blue eyes narrowed. "What does that mean?"

"It means that Vice President Ferguson has apparently decided to make you his scapegoat."

"Bull."

"It's true." She waved her cell phone around. "I just got off the phone with Nick. Ferguson claims that you approached him with the idea of experimenting with biological weapons. He's pointing the finger right at you." Genuine regret fluttered in her belly. "You'll go away for a long time for this. If it even goes to trial."

Fear flickered in his gaze. She knew what he was thinking, because she was thinking it, too. Cover-ups that ran this deep didn't end in highly publicized court cases. They were swept under the rug—usually in the form of a dead body or two, and a clever frame job.

"He sold you out," she said softly. "I think he's going to order Secretary Barrett to turn you over to Homeland Security."

McAvoy's expression conveyed a flood of panic, but along with it came a flash of rage. "That bastard can't put the blame on me. This was *his* doing."

"It's your word against his, Fred. Barring any actual proof of Ferguson's involvement, I'm pretty sure President Howard will side with the veep over the dep sec def."

"Good thing I have proof, then," McAvoy replied in a smug voice.

She arched a brow. "Interesting, because you never mentioned this proof before."

"I was saving it for my lawyer," he muttered. "For leverage."

"Smart," she had to concede, "but that evidence would've made things a heck of a lot easier for Secretary Barrett when he went to confront Ferguson tonight. Now it might be too late."

Again, he shot out, "Bull. You're Rebecca friggin' Parker! You can help me."

"How?"

"Expose that son of a bitch Ferguson! Put it all on the air!"

"Exposing him means exposing you, too," she pointed out.

Bitterness hardened his features. "I'm already going down for this and you know it. But if I go down, I'm taking Ferguson with me. I'm not his scapegoat. Help me take him down, Parker."

She paused. "What kind of evidence do you have?"

"Transcripts and recordings of nearly every conversation I had with Ferguson about Project Aries. Emails, phone calls, memos. I saved it all."

Her brows shot up. "That was risky."

"It was necessary."

"Where is all this proof now?"

"The safe in my study."

Rebecca sighed. "You kept the evidence at your house? Isn't that Amateur 101?"

"I work for the DoD, Ms. Parker. Believe me, I made several copies of everything I have. Some are in various safe-deposit boxes, one is with my lawyer, but the copy in my safe will be the easiest to access at ten o'clock at night." He cocked his head. "So? Will you help me?"

She didn't need much time to think it over. Nick and his father were at the White House at this very moment, getting nowhere with Ferguson and with absolutely no way to weasel the truth out of him. But if McAvoy really did have proof of Ferguson's wrongdoing, then Rebecca could deliver it to Nick and they could use it to get a confession from the VP. Or heck, they could just hand over the proof to President Howard himself and let *him* clean up this mess.

Nick ordered you to stay put, a singsong voice reminded her.

Indecision had her hesitating again, but not for long. Screw Nick's orders. This was to help *him,* darn it, and it wasn't even that dangerous a task. She'd take Connor along, and they would simply drive over to McAvoy's house, grab the proof from his safe, and then Connor could drop her at the White House and head back to the motel with McAvoy.

Easy as pie. Safe as a home-run hitter.

She met McAvoy's expectant gaze. "Yes, I'll help."

"I'm sorry, gentlemen, but it's time for me to get ready for my speech," Troy Ferguson announced, injecting a note of regret into his voice.

But inside, he did not feel regretful. Oh, no, he was seething. He hadn't wanted to attend this gala in the first place, but any deviation from his regular schedule might be construed as suspicious, so he'd forced himself to put on a happy face and work the ballroom.

Kirk Barrett had a lot of nerve springing this on him at a White House event. Ferguson would have the man's job for this. Yes, somehow in the near or distant future, he would make sure Barrett paid the price for his insolence. Both of them, he thought, as his gaze moved to the younger of the two men.

Nick Barrett had been the biggest headache of all this past year. Of all the military units that could have been dispatched to that village in Corazón, it just *had* to be Barrett's. The son of one of Howard's most trusted advisers.

Ferguson hadn't wanted to eliminate the younger

Barrett. He hadn't wanted to put Kirk through that. Truth was, he'd always considered Kirk an ally; they both placed the same value on national security, even though Ferguson hadn't necessarily been able to voice his support over the years.

So yes, he hadn't wanted to kill the man's son. But now he feared he might need to take out the father, too.

"We'll discuss this in more depth after the gala," he told the secretary of defense. "I'd like to bring President Howard into the discussion, if you don't mind."

Both Barretts looked startled by that.

That's right, you bastards. Didn't think I'd do it by the book, huh?

Their surprised expressions only intensified his ire. Clearly his explanation, in which he'd blamed the whole Meridian virus fiasco on Fred McAvoy, had convinced neither father nor son.

But Ferguson was confident that his tracks were thoroughly covered. McAvoy would take the fall for this and now it was just a matter of riding out the impending media storm until this Meridian crap eventually died down.

"I think that's a wise idea," Kirk said with a nod of approval. "The president needs to be brought into the loop."

Ferguson approached the door and rapped his knuckles on it to alert his guard that he was ready to go.

Alfred opened the door. "Mr. Vice President?"

"Please ask one of your men to escort Secretary Barrett and his son back to the ballroom." He extracted a set of cue cards from the inner pocket of his tuxedo jacket. "I'd like a few moments alone to go over my speech."

The secretary left the office first, but the younger Barrett lingered, those thoughtful brown eyes focused on Ferguson with such intensity that he experienced a genuine tug of discomfort.

"Mr. Vice President," Nick Barrett murmured, then nodded and slid out the door.

The moment he was alone, Ferguson pulled out his secure phone and called Carraway.

"We've got a problem," he snapped when the former army captain picked up.

Carraway had been a friend of Ferguson's brother, another former military man who worked in the private sector now. Carraway had left the army several years ago and now ran a profitable soldier-for-hire company that Ferguson had made use of on more than one occasion. At the moment, however, he was not at all pleased with the caliber of Carraway's soldiers.

"You were supposed to post a guard on McAvoy's house and keep an eye on him when he returned from China."

"I did, but the Barretts must have gotten to McAvoy before you ordered the watch detail. My man said there hasn't been any activity at McAvoy's house for the past twenty-four hours."

"Kirk and his goddamn son have him hidden away somewhere," he muttered. "I want you to find McAvoy. We can't have him running his mouth anymore. Post a couple more men on his house. I'll send some agents to the Pentagon under the guise that I want to be briefed on McAvoy's trip. If he's locked up in federal custody somewhere, I'll know. But if he shows up at his house, it's your job to take him out. Understood?"

"Understood," Carraway said briskly.

Ferguson disconnected the call. Damn it. This situation had suddenly become even more precarious. He needed to tread carefully from this point on. Placate

Barrett and his son. Play dumb and horrified when they brought Howard on board.

And make sure Fred McAvoy couldn't cause any more damage.

"We've got company," Connor announced as they approached McAvoy's house.

Rebecca glanced out the car window but didn't glimpse anything that set off her inner alarms. "Are you sure?"

The bodyguard nodded. He drove right past the house and parked several doors down, almost in the exact spot where Nick had parked during their last visit.

"Wait in the car," Connor said in brusque voice, unholstering his gun before he'd even unbuckled his seat belt. "Let me see what we're dealing with."

Rebecca experienced a sense of overwhelming déjà vu as Connor disappeared into the shadows shrouding the residential street. Last time she'd been here, Nick had slunk off to disable the gate, and then the two of them had gone to confront McAvoy about his role in all of this.

This time, McAvoy was in the backseat with his wrists handcuffed behind him, and Nick wasn't with her.

In fact, after tonight, Nick would never be with her again.

Ignoring the clench of pain, she peered out the window in hopes of figuring out what Connor was doing, though she didn't doubt that the man was perfectly capable of handling himself. She'd discovered during the car ride that not only had he been a DoD agent for ten years, but he'd also been Delta Force at one point and a heavyweight boxer at another. Needless to say, she had the utmost confidence in Connor's ability to take care of himself.

Sure enough, when he returned five minutes later, there wasn't a scratch on him. Didn't look like he'd even broken a sweat either.

"What happened?" Rebecca demanded.

"I took care of our little problem." His expression revealed nothing.

"Who was he?"

"Mercenary."

"Are you sure?" she said sharply.

Connor nodded. "He wasn't military. Certainly not government. Definitely a merc."

She didn't ask him how he'd "taken care" of the mercenary, but she had a pretty good idea.

In the backseat, McAvoy spoke up uneasily. "Hurry up," he said as Connor slid into the driver's seat. "If they sent one man, they might send another. Especially if this one doesn't check in soon."

The man had a point, and Rebecca was feeling anxious herself as Connor drove in reverse toward the gate, which was still gaping open from Nick messing with the wiring. They drove right through it and parked by the front door.

The three of them hopped out. McAvoy stumbled slightly, then attempted to regain his balance, a difficult task with his hands yanked tightly behind him. Rebecca took pity on the deputy secretary and grabbed his arm to steady him, which earned her a look of grudging gratitude.

"Thank you," he muttered as they climbed the porch steps together.

Connor went in first to do a sweep of the house, then

returned to collect them and the three of them marched into the study.

Rebecca's gaze roamed the various oil landscapes hanging on the wood-paneled walls, then focused on the majestic deer head mounted over the fireplace, a slightly terrifying visual she hadn't paid much attention to during last night's visit.

But now she paid *a lot* of attention, because that taxidermy head was precisely what McAvoy made a beeline for. Then he halted and turned to scowl at his keepers. "You'll need to uncuff me," he said darkly.

After Connor removed the cuffs, McAvoy turned back to the mantel and ran his fingers along the bottom of the wooden frame the deer was affixed to. Rebecca's brows soared when the wood panel popped out to reveal the gleaming stainless steel vault behind it, and just when she thought her eyebrows couldn't go any higher, she noticed the small panel next to the safe's keypad and her brows pretty much collided with her hairline.

"I feel like I'm in a James Bond movie," she remarked as she watched McAvoy bring his left eye close to that electronic panel.

The unit emitted one continuous beeping sound as it scanned the man's eyeball—whose personal safe required *eye scans,* for Pete's sake?—and then it beeped three times and flashed a green light. McAvoy proceeded to type a long series of numbers on the keypad before the safe finally opened.

He didn't waste any time reaching inside and rummaging around. His hand emerged with a small black case, roughly the size of a cigarette pack. He flicked it open, peered at the contents and nodded as if pleased with what he saw.

Narrowing her eyes, Rebecca approached him and

peered over his shoulder to find two flash drives secured inside the case.

"The data on these are identical." To her surprise, McAvoy pried one out and handed it to her. "Keep this on your person. I'll hold on to the other."

He tucked the black case into his pocket while Rebecca shoved the little drive into the front pocket of her jeans.

"Let's get out of here," she told Connor, who was watching the door with a vigilant eye.

A minute later, they were rushing out the front door with Connor in the lead, McAvoy right beside her and no longer handcuffed.

The gunshot came out of nowhere.

It exploded in the night air and made Rebecca's ears ring, adding to the confusion taking flight inside her. Her heart pounded, then stopped altogether as the man in front of her collapsed facedown onto the porch floor.

Oh, God. Connor. He'd been *shot*. He was…dead, she realized as his limp body rolled down the porch steps and landed in a motionless heap on the driveway. Blood pooled around his head, bringing a rush of nausea to Rebecca's throat.

Another shot cracked in the air and suddenly McAvoy was no longer beside her.

Rebecca instinctively flattened herself on the ground and began crawling toward Connor's body, her gaze zeroing in on the silver key in his lifeless hand. The car key.

McAvoy's cry of pain and surprise was cut short by a second gunshot, then a third. A fourth. And then silence.

No, not silence. Footsteps.

Someone was running toward her.

Rebecca grabbed the key from Connor's hand and heaved herself to her feet. Something hot whizzed by her ear, but she didn't stop, didn't turn around.

She threw herself into the driver's seat and stuck the key into the ignition. There was a blur of movement in the rearview mirror. Two men were running toward the SUV. Both held gleaming black guns in their hands.

Drive, darn it!

Her foot slammed on the gas pedal, her heart sticking in her throat as the SUV lurched forward and peeled away from McAvoy's house.

She sped through the gate and went right over the curb, bouncing so hard that her head nearly smashed into the roof of the car. When her hands started to tingle and her lungs started to burn, she realized she wasn't breathing.

Oh, God. Connor. McAvoy. Both of them dead.

She sucked in a deep breath and got so light-headed she nearly went off the road.

Keep it together, Becks. Get to Nick. Expose Ferguson.

She repeated the plan over and over again in her head, clinging to it, needing it to stay calm. Her foot continued to shake over the gas pedal, but somehow she managed to drive in a straight line. Somehow she managed to speed away from McAvoy's neighborhood without passing out. And without being pursued by some ominous black van.

Inhaling another breath, Rebecca went over the plan again. Get to Nick. Expose Ferguson.

But first...she just had one little stop to make.

Chapter 19

"McAvoy's dead. Parker got away."

The report came five minutes after Ferguson stepped off the podium to the thundering applause from the guests gathered in the ballroom. He'd ducked into the corridor to take the call, and now he couldn't decide whether to feel satisfied or enraged.

"What do you mean she got away? Why was she there in the first place?" he hissed into the mouthpiece.

"I don't know. All I know is what my man reported. McAvoy showed up at the house with Parker and a DoD agent. My men engaged and eliminated two of the targets. Parker managed to escape."

Panic seized his throat. He lowered his voice, barely above a whisper. "She saw McAvoy and a federal agent get gunned down?"

There was a pause, then, "Yes."

Son of a bitch.

This was a disaster. Fred McAvoy and the threat he'd posed had been eliminated, but now an even bigger threat loomed on the horizon. The star correspondent for the country's number-one news network had witnessed the murder of two government employees.

"You have to find her. Now."

"I've already got my people on it, but you should be prepared. There's a chance she might go to the Barretts for help, in which case, she'd be heading your way, sir."

He tamped down his panic by drawing in a deep breath. "I'll tell my staff to detain her if she shows up here. Did your men clean up the scene at McAvoy's house?"

"They staged it as a home robbery. Maybe you can explain away the agent's presence by saying McAvoy requested heavier security because of some trouble he ran into in Beijing." Carraway's tone became apprehensive. "There's one more thing. My men found a flash drive on McAvoy's body."

His chest stiffened.

That little rat.

Clearly McAvoy had somehow managed to compile evidence against him. Jesus. Well, luckily Carraway was in possession of the flash drive now. That was good news at least.

"But the case he was holding it in had slots for two drives," Carraway went on. "There's a chance Parker might have the second drive."

His stomach dropped. So much for good news.

"Find her," he growled.

"Yes, Mr. Vice President."

Ferguson hung up without another word, then gathered the pieces of his shattered composure and walked back into the ballroom.

* * *

Throughout Ferguson's heartwarming speech about patriotism and heroism and every other "-ism" relating to the troops, Nick had stood next to his father and studied the vice president's every move. He had to admit, Ferguson was skilled at captivating a crowd. He made them laugh, made them smile, made them cry. By the time the man left the podium, he'd succeeded in making every person in the ballroom love him.

"He lied to us," Nick muttered. "I don't care how convincing his story sounded. My gut is telling me he was the one behind Project Aries."

"Mine, too," his father admitted. "But I'm not sure what more we can do tonight."

"Do you really think he'll brief the president about this?"

"If he does, then he must be extremely confident that he's covered his tracks and can never be tied to the Meridian virus."

Both men's head shifted in a sharp motion as Ferguson began walking toward the ballroom doors. With the Secret Service agents flanking him, it was hard to be sure, but Nick thought he saw the VP taking a sleek black phone out of his pocket.

Nick took a step, but his dad shook his head in warning. "Be smart, son."

He forced himself to stay rooted, knew his father was right. He couldn't just go running after the vice president and try to spy on the man in front of a room full of people. He ended up using Ferguson's brief absence as an opportunity to check his phone, but there was no message or missed call from Rebecca. She was still at the motel, then, tucked out of sight with McAvoy. Good.

"Somebody's upset," Secretary Barrett said in a low voice.

Nick's father was right—Ferguson had just returned to the ballroom, and although he had a smile pasted on his face, his gray eyes revealed a flicker of unease.

Nick frowned. "Something's happened."

No sooner had the words left his mouth than a skinny male aide hurried over to the vice president and whispered something in his ear.

There was no mistaking the way Ferguson's shoulders stiffened, or the discernible gleam of triumph in his eyes. He'd just received some important news.

Very important, Nick amended as Ferguson immediately marched toward the doors again.

This time, he didn't allow his father to stop him. His instincts were buzzing again, telling him not to let Ferguson out of his sight.

Without a word, Nick left his father's side and threaded his way through the crowd toward the exit. He tried to keep his gait fast but relaxed, a difficult feat, but it was better than the all-out sprint his brain was ordering him to employ. He emerged into the wide hallway just in time to see Ferguson and his security detail round the corner at the end of the hall.

Two agents stood guard outside the ballroom. Nick attempted to look nonchalant as he walked past them, but the men weren't fooled.

"Stop," one of the agents barked.

Nick ignored him and picked up the pace.

"Sir, you were asked to stop!"

He was practically running now, praying that neither man drew his gun and shot him in the back before he reached the end of the hall. Fortunately, he remained bullet-free as he rounded that same corner where Ferguson and his guards had disappeared.

"Let go of me!" A female shout bounced off the walls.

He halted in his tracks, and his heart jammed in his throat when he spotted a flash of red amid the array of black across the hallway.

Rebecca.

Wishing like hell that he had a weapon, Nick lunged toward the source of the commotion, then skidded to another stop when half a dozen weapons snapped up in his direction.

"Nick," Rebecca cried out when she spotted him.

He had a clear view of her now. She stood there surrounded by six agents, three of whom had their guns pointed at her while the other three kept theirs trained on Nick.

Rebecca wore the jeans and tank top she'd had on back at the motel, but her long hair was a tousled mess and there was a smudge of what looked like motor oil on her cheek.

"Detain her," Ferguson snapped. "Him, too."

The vice president took a step away from his horde of agents, then shot Nick an irritable look.

"I took the time to listen to your accusations tonight, son, even though it was highly insulting, and frankly, humiliating." Those gray eyes blazed with anger. "But enough is enough. I can't have the two of you spreading lies and slander—"

"Go ahead and arrest me," Rebecca interrupted. "It's already too late."

A suspicious groove appeared in Ferguson's forehead, but he didn't ask her to clarify. Instead, he glanced at his guards. "Detain them," he said again.

To Nick's dismay, Rebecca took a step toward Ferguson, completely unfazed by the weapons being pointed at her. The damn woman stalked right up to the vice president of the United States and crossed her arms over her chest.

"The truth is out," she announced, sticking out her chin as if to dare Ferguson to argue with her.

Nick's heart did a little proud somersault. Christ, he loved that stubborn jut of her chin. Loved that she was totally oblivious to her diminutive stature, that she had no qualms about squaring off with men twice her size.

And her enthusiasm. He loved that, too.

Not to mention her determination. Her fearlessness. Her fire.

Aw, hell.

Had he fallen in love with her?

The startling thought slid into his consciousness in one rapid swoop, but he just as rapidly pushed it away. This was *not* the time to sift through the confusing emotions swimming around in his stomach.

"You can arrest us if you want," she went on, her green eyes glittering with satisfaction. "But it won't change a gee-dee thing—"

Despite himself, Nick's lips twitched in amusement.

"The whole world will know the truth in about two minutes, if the news hasn't already broken. In that case…" She just shrugged.

"The truth about what?" Ferguson asked coldly, continuing to play dumb.

"That you conducted biological weapons testing on innocent people. That the Meridian virus was your brainchild."

"Lies," he snapped. "That was McAvoy's doing."

"Oh, McAvoy?" Her lips twisted in anger. "You

mean, the man you just ordered to be shot to death in his own home?"

Nick's shoulders set in an ominous line. McAvoy was dead? When he studied Rebecca's somber expression, he knew she was telling the truth.

And he also knew something else—if McAvoy had been shot at his house, then that meant Rebecca had disobeyed orders. Again.

Why was he not surprised?

"I've had enough of this nonsense," Ferguson muttered.

He turned to his guards, no doubt to bark out another order to detain them, but Rebecca interrupted in a cheerful tone. "Is there a TV around here?" she asked. "There's gotta be, right? I mean, look at the size of this place."

Nick found himself grinning.

"Because I really think you need to get to a television," she told the VP. "I think you'll be singing a different tune once you see ABN's eleven-o'clock segment."

Ferguson's face turned red, his eyes burning with fury. Without a word, he stalked toward one of the doors in the hallway and threw it open. Two of his agents went with him, but the rest stayed with Rebecca and Nick out in the corridor.

With Ferguson gone, Nick glanced at the redhead with a wry smile. "What did you do, Red?"

"Nothing much." Her gorgeous green eyes twinkled. "McAvoy had incriminating evidence against Ferguson on a flash drive. He gave it to me before he died." The twinkle faded into a dull gleam. "Connor's dead, too. But I managed to get away."

Fear and satisfaction mingled in Nick's blood, though he discovered that the latter overpowered the former.

The thought of Rebecca in the middle of a gunfight scared the living hell out of him, and yet at the same time, he suddenly realized he wasn't at all surprised that she'd managed to escape.

Rebecca was smart.

Resourceful, strong, brave.

Of course she'd made it out alive.

Something hot and painful squeezed his chest, but he ignored it and focused on what Rebecca was saying.

"I stopped at an internet café on the way here and emailed all the transcripts on that drive to the network."

Nick took a step toward her, then froze when two Secret Service agents cocked their weapons.

"Relax, fellas," he said with a sigh. "We're not the bad guys here. You'll find that out soon enough."

None of the men blinked or responded.

Rolling his eyes, he glanced back at Rebecca. "So you sent ABN the evidence. Good thinking."

"Oh, I didn't just send it to ABN. As of right now, every media outlet in the country, as well as a few key markets abroad, has a copy of every email and phone call Ferguson exchanged with McAvoy."

A smile stretched across Nick's face. "Nice."

Rebecca spared a pithy look at one of the agents. "The whole world now knows that Ferguson was responsible for creating a biological weapon, testing it on innocent people and accidentally allowing it to be released on U.S. soil."

She turned back to Nick, her expression becoming defiant. "I'm not going to apologize, by the way."

He frowned. "Apologize for what?"

"Not staying put at the motel. I know I took a risk by bringing McAvoy to his house, but we needed to get our hands on that flash drive." She stuck out that sassy chin of hers again. "And by disobeying your orders, I exposed Ferguson, so I refuse to be sorry for that, Nick. I don't care if tonight reinforces every last thing you think makes us incompatible, but I won't say I'm sorry."

She finished in a rush, and he lifted a brow at her. "You done?"

"Yes," she grumbled.

"Good, because I wasn't expecting an apology." He shrugged. "And I'm not sure I want one."

Her eyes widened. "For realsies?"

A laugh bubbled in his throat. God, he loved this woman.

Yep, he *loved* this woman. He frickin' loved her to death.

"For realsies," he confirmed. "You got the proof we needed, darling, and you showed it to the world. There's nothing left to cover up. Ferguson can't kill us and make up some bogus reason for our deaths. He can't do a damn thing to us now."

Rebecca's mouth lifted in a smile. "Damn right, he can't." She suddenly clapped her hand over that sexy mouth. "Crap. I swore."

"Don't worry, I won't tell." With a dry expression, he glanced at the army of guards who didn't seem inclined to lower their weapons. "I'm sure these dudes won't either."

He could have sworn he saw a muscle twitch in one of the agents' jaws, but when he peered closer, the man was once again stone-faced.

Ferguson was still behind that door, and Nick could now hear the faint murmur of voices. They were most likely wafting out of the television the VP had turned on, the television that was tuned into the ABN newscast, which was, at the moment, airing Troy Ferguson's dirty laundry and unconscionable actions to the entire country.

And even though Nick knew that now was definitely not the time to have a heart-to-heart—what with the armed men surrounding them—he couldn't stop himself.

Besides, it seemed comically apt to be having this conversation during a situation that just oozed danger.

"I'm an idiot," he told Rebecca.

She looked flabbergasted. "Why?"

His voice grew hoarse, thick with emotion. "Because I was so busy thinking about what 'the one'—" he used air quotes to emphasize the words "—ought to be like, that I didn't realize she was standing right in front of me the whole time."

Rebecca's breath hitched in pleasure, but then she faltered. "Wait. Is it me? You mean me, right?"

A soft chuckle filled the air, and they both turned to stare at the Secret Service agent who'd made the amused sound. The man guiltily cast his gaze downward, and when his head lifted again, his face had reverted back to robotically expressionless.

Fighting his amusement, Nick grinned at Rebecca. "Yes, I mean you." His voice thickened again. "You're the one. The right woman for me. I was just too blind and stupid to see it."

"But…" She bit her bottom lip. "What about my job? Nothing's changed. I'm going to keep covering the stories that intrigue me, even if they're dangerous."

"Look around us, Red." He swept his arm at the handful of guns. "We're splat in the middle of dangerous, and you're handling yourself just fine."

"I always do," she said gently.

"I know." He swallowed. "I was a real ass. An overprotective ass. And I was wrong, because you know what? If you hadn't ignored my orders tonight, Ferguson might have gotten away with everything. And you know what else? I *love* how fearless you are. It's downright inspiring. And even though it took me a while to figure it out, I also love the way you challenge me."

He took a breath, suddenly feeling embarrassed about spilling his guts in front of four armed men. But Rebecca's green eyes were swimming with such joy that he couldn't stop now. Couldn't leave her hanging.

"I don't want to change you," he said huskily. "Actually, I'm pretty sure that if you weren't the way you are, I might get bored after a while."

She studied him warily. "Do you really mean everything you're saying, or are you just getting caught up in the emotional urgency of the situation?"

"The only thing I'm caught up in is you."

Oh, brother. He regretted the words before they even left his mouth. Not because he didn't mean them, but because he now looked like a total sap in front of all these beefy, broad-shouldered Secret Service guys.

And yet when he unintentionally met the eye of one agent, he could swear he saw approval reflecting back at him.

"That was smooth," Rebecca said frankly. "I think my heart did a little flip. Write that line down, Nicky. You can say it to me every night before we fall asleep. It can be our 'thing.'"

He laughed. "Deal."

She opened her mouth like she wanted to say more, but the sound of footsteps cut her off. All heads swiveled to find the secretary of defense striding toward them.

"Lay down your weapons," Secretary Barrett ordered, looking stunned by the scene he'd stumbled on.

None of the agents obeyed.

"I'm sorry, Mr. Secretary, but we take our orders from the vice president," one of the guards said, but his voice contained a note of genuine regret.

"Are you telling me that the vice president ordered you to hold two civilians at gunpoint, out in the open where anyone who wanders out of the ballroom could see you?" The secretary sounded livid. "Where is the VP?"

Nick cocked his head to the closed door ten feet away. "In there."

"He's watching the news," Rebecca told Nick's father. "Seems like all you ever see on the news these days is stories about corruption and cover-ups."

A knowing gleam entered the secretary's eyes. "It's a shame," he agreed. "But how convenient is it that we are now able to get a news update with the touch of a button?" As if to illustrate that point, Nick's father held up his cell phone.

The screen was opened to the ABN website.

Nick choked down a laugh.

"I do believe President Howard is boarding Air Force One as we speak," Secretary Barrett added. He glanced at the guard who'd spoken to him. "I also believe you'll be receiving new orders from the director of Homeland Security soon."

As if on cue, the lead agent suddenly touched his earpiece. He furrowed his brow, listened for several long moments, then muttered, "Yes, sir," before finally ordering the others to stand down.

Nick breathed a sigh of relief as every weapon was lowered and the agents backed away from him and Rebecca.

The redhead immediately launched herself into his

arms, and he held her tight, breathing in the sweet scent of her hair.

"You okay?" he murmured. "You sure you weren't hurt at McAvoy's house?"

"I'm fine." She kissed his clean-shaven cheek. "By the way, you look incredible in a tux."

He chuckled, then wet his thumb with his tongue and wiped away the spot of grease on her face. "By the way, there's one more thing I forgot to say."

"Which is?"

He brought his mouth to her ear and murmured, "I love you."

Rebecca didn't even get to bask in the sheer awesomeness of Nick's declaration of love. No, because the second she opened her mouth to order him to say it again—and then ten more times after that—the door that Ferguson had disappeared behind swung open, and the vice president stepped out into the corridor.

He was sandwiched between two agents again, but their posture no longer seemed protective. There was a combative feel to them now, as if they'd been ordered not to let Troy Ferguson out of their sight.

When Rebecca met the vice president's gray eyes, she didn't miss the cloud of defeat darkening them.

He knew he was beaten. No more cover-ups, no more hit squads. The second Rebecca had downloaded the contents of that flash drive and pressed Send, she'd known she was signing Ferguson's walking papers.

It came as no surprise that he didn't say a word to her or Nick, but he did address Secretary Barrett. "You know I was right to do it, Kirk. He's too damn lenient. Too damn forgiving."

Nick's father released a tired breath. "There were

other ways to push our agenda, Troy. If you'd only come to me, sat down in my office for an hour or two, the two of us could have designed a defense plan so rock-solid that Howard wouldn't have been able to veto it."

"Hindsight," the VP murmured ruefully.

The Secretary shook his head in disappointment, but he didn't have an opportunity for further comment because the Secret Service agents began to lead Ferguson away, most likely on the orders of President Howard himself.

The other guards dispersed, leaving Rebecca alone with the two Barretts.

The senior Barrett cast a pleased smile in her direction. "Good work, Parker. He would have tried to lay the blame on McAvoy's shoulders if you hadn't found that evidence." Now he glanced at his son. "Tell Tate and Stone to come home, Nicholas. They'll need to be debriefed."

"Yes, sir."

The secretary turned back to Rebecca. "I'll give you two a moment alone. I'm sure my son would like some privacy when he yells at you for leaving the motel, and I'm equally certain you'll want some privacy yourself when you staunchly defend your actions."

Laughing, Rebecca waved a dismissive hand. "Oh, we already had that fight, sir. It's time for the kiss-and-makeup part."

Nick's dad chuckled. "I'll leave you to it, then."

After the older man marched off, she grinned at Nick and said, "Anyway, back to what you were saying before…"

"What was that again?"

"Don't be a jerk. You know exactly what you said."

"Ah, you mean the I-love-you part."

"Yep." She crossed her arms. "Say it again."

"Well, aren't you bossy." He raised his eyebrows. "Correct me if I'm wrong, but I don't remember your returning the sentiment."

She raised her eyebrows right back. "That's because I'm still not sure if you meant it."

The wounded look on his face caught her off guard. "Of course I meant it."

"You really love me?" She narrowed her eyes. "Even though I'm a risk taker?"

He nodded.

"Even though I don't plan on quitting my job, not now, and not after I have kids?"

Another nod.

"Even though I'll probably always argue with you about every little thing?"

A nod, this one accompanied by a smile.

"Even though—"

He silenced her with a kiss, and God help her, but she couldn't muster up any irritation at being interrupted. Instead, she sank into his strong chest and kissed him back. His tongue slid into her mouth, teased her with a few sensual licks, and then he tore his mouth away.

"I love you, Rebecca," he said softly. "And I wouldn't change a damn thing about you."

Warmth exploded in her chest, circling her heart and bringing tears to her eyes. "I love you, too."

"Finally, she says it. Took you long enough."

"You deserved to sweat for a bit after your big you're-not-right-for-me speech."

Guilt flashed across his face. "I'm sorry about that. I was an idiot."

"You were, but that's okay. I forgive you."

She couldn't seem to stop smiling, and she knew she

must look ridiculously goofy and starry-eyed at the moment. But it was simply impossible to control the sparks of happiness dancing through her body.

"So we're really going to do this?" she asked, her voice going serious. "We're going to see where this whole relationship thing leads?"

"No."

Her mouth fell open. "What do you mean no?"

"Darling, just because I'm willing to amend the qualities I want my perfect woman to have doesn't mean I'm not a gentleman anymore." His smile was self-deprecating. "I think I'll always be that old-fashioned good guy you like to tease me about being. And the good guy in me wants more than an affair from you. He wants to put a ring on your finger."

"Are you asking me to *marry* you?"

"Would you say no if I did?"

Rebecca pondered that for a moment, wondering why the idea of getting engaged wasn't freaking her out in the slightest.

"Don't worry, it'll be a long engagement," Nick assured her. "It'll take me a while to reintegrate into society. After all, I've been living in crumbling fortresses and beach shacks this past year."

The little grin he gave her was so adorable she almost melted into a puddle at his feet. God, she loved this man. She never would have dreamed that she'd fall in love with someone so sweet and respectable—an old-fashioned gentleman, as he apparently liked to refer to himself.

And yet she'd fallen. Hard. And she had no intention of letting Nick Barrett go.

"Okay, fine, but only if I get to pick out the ring," she said with shrug.

"I propose to you and you respond with 'Okay, fine'?" He shook his head in dismay. "What am I going to do with you, Red?"

"Lots of things," she answered cheerfully. "Trust me, we're going to have a blast together."

"I don't doubt it, Sherlock."

She met his gorgeous eyes, genuinely touched. "Oh, my gosh. Are you officially agreeing to be my side-kick?"

"Well, I'm thinking we can take turns being Sherlock, but we'll always be partners. How does that sound?"

Still smiling—because she truly couldn't stop—Rebecca raised herself up on her tiptoes and kissed him. "It sounds effing awesome."

Epilogue

One Month Later

"Are you serious? After a year on the run, we're finally able to return to civilization and you choose to live *here?*" Sebastian Stone grumbled. "Jeez, the places we stayed in when we were hiding out weren't half as isolated as this property."

Captain Robert Tate offered his trademark I-don't-give-a-damn shrug. "Eva and I like living in the country. Deal with it."

Tate reached into the cooler and pulled out a couple beers. He handed one to Nick, who twisted off the cap and took a sip. "Thanks, Captain. Man, it's hot out today. It wasn't this humid in D.C."

"Speaking of D.C., is Rebecca planning on covering Ferguson's impeachment proceedings, or will ABN assign someone else?" Sebastian asked, curious.

"She's covering it," Nick replied. "When her new producer suggested that her personal connection to Ferguson and the scandal might affect her ability to remain objective, she almost bit his head off."

He couldn't help but chuckle. Rebecca had been covering the scandal since it had broken at the Veterans Gala and Nick knew she'd never give it up now. This was her exclusive, her scoop, and he didn't blame her one bit for clinging so hard. She'd suffered for this, bled for it, lost her friends and coworkers for it.

His gaze drifted across the backyard. Well, not so much a backyard as a stretch of rugged land lined with trees in full bloom, gentle hills and a narrow creek that he could hear gurgling even all the way from the huge cedar deck behind Tate and Eva's enormous North Carolina country house.

Rebecca was sitting on the grassy bank near the creek, swinging her bare feet in the water as she laughed at something Julia Davenport had said. Her red hair shone in the afternoon sunlight, and those green eyes were animated as usual. She and Julia had hit it off from the second they'd met, which didn't really surprise Nick. Julia was as outspoken as Rebecca, and had that same type of sarcastic humor that Rebecca possessed in spades.

The two women had been chatting on the grass for the past hour, and now they were joined by Eva Dolce and her three-year-old son, Rafe, who made a mad dash for the water's edge.

Rebecca caught the toddler around the waist before he could dive headfirst into the water, and the sight caused a rush of warmth to travel through Nick's chest. Did it make him a total softie that he liked seeing a child in Rebecca's arms?

Not that he planned on knocking her up anytime soon. No, children would come in time, way into the future; although if his father had anything to say about it, Rebecca would already be shopping for maternity clothes. Secretary Barrett had a lot on his plate at the moment dealing with the fallout from McAvoy's and Ferguson's actions, but that hadn't stopped him from harassing Nick to make things official with Rebecca. The secretary was absolutely crazy about the woman, and didn't try to hide it.

Nick was pretty crazy about her, too.

"So you two are staying in D.C., then," Sebastian said. "Did you accept that job at the DoD yet?"

"No, I'm still considering it." Nick knew he'd end up taking the gig, though. Returning to the military held no appeal for him anymore.

He glanced at Tate. "What are you up to these days? Are you and Eva still planning on becoming carpenters?"

Tate rolled his eyes. "Get it straight, Nicky. Eva is planning on designing security software. *I* might dabble in some carpentry. Tomorrow morning I'm going to build a chair."

Sebastian snickered.

Nick snorted.

Their former commanding officer glared at them and flashed both his middle fingers. "Eff right off."

"Wait, are you fake-swearing, too, now?" Nick demanded.

Resignation washed over Tate's moss-green eyes. "That's what happens when you live with a three-year-old."

Nick sighed. "I live with a twenty-seven-year-old. I

shouldn't have to censor my language, but that infuriating woman insists on it."

"You two are already living together?" Sebastian said in surprise.

"Yeah, I moved into Rebecca's place in Arlington." He rolled his eyes. "And don't give me that look, Seb. You and Julia have been joined at the hip for months."

Tate glanced at the sandy-haired man. "You still heading to Africa at the end of the month?"

Sebastian nodded, and his gray eyes softened as he glanced across the yard at Julia. "The doc's got a new post, a six-month stint in a village in northern Somalia. I'm tagging along."

Nick couldn't help but feel amazed that they were standing around discussing their plans. They'd been living day-by-day this past year, trying to figure out why their unit had been targeted, and now this frustrating ordeal was finally behind them.

And somehow, during that year of hiding, all three had managed to find women who loved them.

Figure that one out.

Nick's gaze drifted to Rebecca again. At that exact moment, she turned her head and caught him staring, and the smile she gave him was so beautiful, so full of joy and mischief that his heart damn near soared right out of his chest.

He smiled back, then focused on the two men he considered his best friends. No, his brothers.

Sebastian raised his beer bottle in the air. "Here's to not having to look over our shoulders anymore."

After the three of them clinked their bottles, Tate's gaze shifted to the raven-haired woman by the creek and he let out a soft laugh. "We made out all right, huh?" he said wryly.

"Yup," Sebastian concurred, his gray eyes focusing on Julia, whose long brown braid rustled in the afternoon breeze.

Nick's eyes found their way back to the redhead who'd bulldozed her way into his life. "We made out just fine," he agreed.

* * * * *

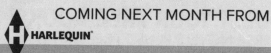

COMING NEXT MONTH FROM
HARLEQUIN®
ROMANTIC suspense

Available June 4, 2013

#1755 CONFESSING TO THE COWBOY
Cowboy Café • by Carla Cassidy

Mary Mathis may hold the secret to the serial killer targeting local waitresses. Will she confess to the hot sheriff before the killer takes her as his final victim?

#1756 ROCKY MOUNTAIN LAWMAN
Conard County: The Next Generation
by Rachel Lee

A Forest Service lawman and an artist face down a dangerous terrorist group in the isolated Rocky Mountains and are driven closer than they ever thought possible.

#1757 FATAL EXPOSURE
Buried Secrets • by Gail Barrett

With innocent lives at stake, a former runaway must stay and confront her secret past. But will the sexy cop on her trail betray her or heal her wounded heart?

#1758 TEMPTED INTO DANGER
ICE: Black Ops Defenders • by Melissa Cutler

Math whiz Vanessa Crosby creates a program that lands her on a crime ring's hit list. But when ICE agent Diego Santero comes to her rescue, danger never looked so tempting....

YOU CAN FIND MORE INFORMATION ON UPCOMING HARLEQUIN® TITLES, FREE EXCERPTS AND MORE AT WWW.HARLEQUIN.COM.

HRSCNM0513

REQUEST YOUR FREE BOOKS!
2 FREE NOVELS PLUS 2 FREE GIFTS!

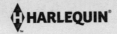

ROMANTIC suspense

Sparked by danger, fueled by passion

Diego unbuckled her harness as Vanessa clutched the helicopter seat's armrests. "What are you doing?"

He pointed across her, out the door. "You have to jump, Vanessa."

Oh, no. Absolutely not.

Clutching the door frame so hard her fingernails ached, she shuffled her feet toward the edge and poked her head out the side to stare at the green water below. Over the roar of the rotor blades, she shouted, "Are you crazy? How high up are we?"

"Fifteen meters. It's as low as I can get with these trees."

Fifteen meters was fifty feet. A five-story building. Her stomach heaved. "There could be barracuda in there, or crocodiles. Leeches, even."

"That's a chance you have to take. There's nowhere else to land. The rain forest is too thick and we're out of fuel. You have to suck it up and jump."

"What about you?"

"I'm going to jump, too, but I have to wait until you're clear of the chopper. And there's a chance my jump won't go off as planned. We're running out of time."

She knew she needed to trust him not to leave her, but it was hard. She'd never been this far out of control of her life and she couldn't stop the questions, couldn't let go of the fear that he'd abandon her to fend for herself. "How do I know you're not going to dump me here and fly away?"

"I thought we went over this. Did you forget my speech already?"

"No." But promises were as fluid as water, she wanted to add. People made promises all the time that they didn't keep.

"You gotta hustle now. We don't have much time left in this bird."

She stood and faced the opening, then twisted to take one last look at Diego. What if he didn't make it? What if this was the last time she saw him? "Diego…"

"Jump into the damn water or I'm going to push you. Right now."

She whipped her head straight. Like everything else that had happened in the past couple hours, with this, she didn't have a choice. She sucked in a breath and flung herself over the edge.

Don't miss
TEMPTED INTO DANGER
by Melissa Cutler

Available June 2013 from Harlequin Romantic Suspense wherever books are sold.

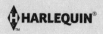

ROMANTIC suspense

CONFESSING TO THE COWBOY
by Carla Cassidy

Small town Grady Gulch has been held captive
by a serial killer targeting waitresses.

Mary Mathis may hold the secret to the killings,
but she risks losing it all if she confides in Sheriff
Cameron Evans, a man who has been captivated
by Mary. Will she confess to the hot sheriff
before the killer takes her as his final victim?

Look for *CONFESSING TO THE COWBOY*
by Carla Cassidy next month from
Harlequin® Romantic Suspense®!

Available wherever books and ebooks are sold.

Heart-racing romance, high-stakes suspense!

HRS278251

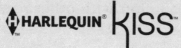

* * *

"WELL, if it isn't the Queen of Coffee!" DeFasio's greeting was one of wary cheer. We sat in his cluttered office in the Sixth Precinct. "I never thought I'd see you again. Not after we arrested your pal, Nate Sumner."

"How is that case going for you, Lieutenant?"

"I'm not at liberty to discuss an ongoing investigation." He lowered his voice. "Off the record: Things have come to a dead stop. Right now the investigating officers are looking at other angles."

"Other *suspects*, you mean?"

"No other suspects. Not yet."

"Then you must be referring to 'angles' like Charley Polaski's heavyset husband, Joe? The guy who fell—or was more likely *pushed*—off the High Line the other night? Anyone check him out for dart marks from a tranquilizer gun? The kind wildlife enthusiasts shoot wolves with in Wyoming to track their migration patterns?"

DeFasio's eyebrow rose. "How could you possibly know—"

"I'm guessing the very same kind of dart was just used in a Chelsea apartment to render the very tall Darren Engle unconscious enough for his head to be bashed in by a dragon slayer statue."

DeFasio went quiet for a long moment. "No wonder Mike Quinn's so sweet on you. Have you got hard evidence, Cosi?"

"I have a way to get it. Or rather, *you* might. You just don't know it yet."

And this is where my *second* shock was about to pay off.

When Anton Alonzo had handed me my THORN phone, he described it as fireproof and shockproof. I hadn't thought much about it until Minnow's phone had survived a major dip in the Atlantic.

That's why I asked DeFasio to get his hands on Charley Polaski's smartphone, the one they'd retrieved from the burned-out remains of Eric's car.

When Charley's phone arrived at his desk, we looked it over. As I suspected, it was a THORN phone. It was also scorched and drained of power with a heat-cracked screen.

"What do you want with this, Cosi?" DeFasio challenged. "We already have what was on it . . ."

As he explained it, the e-forensics people hadn't bothered tinkering with the phone itself because they'd already downloaded a duplicate of its digital files from the backup server at THORN, Inc.

"Please, Lieutenant, humor me. I want to see what's on this phone."

"That phone's not going to start, Cosi, look at its condition."

"You don't understand. It's a THORN phone. It's built to be indestructible. I'm sure, even with the external damage, the data will be accessible once the device is recharged."

"Okay, you got me. But how do we recharge the thing? The pin configuration won't fit a standard—"

"Try this." I handed him the charger for my own THORN phone.

"You have an answer for everything, don't you?"

"I try."

"Then why do you think we'll find new evidence in the dead chauffeur's phone?"

"You know Charley was more than a driver, right?"

"Yeah, she was working undercover as a PI."

That's when I told DeFasio what Joe Polaski had told me—I finally understood what he meant that night he grabbed me. Charley had a routine. She gathered information, took notes, and stored them on her THORN phone. Then she transferred those notes to Joe, who agreed to keep them safe for her.

After the info was safely transferred, she deleted the data before the THORN server performed its daily backup, pulling the day's data into its archives.

"The backup happens at midnight, according to the instructions for my own phone, so Charley was erasing her phone logs daily to make sure no one at the company, not even Eric, could read her files and find out what she'd learned."

"I get it . . ." I could feel DeFasio's excitement. "Charley was killed before she could erase what she'd discovered on the day of her murder."

"Exactly."

"You really think that phone is still functional? And the data is still there?"

"Let's hope."

"Okay, then. Let's see . . ."

I thanked DeFasio and he saw me to the door, adding a sheepish request of his own. "Some of the guys wanted me to ask: can we get a few more samples of that Baileys Irish Cream Fudge?"

"Listen, if your squad can help clear Nate Sumner and Minnow Tork, I'll personally deliver enough to get all of us bombed."

Sixty-nine

~~~~~~

So much happened over the next two days that my impromptu trip to Brazil felt like ancient history.

After DeFasio fully recharged Charley's THORN phone, he found incriminating evidence.

Just as I'd thought, the evidence pointed to Eric's sister, Eden Thorner.

Eden must have sensed it was over because she'd completely disappeared. She'd ditched her credit cards and deactivated her phone, along with its GPS tracking, leaving no way to trace her movements.

When Eric returned from Brazil, he and Anton Alonzo searched for Eden in her Manhattan apartment, her summer house in the Hamptons, and her country home in Connecticut, but she was gone without a trace.

"I wonder where she went."

Matt shrugged, gaze glued to his smartphone. "Probably some country without a U.S. extradition treaty."

We were back at the Village Blend, and things had finally returned to normal—normal for my coffeehouse, anyway.

The morning rush had ended, and I took a break. As I sunk into a stool beside Matt, Esther approached, two espresso cups in hand.

"You've got to try this, guys! Don't ask what it is. Just taste it."

Esther set the steaming demitasses in front of me and Matt, then stepped back to gauge our reactions.

I sipped, and found the espresso rich, dark, nutty, with hints of walnut *and* almond, topped by an amazing crema. As it cooled there were notes of raspberries, maple syrup—and was that pancake batter?!

"Brilliant!" I said after my third compulsive gulp.

Matt nodded. "Very nice."

"This cup tastes like a country breakfast," I said. "What did you do, Esther? Break into the Red Hook warehouse and roast one of those rare beans Matt imported for Eric?"

"It's just our own Morning Blend, boss. I've been practicing 24/7 with the new Slayer; I can vary the pressure and express time so even those old, familiar coffees we've always served have flavors we never knew existed."

"FEI," Nancy said. "Weekend business picked up plenty since we started using the Slayer. Dante and I had to close an hour late on Saturday because we had so much last-minute traffic."

"FEI? Nancy, don't you mean FYI? As in *For Your Information?*" Esther asked.

Nancy shrugged. "What I said was for *everyone's* information."

I laughed, Esther slapped her forehead, and Tucker rushed through the front door—accompanied by an early spring breeze and the excited tinkling of our old familiar doorbell, lost after the explosion wrecked our shop but found again by intrepid members of the NYPD.

The Bomb Squad located the dented brass bell in the

evidence bin when they retrieved Charley's phone. Sergeant Spinelli returned it to us and I handed over a double batch of my Baileys fudge—a happy trade for all parties.

"Hot off the presses!" Tuck said, dropping an open *New York Times* in front of me, Matt, Esther, and Nancy before shedding his coat.

I read the headline and scanned the first few paragraphs, but as an insider, I already knew everything in the report.

Officially Eden Thorner was wanted for embezzlement, because she pilfered millions of corporate dollars in the months before she fled. Unofficially, she was the prime suspect in the murders of Charley and Joseph Polaski, and Darren Engle—her intern.

My theory: the brilliant, young rocketeer had made the car bomb for her and even helped her murder Joe. *"Your wish is my command, Milady . . ."*

The words I'd heard at THORN's Appland echoed sadly in my mind.

Darren must have been in love with Eden, and she'd used him to her own ends. Everything was fine with Nate arrested, but when her brother started working in Nate's defense, she clearly became nervous about how much Darren knew, so she killed her accomplice in an attempt to frame Minnow for all of the murders.

Of course, this whole murderous mess started with the death of the young, gorgeous actress with a drinking problem—Bianca Hyde, the girl who'd gotten bombed before she got bashed, which resulted in the LAPD ruling the death accidental.

I still wasn't sure why Eric's sister had killed Bianca. I had my theories, but I didn't care about espousing them any longer because my personal quest was over.

Little Minnow was off the hook. And all charges against Nate Sumner were dropped. The head of Solar Flare would be released from jail by noon.

Madame was planning to meet Nate at the courthouse, and she was probably going to wear go-go boots, too.

I was very pleased. Madame and Nate had a happy ending and so did Eric and Minnow.

Unfortunately, my detective boyfriend (turned Justice Department G-man) remained out of touch, so I was still waiting for mine.

An hour later, I was working behind the counter again when the bell rang over the door. A cheerfully familiar voice called out—

"Hey, Coffee Lady!"

A giddy grin was plastered across Sergeant Emmanuel Franco's rugged face; his muscular arms were hauling several suitcases and a shoulder bag.

"Manny, what's going on?" I asked, worried. "Are you leaving town?"

"Wrong conclusion, Madam Detective. I'm here to make a special delivery."

He set the suitcases down and tugged a pink backpack off his arm. I saw the Hello Kitty logo emblazoned across that bag and my heart stopped.

"That's not yours! That pack belongs to—"

My daughter's grinning face peeked around Franco's muscular shoulder.

"Hi, Mom!"

"Joy!"

We couldn't rush together fast enough.

"See, Mom, you're not the only one full of surprises!"

After more hugging and a few tears, Franco cleared his throat.

"I hate to interrupt this sweet reunion, but I have to get back to the precinct." Then his eyes met Joy's and he lowered his voice. "Will I see you tonight?"

Joy glanced at me uncertainly. "I don't know, I just got home and—"

"Of course, Joy will see you tonight," I said. "If you pick her up after eight, my daughter and I will have the whole afternoon to catch up."

OVER lunch in my duplex above the Blend, I asked Joy *The Question*—

"When are you coming home for good?"

Her answer was clear—and complicated.

Joy absolutely planned to move back to New York City to settle down. The complicated part was *not yet*.

As she explained it, her work situation in Paris had improved a great deal. The night she impressed the chef at L'Ambroisie, he offered her an apprenticeship. She didn't want to take it, but (being Madame's grandchild) she used the situation to her advantage. She told her current boss at Les Deux Perroquets about the offer, and he hit his vaulted ceiling.

Without Joy and her contributions to his menu, the man knew that Michelin Rising Star might not be so easy to attain. To keep her in the fold, he granted Joy's requests: her cancelled vacation time was immediately reinstated; her temporary promotion was made permanent; and the owner actually agreed to hire more kitchen help to give his brigade a reasonable chance of keeping up with the customer crush—and having restorative time off.

I did ask Joy why she passed on the chance to apprentice at a Michelin four-star restaurant to stay at one with a lowly Rising Star award.

Her logic was simple. "It will mean much more to me to help earn that Michelin star for everyone at Les Deux Perroquets, and for my adopted home of Montmartre. I've made so many friends there . . ."

But I knew Joy needed to earn that star for herself, as well. The victory would prove she'd risen to the challenges of

moving to France. Then she could return to her chosen field
in her hometown and put her troubled past behind her with
her reputation restored.

"I'll give it a year, Mom. If we earn the star, my standing
will be huge, and I will easily find a place in a Manhattan
kitchen. If we lose, I'll come back home and take any job I can
find—I'll even work for you if you'll have me." She grinned.
"Either way, I promise I'll come back in the next twelve
months. Believe me, I made the same promise to Manny."

As I brushed away a tear, Miss Phone's fembot voice delivered more good news—

"Clare, this your programmed alert. You have received a
text message from Michael Quinn."

With shaky hands, I snatched the phone to call up the
message, which I read aloud to Joy.

Out of touch for the rest of the afternoon. Meet me at
Dynasty Pier on the West Side at nine o'clock for an intimate dinner cruise. Love, Mike!

There was no stopping my tears now, but they were tears
of relief.

"Looks like we both have dates tonight, Mom!"

I nodded and immediately sent a return note to him—

Looking forward to our big date at Dynasty Pier! See you
tonight!

"Thank goodness," I whispered. "Now Mike and I can
finally get back on track."

Seventy

~~~~~~

WHEN I exited the cab, Dynasty Pier's front gate appeared brightly lit and its boathouse glowed cheerfully in the night.

Next door, Chelsea Piers had been docking transatlantic ocean liners and cruise ships for over a century. Dynasty was designed to accommodate much smaller vessels. The pier was little more than a concrete walkway extending a hundred feet into the dark waters of the Hudson River.

As I approached the entrance, I delighted in the sound of the tide slapping against the piles. A frosty spring wind came off the dark river, giving me a slight chill. My new black silk dress was dripping with lace; elegant, innocent, and sexy all at once—but not much for warmth, and I tightened the belt on my wool coat.

I saw no one, but someone must have seen me because a buzz sounded and the steel gate automatically unlocked. I pushed through and the door clanged behind me. I walked eagerly toward the boathouse, my high heels clicking on the concrete.

The boathouse door was locked, so I firmly knocked. When no one answered, I peeked through the slats. I spied a desk and a radio, but the single-room structure seemed deserted, so I approached the only ship at the pier tonight. It wasn't very large, maybe a forty-footer, and I doubted the vessel could accommodate more than fifteen people.

Mike wasn't kidding when he said this would be an intimate meal. Did he charter this boat all by himself? More likely it's a VIP cruise. Maybe his DC colleagues are joining us . . .

With a few more steps forward, I noticed the name on the ship's bow.

BLUE ROSES.

I stopped dead. On the black water, a lone barge blew its horn as it floated past, and I got a bad feeling. *Something's very wrong here.* There was no way Mike would have invited me aboard a ship christened with that name, not after the poem he'd sent.

Roses white and red are best . . .

I quickly turned to leave—and found the Metis Man blocking my retreat.

Wearing a fur-trimmed sealskin parka, high boots, and a bandolier slung over one shoulder, Garth Hendricks looked like an Alaskan native on a bear hunt. The very large gun he clutched in one gloved hand told me he was loaded for bear, too.

With my exit blocked, I had nowhere to go but the water. I was willing to jump, but I never got the chance.

He shot me.

The dart pierced my coat and sunk into my shoulder. The impact of the flying syringe rocked me, and the needle stung, too—but only for a second. Then my right side went numb.

I knocked the dart aside with a clumsy swipe of my left hand and the empty syringe bounced off the concrete.

"You won't get away with this," I told him—only it came

out sounding more like "Ooop coat way be fist," because my tongue had stopped working.

I was having trouble breathing, too, and my mouth gaped like a fish out of water. Finally my knees got wobbly and I sank onto the frigid concrete, paralyzed but still conscious.

"I shot you with a tranquilizer gun," Garth explained, his tone matter-of-fact. "You'll have some trouble breathing—Etorphine affects the respiratory system—but you probably won't die. Not from the sedative, anyway."

Garth nudged me with his boot. Then he placed the barrel of his gun against my forehead.

"Eden used this dart gun to shoot wolves in Wyoming." He smiled. "She also used it to paralyze Joe Polaski, so that dumb obedient Darren could help me chuck him over the side of the High Line. Joe was just like you, Clare. Conscious, but completely helpless."

Garth stepped out of view and I heard a rumbling sound. A moment later he wheeled a flatbed dolly into view and parked it beside me. With a grunt, he rolled me onto it.

"You see, Eden ruined a good thing when she acted on her own initiative, and tried to electrocute you with Darren's help. It's only a matter of time before OSHA discovers how the electrical system was rigged, but dear dead Darren can take the fall for that. I'll miss the boy—he was so eager to please—but there are plenty of young, eager interns out there . . ."

Of course. Fits right in with your "fun sweatshop" philosophy!

Garth continued his arrogant babble while he wheeled me up the gangplank and onto the deck.

"Did you know? As soon as Eric inherited his father's business, he sold it out from under his older sister. There was nothing she could do. Her father left the little freak everything. Then Eric used his stake to make himself a billionaire . . ."

Garth untied the ropes, releasing the ship from its moorings.

"Eric made up for his lost youth, too, by serially dating bimbo models and starlets. He even wanted to *marry* one of those tramps. She didn't like me much or Eden—and Eric actually started *listening* to her and cutting us out. We couldn't let that happen, so Eden and I made a plan—and a pact. She and I would control Eric through his women. That's why we dangled Bianca Hyde in front of Eric—and like a good fish, he took the bait. Bianca might have been sleeping with Eric, but Bianca was working for us . . ."

I tried to muster my voice, but all I could manage was a rasp.

"What's that, Clare? Oh, no, we didn't have to use the tranquilizer gun on Bianca. That stupid little whore managed to kill herself right in front of Eden. I wasn't there at the time, but it turned out to be a lesson for both of us. *Murder* could be the solution to any problem—the Occam's Razor that would cut through human tangles with elegant finality."

Garth rolled the dolly through a narrow door, into a room off the boat's main cabin. With a sharp kick to my ribs, he knocked me off the flatbed and onto the carpeted floor.

"Bianca didn't love Eric. She barely liked him, but she was a very good actress, and she figured the act would pay off—if she did exactly what Eden and I told her . . ."

Garth stepped out of range, and I heard the rasp of a zipper.

"With a few carefully planted surveillance devices, we gained access to Eric's secret bank accounts and began to siphon money. A few million here, a few there. You'd be surprised how fast it all added up. Once we had access, losing Bianca didn't matter so much. Then Charley came snooping, and she had to go, too."

Garth dropped a heavy object on the floor. Then he stood over me, a hypodermic needle in hand.

"And now here you are, *another* nosy snoop. Oh, yes, Clare. I read Eric's file on you, and I know all about your little hobby. I don't know if you're working for the police, the Feds, or some private individual, and I don't care. You can't be around Eric any longer, watching his back, asking questions. In time, I'll take care of his new little infatuation with Minnow. But right now, it's time for *you* to go—"

I felt a slight sting as the needle bit into my arm. Then Garth's smirking face disappeared and my world faded to black.

Seventy-one

~~~~~~

Consciousness crashed down on me like a hammer and I awoke to the sound of my own scream.

I sat upright, felt spiderwebs tickling my arm, and hastily slapped them away. Garth's syringe, marked *Diprenorphine*, dropped to the carpet beside me.

I didn't have a clue what diprenorphine was meant to do, but I was happy the needle didn't contain arsenic or strychnine. I had a disquieting feeling Garth wanted me awake and alert.

My mouth was papery and I felt hazy from the drugs. Standing was an issue, too. The boat rocked under my high heels, and the gentle motion was enough to throw me off balance, so I kicked off my high heels and gripped the carpet with my toes. Garth had already pulled off my coat and scarf, so I added my footwear to the pile.

Illuminated by the dim glow of scarlet emergency lights, the cabin was free of furniture. I peeked through the only portal (too small to crawl through, alas). Nothing was visible beyond dark skies and black water.

Crossing to the exit, my foot brushed a large bundle on the floor. Ignoring it, I continued to the door, which was, of course, locked.

I pounded on the door and yelled for Garth, but the silent response was eerily complete. Not even the rumble of the engine could be heard above the muted sound of slapping water.

I had the sudden, sickening realization that I was alone.

I stumbled back to my coat, desperate to find my purse. But my bag was missing along with my wallet, keys, my IDs and credit cards, and my THORN phone.

That damn phone!

I thought back to my day at Appland and how Darren Engle had "fixed" my phone for me. Sure, he'd unblocked calls from Mike Quinn, but he'd obviously added an alternate phone number under Mike's listing in my address book.

Garth must have used that number to send the fake text message as Mike—and I fell for it!

I was so angry (and freaked out and groggy) that I didn't notice the steady, ominous sound of a ticking clock. Not right away. But when I did . . .

Oh, no.

I crawled to the bundle I'd nearly tripped over—it was a worn canvas knapsack plastered with airport stickers and comic book superheroes. The name *Darren* was embroidered on the flap.

My hands were trembling from the double-dose of drugs, and the zipper was stubborn. When I finally got to peek inside, my worst fears were confirmed.

I was no expert, but I knew I was staring at a bomb.

The digital alarm clock displayed the time at seventeen minutes to midnight. The alarm was set to go off at twelve. Quick calculation: I'd been missing for nearly three hours, and I had seventeen minutes to live.

I fought down a panicked urge to tear the bomb to pieces, and studied the device instead. Three wires led from the clock to a little black box. The box was connected by more wires to a bunch of green bottles filled with clear liquid.

In the movies the bomb defuser always cuts a wire. But it is always the right wire, and I had nothing to cut with, anyway.

I blew on my cold hands, thought about putting on my coat and gloves—

Gloves! Oh, thank God. I have my glove phone!

My gloves were still in my coat pocket, and I slipped the left over my trembling hand, then put it to my ear. "Miss Phone?"

For a chilling second I thought I might be out of range.

"Hello, Clare. Would you like to make a call?"

"You bet I would."

Lieutenant Dennis DeFasio answered after the first ring.

"Where the hell are you?" he yelled. "Mike Quinn has been tearing up the docks looking for you! He said you were set up?"

"I was!"

"We've got FBI, Homeland Security, even the freaking Coast Guard crawling all over this town. How could you do this to me, Clare? You know how I feel about Feds—"

"I sympathize with your plight, Dennis, but right now I need to defuse a bomb."

"What!" DeFasio muttered a particularly nasty obscenity. "Talk to me—"

In fifty words or less, I explained my dilemma. Once or twice DeFasio interrupted me to talk to someone on his end. I heard words like *triangulation*, *signal strength*, and *Coast Guard*.

"Describe the bomb," DeFasio abruptly commanded.

"There's an alarm clock connected by three wires to a black box, which is connected to nine little green bottles containing some kind of liquid. Is this a firebomb like the one that blew up Charley?"

"Unfortunately, no," DeFasio replied. "Our boy graduated to the big leagues."

"Our boy?"

"Darren Engle. I'll tell you more after you follow my instructions. Tell me, do you have any flexible rubber on you?"

"You mean—"

"I mean a condom. You know, like some ladies carry in their purses in case they get lucky on a—"

"No! I do not have a condom!"

"Okay, how about non-conductive cloth—"

"My dress is silk, and I have a wool coat and scarf."

"Won't work. We're trying to avoid a spark. Even static electricity could set off the nitroglycerine."

"Nitroglycerine?!"

"How about cotton. Honey, are your undies made of cotton?"

"Yes," I reluctantly replied.

"Great. I want you to take them off—"

Oh, good grief. "Condoms, panties—this call's starting to sound like Bomb Squad phone sex."

"Cut the wisecracks and take off your panties!"

"Oh, all right . . ."

I reached under my dress, slipped off my pantyhose, then my cotton panties. Yes, it was embarrassing (and chilly), but I had less than eight minutes before the ka-bloom, so I threw modesty to the wind.

"Now what?"

"Tear your panties into strips. Enough to cover all three wires leading from the clock to that nasty black box, which is the detonator. That's what you're going to do, wrap each wire in cotton so there is *no possibility* that their ends will touch when you pull the wires out."

"Use one hand, one finger if you can, and work carefully. You want to avoid a spark, and you don't want to jar those wires too much, either."

"I'll wrap with my right hand, and talk to you with my left. Now, please distract me by telling me more about Darren Engle."

"Engle built the bomb that killed Charley and framed Nate Sumner. The investigators found evidence that the sneaky little punk attended Solar Flare meetings, and after each one he collected Sumner's discarded iced tea cans, with the professor's fingerprints all over them. Darren used those cans to build his bomb."

While DeFasio spoke, I covered one wire and I started working on the second. I had six minutes left.

"You said Darren graduated to the big leagues?"

"He used his rocket-building skills to construct his first bomb. Two iced tea cans filled with liquids that combine to produce a flammable explosive in a third can. It's just like a rocket engine, but it's meant to explode, not propel. The little bastard even used compressed air capsules to push the liquids into the mixing chamber. Really ingenious—"

"Can we focus on my bomb, Lieutenant?"

"I'm getting to your bomb. We found traces of nitroglycerine in Darren's apartment. We think that's where he built the device you are defusing right now."

"Darren's dead. I wonder what this bomb was supposed to be used for . . ."

DeFasio paused to listen to someone on his end.

"Good news!" he cried. "We've pinpointed your signal. A Coast Guard helicopter has been dispatched to your position, and a boat is on the way. They should both arrive in five minutes—"

"Which is two minutes after this bomb goes off."

"We're not going to let that happen, Clare."

"I hope you're right, Dennis."

"I better be. I've got a whole squad waiting for more fudge."

I took a breath. "I've covered all the wires. What do you want me to do now?"

"You're going to pull those wires out of that black box in one clean yank. I want you to place your left hand on top of the box, and tug the wires free with your right. Pull it real hard. I'll talk to you when it's over."

I paused. "Dennis?"

"Yes?"

"If I don't do this right, I want you to tell my daughter that I love her and want her to be happy. And please tell Mike Quinn that I loved him, with all my heart. And tell my ex-husband that I never—"

"You tell them, Clare. You have less than two minutes."

I got into position, and closed my eyes. Trembling now, I held my breath and yanked the wires as hard as I could.

Cautiously, I opened one eye, then the other. The clock dangled from the wires in my hand. I heard lapping water, the sound of a distant helicopter, and no explosion!

Brrrrring! The alarm clock loudly jangled.

I screamed and smashed it against the bulkhead. Then I steadied myself, and gave DeFasio the good news.

I heard cheers erupt around him.

Never knew a bunch of guys so excited about getting Irish Cream fudge.

Outside the night was rocked by the blast of a boat horn. Through the portal I spied a white hulled speedboat pulling up beside *BLUE ROSES*. Then footsteps pounded on the deck. Thirty seconds later, something heavy slammed against the cabin door.

"I'm here!" I screamed. "The bomb is defused. Please get me out!"

Another crash, and the door sagged. A final kick smashed it open, and a familiar silhouette filled the doorway.

"Mike!"

"Clare . . ." For a nanosecond, he stood staring, the look of fear still on his face. Then he opened his arms, and I couldn't run into them fast enough.

Seventy-two

~~~~~~

"MACBETH," I said, lying in bed the next morning. "That's what it all comes down to—the struggle over control of a crown."

Mike yawned. "I buy that theory . . ."

"Of course, that crown turned out to be one of THORN."

"Ouch."

"I hope that's exactly what Garth Hendricks said when they arrested him."

"I'm sure he said a lot more—and then clammed up. It won't help. You're still alive, and are now the star witness against him."

"You bet your sweet nitroglycerine knapsack I am."

"And I'm sure they'll find plenty of physical evidence on Eden Thorner's body . . ."

The cops found her corpse under a tarp near the stern. Garth had planned to blow her up with me—continuing his frame job on Eric's sister.

Garth's so-called "pact" with Eden Thorner had ended the

day she acted on her own (with Darren's help) and tried to electrocute me at Appland—unsuccessfully.

Garth knew Eden had blown it then. And when she and Darren continued their bumbling, trying to frame Minnow (again, unsuccessfully), the Metis Man knew what he had to do: frame Eden Thorner for everything and then kill her to make sure she never talked.

"That nitro-packed knapsack I defused was built by Darren," I noted, "but he was already dead, which is why I think Garth and Eden were planning an even more sinister crime."

"I can guess exactly what they were planning."

"When Eric disappeared with me and Matt on that world coffee tour, they must have panicked. They'd lost control of Eric yet again—over a woman. So they decided to cut through all of their problems with the most elegant solution of all."

Mike nodded. "They decided to kill the boy billionaire. With a nitro pack that size, they were probably going to blow him up in his plane or that yacht.

"*Boom*, no more headaches trying to control him."

Mike grunted. "Without a wife or children, Eden would inherit the company and all the money."

"Garth was her partner in crime, and likely the bedroom, so he would run the company, which he clearly thought he was better at than Eric, anyway. And Darren was the kid they were going to frame—and kill—after they'd assassinated the young King of Appland."

"You're right." Mike stretched and rolled toward me. "It does sound Shakespearean."

"Except for the sliding boards."

He nuzzled my neck. "Well, I for one am glad you had cotton panties . . ."

"And I'm glad the first thing you did when you got out of that committee hearing was check your text messages . . ."

Mike had been on Capitol Hill when I'd replied to his text message about meeting him at Dynasty Pier. The hearing was top secret, the room secured from external signals. By the time he got out, I'd already been *tranked* by Nanook of the North.

When Mike couldn't reach me, he confirmed my "plan to meet him at the pier" with Joy—and went absolutely nuts. He'd been in law enforcement long enough to know a setup when he saw it.

In my own defense, my guard was down for a simple reason. I thought the bad guy was gone . . . or rather, the bad girl. And she *was* gone. Garth had sent her to an early grave; I simply didn't realize that the infamous "they" Joe Polaski had tried to warn me about weren't Eden and Darren. It was Eden and Garth Hendricks.

"So . . ." Mike said, between delicious little kisses, "are you done with world coffee tours, South Beach yachts, and forbidden plantations?"

"For the time being. Are you done with top secret conferences?"

"For the time being."

"Then how about we take some time for ourselves and make the most of it?"

"Billionaires and bosses be damned?"

"Exactly."

"Sweetheart, you've got a deal."

EPILOGUE

∿∿∿∿∿∿∿∿∿∿∿∿∿∿∿∿∿∿∿∿

"In honor of the work he has done to improve our island nation, I present Mr. Eric Thorner with the Gold Cross of Costa Gravas!"

Behind the podium, a grinning Eric accepted his award from the island's ambassador. After a short speech, Eric departed the embassy's stage to enthusiastic applause.

Matt, Madame, and I watched the presentation from the front row. Mike Quinn was beside me, my oh-so-handsome G-man date, looking dashing in his formalwear. (I was back in Madame's vintage beaded Chanel—and happy to say Mike couldn't take his eyes off me.)

After the presentation, we all moved to the reception room.

Another round of applause greeted Eric when he entered, Wilhelmina Tork on his arm.

Wearing a blue velvet dress that elegantly showed off her lush figure, Minnow drew many appreciative stares. Even Matt did a double take, astonished at the girl's Cinderella-like transformation from techie tomboy to self-confident princess.

Anton Alonzo appeared, bearing champagne for me and Mike. The three of us toasted the couple.

"You know I had that gown made for you, Clare Cosi," Anton informed me.

"It suits Wilhelmina much better," I said, glancing uneasily at Mike. "She looks so amazing. Eric can't take his eyes off of her. And . . . am I right to suspect there's a Barbie among all those lonely Ken dolls now?"

"It's true," Anton said, then shook his head. "But though Wilhelmina has her virtues, she is still very inexperienced and unsophisticated. Minnow has much to learn."

I touched his champagne flute with mine. "She'll find no better teacher than you, Anton."

"But when will I find time for tutoring?" Anton complained. "Eric's gaming division is now merging with Grayson Braddock's publishing group, so Minnow has a host of new properties to manage. Did you know Eric's promoting her to lead the entire Braddock-Thorner digital gaming unit?"

"You'll both manage. I expect great things from Minnow, and from you."

Anton took my hand and bowed over it before excusing himself. "I do hope we meet again, Ms. Cosi."

"Me too, Anton. Me too . . ."

Minutes later, Mike pointed out another lovely couple: Nate Sumner with Madame at his side. The head of Solar Flare had been invited to attend the afternoon reception by the group's new corporate sponsor, THORN, Inc.

Though Eric insisted that Nate's organization would remain an independent advocacy group, Matt rather cynically reminded me of Michael Corleone's famous maxim: "Keep your friends close and your enemies closer."

Nate Sumner was certainly in a better place than Garth Hendricks, the man who tried to frame him and kill me.

Garth was now officially charged with multiple murders. Of course, he hired the best criminal defense lawyer in the business. But he'd been denied bail because he was a flight risk, and the evidence against him was overwhelming. This morning's *Washington Post* reported a plea deal was imminent, one that would likely put Garth away for a very long time—enough time to write more books, no doubt, although I didn't think anyone would be listening to his business philosophies. After all, he didn't get away with anything. Maybe he'd try his hand at crime fiction.

By now, I'd finished my champagne, and Mike headed to the bar to get us refills. He'd barely stepped away before a glass brimming with bubbly appeared in front of me, courtesy of Eric Thorner.

"You're always giving me things. It's a bad habit. Spoil Minnow from now on."

Eric laughed. "I just gave her the whole gaming division."

"And the lifestyle apps?"

"I'm still in charge. The Billionaire Blend debuts at the potluck, and we're releasing the exclusive billionaire lifestyle app that same week. The Billionaire Blend will be the very first product we offer."

It was hard to believe, but after an astonishing amount of money, and untold hours of experimentation, our Billionaire Blend was finally going on sale. It was *the* most monstrously expensive coffee on the planet. That's what Eric wanted, because he knew his consumers.

Only the wealthiest portion of the human race could afford to sip a cup of it, which didn't sit all that well with me. But I took comfort in the knowledge that the farmers who grew those special, select cherries would ultimately benefit more than the billionaire connoisseurs who consumed it.

"Of course, being in charge these days doesn't mean I'm stuck at corporate headquarters," Eric continued. "I'm building a digital infrastructure on Costa Gravas and I'll be spending a lot of time there, so I decided to buy a fallow plantation to cultivate Ambrosia beans."

"Freed from the tyranny of the sliding board, eh?"

Eric laughed. "I'm free from a lot of things, thanks to you. I would have never known about Minnow if—"

"Propinquity and intensity, Eric. You and Minnow worked side by side for years. It would have happened someday."

"Not with Garth around . . ." He fell silent a long moment, and I knew the blackness of Garth's crimes—and his sister's, too—were still weighing heavily on him. "I didn't see it coming," he said softly. "Not from that direction."

"Neither did I—but it's over now, and you can start over with Minnow by your side. She deeply loves you, Eric. And she's the kind of girl you can truly count on to watch your back."

"Like you, Clare Cosi."

"Well, we *were* both Girl Scouts."

"I know." Eric arched an eyebrow. "It's in my file."

"Speaking of that file—the one you have on me? Did it happen to include reports of my past amateur sleuthing activities?"

Ever the player, Eric shrugged. "Could be."

"That wouldn't be the real reason you chose my coffeehouse to create your Billionaire Blend, would it?"

"Let's just say . . . it was a contributing factor."

Members of the press were finally admitted, and they ringed Eric, peppering him with questions.

I wandered off, searching for Mike and found him by the bar, speaking with a stunning woman in her thirties.

She was tall and lithe in a shimmering gray sheath. Her skin was alabaster, her long strawberry blond hair coiled into a twist. When Mike saw me approach, he paused and smiled.

"Michael?" snapped the woman, realizing she lost his attention.

"Give me a minute," he replied.

The woman's steel gray eyes stared daggers at me as Mike bussed my cheek. "You look beautiful tonight, sweetheart, did I tell you that?"

"Yes. Who is that woman, Mike?"

"My boss."

"*That's* Katerina Lacey? You told me she was a battle-ax!"

"She is."

"She's gorgeous—and young!"

"Listen, Cosi, I told you before. You've been gallivanting all over the world with a boy billionaire. The fact that my boss is a woman shouldn't be an issue, no matter what she looks like."

"But I've been honest. You have *not*."

"I trusted you," Mike shot back. "I gave you the time and the space it took for you to come to your senses. Now the question is: Do you trust me?"

"There's really nothing going on between you and your boss?"

"No. And there never could be."

"Not even with plenty of propinquity?"

He grunted. "You don't know her, Clare. Lacey's a creature. A political animal, completely focused on the next rung up the ladder with very little regard for who she steps on as she goes. I could never give my heart to a woman like that."

At the mention of his heart, Mike took my hand—the one wearing his Claddagh ring—and gently caressed it.

"Michael!" Lacey impatiently called, snapping her fingers as she waved him over.

"Clare!" Eric suddenly beckoned from the opposite side of the room.

Mike put his lips to my ear. "Let's you and I get out of here. Right now. Together. What do you say?"

I didn't hesitate. I took his hand and tugged him toward the embassy's front door. Outside, in the fresh spring air, we paused long enough to inhale the aroma of cherry blossoms—and send our bosses identical text messages.

Called away on personal business. See U Monday.

Then we shut off our smartphones (for a little while anyway), left the cyber-world behind, and set out to enjoy the real one.

Blue Roses

Roses red and roses white
Plucked I for my love's delight.
She would none of all my posies—
Bade me gather her blue roses.

Half the world I wandered through,
Seeking where such flowers grew;
Half the world unto my quest
Answered me with laugh and jest.

Home I came at wintertide,
But my silly love had died,
Seeking with her latest breath
Roses from the arms of Death.

It may be beyond the grave
She shall find what she would have.
Mine was but an idle quest—
Roses white and red are best.

—RUDYARD KIPLING

RECIPES & TIPS
FROM THE VILLAGE BLEND

Visit Cleo Coyle's virtual Village Blend at
CoffeehouseMystery.com
for even more recipes including:

* Baileys Irish Cream Poke Cake
* Triple-Chocolate Italian Cheesecake
* *Canelé* (little caramelized French cakes)
* Nuts on Horseback
* Frito Shepherd's Pie
* Blueberry Blondies
* Joy's Hazelnut Brittle (and Praline)
* Baby Billionaire Candy Apples
* Flourless Peanut Butter Cookies, dipped in . . . Chocolate-Peanut Reese's Nutella and Almond Joy Nutella
* Norwegian Egg Coffee (an easy way to . . .)
* Make Your Own Holiday Spice Coffee Blend
* Clare's Cloudy Dream *Pousse-Café*
* Hazelnut Orgasm
* Paleo Pizza with Cauliflower Crust

RECIPES

What lies behind us and what lies before us are
small matters compared to what lies within us.
—RALPH WALDO EMERSON

Off-the-Menu Coffee Drinks

When the Quiz Master tested Clare Cosi's baristas by ordering
exotic, off-the-menu drinks, Clare thought he was trying to
steal away her staff. In the end, it was Clare who got swept
away—into the world of this mysterious Internet billionaire.
The following is a short guide to real drinks that coffeehouses
will make for you—whether or not they're on the public menu.

The Basics—All coffee drinks start out with brewed coffee,
or, more often, espresso. Other ingredients could include a
dairy product (milk, cream, sweetened condensed milk,
half-and-half), sweeteners (sugar, honey, or syrups), spices
(cinnamon, nutmeg, cocoa powder), or other flavorings
(chocolate, vanilla, fruit syrups, etc.).

Espresso—The Italian word literally means "express."
Espresso starts with a darkly roasted coffee (an "Italian" or
"espresso" roast), which is ground very fine and packed
tightly into the "portafilter" handle of an espresso machine.

Scalding-hot water is forced through these packed grounds at high pressure. The contact time between the water and the coffee is very short, about twenty-five seconds. When an espresso is made correctly, you should see a reddish-brown "crema" at the top of your cup. This foam is the most important thing to look for in a well-made espresso. It tells you the oils in the coffee have been released and suspended in the liquid. A single serving of espresso is called a "shot." Two shots is a *doppio* ("double" in Italian).

Latte—Italian-style drinks in a gourmet coffeehouse start with at least one shot of espresso, and the latte is no exception. Short for "café latte," this is the most popular drink served in American coffeehouses. It's made by adding steamed or hot milk to one or more espresso shots. Americans top their lattes with foam; Italians do not. A **Mocha** is a chocolate variation of a latte.

Cappuccino—Like a latte, the "cap" starts with espresso, but much more foamed milk is added than you'll find in a latte— the usual ratio is one part each of foam, steamed milk, and espresso. You can order a cappuccino two ways: a "dry cap" (more foamed milk and less steamed milk) or a "wet cap" (with less foam and more steamed milk).

Beyond the Basics—It's blue skies and a world of experimentation. From New York to Seattle to Italy to Hong Kong, new coffee drinks are created every year and no rundown can be complete. Here's a list of the exotic coffee beverages that the Quiz Master requested, followed by a short description.

Affogato—The Italian word for "drowned," which refers to the act of topping a drink or dessert with espresso.

Antoccino—A single shot of espresso with an equal amount of steamed milk.

Baltimore—An equal mix of caffeinated and decaffeinated brewed coffees. Not to be confused with a Half-Caf, made from decaffeinated and caffeinated beans that are mixed *before* brewing.

Black Eye—Brewed coffee with a double shot of espresso.

Bombón—An espresso served with sweetened condensed milk, also called a Café Bombón.

Breve—A shot of espresso with steamed half-and-half instead of milk.

Caffé Affogato—A scoop of gelato or ice cream topped by espresso. Can be a served as a beverage or as a dessert. Sometimes caramel sauce or chocolate sauce is added.

Caffé **Americano**—A shot of espresso mixed with hot water. An Americano has the strength of brewed coffee but with a heartier taste.

Café au Lait—One part double-strength brewed coffee, or espresso, one part scalded milk.

Café Mélange—Brewed, black coffee topped with whipped cream.

Café Miel—A shot of espresso, steamed milk, cinnamon, and honey; from *miel*, the French word for "honey."

Café Noir—A single shot of espresso as it is ordered in France.

Coffee Milk—Cold milk mixed with sweet coffee syrup to taste; the official drink of Rhode Island.

Café Mocha—A latte with chocolate syrup.

Café Noisette—An espresso with enough cream to give the beverage a rich, brown, hazelnut color and a smooth, nutty taste. *Noisette* is the French word for "hazelnut."

Café Zorro—Double espresso added to hot water.

Chocolate Dalmatian—A white-chocolate mocha topped with java chips and chocolate chips.

Cortado—An espresso with an equal portion of warm milk added to the shot after pulling. This drink is called a **Gibraltar** in North America.

Cowboy Coffee—Brewed coffee made in a pot by adding fine coffee grounds to water and boiling. Cold water is added at the end of the process to settle the grinds.

Gibraltar—The American name for a **Cortado**.

Green Eye—Brewed coffee with a triple shot of espresso, also called a Triple Death.

Eiskaffee—"Ice Cream Coffee" is a German beverage consisting of chilled coffee, milk, sweetener, and vanilla ice cream topped with whipped cream.

Frappuccino—A line of blended coffee-and-ice beverages trademarked by Starbucks. (To find Clare's easy, home version of this popular drink, visit CoffeehouseMystery.com.)

Guillermo—An espresso shot poured over slices of lime. It can be served hot or over ice and with a touch of milk.

Hong Kong–Style Milk Tea—Black tea with sweetened condensed milk or evaporated milk. Can be served hot or cold.

Lillylou—Equal parts mocha and white mocha topped with espresso and steamed half-and-half. Served without foam; whipped cream optional.

Macchiato—An espresso with a dash of foamed milk, from the Italian word for "stained."

Norwegian Egg Coffee—Cowboy Coffee with an egg added to cut down on bitterness.

Mocha—A latte with chocolate syrup, sometimes topped with cocoa powder.

Marble Mocha—Equal parts white-chocolate mocha and regular mocha.

Peppermint *Affogato*—A shot of espresso over peppermint ice cream, topped with crushed candy canes.

Red Eye—Brewed coffee with a single shot of espresso, also called a Shot in the Dark.

Red Tux—A Zebra Mocha with raspberry syrup.

Regular Coffee—In New York City, Boston, parts of New Jersey, and the Philadelphia area, a regular coffee is brewed coffee with milk or cream, and sugar.

Shakerato—an espresso poured into a cocktail shaker over ice, with simple syrup for a sweetener. Shake until frothy and serve in a cocktail glass.

White Chocolate Mocha or **White Mocha**—a mix of espresso, steamed milk, and white-chocolate syrup topped with whipped cream.

Yuanyang—Three parts brewed coffee; seven parts Hong Kong–Style Milk Tea; also called a *Ying Yong.*

Zebra Mocha—A mixture of regular mocha with a white chocolate mocha, sometimes called a Black Tux. See also **Red Tux**.

Clare Cosi's Coffeehouse Billionaire Bars

After Clare's brash brushes with not one, but two billionaires, she dreamed up this multilayered treat for her coffeehouse customers. Since her life was nearly cut short, she started the dessert with a classic shortbread base. Several sticky situations inspired the chocolate-caramel layer. And because coffee and crazy-nuts collided, she added a hazelnut latte cream. Finally, the chocolate layer on top is a reminder of the very sweet time she spent with her daughter, Joy, which (nearly) made the rest of what she went through worth it. If you enjoyed Clare's story, she hopes you'll also enjoy the culinary creation it inspired. Behold Clare Cosi's Coffeehouse Billionaire Bars.

Makes 16 bars

Shortbread layer:

> 6 tablespoons unsalted butter, softened
> ⅓ cup granulated sugar
> 1 teaspoon pure vanilla extract
> ½ teaspoon kosher salt or ¼ teaspoon table salt
> 1 cup all-purpose flour

Chocolate-Caramel layer:

> 25 soft caramel candies, unwrapped
> 2 tablespoons heavy cream
> ½ cup semisweet chocolate chips

Hazelnut Latte Cream:

> ½ cup unsalted butter, softened
> ½ cup light brown sugar
> ¼ cup granulated sugar
> 2 tablespoons heavy cream
> 1 teaspoon pure vanilla extract
> ¼ teaspoon kosher salt or ⅛ teaspoon table salt
> ¾ cup all-purpose flour
> ½ cup chopped hazelnuts, toasted

Sweet Mocha Glaze:

> *1 cup semisweet chocolate, chopped, or chips*
> *½ teaspoon espresso powder*
> *2 tablespoons heavy cream*

Step 1—Prep oven and pan: Preheat your oven to 350° F. Line a 9-inch-square baking pan with parchment paper, allowing extra paper to hang over two sides to create handles. Set aside.

Step 2—Make the shortbread layer: Using an electric mixer, cream together butter and sugar. Add in the vanilla and salt and blend to combine. Finally, blend in the flour and mix into a crumbly dough. Using hands, form dough into a smooth ball. Press firmly into your prepared pan. Poke shallow holes into the surface of the dough with a fork or skewer. Bake for about 15 minutes. You're looking for the shortbread edges to turn a golden brown. Remove from oven and cool.

Step 3—Make the chocolate-caramel layer: Warm the little caramel candies, cream, and chocolate chips over medium heat in a small saucepan, stirring until melted. Pour the warm chocolate-caramel mixture over cooled shortbread crust and spread evenly. Chill the pan in the fridge for at least 1 hour. The chocolate-caramel layer must be set before you proceed.

Step 4—Make the Hazelnut Latte Cream: Using an electric mixer, cream the butter and sugars. Blend in the heavy cream, vanilla, and salt. Blend in the flour. Fold in the chopped and toasted hazelnuts. Spread cream layer onto the *cooled* chocolate-caramel layer. Use the back of a spoon to even out. Place in the refrigerator to chill while you prepare the Sweet Mocha Glaze.

Step 5—Make the Sweet Mocha Glaze topping: Over a double boiler of simmering water, heat all ingredients until completely melted and smooth, stirring occasionally. Spread the warm glaze over the chilled Hazelnut Latte Cream layer and chill until set, about 1 hour. Using the parchment paper handles, lift the block to a cutting board and slice into small squares, and eat with a *wealth* of joy!

Glazed Pumpkin Spice Latte Muffins

When the chill of fall descends on New York, Clare's customers demand the return of the Pumpkin Spice Latte Muffins to the Village Blend menu. Clare developed this muffin as a celebration of her customers' longstanding love of these classic American fall flavors—with a hint of coffee, of course. (Look for it in the muffins' sweet finishing glaze.)

12 tablespoons (1½ sticks) unsalted butter, softened
1½ cups firmly packed light brown sugar
2 large eggs, room temperature
¾ cup canned pumpkin (pumpkin puree, not pie filling)
2¼ cups all-purpose flour
2 teaspoons pumpkin pie spice (or make your own, page 363)
¾ teaspoon baking soda
Pumpkin Spice Latte Glaze (page 363)

Step 1—Make the batter: Preheat oven to 350° F. Line 12 muffin cups with paper liners or grease with butter or oil, or coat with nonstick cooking spray. Set aside. Using an electric mixer, cream butter and sugar until light and fluffy. Add eggs and pumpkin puree and mix until well blended. Add in flour, pumpkin pie spice, and baking soda, and mix just until flour is fully incorporated into batter; do not overmix.

Step 2—Bake: Spoon batter into prepared cups, and bake for 18 to 20 minutes. Muffins are done when a toothpick inserted comes out with no wet batter clinging to it.

Step 3—Glaze: When muffins have cooled, dip the tops of the muffins into the Pumpkin Spice Latte Glaze to finish.

Pumpkin Spice Latte Glaze

2 tablespoons unsalted butter
4 tablespoons espresso or strong coffee (or water)
1 teaspoon pumpkin pie spice (see receipe below)
1 teaspoon vanilla extract
2 cups confectioners' sugar

Step 1: In a medium saucepan, combine butter, coffee, pumpkin pie spice, and vanilla. Heat slowly, stirring until butter melts. Be careful not to allow the mixture to simmer or boil.

Step 2: Add the confectioners' sugar and stir until it all completely melts into the liquid. Whisk to remove any lumps and blend into a smooth, thick glaze. If the glaze is too thick, whisk in a bit more coffee. If the glaze begins to harden, simply return the pan to the stovetop and warm the glaze while whisking. Add a bit more coffee, if needed, to thin the glaze back to the proper consistency for dipping the muffin tops.

MAKE YOUR OWN PUMPKIN PIE SPICE: Pumpkin pie spice is available in most grocery store spice sections. To make your own, simply mix the following ground spices for

1 teaspoon of pumpkin pie spice: ½ teaspoon cinnamon, ¼ teaspoon ginger, ⅛ teaspoon ground allspice or ground cloves, and ⅛ teaspoon ground nutmeg.

Joy's French Apple Cake Squares

These fragrant apple bars are the perfect treat for breakfast with a fresh cup of hot coffee. Joy Allegro developed the recipe for her mother's coffeehouse. The alchemy of the oven gives the apple layer a custard-like texture while the top bakes up as a soft, sweet, sugar-crusted cake laced with the fragrances of vanilla and rum. As Clare likes to say to her customers, "When you take your first bite of these, you'll know joy (and thank her)!"

Apple filling:

6 Granny Smith or Golden Delicious apples (about 3 pounds in weight)
1 teaspoon freshly squeezed lemon juice
2 tablespoons water
5 tablespoons light brown sugar
1 vanilla bean, halved (optional)

Basic batter:

1¾ cups all-purpose flour
1¼ cups granulated sugar, divided
3 teaspoons baking powder
1 teaspoon kosher salt or ½ teaspoon table salt
2 large eggs, beaten with fork
1½ cups canola, vegetable, or cold-pressed coconut oil
1 cup whole milk
¾ cup sour cream or crème fraîche

2½ teaspoons vanilla extract
1 tablespoon dark rum or 1½ teaspoons rum extract

Apple Custard layer:

3 large egg yolks

Step 1—Prep pan: Line a 13 x 9-inch baking pan with parchment paper, allowing some of the paper to hang over the long ends to create handles (these will allow you to lift the bars out after baking). Lightly coat the paper with nonstick cooking spray and set aside.

Step 2—Prep apples: Peel and cut apples into thin slices and place in a saucepan with lemon juice, water, and brown sugar (and throw in a vanilla bean here if you like). Over medium heat, cook and stir gently for about 15 minutes to soften the apples and caramelize them. Drain excess liquid and set aside to cool. Remove vanilla bean, if using.

Step 3—Create basic batter: Preheat oven to 325° F. Add flour, 1 cup granulated sugar, baking powder, and salt into a bowl and whisk together. Make a well. Add eggs, oil, milk, sour cream, vanilla, and rum (or rum extract). Whisk until well blended but do not overmix, or you will develop the gluten in the flour and your cake will be tough instead of tender.

Step 4—Create apple custard layer: Remove 1½ cups of batter from the mixing bowl and pour into a separate bowl. Whisk in egg yolks (this will help give your apple layer a more custard-like texture). Gently fold the apples into egg batter, pour into prepared pan, and even out the layer.

Step 5—Finish and bake: Pour the remaining (cake-layer) batter over the top of the apples. Sprinkle remaining ¼ cup granulated sugar evenly over the top of cake to help create a crust while baking. Bake about 1 hour (you may need another 15 or so minutes). You're watching for the top of the cake to turn a golden brown, the center of cake to set, and a toothpick inserted in the center should come out with no wet batter clinging to it. Remove from oven and cool completely. While very warm the bars may not stay together, but once cool, you will be able to slice into squares and serve (with joy!). For a finished look before serving, dust lightly with confectioners' sugar.

Clare Cosi's Skillet Lasagna (for Mike)

On the night of the explosion, Clare was craving the comfort food of her childhood, namely her nonna's hearty lasagna. Without the time (or energy) to make her grandmother's many-layered casserole, she whipped up this quickie skillet version for herself and Detective Mike Quinn.

Given Quinn's interest in other kinds of comfort that night, they didn't actually eat this meal for many hours after it was cooked. No worries. Clare Cosi's Skillet Lasagna tastes even better as a leftover dish. "Heat and reheat"—good advice for this dinner, as well as Clare and Mike's weekend-to-weekend relationship.

6 ounces curly lasagna noodles
1 yellow onion, finely chopped
1 cup baby bella mushrooms (optional), chopped
2 cloves garlic, minced
½ pound lean ground beef
½ pound ground pork (or chicken)
1 (28-oz.) can whole peeled tomatoes, drained and chopped (you can use a food processor for this)
¼ cup tomato paste

1 tablespoon Italian seasoning or a mix of dried rosemary, basil, and
oregano
Handful of fresh, Italian (flat-leaf) parsley, chopped
¾ cup ricotta cheese (whole milk will give the best flavor)
½ cup mozzarella cheese, shredded (whole milk will give the best
flavor)
Sprinkling of grated Romano or Parmesan cheese (to taste)

Step 1—Boil lasagna noodles: Bring a large pot of water to
a boil. Break lasagna noodles into 3-inch pieces and cook
according to the package directions. Drain well and set aside.

Step 2—Meat and veg: Lightly coat a large skillet with olive oil
and set over medium heat. Add chopped onion. Cook and stir for
5 minutes, until translucent. Add the mushrooms and garlic and
cook another 2 minutes. Stir in ground beef and pork, breaking
up and cooking until meat is browned and no longer pink, about
5 to 7 minutes. When the meat is cooked, add chopped tomatoes, tomato paste, and Italian seasoning, stirring frequently,
until thickened, about 6 minutes. Stir in parsley.

Step 3—Finish with noodles and cheese: Add in the cooked
lasagna noodles and gently stir until heated through, about 5
minutes. Use a spoon to evenly top the mixture with big dollops
of ricotta. Sprinkle the shredded mozzarella on top. Cover and
cook a few more minutes, until everything is heated through.
Dish out helpings and garnish with a sprinkling of grated
Romano or Parmesan cheese and a bit of parsley on the side. To
reheat, add more mozzarella, cover, and melt. *Molto bene!*

How to Make an Irish Car Bomb

*On the night that Mike Quinn took Clare to visit the NYPD Bomb
Squad, he told her the story of the first time he worked with the*

squad's lieutenant, Dennis DeFasio. At the close of the case, DeFasio and his crew took Quinn to a pub for a night of Irish Car Bombs (the kind you drink).

The "Irish" refers to the traditional ingredients: Guinness Stout, Baileys Irish Cream, and Jameson Irish Whiskey. As for the bomb, this is a "bomb shot" drink like the notorious Boilermaker. You must chug it immediately or the Baileys Irish Cream will curdle.

Don't expect to find this beverage in a Dublin pub; this is an American concoction. An interesting note: the coffee liqueur Kahlúa was once part of the original recipe, but is now considered optional. When Clare's homemade Kahlúa (page 378) is involved, however, Quinn goes old school.

Makes one heck of an explosive serving

> ½ ounce Irish cream (Baileys)
> ¼ ounce Irish whiskey (Jameson)
> ½ pint Irish stout (Guinness)

Pour the Irish cream into a shot glass, then carefully pour the whiskey on top—go slowly and it should float. Pour the Irish stout into a tall beer glass and drop the shot glass into it. Drink immediately, drain the glass, and make sure someone in your group is a designated driver (or you have cab fare home).

Baileys Irish Cream and Caramel-Nut Fudge

Yes, this is the very buttery caramel fudge (with an Irish cream kick) that Clare used to bribe NYPD Bomb Squad Lieutenant DeFasio and his crew. That night, she made it in an 8-inch-square pan and cut it into bite-sized pieces for sharing. If you don't expect to consume it in one night, however, Clare suggests making the fudge in *a loaf pan. Then you can remove the fudge block, wrap it in plastic, and store it in the fridge. Over the course of many evenings, you can take out the block, cut off slices to enjoy with coffee, and rewrap it to keep fresh for the next time you'd like a wee nip of edible joy.*

²/₃ cup evaporated milk
1 cup light brown sugar
¹/₃ cup granulated sugar
2 tablespoons unsalted butter
½ teaspoon coarse sea salt (do not substitute table salt)
2 cups mini marshmallows
1 teaspoon pure vanilla extract
¼ cup Baileys Irish Cream
2 tablespoons pure maple syrup (not pancake syrup, which is
flavored corn syrup)
1½ cups white chocolate chips (or 9 ounces of white chocolate discs)
¾ cup plus ¹/₃ cup chopped, toasted walnuts

Step 1—Prep pan: Use an 8-inch-square pan or an 8½ x 4½-inch loaf pan. Line the pan completely with parchment paper and allow the paper to extend beyond at least 2 sides to create a sling with handles. You'll use these to easily lift the fudge from the pan.

Step 2—Bring to a boil: Combine evaporated milk, sugars, butter, and salt in a large saucepan. Place over medium heat and stir occasionally to prevent burning. When the mixture comes to a full, rolling boil, set the timer for 5 minutes and stir constantly.

Step 3—Stir in final ingredients: Pour in the mini marshmallows and stir rapidly to melt. Remove from heat and stir in the vanilla extract, Baileys Irish Cream, and maple syrup. Add the white chocolate chips and stir until melted. Fold in ¾ cup chopped walnuts.

Step 4—Pour, garnish, and chill: Pour fudge mixture into prepared pan. Sprinkle the remaining ⅓ cup chopped walnuts across the top to decorate. Allow to cool completely at room temperature.

Step 5—WARNING: Do not cover the top of the pan with plastic wrap until the fudge has completely cooled; otherwise, steam will condense and your fudge will become soggy. Once the fudge loaf is cool, loosely cover the top of the pan with plastic wrap or foil and place the pan in the fridge, chilling until firm. Remove pan from fridge and lift the fudge out of the pan using the parchment-paper handles. Slice to enjoy. To store, rewrap the fudge tightly in plastic and place back in the fridge.

BAILEYS BUYING NOTE: If you're not a big drinker, simply buy 2 mini-bar bottles of Baileys. Inexpensive, single-serving bottles come in sizes of 50 milliliters, and 2 bottles will allow you to measure out the amount needed for this recipe.

Baileys Irish (Butter) Cream Frosting

This is one of Clare Cosi's favorite go-to frostings when she's making no-frills cupcakes for Mike. The frosting brings the party—and the flavor.

To get Clare's Irish Cream Poke Cake recipe, a fantastic (and easy) "wow" of a party cake that will sit beautifully beneath this frosting, drop by author Cleo Coyle's online coffeehouse at CoffeehouseMystery.com.

Makes about 2 cups (amazing!) icing, enough to frost a 2-layer cake or 24 cupcakes

1 cup (2 sticks) unsalted butter, softened
2 tablespoons Baileys Irish Cream

1 teaspoon pure vanilla extract
3 cups confectioners' sugar

Using an electric mixer, cream the softened butter. Add Baileys Irish Cream, vanilla extract, and 1 cup confectioners' sugar. Beat until the sugar is dissolved. Scrape down the bowl, add 1 cup confectioners' sugar, and beat until dissolved. Add the remaining 1 cup sugar and beat until smooth. If frosting is dry, add a bit more Irish Cream until you get the consistency you like.

Clare Cosi's Crunchy Almond Biscotti

(Easy Food Processor Method)

Clare proudly served these goodies to her esteemed (and beloved) employer, Madame Dreyfus Allegro Dubois. Like the gelato makers of Sicily, Clare developed this recipe with the goal of making the cookie taste exactly like the star ingredient. Bite into these crunchy, twice-baked fingers and the fragrance and flavor of almond will envelop you. Dip them in chocolate and your mouth will believe it's filled with chocolate-covered almonds.

Makes about 2 dozen finger-sized biscotti

½ cup whole, shelled almonds, skins on
1 cup all-purpose flour
⅓ cup granulated sugar
¼ teaspoon baking powder
¼ teaspoon baking soda
⅛ teaspoon kosher salt or pinch table salt
1 large egg
1 egg yolk

1 teaspoon pure vanilla extract
1 tablespoon canola or vegetable
or (cold-pressed virgin) coconut oil, liquefied
½ cup sliced almonds
1 egg white

Step 1—Make the dough: Preheat oven to 350° F. Line a baking sheet with parchment paper and set aside. Place whole almonds into the food processor and pulse until texture resembles sand. Add flour, sugar, baking powder, baking soda, and salt to the bowl and pulse until well mixed. Add egg, egg yolk, vanilla, and oil. Process and/or pulse until a dough forms. Transfer the dough onto a flat surface, knead, and shape into a disc. Add the remaining ½ cup sliced almonds and knead with your hands until the nuts are mixed in.

Step 2—Shape into logs and bake: Divide the dough in half and roll between your palms to create 2 long cylinders. Place these cylinders onto prepared baking sheet, leaving plenty of room in between, and flatten them, shaping into long rectangles. Brush tops and sides with egg white whisked with a little water. (This helps prevent crumbling when sliced and gives the cookies a nicer crust.) Bake for 20 minutes. Remove from oven and allow to cool 15 minutes. While warm, the logs are fragile; handle carefully. The best way to transfer them is to *slide the parchment paper* off the pan and onto the cutting board or flat surface. Reduce oven temperature to 300° F.

Step 3—Slice: Using your sharpest knife, slice the logs on a sharp diagonal into finger-thick cookies, about ½ inch. *No sawing!* Slice down *hard* in one motion to cleanly cut through any crunchy almonds. *Cutting tip: This is often why the cookies crumble at this stage. If you were to saw back and forth on the log or only gently cut, when you hit a hard nut, you'd*

merely agitate the nut instead of cutting through it and that agita-
tion will crumble the cookie around the nut. So be sure to cut down
hard.

Step 4—Add the "bis" to biscotti by baking again:
Reusing your parchment paper, place the cookies on their
sides on the baking sheet and bake for an additional 10 minutes. Flip and bake for another 10 to 12 minutes. Remove
from oven. The cookies will get crispier and crunchier as they
cool. Store in a plastic container. There is no need to refriger-
ate, but you must allow biscotti to cool completely before
storing or the cookies will end up soggy from condensation.

CHOCOLATE-COVERED ALMONDS: That's what these
deliciously crunchy biscotti will taste like when you dip
them in chocolate. Clare likes to dip half the cookie (length-
wise) so chocolate can be tasted in every bite. Simply place 6
ounces of semisweet chocolate, chopped (or 1 cup chips), and
about 4 tablespoons heavy cream into a microwave-safe bowl.
Stir well. Heat for 20 seconds and stir, repeating until chocolate
is melted. Chocolate burns easily and you do not want to nuke
the chocolate until it's completely melted or you will risk burning it, so take care.

Clare Cosi's Chocolate-Crusted Banana Bars

"Lovin' from the oven" is how Matt described these fresh-baked
squares, and he was right. The chocolate layer adds a nice twist to
the traditional banana bar recipe. Clare adds a bit of earthy espresso
powder to that bottom layer as well. Yes, she's a coffee fiend, but
here's the truth: you won't taste coffee, only a more powerful note of
chocolate. Espresso powder is a baker's secret to deepening the flavor
of chocolate in recipes.

Yield: 16 squares (from one 9-inch-square pan)

2 cups mashed ripe bananas (about 4 large)
¼ cup sour cream
¾ cup canola oil (or cold-pressed coconut oil)
½ cup light brown sugar
1 egg, lightly beaten with fork
1 teaspoon pure vanilla extract
1½ teaspoons baking powder
1 teaspoon baking soda
½ teaspoon kosher salt or ¼ teaspoon table salt
1½ cups all-purpose flour or 1 cup all-purpose flour and ½ cup spelt,
amaranth, or whole wheat flour
¼ cup baking cocoa
½ teaspoon espresso powder
½ cup chocolate chips
½ cup chopped walnuts (optional)

Step 1—Make batter: Preheat oven to 350° F. Line the bottom of an 9-inch-square pan with parchment paper and butter the paper; set aside. Combine bananas and sour cream with a fork. Add in oil, sugar, egg, vanilla, baking powder, baking soda, and salt. Mix until smooth. Add flour and mix until a batter forms.

Step 2—Create chocolate bottom: Remove 1 cup batter and place in a separate bowl. Add cocoa, espresso powder, chocolate chips, and chopped walnuts, if using, and mix until blended. Be careful to not overwork batter or you'll develop the gluten in the flour and your bars will be tough instead of tender.

Step 3—Assemble and bake: Spread the chocolate batter evenly across the bottom of prepared pan. Spoon remaining batter on top, and even out using the back of a spoon. Bake 25 minutes or until a toothpick inserted near the center comes out clean. Cool on a wire rack.

Clare's Billionaire Twinkie Cupcakes

Clare Cosi's dinner at the Source Club ended with a nasty scene and no dessert, which meant Clare and Eric never had a chance to sample Chef Clarke Harvey's Billionaire Twinkie. But her hankering for that golden cake with gooey marshmallow crème filling wouldn't go away, so Clare dug up her old "In the Kitchen with Clare" column recipe for Twinkie Cupcakes and baked them up for the billionaire's cyber crew. Here's her recipe, so you can enjoy them, too . . .

Makes 12 cupcakes

Cupcakes:

> 1 box yellow cake mix* (see Note below)
> 1¼ cups water
> ⅓ cup canola oil
> 4 egg whites (room temperature is best)

Filling:

> 6 cups (1 10-oz. bag) mini marshmallows
> 2 tablespoons corn syrup (or vanilla-flavored corn syrup)
> ½ cup confectioners' sugar
> 2 tablespoons unsalted butter, softened
> 1 tablespoon milk
> ½ teaspoon vanilla extract (tip: for a whiter filling, use "clear vanilla" extract)

*A note on the cake mix: I use Betty Crocker plain yellow cake mix (not butter yellow) for this recipe. This recipe should work with any brand of yellow cake mix. Be sure to pick up a mix that lists oil in the directions and has "pudding in the mix" as a feature. (FYI: When you use oil in a cake recipe, your cake will stay fresher for a longer period of time.)

Step 1—Mix the batter: Preheat oven to 350° F. Spray a 12-cup muffin tin with nonstick spray or line with cupcake liners, and set aside. Into a large mixing bowl, combine cake mix, water, and oil. Beat with an electric mixer for about 1 minute until a smooth batter forms. Be sure to scrape down the bowl as you mix. Place in the fridge until you complete the next step.

Step 2—Beat the egg whites: In a clean and dry glass, metal, or ceramic bowl (do not use plastic, which holds grease), beat egg whites until soft peaks form.

Step 3—Fold the eggs into the batter: Using an electric mixer on a low speed, fold the egg whites into the cake batter. Do not overbeat—just mix enough to smoothly incorporate the egg whites. You should no longer see white, just the yellow batter.

Step 4—Fill the pan and bake: Fill each cup with ¼ cup batter. Then go back and add 1 tablespoon more to each cup. Do not fill cups to the top.

This should give you 12 cupcakes with a little batter left over for a 13th cupcake (if you want a baker's dozen). When you fill the cups as described, they should bake up uniformly with little, golden domes. Bake for 15 to 17 minutes. Transfer pans to a cooling rack and allow the cupcakes to cool in their pan.

For the filling:

Step 1—Make the marshmallow crème: Place mini marshmallows into a microwave-safe bowl. Add corn syrup and heat in the microwave for about 30 seconds (adding 15-second increments if needed). Do not completely melt the marshmallows in the microwave. You are watching for them to become very soft. Then stir them up and . . . voilà, you have made marshmallow crème (aka Fluff). Set mixture aside to cool.

No Microwave? To complete this step without a microwave, simply create a double boiler by placing a heatproof bowl over a pan of simmering water. Warm the mini marshmallows and corn syrup, stirring until they've melted into marshmallow crème (aka Fluff).

Step 2—Make the filling: Add the confectioners' sugar, butter, milk, and vanilla extract. Using an electric mixer, beat filling until smooth and blended, scraping down the bowl as you mix.

Assemble the cupcakes:

Step 1—Make sure the cupcakes don't stick: You must fill each cooled cupcake while it rests in the cupcake pan. But . . . first be sure your cupcakes will come out of the pan easily. If you are not using cupcake liners (or a silicone baking pan), gently run a knife around the outside edge of each cupcake to free it gently from the metal pan. Then place it right back into the well.

Step 2—Cut the hole: Using a small, sharp knife, cut a cone-shaped hole into the top of each cupcake. Remove the cone and fill the hole with the copycat Twinkie filling. The filling is very sticky so lightly coat your spoon with non-stick spray. You can also use a pastry bag for this job. Or, spoon the filling into a Ziploc plastic bag and use a scissors to snip off one corner, which will turn it into a pastry bag.

Step 3—Fill and finish: Slice off the "top" of your cupcake cone and place it back on the filled cupcake. You can serve the Twinkie Cupcake as is or use some of the filling to frost the top. If you like, as an added garnish, you can crumble the extra crumbs (from the bottom of the cone) over the frosted top. The filling is gooey and delicious. If you prefer a stiffer filling, simply chill the cupcakes in the fridge after filling.

Clare Cosi's Kahlúa

(Homemade Coffee Liqueur)

On the night of the Source Club dinner, Matteo Allegro sees that his ex-wife needs something to calm her nerves (and his), so he whips up espresso martinis using Clare's homemade Kahlúa. This sweet, rum-based coffee liqueur is easy to make. It also makes a lovely gift, and Clare is happy to share her recipe. (Matt's Espressotini recipe can be found on page 379.)

Yield: About 3 cups

2 cups brewed coffee or espresso
1 cup granulated sugar
1 cup dark brown sugar
5 teaspoons espresso powder (see page 379)
2 cups light rum
2 teaspoons pure vanilla extract (or 1 vanilla bean, split)
1½ tablespoons chocolate liqueur

Step 1—Mix and simmer for 1 hour: In a large saucepan, mix together the coffee, sugars, and espresso powder. Do not add any other ingredients at this time or the cooking process may destroy their flavors. Bring the mixture to a boil. Reduce heat and simmer uncovered, stirring occasionally for at least 1 full hour until mixture thickens slightly. (Again, you should not be boiling the mixture. It should be cooking at a simmer and thickening.)

Step 2—Add final ingredients: Take the mixture off the heat and cool for 5 minutes. Stir in rum, vanilla extract, and chocolate liqueur. You are adding these ingredients off the heat to preserve their flavor.

Step 3—Store and age: Pour your homemade Kahlúa into a glass storage container. You may sample it now, but for the best flavor, it should be aged about 3 to 4 weeks. Keep the container in a cool, dark place and stir every week or so. (If using vanilla bean, remove after the storage period. Store the bean with sugar for additional flavor in your coffee.)

ESPRESSO POWDER: Espresso powder is made from roasted espresso beans that have been ground, brewed, and freeze-dried. Espresso powder dissolves in water to create instant espresso. While Clare would never drink espresso made from freeze-dried powder, she highly recommends using good-quality espresso powder (rather than freeze-dried instant coffee) to add coffee flavor to your baking and cooking. Look for espresso powder in the instant coffee section of your store. Popular brands include Medaglia D'Oro Instant Espresso Coffee and Ferrara Instant Espresso Coffee.

GIFT IDEA: Clare often gives small, decorative bottles of her homemade Kahlúa to friends and customers. If you don't have time to age your Kahlúa before giving it as a gift, simply transfer the finished liqueur to decorative bottles, seal them, and tie on a pretty tag that asks recipients to age the newly made liqueur 3 to 4 weeks before drinking.

Matteo Allegro's Espressotini

An espressotini is an espresso martini. Given Matt's lifelong relationship with coffee, this is one of his favorite cocktails. He fixed a double for Clare (and himself) on the night of the Source Club dinner. Enjoy this recipe for a single.

Yield: 1 espresso martini

1½ ounces vodka (Matt prefers vanilla-flavored)
1½ ounces Kahlúa (Matt uses Clare's homemade)
1 ounce espresso (chilled to room temperature)
1 ounce white crème de cacao (or Baileys Irish Cream)

Fill a cocktail shaker with ice. Pour all ingredients over the ice. Shake well. Strain into a martini glass rimmed with a mixture of cocoa and sugar or fine shavings of chocolate.

FYI: 1 ounce of liquid measure equals 2 tablespoons or 6 teaspoons.

Matt Allegro's Ugandan Chicken Stew with "Groundnuts" (Peanut Butter)

Matt introduced billionaire Eric Thorner to this fragrant, one-pot stew in Uganda, the first stop of their world coffee tour. Because this East African nation is landlocked with limited livestock and fisheries, groundnuts (aka peanuts) have become an important source of protein for Ugandans. It is the women who traditionally gather and sort the legumes, and many of their recipes contain these nuts. Guests are also served the nuts as a welcome food.

During his early years traveling the continent of Africa, Matt learned to prepare a version of this simple, hearty stew while staying in the home of a Ugandan friend. He especially enjoyed preparing it for Clare during the early years of their marriage, exciting his young wife's taste buds with savory flavors while entertaining her with equally savory tales of his African travels.

Serves 6

2–3 pounds chicken
½ tablespoon salt

½ tablespoon black pepper
1 cup (2 sticks) unsalted butter
1 cup onion, chopped
5 cloves garlic, chopped
2½ cups chicken stock
²/₃ cup peanut butter
2 egg yolks
3 tablespoons chopped parsley (for garnish)

Step 1—Prep the chicken: Cut the chicken into 2- to 3-inch pieces. Discard the small bones (ribs, wings, and neck bones) but leave the larger bones in the stew for richness. Rub the chicken pieces with salt and pepper and set aside.

Step 2—Start the simmer: Melt butter over medium heat in a large, heavy skillet or stew pot, and add the chicken and onion. Add a small amount of stock and cover. Reduce heat and simmer over lowest heat possible for 20 minutes, periodically adding chicken stock until it is all used.

Step 3—Add the peanut butter: Remove ½ cup liquid from the pot and add it to the peanut butter. Mix to create a paste. Return the peanut butter paste to the pot and bring to a boil, then reduce heat and simmer for five minutes.

Step 4—Thicken with egg yolk: Further reduce heat and remove ½ cup cooking liquid and set aside to cool for a minute or so. Break the eggs and separate the yolks. Whisk the slightly cool liquid into the egg yolks, and then add the egg mixture to the pot and mix into the stew.

Step 5—Finish the stew: Simmer gently until chicken is done, about 15 minutes. Do not heat the stew above a simmer from this point or the eggs will clump instead of thicken. Garnish with parsley and serve over white, brown, or basmati rice.

Cleo Coyle's Queso Fundido

(Mexican Cheese Dip)

Clare faced a dilemma while catering the Appland party. Some staff members had issues with eating dairy or gluten. Others were junk food junkies, still hooked on college computer-lab fare of 24/7 candy bars, pizza, and nachos. When Clare spied Doritos on Eric Thorner's Gulfstream jet, she knew he and his gang would be up for this gooey, delicious Mexican-American dip.

Because eating fundido *is a whole lot of fun, one might get the impression that that's where the name originated. In truth,* queso fundido *means "melted cheese" in Spanish. The dish, which combines the bubbly flavor of warm cheese with the bright, malty flavor of Mexican beer, originated along the borders of Northern Mexico and the Southwestern United States.*

Serves 4

1 plum tomato, chopped
1 yellow onion, chopped
1 jalapeño pepper, seeded and chopped
1 tablespoon dried oregano
¼ teaspoon sea salt
Dash black pepper
½ cup Corona or other pale lager beer
6 ounces Monterey Jack cheese, cut into
1-inch chunks
6 ounces extra-sharp Cheddar cheese, cut into
1-inch chunks
Tortilla chips
Chorizo, your favorite sausage, or bacon bits
(optional, for topping)

Step 1—Roughly chop the cheeses: Break block cheeses into 1-inch pieces, and set aside.

Step 2—Prep the veggies: Chop tomato, onion, and jalapeño pepper. I recommend using only the green part of the jalapeño, discarding the seeds and the white membrane, which hold more heat than flavor. (For tips on working with jalapeños, and suggestions for other peppers to use in this dish, see note at the end of the recipe.)

Step 3—Cook the veggies: Heat a nonstick, oven-safe saucepan, or a well-oiled, cast iron saucepan over medium heat (if you do not have a nonstick, oven-safe saucepan, see note in Step 6). Sauté veggies until the onions are soft and translucent, about 6 minutes.

Step 4—Simmer: When the veggies are soft, add the oregano, salt, and pepper to the saucepan. Add beer and heat the mixture to simmering, stirring occasionally and scraping browned bits that may stick to the pan. Let simmer 3 to 5 minutes, or until the liquid is reduced by half.

Step 5—Add the cheese: Add cheese chunks, a handful at a time, while stirring vigorously. Allow each addition to melt and the mixture to become blended and smooth before adding more. When all the cheese is added and mixture is smooth, you're ready to finish. You can serve now or save it for a few hours before service. Add chorizo, sausage, or bacon bits, if using (for directions on how, see note at the end of recipe).

Step 6—Finish under the broiler: With the cheese melted and blended, you can now finish by broiling and serving in the same pan in which you cooked it. *If your pan is not oven-safe, transfer the dip to a casserole, pie plate, or another ovenproof container before placing it under a broiler and serving. Be sure to grease the new pan with oil to prevent the cheese from sticking.* Broil until the top just turns golden brown, about 2 to 5 minutes. Serve immediately, while mixture is bubbly and hot.

Beer Measuring Tip: Never measure the foamy white head when using beer in a recipe. Allow the beer to settle first.

Variation: For white Cheddar dip, replace extra sharp Cheddar with 6 ounces of *queso blanco* (or white Cheddar).

Serving tips and chorizo topping: Use tortilla chips for dipping. You may also garnish the finished *fundido* with cooked chorizo, sausage, or bacon bits. For the chorizo or sausage, slice open the casings, and cook the meat inside, mashing with a fork until it resembles ground meat. Drain the meat and sprinkle it over *queso fundido* before it goes under the broiler.

How to reheat: Simply warm the *fundido* over medium heat; stirring until melted and bubbly once again.

Pepper options: Jalapeño is traditional for this dip, but if you'd like zero heat, go for a bell pepper. For milder heat than a jalapeño, use a banana, cherry, or poblano pepper. For more heat than a jalapeño, try a fresh Serrano, or sprinkle in some dried cayenne. Suicidal heat? Try a Thai chili, Scotch bonnet, or habanero.

Pepper safety: Take care when cutting jalapeños or any hot pepper. The capsaicin in the peppers can burn skin. If you have a tiny scratch or winter-chapped skin, the burn can be painful. Should you absently touch your nose, lips, or your eyes while cutting hot peppers, you will surely regret it (ask me how I know). Use latex gloves to protect chapped hands; otherwise, work with care.

Clare Cosi's Italian Beignets

The Appland crew missed out on this treat, but you can enjoy them by following this recipe. Clare's grandmother used this basic dough to make a sweet treat and also a very traditional recipe—a savory Italian snack called anchovy fritters. While Clare's father loved the fritters, Clare was not a fan. She preferred the sweet, fried dough treats that her nonna made from this dough. They taste like donuts but crispier. They puff up like a French beignet and are finished with confectioners' sugar, but they're not exactly that, either. Whatever you want to name them, once you taste them, you'll call them delicious.

Yield: About 3 dozen fried dough treats (depending on size)

Easy yeast proofing:

> ¼ ounce dry instant yeast
> ¼ cup warm (not hot) water
> 1 teaspoon sugar

Beignet batter:

> 3 cups flour
> 1 teaspoon sugar
> Pinch salt
> 1 egg
> 1¾ cups water
> 1 tablespoon oil (canola or vegetable oil), plus additional for frying
> Confectioners' sugar (for dusting)

Step 1—Proof the yeast: To see the *proof* that your yeast is alive before mixing it into the dough, combine the instant yeast in a small bowl with the water and sugar. If the bowl does not foam up after 5 minutes, dump it and start over with a new batch.

Step 2—Mix the dough: Meanwhile, in a mixing bowl combine the flour, sugar, salt, egg, water, and 1 tablespoon oil. Add proofed yeast mixture and mix well. Dough will be shaggy. Cover and allow to rise, about 2 hours, until doubled in size.

Step 3—Cut the dough: When dough has risen, pull off a piece, knead with lots of flour, then use a rolling pin to create a very flat, very thin sheet. Use a pizza cutter to cut out long strips, rings, or squares. (Clare's favorite shape is long strips—which creates a treat on the crunchier side. Squares will give you a softer, pillowy treat.) Experiment with which shape gives you the most satisfying level of flavor, crunch, or softness.

Step 4—Fry the dough: Pour a few inches of oil into a skillet with high sides. Place the dough pieces in hot oil. They will float to the top of the oil and turn light golden brown (for the best flavor, do not allow the beignets to brown too much). Flip and fry on the other side. Drain on paper towels, dust both sides with confectioners' sugar, and eat with joy.

Don't Miss the Next
Coffeehouse Mystery by Cleo Coyle

*Join Clare Cosi for a double shot of danger
in her next coffeehouse mystery!*

**For more information about the
Coffeehouse Mysteries
and what's next for Clare Cosi
and her baristas at the Village Blend,
visit Cleo Coyle's website at
CoffeehouseMystery.com**

Holiday time is party time in New York City, but after a sparkling winter bash ends with a murder, Village Blend coffeehouse manager Clare Cosi vows to put the killer on ice...

From New York Times Bestselling Author

CLEO COYLE

HOLIDAY BUZZ

A Coffeehouse Mystery

At the Great New York Cookie Swap, pastry chefs bake up their very best for charity. Clare is in charge of the beverage service, and her famous Fa-la-la-la lattes make the gathering even merrier. But her high spirits come crashing down to earth when she discovers the battered body of a hardworking baker's assistant.

Police suspect a serial attacker whose escalating crimes have become known as "the Christmas Stalkings." Clare's boyfriend, NYPD detective Mike Quinn, finds reason to believe even more sinister forces are involved. Clare isn't so sure—and when she finds a second bludgeoned baker, she becomes a target. Now Clare is spending the holiday season poring over clues, and she's not going to rest until justice is served.

INCLUDES HOLIDAY AND COOKIE RECIPES!

"Highly recommended for all mystery collections."
—*Library Journal* (starred review)

"[A] frothy cast of lovable eccentrics."
—*Publishers Weekly*

facebook.com/CleoCoyleAuthor
facebook.com/TheCrimeSceneBooks
penguin.com

*Greenwich Village coffeehouse manager Clare Cosi
is rolling with a popular new trend,
until someone close to her is driven to kill . . .*

From *New York Times* Bestselling Author
CLEO COYLE

A Brew to a Kill
A Coffeehouse Mystery

The Village Blend's *Muffin Muse* coffee truck is all the
rage. But a fatal hit-and-run followed by a mysterious
death at a food truck–catered wedding give Clare a clue
that something bitter is brewing.

Then she opens a bag of imported coffee beans and
finds ten pounds of rocks—the kind that will earn you
a twenty-year jail sentence. Is her ex-husband and business partner smuggling Brazilian crack? Is her staff
now in danger?

To clear up this murky brew, Clare must sweet-talk
two federal agents, dupe a drug kingpin, stake out a
Dragon Boat festival, and teach a cocky young undercover cop how to pull the perfect espresso—all while
keeping herself and her baristas out of hot water.

Coffee. It can get a girl killed.

Includes coffee cake and muffin recipes!

facebook.com/TheCrimeSceneBooks
penguin.com